A HOPEFUL CHRISTMAS

A REGENCY ROMANCE COLLECTION

Cover image: Malgorzata Maj © Arcangel

Cover design copyright © 2020 by Covenant Communications, Inc.
Cover design by Hannah Bischoff

Published by Covenant Communications, Inc.
American Fork, Utah

Printed in the United States of America
First Printing: October 2020

26 25 24 23 22 21 20   10 9 8 7 6 5 4 3 2 1

ISBN:1-978-52441-362-0

A HOPEFUL CHRISTMAS

A REGENCY ROMANCE COLLECTION

ANNEKA R. WALKER

SIAN ANN BESSEY

CARLA KELLY

KRISTA LYNNE JENSEN

Covenant Communications, Inc.

OTHER BOOKS AND AUDIOBOOKS
BY ANNEKA R. WALKER

Love in Disguise

The Masked Baron

LOVE IN DISGUISE

ANNEKA R. WALKER

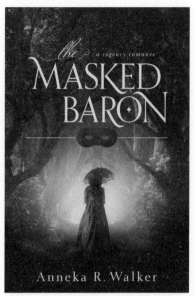

PRAISE FOR ANNEKA R. WALKER

"A sweet reminder that love has the power to change everything—especially when Christmas is in the air."

—Sian Ann Bessey, author *The Noble Smuggler*

"Just what is the appeal of Christmas stories? I believe it is hope, hope that complications large and small will work out for the best. Anneka understands this; it shows in what she writes."

—Carla Kelly, author *The Unlikely Heroes* (coming 2021)

"A touch of mystery, rebellion, and sweet romance for Christmas!"

—Krista Lynne Jensen, author *Kisses in the Rain*

LORD BLAKELY'S GIFT

ANNEKA R. WALKER

To Jonathan
You inspire me to be a better person—
just another reason why I love you.

$\mathcal{A}$CKNOWLEDGMENTS

MY HUSBAND LOVES A HEARTWARMING Christmas story—so, of course, I had to write him one. I'm thankful for the example he sets as a true gentleman, one who loves both his family and his Savior. Thank you to Shawna, Heather, and my mom, Heidi, for being my early readers. Rough drafts aren't ideal reading. My mother-in-law, Jan, supplied child care on a few occasions, helping me meet my deadlines. My kids have the best grandmothers! Thank you to Martha Keyes and Krista Jensen for their valuable critiques. I love working with Covenant Communications and appreciate all the help my editor, Kami Hancock, gives me. She is fabulous to work with! Amy Parker, thank you for getting my books into the hands of readers!

My whole heart overflows with gratitude for my Savior, Jesus Christ. He is the reason we celebrate, and His grace continues to amaze me. Merry Christmas!

CHAPTER ONE

Northamptonshire, 1811

IVY WASN'T RUNNING AWAY—NOT EXACTLY. She only desired to help.

"Visiting your estranged grandmother is not more important than receiving a proposal of marriage," Aunt Morris said, pacing in front of the drawing-room fireplace. Her distress was causing her normal poise to crumble.

"If Mr. Beales wanted to propose, he would have done so already," Ivy argued.

Aunt Morris's eyebrows arched, and the points in the middle disappeared under her perfectly coiled brown curls. "He is shy. A man like him needs a little encouragement."

Forcing a relationship simply felt wrong. Ivy prided herself in following her conscience. Right now, her conscience said to be with her grandmother.

"Oh, do let her go," her youngest sister, Alice, said with unfettered exuberance. "You know how she adores championing a good cause." Alice turned to Ivy. "You would have made an excellent knight."

It was a relief someone was on her side. "Thank you, Alice."

"Have you thought this through?" her more serious sister, Julia, asked.

"Grandmother has never requested a visitor before. Someone should go." Ivy was sandwiched between both her sisters on the sofa, and she reached over on either side of her and clasped their hands. "It's only fair since we have each other the rest of the year." It would be hardest to leave these two. They had always spent the holidays together.

"Better for her to go than me," Father grumbled from behind his newspaper. "I wish I could light a match and burn all memories of Amorwich from my mind." It was no secret Father abhorred the town her grandmother lived in, and would never return, which was why Ivy felt compelled to go instead.

"I have never felt as strongly about something as I do now." Ivy could not explain why she wanted to go where no one else did. Sometimes doing a good turn was worth a small sacrifice of convenience. Wasn't it?

"You won't fall in love with someone while you are away?" Aunt Morris pinned Ivy with her unflinching gaze—one employed often to intimidate her nieces, or anyone else for that matter, when determined to get her way.

"I will be gone only for the month of December," Ivy said. "It's hardly enough time to convince a stranger to love me."

"She wouldn't dare." Her father crushed the corner of his paper beneath his tight grasp. "She knows I will not abide a connection to such a wretched place."

Aunt Morris sighed. "Very well. If you promise not to fall in love without my express permission, I will concede."

The idea of her falling in love so quickly was so unlikely Ivy easily agreed. Helping Grandmother was the right thing to do.

Ivy had made a terrible mistake.

She sat awkwardly in an embroidered chair near Grandmother's bedside, searching for something to say to the woman she hardly knew. The white of Grandmother's hair matched the linens on the bed; her pallor was nearly the same shade. A patched quilt was tucked around her small, sickly frame.

There had been no mention before of Grandmother's illness.

"I . . . know you expected my father, but I very much wanted to visit." Ivy unclenched her clasped hands and forced her rigid posture to relax.

Grandmother's sad eyes blinked, but she did not respond, not even a simple greeting.

Some ideas were better in Ivy's mind than in real life, but there had to be some way she could help—even if she wasn't the desired guest. She tried a compliment next. "You have quite a lovely house." This was not an outright lie. She had always wondered what her father's boyhood home had looked like. Ravencross, the rambling manor house, was clean and well-furnished. It was more the feeling that permeated every room that she did not care for. A somber pall draped over everything like the hush after a funeral, though it had been ten years since Grandfather's death.

How could she survive being here for an entire month?

When Grandmother again said nothing, Ivy switched tactics. "I am very good at reading out loud. I could read something to your liking."

Grandmother sighed and shook her head, her tired eyes saying more than her mouth did. When Ivy was much younger, Grandmother had visited her family often. Ivy distinctly recalled the woman's spirited nature, one Ivy had been told she had inherited. Grandmother's despondency now was quite worrisome.

By the morning of her third day at Ravencross, Ivy began to question her ability to do any good. As she sat again by Grandmother's side, her secret hope for a relationship with this woman now seemed impossible. The many quiet hours in her company did not seem to offer any comfort or improvement in her health. Ivy's resolve to stay waned. She missed her sisters and was tempted to take the half-day journey back home—even if it meant facing Mr. Beales. She grimaced. Her thoughts were becoming nonsensical. She wasn't ready to give up. Not yet.

After a few maddening minutes of silence at Grandmother's bedside, Ivy knew she required fresh air. "Have you any objection to me walking to town?" Ivy waited, hoping Grandmother would give her consent.

Grandmother turned toward the window, possibly to gauge the weather, but the drapes were pulled tightly closed. "Dress warm," she finally said, her dull voice barely above a whisper.

Ivy promised to do so and rushed from the room. Escaping Ravencross would surely refresh her mind to new ways to help Grandmother. The dark house seemed bound to absorb every last shred of happiness. Was this why Father had not returned in more than twenty-five years? Ivy tied her bonnet under her chin and buttoned her blue spencer. Last came her kid gloves and winter cloak. The bitter chill in the air would not keep her from her walk.

She had seen the small town of Amorwich on her way to Ravencross and knew that the road, a fairly straight line of frozen brown, would take her directly there. When she arrived, nothing seemed familiar, and a stab of homesickness wrenched in her stomach. She turned down Barron Street, which looked to be the main hub of the village, and noticed a sign for a tearoom.

She started in that direction but never made it there.

A bleating goat caught her attention. He was tied to the side of a market stall that sold cheese and milk. The burly dairyman chastised his bellowing goat and then, after a moment of wrestling, unexpectedly maneuvered the animal into an unnatural sitting position. The goat's legs stuck out beneath him like he was a person, and his head lolled to the side.

Had the dairyman just killed his animal right in the middle of the street? Aunt Morris would be appalled! No wonder Father had such contempt for the town. Ivy didn't believe she could continue without saying something. Sometimes even an animal needed an advocate. A rain barrel stood between her and the stall, and as she moved to walk around it, her foot caught on something. She moved her skirts out of the way, and the fabric brushed the leaves back to reveal a rather plain-looking miser purse hidden next to the barrel.

If everyone was like the dairyman, she doubted they would care to see it returned, but she picked it up to see if she might find its owner anyway. Ivy finished circling the barrel and turned to the dairyman again, this time with two questions on her lips. She had only just opened her mouth when a man's shoulder bumped hard into hers. She stumbled, but the man's strong arms wrapped around her to keep her from falling.

"You should watch where you are going," the man said, his voice more annoyed than apologetic. Her eyes connected with his, and her breath caught. She was surprised to see he was a gentleman. His tight lips and furrowed dark brow softened at the sight of her. He might have been exceptionally handsome—especially from her close view—but his appearance did not detract from his rudeness. The manners in this town were shameful!

"I apologize," she said, more than a little flustered, "though I am quite certain the incident was no fault of my own." She put both her hands on his chest and pushed away from him, the force of the push causing a misstep. The error knocked her off-balance and sent her falling against the wooden stall and onto her backside. The dairyman's stall shook. Ivy looked up at the same time a bucket overturned, and cold milk poured over her bonnet, face, and gown. She changed her mind. It seemed the silence of Ravencross was preferable to the village after all.

"You are very right," the gentleman said, holding back a laugh. "The first was entirely my fault. But this . . ." He chuckled while waving his hand toward her. "I declare my innocence."

A tug on her bonnet caused her to turn away from the irksome gentleman, and she found herself face-to-face with a scruffy white goat—the one she'd thought was dead. She yelped and pushed back against the stall, causing cheese curds to tumble onto her lap.

The dairyman hurried around the stall and extended his hand to help her up the exact same time the gentleman did. She looked at the men—both in need of a lesson in manners—and accepted the hand of the dairyman. He, at least, might not know any better. Once righted, she removed her dripping bonnet, and her mouth turned down in an unrepentant frown. Taking a step away from the stall, she assessed the damage to her milk-stained kid gloves.

"Forgive me," the gentleman pleaded, his tone now contrite. "I was reading the paper while walking." He nudged the sodden paper with the toe of his boot right before the goat began to eat it. "Most know my strange habits and tend to stay out of my way while I am in the village. You must be new here."

Ivy nodded, her anger deflating with his sincere apology, and dropped her ruined bonnet to her side. "I am visiting Ravencross for the holiday."

"Ravencross?" His eyes widened. "Are you a relation to Mrs. Hunt?"

"Mrs. Hunt is my paternal grandmother." Now it was her turn to humble herself. "And I, too, apologize. I was not paying attention in the least when we collided. I was about to ask after—"

"You wanted milk?" His lips twitched in humor.

"No," she said, fighting a smile of her own. "I shan't have a taste for milk again for some time. It was the goat, actually."

"The goat?"

"Yes." She pointed to the animal, who did not seem at all ashamed of nibbling a hole into her bonnet. "He was sitting like a person, and I could have sworn he was dead."

The gentleman raised one brow in disbelief. "You must have hit your head harder than I thought. Perhaps I should call for a doctor."

Ivy shook her head. "I am being perfectly honest. Ask him." She pointed to the dairyman.

The gentleman clasped his hands behind his back and turned to the dairyman. "Mr. Bryant?"

Mr. Bryant wore a trim black beard and a once-white apron. He was built for hard labor, and his meaty hands yanked his unruly goat away from the milk. After several attempts, he maneuvered the goat back into his sitting position. Immediately, the goat's limbs went limp and his head relaxed to one side. "It's a li'l trick to help Chester behave."

"How very strange," Ivy said, stepping closer. "Does it hurt him?"

"Not at all, miss," Mr. Bryant said.

"Then a goat truly was behind all this chaos." The gentleman shook his head in amusement.

She faced the gentleman. "As well as my slight preoccupation with this purse I found on the other side of that barrel." She lifted it in proof, though she was surprised she'd managed to hold on to it.

"Interesting." The gentleman accepted the purse and turned it over in his hands.

Ivy examined it at the same time. The long wool stocking had two rings in the middle to close the opening. The dyed burgundy color was absent of softness, tassels, and beads like the purses of the upper class. However plain it may be, it was heavy and full of coin. Someone would miss it.

"Mr. Bryant, have you seen this before?" The gentleman held up the purse.

"No, Your Lordship," the dairyman said as he wiped the last of the milk remains off the stall tabletop. "Don't recall seeing anything like it."

Lordship? Ivy cringed as she accepted the purse back. Not only had she made a fool of herself in front of a handsome gentleman but a titled one at that.

"Inquire around, will you, Mr. Bryant? And . . . I will see you are compensated for your loss today." His voice seemed stilted, almost uncomfortable.

"Let me pay the man," Ivy said, holding up her reticule. "It was my doing, after all."

"Nonsense," His Lordship said, clearing his throat and regaining a tone of authority. "Mr. Bryant is my tenant and my responsibility. Do you have a carriage I can walk you to? You will catch cold if you stay wet."

Just the mention of it brought a shiver to her shoulders. "I walked, my lord."

"No matter. I shall escort you home in my carriage. Come."

Several villagers were already staring at her. A closed carriage sounded exceptionally appealing. Ivy matched her gait with that of her escort and took a moment to examine him out of the corner of her eye. He was maybe five years older than she was, but not more than ten. She liked how his thick ash-brown hair curled beneath his top hat. With her best posture, she reached his shoulder, but she was not the tallest of women.

Besides his appealing physical traits, there was a sensible air to him. His smile was not as ready as some people's, but he did seem kind. He'd also seemed annoyed with their collision, but then again, so had she been. This thought led her back to her face-off with the goat. She batted her eyelashes to clear the mental image and focused on the carriage instead. Painted on the door was a unique crest with a sword and rose crossing each other, both surrounded by bay leaves. The emblem reminded her that no matter what positive qualities this gentleman possessed, she was not quite his equal.

"Do you have a maid with you?"

Ivy bit her lip. "You must think me improper, but I did not think to ask for one. I was determined to take a walk and—"

He put up his hand to silence her. "Propriety must bow to unfortunate mishaps caused by men who don't pay attention."

A footman stepped forward and opened the door, but His Lordship was the one to help Ivy inside. Then he took the seat across from her and gave her a small but encouraging smile.

"Do you live far?" Ivy asked. "I would hate to inconvenience you."

"Not at all. I live a few miles from Ravencross. When you walked here, you passed a bridge, and the path forked. Right leads to my home at Fairmore, and straight takes you to town."

"I remember the bridge and the division in the road," she said. "Perhaps I should have turned and avoided this mess." She tried to keep her tone light, but the smell of milk on her clothes kept her humiliation fresh.

"Then I would have missed out on our memorable meeting. I won't soon forget you now . . . or Chester the goat." The gentleman's almond-shaped eyes crinkled with amusement. They were not brown, like she had first assumed, but hazel.

She might need a day for the heat to leave her cheeks before she could laugh with him. Though, she wondered if she blushed from his attention or from embarrassment. She fingered the miser purse again. "Please let me know if Mr. Bryant locates the owner of the purse. Do you think it will be a formidable task for him? Christmastide is a terrible time to go without."

"I will send word if I hear of anything. I wouldn't worry."

"Thank you." Ivy could already imagine a young family retracing their steps in desperate search of the purse. Perhaps this was the real reason she had felt compelled to come to Amorwich. "I am not one to needlessly fret, but I cannot be at ease until the money is restored to its owner. I plan to return to the village tomorrow and ask around myself."

The gentleman eyed her. "I should have known by your red hair that you would be the determined sort."

"Auburn hair," Ivy corrected. "I would resent such a comment, but I have long heard the Hunt women are a determined lot. Whether it is caused by our hair color, I cannot say."

The gentleman studied her for a moment and then chuckled. "I'm sorry if my comment about your hair offended you when truly I find it enchanting, even if it is auburn and not red. I heard tell once that red hair is the mark of a pure heart . . . if you change your mind about the exact shade."

Ivy shook her head, although inwardly she was amused. "We were discussing the purse, not my hair."

"So we were. I recall your insistence to stop at nothing until the money is returned. And I was about to assure you the matter will likely take care of itself and not to bother thinking on it again."

This would not do. Ivy folded her arms across her chest. "Isn't this the time of year for Christians to rise to the occasion? Out there is a poor man or woman likely beside themselves with worry. I cannot return home in good conscience without promising to help."

He eyed her curiously. "Very well; I cannot distract you from your cause. And I cannot in good conscience let you complete the task alone. I have some business matters to see to in the morning, but then I will ask around as well."

"Thank you," Ivy said, grateful for whatever assistance the man might offer. He knew the people and the village much better than she did. "Please be sure to not reveal the description of the purse. I would not want someone to claim it dishonestly. Let them tell you what it looks like."

The carriage stopped, and the footman opened the door and helped Ivy down. "Thank you for the use of your carriage," she said, dipping into a curtsy. It had been a godsend, but she was not sure what she thought of the gentleman just yet.

CHAPTER TWO

CURTIS'S MOTHER, LADY BLAKELY, WOULD not like him escorting home Mrs. Hunt's granddaughter. His mother was above reproach, except for one black spot—her feelings for the Hunts. But as soon as he'd taken in Miss Hunt's deep green eyes, rimmed with blue, he had forgotten himself. The beautiful Miss Hunt was a series of delightful surprises. First, her fiery spirit as she'd pushed out of his arms, then the absurd milk-and-goat incident, and lastly her insistence to do her duty concerning the lost purse.

"There you are," Mama announced as he entered through the front door of Fairmore. "I expected you at tea, and you were well aware of your obligation to me."

Curtis's lips pulled upward; he would not fold for a moment. "You were well aware that I refused your invitation to meet Miss Buxton."

"You seem much too happy after abusing your mother," she said, her pout more pretense than real.

"Mama," Curtis said. "I have no intention of allowing you to arrange my marriage. I told you I will find a wife all on my own."

"Will you? I am beginning to wonder."

"Yes, I might even bump into her unintentionally in the village. She will fall at my feet, with or without milk on her head, and it will be love at first sight."

His mother blinked a few times. "Have you been in your cups?"

Curtis chuckled. "I am not foxed. I am simply reassuring you that I have things well in hand."

"I do wonder, but I shall let it be this time." She sighed. "But do not forget the card party on Thursday. I will not be so forgiving if you miss that."

Curtis bowed. "Yes, Mama. I promise to come." Her exasperation made him want to laugh again, but at least she did not press him about his time in the village. While he was certainly happy to meet a lovely young lady, he knew bringing up her name would cause a greater argument than did missing tea. When Mama disappeared into the drawing room, he breathed out in relief. Now he could think on Miss Hunt again without any feelings of guilt.

Why the young lady wanted to help some poor villager was beyond him. It was the noble thing to do, to be sure, but it was not pressing like she made it out to be. For him, helping people was more uncomfortable than anything. He even avoided checking on the welfare of his tenants. His father had been the opposite; he ought not to have died prematurely. The pressure to follow in the footsteps of such a dignified man overwhelmed Curtis.

His younger brother, Esmond, should have been the firstborn since he naturally cared for everything around him. Curtis tended to avoid social situations, his tenants, and all the responsibilities that forced him to deal directly with people. Why disappoint them? But thoughts of Miss Hunt defied his normal rationale. For some unexplainable reason, Curtis would risk a few awkward conversations if it meant another meeting with her.

A clean milk-free cloak was something to be grateful for when there was little else to bring Ivy joy. The doctor had called that morning, and he'd reported Grandmother unchanged. She suffered from an inescapable case of old age. There was nothing to be done but keep her comfortable.

As Ivy pinned the blessedly clean cloak closed at her throat, her thoughts circled to past Christmases when she'd been surrounded by her father and sisters. What were they doing back in Peterborough? Did they miss her as much as she did them? Nothing here had gone as she had planned. She pushed her melancholy thoughts aside and stopped once more at Grandmother's room.

The poor woman's frail body sat in her bed, propped up by pillows. A neatly folded handkerchief lay in her hands, and her unfocused eyes seemed to sharpen with Ivy's arrival.

"Can I sit with you this morning?" Ivy asked.

"No, you *may* not."

Ivy had anticipated being ignored, which was why she had already pinned on her cloak, but this response was new. It was a trace of the grandmother she had once known, even if her words lacked their usual fire.

"Do you mind if I go out again this morning?"

"Go on," Grandmother said. She coughed once and closed her eyes.

Ivy stood in the threshold of the room, filled with inadequacy. What more could she be doing? She held back a sigh. At least she was here and available. It seemed doing the right thing also meant doing the hard thing— and acting in her father's stead was no exception. It saddened Ivy to think her father's hatred for a place would prevent him from being with his mother at the end of her life. She would do her best to cheer her grandmother any way she could.

"Would you like me to bring you something from the village?"

Grandmother's head swayed almost imperceptibly from side to side.

Ivy's shoulders drooped with disappointment. "Very well. I do hope you feel better by this evening." Maybe rest would help where she could not. She made her way out of the dreary house and began her walk to the village. When she passed the fork in the road, her thoughts drifted to the gentleman she'd met the day before. Now, there was something enjoyable to think about.

He'd been uncommonly handsome. Dare she hope to catch a glimpse of him? And would he really help her find the owner of the purse? She'd seen the look of amusement mixed with doubt in his eyes. Regardless of whether or not he wanted to help, Ivy would search every day of her holiday if she had to. She'd never forgotten a peasant family's forlorn expression when they'd come begging for a few cups of corn on St. Thomas's Day last December. The children were starving, and Ivy would not let another family suffer if it was in her means to help.

"Good morrow," a farmer said as his cart passed by Ivy.

"And to you. Pardon me, but have you lost a purse?"

The man slowed and looked back. "A purse? Was it full of blunt?"

"Yes."

He rubbed his scruffy chin. "Not mine, then. Mine's full of holes, see. But I'd be careful spreading about town that you're toting a fat purse. Wouldn't be safe for you."

Ivy pulled her reticule tight against her stomach as the farmer bid her adieu. While she'd left the coin purse at home, she did carry some pin money of her own. The farmer appeared to be genuine in his carefulness, but his words reminded her that again, in her haste, she had left without a maid. Her aunt would be furious, but Ivy wasn't turning back now. At home she never had to worry about such a precaution since she always had a sister by her side. Regardless of how important her errand might be, she must guard her reputation. And as the kindly farmer had pointed out, once the word was out that she had money on her, she would be susceptible to all sorts of trouble.

Ivy made her way to Barron Street toward Mr. Bryant, the dairyman. "No doubt you remember me from yesterday."

"I do indeed," Mr. Bryant said with a crooked grin. "No harm came from your tumble, did it?"

"No. I am perfectly well, thank you. But I am sorry about the spilled milk."

"I'm not," Mr. Bryant said with a chuckle. "Haven't seen His Lordship smile before. And I was paid thrice the worth of the milk. It was a good day for the wife and me."

Ivy recalled the unnatural way the gentleman had spoken to his tenant. She filed it away to think about another time. "I am glad you received such generous compensation. By chance, did anyone come back for the lost purse?"

"No, miss. I asked some of the shop owners, but none of them lost anythin'. I'll keep an eye out for you."

"Thank you, Mr. Bryant. I appreciate your helpfulness." Since Mr. Bryant had already asked the shop owners, Ivy was left without a plan. She wished him a good day and went in search of something to bring back for Grandmother. Ivy found her way into the haberdashery and purchased a rust-colored ribbon while she thought of what to do next.

"Why would you buy a ribbon a shade so near the color of your hair?" a voice asked from behind her.

Ivy turned away from the shop's counter to face the gentleman from the day before. Her stomach unwillingly tightened in anticipation. She quickly curtsied. "Good day, my lord. I was not sure I would see you today."

"I saw you come in. I hope you don't mind."

"No. On the contrary, I wanted to see you again. I mean . . ." Her admission apparently surprised him almost as much as it did her.

"I understand." He opened the door, and a brisk chill greeted them as they exited the shop. "You are referring to the lost purse, I assume. I am sorry to report I've learned nothing since yesterday."

"Nor I," Ivy said. "Mr. Bryant claims the shop owners have heard nothing either."

"There are several outlying homes we could try next."

"We?" she asked, betraying her eagerness.

The gentleman realized his mistake and smiled sheepishly. The dairyman had to have been wrong about never seeing His Lordship's smile. Ivy had seen it several times now herself.

"Now that I think of it," the gentleman said, "my schedule this afternoon is free—if you would care for my company."

"I would be delighted. But there is one problem. We haven't even been introduced."

"Ah," the gentleman said. "You are Miss Hunt, I presume. And I am . . . Lord B."

"Lord B.?" Her brow furrowed.

He moved his gloved hand to his mouth and coughed to hide the amusement that was so clear in the twinkle of his eyes. "Please, call me Lord B. until our errand is finished today. I will reveal all at the end of the day."

Ivy folded her arms across her chest. "I learned not a half hour ago that I am too trusting. I came to town without my maid again and naively advertised the money I carry. Then I almost agreed to let you—a mere stranger—accompany me. My judgment is in question. Who is Lord B., and can I trust him?"

"Lord B. is a gentleman in title and in manner, I assure you. I will provide a character witness at the first opportunity to ease any concern."

Ivy had to hide her smile now. "I will have to insist on this witness—if we are to continue to walk together, that is."

"Your mother trained you well," Lord B. replied.

Ivy dipped her head, ignoring the cool gust of wind that pulled at her skirt. "My mother died twelve years ago. My two sisters and I had an adequate governess and a smothering aunt who owns the credit for our upbringing. My father loves us enough for two parents but says his club is no place for the rearing of ladies."

"I am sorry to hear about your mother. My father died two years ago, so I can sympathize with your grief."

"Oh, now I am sorry. Your loss is fresh. Though, I appreciate the kinship your similar experience offers. People with two parents don't quite comprehend what life is like with just one. Does that sound uncharitable?"

"Not at all," Lord B. said as he leaned against the outer brick wall of the haberdashery. "Loss is never easy. I always knew I'd inherit the responsibilities of a baron, but I'd expected to be much older when I did. I'm still fumbling through my obligations. Life would be far simpler if my father were still alive."

"If he were, which tenant would he visit first?"

Lord B. gave her a sideways look. "What an interesting question. Let me think. Oh, he would check with Mr. and Mrs. Humphrey."

"Then, we must go there right away," Ivy said, repressing thoughts of propriety for the sake of a good cause. "We wouldn't want the Humphreys to be without their purse, now, would we?"

He chuckled. "No, we wouldn't."

Ivy let Lord B. help her into his carriage once the directions were passed to the driver.

"Why the Humphreys before the other tenants?" Ivy asked as the carriage bounced down the dirt road away from the village.

Lord B. looked through the window, drawing Ivy's eyes to the passing trees, bare of leaves and color. "Mrs. Humphrey was the nursemaid for my younger brother and sister and myself. Mr. Humphrey is our gamekeeper. They have served my family for as long as I can remember."

"Do you visit them often?"

"Who, me? No, never. I have no reason to."

"Not even to inquire about their welfare?"

"They are paid adequately for whatever services they render my family. The rest of their lives is really none of my business."

Ivy couldn't quite understand. Lord B. seemed generous in his efforts to help her but aloof toward his tenants. She imagined the relationship between master and tenant was usually this way, but for some reason, it felt wrong to be that way for Lord B.

"Well, I am sure they will enjoy seeing you today." She smiled, and he returned it, a single dimple appearing in his left cheek. His simple smile felt like butterfly wings tickling her arms and dancing in her stomach. Never had any man, especially Mr. Beales, created such a sensation.

The carriage pulled up to a stone farmhouse with a thatched roof and smoke rising from the chimney. The garden was small but neat and tidy. Ivy fingered her reticule, thinking of the miser purse. Were the Humphreys the owners she and Lord B. searched for?

CHAPTER THREE

CURTIS KNOCKED ON THE HUMPHREYS' door. He ran his hands down his coat, hoping to rid himself of his sudden anxiousness. It had been too long since he'd greeted the older couple, even though he had no obligation to do so. Miss Hunt glanced his way but did not say anything. He could thank her for that. She had cast a spell on him with her sweetness and tricked him into coming, but the awkwardness of their visit would be entirely his own fault.

The door pulled inward, revealing the jovial smile of Mrs. Humphrey. She looked the same, though with a few more wrinkles and more gray in her bun than Curtis remembered.

"Well, bless my soul! What do I owe the honor of this visit?"

"Mrs. Humphrey," Curtis began, "might we trespass for a moment?"

"Indeed, Your Lordship. Come in out of the cold."

"Thank you." Curtis led Miss Hunt inside the small but tidy room. She paused to warm her hands by the crackling fire.

"Miss Hunt, may I introduce Mrs. Humphrey?"

"A pleasure," Mrs. Humphrey said, dipping into a curtsy. She ushered them to her table and said, "Tea, anyone?" while they sat. She was already pouring two cups before they could object.

When the woman handed Curtis a cup, he took a sip and said, "I hate to intrude, but—"

"Nonsense." Mrs. Humphrey cut him off. "You are always welcome. With my husband gone trapping, I am alone far more often than I care to be. I hoped you would someday spare a minute to visit your old nurse—not that you would even think to." She paused, clearly regretting her hurried words. "I'm talking too much, aren't I?"

"No, not at all," Miss Hunt assured her.

"I think you misinterpreted our request to come in," Curtis said.

"Yes," Miss Hunt added. "Lord B. has been meaning to visit, but he is so very busy, you see."

Curtis cut a look at Miss Hunt. Why was she lying for him? He had not been meaning to visit . . . ever.

Mrs. Humphrey's thick cheeks lifted into a smile. "Lord B.? I do like that. And I understand why he cannot visit. His Lordship is an important man now, like his father."

Miss Hunt nodded. "But you were the first on his list to see today. Isn't that so, Lord B.?"

Lord B. sounded like a silly name to have given now that Miss Hunt insisted on calling him it while in company. It served him right. "Yes, you were first on our list." He smiled, but his social smile usually felt like more of a grimace. He couldn't help his awkwardness, though Miss Hunt seemed perfectly at ease in their current situation.

"We heard rumors of a lost purse, Mrs. Humphrey," Miss Hunt said. "I do hope it wasn't yours."

"No, miss. The ribbon might not run as thick here as it does in some houses, but we've sufficient to see us through."

Curtis was glad to hear it. He didn't want the Humphreys to go without. He scooted his chair back and made to stand, but Miss Hunt put her gloved hand on his to stop him. It was there for just a moment, but the small gesture made him freeze in place.

Miss Hunt gave Mrs. Humphrey her full attention. "Do you celebrate Christmas? I admit I love it more than Twelfth Night."

Miss Hunt's question perplexed Curtis. Not ten minutes ago, she was eager to search for the owner of the purse, and now all she wanted to do was gab the day away.

"Yes, but we're simple folk," Mrs. Humphrey said. "There is always Christmas pudding, and we used to have . . . that is . . ."

"Well?" Curtis prompted.

Mrs. Humphrey's cheeks blotched with patches of red. "Your father—he, ah, used to insist we keep a goose for our table. He was a generous man."

Curtis wondered why no one had ever told him. "By all means, you should have a goose this Christmas too."

Mrs. Humphrey smiled. "I told the other families you would come around."

"Come around?" He frowned. What could she mean?

"Ever since you were a small boy, you were wary of people. Always sweet but kind of nervous-like when others were visiting."

Now Curtis's cheeks were surely red. Mrs. Humphrey had him pegged. "I am not easy in company, which reminds me, Miss Hunt, it is time we visit the Pools before my enthusiasm wanes."

Miss Hunt bit back her smile. "Yes, we don't care to neglect the Pools. Thank you for the tea, Mrs. Humphrey."

"You're very welcome. I hope you and, er, *Lord B.* come see me again soon."

Miss Hunt assured her that even if she could not come, Lord B. would. As soon as they were away from the Humphreys' cottage, Curtis turned to Miss Hunt. "Why would you promise the woman I would return?"

Miss Hunt laughed lightly. "Of course you will return. Why ever would you stay away? I could have remained for hours, you know, eager as I was to hear stories about you as a child."

"You don't even know my full name, and you were eager to hear about me as an awkward youth?" Curtis wanted to be annoyed, but Miss Hunt was as charming as a sunset in the Lake District.

"I would never believe you to be awkward," Miss Hunt assured him. "You have a quiet confidence, even when you are uncomfortable. That sort of self-assurance will be an asset to you in running your estate."

"You think so? Are you an expert on the subject?" he teased, although he was pleased with her compliment.

"Yes," she said with conviction, and then her face fell, revealing her obvious bluff. "Actually, I know nothing about running an estate. I do know about people, though, and Mrs. Humphrey provided me with an excellent character witness. In other words, you may accompany me to the Pools' home."

He laughed. "How fortunate I am to deserve your company. Come, let's walk and leave the carriage here. The Pools do not live far."

The two of them approached the Pools' door a few moments later, and Curtis knocked. This house was much smaller than the Humphreys' home, and instead of stone, it bore white plaster on the outer walls and a thatched roof. Curtis knocked again, but no one answered.

Miss Hunt pressed her ear to the door. "Do you hear someone coughing?"

"I don't think it proper to eavesdrop, Miss Hunt." Though he thought he heard a muffled noise, he could not say whether it was a cough.

She narrowed her eyes as she listened. "I am certain I hear coughing." She turned the handle before he could stop her, cracking the door open. "Anyone home?"

Curtis heard the hacking cough rather clearly now. A voice called to them, but he could not make out the words.

"I think we've been invited in."

"How can you be sure?" Curtis regretfully followed her inside. Odd; the room was the same temperature as the outside. Sure enough, there wasn't a fire in the grate.

Miss Hunt led the way to the other side of the room, where a drape separated the sleeping area from the main room. She pulled it back and gasped.

Curtis hurried to the bedside. "Mrs. Pool!" The pale young woman was shivering in her bed with blankets up to her chin. She coughed again, but her eyes did not seem to register Curtis's or Miss Hunt's presence.

Miss Hunt joined him and put her hand to Mrs. Pool's forehead. "She's burning with fever."

"Where is her husband?" Curtis asked—a ridiculous question since Miss Hunt knew less than he did about Mr. Pool's whereabouts.

"I'll get Mrs. Humphrey to help, but perhaps a fire would be appropriate first."

Grateful for a task, Curtis moved to the fireplace, but there was no wood in the box. He searched the side and back of the house, but there wasn't any wood to be found anywhere. Miss Hunt came out, and he followed her to Mrs. Humphrey's. "I will have to borrow some of the Humphreys' wood. I don't see an ax, let alone tinder for a fire."

It took only a few minutes to backtrack to the Humphreys'. Curtis sent his driver to find the doctor before hurrying up the walk. This time, Curtis knocked harder and without the same trepidation.

"You're back." Mrs. Humphrey's mouth turned from a smile into a frown of concern. "Oh dear. By the looks on your faces, something must be wrong."

"Mrs. Pool is fevering," Miss Hunt said.

"And we'll need to borrow wood," Curtis added.

Mrs. Humphrey invited them in. "I will grab some herbs and things. Miss Hunt, could you carry over the teapot? It's still warm."

They all separated and gathered back at the Pools'. Miss Hunt acted like a true nurse and danced around Mrs. Pool as Mrs. Humphrey shot out instructions. Curtis coaxed a fire to life and then stood back and watched.

"The doctor should be here within the hour," Curtis offered lamely. Never had he felt so useless.

"It's a blessed thing you found her, or she would surely have died in the night." Mrs. Humphrey attempted to get some tea into Mrs. Pool's mouth.

"Where is her husband?" Curtis asked.

"Took off a fortnight ago," Mrs. Humphrey said. "My husband and I offered to help, but Mrs. Pool wouldn't have it. She's awfully prideful. Threatened us harm if we ever stepped foot near her again. I left a basket last week, but Mrs. Pool returned it without taking so much as a crust of bread."

Curtis looked at Miss Hunt as he realized the graveness of Mrs. Pool's situation. "I never heard Mr. Pool left."

Mrs. Humphrey gave him a sympathetic glance. "He's taken off before, so it's likely he'll return before the month is out. I'm only glad they haven't any children yet, or I'd worry even more."

They waited for the doctor to come, and when he finally arrived, they all breathed more easily. Miss Hunt hugged herself. "Is there anything more we can do?"

The doctor shook his head. "Better leave before you catch the illness yourself."

The very idea caused Curtis to act. He put his hand on the small of Miss Hunt's back and directed her to the door, leaving Mrs. Humphrey to take charge. "You heard the doctor," he said. "I won't let you risk your health."

"I'm simply worried. Mrs. Pool was too weak to even take a sip of tea."

"I know." Curtis was worried too. He accompanied Miss Hunt back to his carriage, helped her inside, then took the seat opposite her. Strange how one day together felt like a week. There was something about working by her side that seemed to connect Curtis to Miss Hunt. "Your grandmother must be anxious as to your whereabouts."

"She is probably sleeping. Her health is declining rapidly."

"I'm sorry to hear it. I thought I saw her in the village not long ago. She seemed perfectly well then."

Miss Hunt's brow rose. "Truly? I assumed she'd been sick for months. None of us were made aware of her illness until I arrived. She'd requested a visitor, and my father thought her in need of company for the holidays."

"It was kind of you to come, then. Are the two of you close?"

"Not at all." Sadness emanated from her eyes. "My father does not speak of Amorwich with any kindness. There was a land dispute between two families, and my father regrets to be on the losing end. This is my first time visiting Grandmother in all my life. She came to Peterborough often enough when I was younger, but she stopped traveling after my grandfather died. When she writes, it's mostly to my father."

Curtis shifted in his seat. He knew of the dispute Miss Hunt spoke of. While the details were murky, the negative feelings between the families had only escalated over the years. He scratched the back of his neck, attempting to hide his unease. How had he involved himself in such a moral dilemma? Despite how impossible it was, he knew he wanted to court Miss Hunt. He looked up just as a lock of auburn hair fell across her cheek. He longed to tuck it behind her ear and tell her how wonderful she was. When the carriage pulled up in front of Ravencross, his confusion piqued. He should not be here, of all places.

"Thank you," Miss Hunt said, "for helping me and your tenants. You are a good man."

Guilt mixed with his confusion and tightened his stomach into a knot. He'd fooled this beautiful, innocent woman into thinking him a magnanimous person. He had done his duty and no more. The welfare of his tenants had never been his first priority, but all he could do was mumble "You're welcome."

Her wide smile unnerved him as she said goodbye, reminding Curtis he didn't like to be unnerved. In fact, all of Miss Hunt's ideas stretched him in ways he didn't care for. With her out of the carriage, his logic kicked in. He wasn't capable of following Miss Hunt's every whim or fancy. No, her goodness had temporarily intoxicated him, and that was why he was suddenly thinking about courting. Tomorrow, he would return to his normal self. He would stay away from the village. He would remain in his office, where he could safely conduct business through ledgers and letters.

CHAPTER FOUR

IVY'S ERROR IN JUDGMENT DID not sit well with her. Her aunt had taught her better than to spend the day with a gentleman unchaperoned. Not that Lord B. had given her any reason to worry. He had been the perfect gentleman and gone along with all of her ideas. Never had she been treated so well by a man. She did not even know his full name. She'd forgotten to ask.

Her concern for Mrs. Pool had been her sole focus. Helping Mrs. Pool renewed Ivy's desire to find the owner of the miser purse. There was too much suffering in the world.

The housekeeper, Mrs. Talbot, met Miss Hunt in the entryway of Ravencross. "A word, Miss Hunt?"

"Certainly," Ivy said, already wondering if Grandmother's health had worsened. Never had Mrs. Talbot seemed at all interested in speaking with her before.

"I saw the family crest on the carriage through the window. I'm afraid I must caution you, miss. Your grandmother would not like you keeping company with the Blakely family, not with bad blood between them." Mrs. Talbot's long face only lengthened with her grim frown.

"Blakely?" Ivy easily connected the name to Lord B. "What bad blood do you refer to?" Then it dawned on her, and she almost forgot to breathe. "The Blakelys are the family feuding with ours! My father always speaks of Amorwich, never the specific family. I had no idea of his connection to . . . I feel simply awful."

Mrs. Talbot nodded. "It isn't my place to gossip, but I thought you ought to know."

"I thank you, Mrs. Talbot."

Mrs. Talbot looked behind her, but no one was there. Then she leaned closer to Ivy. "Such news of you with His Lordship could send your grandmother to her grave faster than any illness ever could. The matter has festered with time. In her condition, we cannot risk her hearing of it."

Ivy appreciated the housekeeper taking her into her confidence, but disappointment still settled on her shoulders. Upsetting Grandmother defeated her purpose for coming to Ravencross. It also meant not continuing her friendship with Lord Blakely. That thought hurt more than it should. But what about the miser purse? And she would worry without news of Mrs. Pool.

She took off her things and went directly to Grandmother's bedroom. The door was open, so she stepped inside. "Are you feeling better?"

Grandmother might have rested all day, but the fatigue in her face seemed more apparent than ever. "Don't worry about me."

More than a little afraid of her grandmother, Ivy approached the bedside with trepidation. "I brought you something from town."

Grandmother's eyes sharpened, and she leaned toward her. "What is it?"

"A ribbon the color of my hair—your hair too, when you were younger. I thought you might like me to tie it into your braid."

Grandmother relaxed back against her pillows and turned her head away, exposing her thin white braid.

Unsure what the silent gesture meant, Ivy hesitated. She remembered Lord Blakely's reluctance to visit his tenants and decided it was always best to act on a kind thought. She bravely reached over and tied a neat bow at the end of Grandmother's hair. There was no "thank you" or "leave me"— just more silence.

Curtis made his valet assist him in dressing well before dawn. Thoughts of Mrs. Pool had kept him from sleeping, and a ride to check on her would be worth the peace of mind. The December morning wind cut through his jacket once he stepped outside, but it only reminded him of the dark fireplace in the Pools' cottage. He was relieved to see a trail of smoke coming from the chimney as he approached in his carriage.

He quietly rapped on the door, feeling foolish for coming at such an hour. It would not do any good to wake Mrs. Pool in her weak state.

The door creaked open, revealing a tired Mrs. Humphrey. "Your Lordship?"

Her vigilance impressed him. "I couldn't sleep. Do you mind if I come in? I only wanted to know if Mrs. Pool was still with us."

Mrs. Humphrey let him in, but she shook her head as he took a seat at the wobbly table. "I would have sent word after breakfast either way. You ought not trouble yourself."

He shrugged. "Might as well give me the news now." He looked at the drape, where on the other side, Mrs. Pool either slept or lay dead.

"The fever hasn't taken her yet, but if we cannot get any nourishment into her, Mrs. Pool won't last another day."

"Is there nothing to be done? Did the doctor leave medicine?"

"Yes, but Mrs. Pool was nearly beyond help when we found her. 'Twill take a miracle."

Curtis frowned. "A miracle? As in an act of God?" He could only utter such a question in the privacy and company of his old nursemaid.

"Miracles happen every day, Your Lordship. But it isn't up to us to grant them, now, is it? All we can do is ask and believe."

"You mean pray." It must be the fatigue he felt, because the pressure of such an idea weighed heavily around him like a coat of chain mail. Curtis hadn't uttered a prayer since the day his father had died.

Mrs. Humphrey didn't hear him. She was setting a pot of water over the fire to boil for tea. Curtis did not consider himself religious. He believed in God but no longer worshipped Him. On Sundays, he attended church for his mother's sake. Speaking to God after all these years felt as unnatural as making small talk at a party. Curtis never knew what anyone expected him to say. But he could spare a few words for Mrs. Pool. The young lady's feverish thrashings struck a chord of sympathy inside him. He closed his eyes and whispered a simple plea. "Spare her, Holy Father."

❄ ❄ ❄

Ivy knew seeing Lord Blakely again was out of the question, but thoughts of the miser purse and Mrs. Pool inevitably brought her mind back to him. She stewed all through breakfast before deciding she'd take a maid and return to the village. They would stop at Mrs. Pool's first, before she had any chance of running into Lord Blakely, and bring the sick woman some fresh bread and soup.

Her lady's maid was shared with her grandmother since her maid in Peterborough could not be spared. Edith did not take kindly to the idea of joining her, but Mrs. Talbot insisted upon sending her and even requested the carriage.

Ivy addressed Edith. "We will stop first at Mrs. Pool's cottage. Do you know her?"

Edith was at least fifteen years Ivy's senior, with wide-set eyes and brown hair that poked out of her mobcap like the bristles of a paintbrush. She kept her opinions to herself, but it was clear she had many brewing inside. "No, miss. Never heard of her."

"She seems close to my own age," Ivy added, but no sign of recollection sparked in the maid's eyes. Instead, Ivy saw barely veiled annoyance there. She hated putting anyone out, but this was absolutely necessary. "Mrs. Pool is very ill, and the doctor said she might not make it through the night. I cannot be easy until I know how she is." And Ivy couldn't be sure Lord Blakely would send word to let her know.

A fresh blanket of snow already contained a few footprints up to the Pools' cottage. Ivy knocked and waited, with Edith standing quietly behind her. To her surprise, Lord Blakely opened the door. His eyes widened, matching her own.

"Well, this is unexpected," he said.

"Yes"—Ivy's smile slipped—"Lord Blakely."

Lord Blakely cleared his throat. "I see you discovered my real name on your own."

"Perhaps we can speak of this after I hear of Mrs. Pool's well-being."

"Oh, certainly." Lord Blakely moved aside and ushered them in.

Mrs. Humphrey poked her head around the drapes. "Oh, miss, you shouldn't be here. Remember what the doctor said? These fevers are known to spread."

Feeling foolish but also determined, Ivy did not move. "I must know how Mrs. Pool is faring. She is still alive, then?"

Mrs. Humphrey clucked her tongue. "Look at the two of you—as worried as a couple expecting their first child. Yes, Mrs. Pool is still with us."

Ivy's cheeks warmed at the notion of her and Lord Blakely being married and with child. "I am relieved to hear it. This is Edith, my maid. We brought a few staples for Mrs. Pool. I would recommend the soup right away."

"Thank you, miss."

"You must be exhausted." Ivy could see the fatigue in Mrs. Humphrey's eyes. "Perhaps we could sit here while you rest."

Mrs. Humphrey sighed, and clearly she was too tired to disagree. "Let Edith sit here, and the two of you take some fresh air while I nap. I won't be putting your health at risk."

Lord Blakely put his bare hand on Ivy's back, the touch warm and familiar from the day before. He gently led her to the door before Ivy's stubbornness could dissuade them. Edith switched Mrs. Humphrey places, and Ivy was convinced she had helped at least in some small way.

"The snow is still coming down." Lord Blakely shook his head. "Here, let me grab the kitchen chairs, and we can sit under the eave of the roof."

Once situated in Mrs. Pool's smallish garden, Ivy laughed.

"What is so humorous?"

"We are."

"Hmm?"

Ivy pointed to the cottage. "Both of us coming here as if we know anything about caring for the sick. I mean, I do know a little, but I hardly know one poultice from another. And you, a titled gentleman. It seems rather silly."

Lord Blakely gave her a crooked grin—one that set her heart to pounding. "And now we are sitting outside in the middle of December so you might avoid getting ill, when you are just as likely to catch a cold out here."

Ivy sighed, but it was a contented one. Until she remembered that she was not supposed to be speaking to Lord Blakely at all. "You know, I did not understand the connection of your family to my own until last evening. I'm not supposed to be in company with you."

His expression turned sheepish. "Nor I with you."

"Did your family really steal the Hunts' land?"

"My family?" Lord Blakely raised one brow. "It had nothing to do with stealing. It was part of an agreement that fell through. No one cheated anyone, but the frustration turned into hate faster than anyone imagined it would. The snub continued decades later. There aren't many influential families in the area, so it is a real shame."

"Then, what I know is correct. A friendship cannot be made between us."

"There is simply too much history to undo." Lord Blakely's tone was casual, but his eyes held some regret. "You and your maid may return home, and I'll send one of my staff to relieve Mrs. Humphrey."

"I plan to return to the village and keep asking after the miser purse."

"That purse again. You cannot forget it?"

Ivy shook her head. "No, not for a moment. Remember, it's—"

"Christmas, I know," Lord Blakely finished. "I've known you for only a few days, and yet, I find myself folding for your desires. If I check with my other tenants, will that satisfy you?"

"Might I join you?"

Lord Blakely chuckled. "You are incorrigible."

She smiled. "I shan't be offended by such a remark—only further emboldened."

"Is tomorrow soon enough? I will have hot bricks and blankets for the carriage."

Ivy hesitated. "Will our families be upset by us working together to help someone in need?" Would Grandmother even blink if Ivy told her exactly how she had spent her time the last few days?

Lord Blakely studied her. "One more day cannot hurt. It's not as if we are courting."

Ivy laughed a little too loudly. "Heavens, no."

"What if you walk to the bridge tomorrow and we meet there?"

"I think the bridge a wise location." Ivy found her cheeks warming, despite the cold. He was looking at her with such intensity.

Lord Blakely cleared his throat. "Well. Shall I take you home?"

Ivy nodded. "And you'll send word if anything changes with Mrs. Pool?"

"I will. And when Mrs. Pool is better, she will have you to thank." Lord Blakely's eyes met hers once more. Ivy could melt under such a gaze.

"The soup will help," Ivy insisted. "Its restorative properties are quite magical."

"Truly?" His brow quirked with an amused curiosity.

"It's not just the superior and diverse flavors. I believe it to be the ideal remedy for everything from a cold to a bad temper."

"Soup does all that for you?" The tops of Lord Blakely's cheeks lifted in amusement as he rose from his chair.

"It's a great comfort to me. More so than flowers, decadent desserts, or words of poetry. It warms me from the inside out and fills all my senses. And it reminds me of my mother. I only hope it will cure Mrs. Pool, but I'm worried she is too far gone." Ivy stood so Lord Blakely could take her chair back inside.

"Perhaps it's the thought behind the soup that has healing properties," Lord Blakely suggested, wrapping his hands around the sides of one of the chairs.

"Like the thought that brought you here today?" She said it teasingly, but she meant it. "I didn't think you enjoyed visiting your tenants."

Lord Blakely moved his hands up and down the sides of the chair as if to avoid her eyes. "I was in the area."

Ivy frowned, trying to make sense of the man. "You have a kinder heart than you give yourself credit for."

Lord Blakely finally met her gaze. His eyes held a mixture of sadness and possibly regret. She knew from their previous conversation that his being here was not natural to him, but she had a strange desire to help him see what he was capable of. After three days of crossing paths, she felt she saw more good in him than he did in himself. If only he were not a Blakely and she not a Hunt.

CHAPTER FIVE

CURTIS DID HIS BEST TO remain patient with his mother. "Can you not ask Esmond or Amelia? I'm much too busy to help you plan your Christmas ball." He could easily carve out some time, but it was wiser to keep himself occupied than to be trapped under his mother's thumb.

Lady Blakely sighed. "I know this is a yearly tradition, but I'm drowning in expectations. It's not as if I'm inviting all of Northamptonshire, just a few affluent families in the surrounding towns, but someone is always unsatisfied. We must have no fewer than sixty dishes prepared for dinner." She didn't stop for him to comment but blazed on with her thoughts. "I'll have a room set up again for billiards and cards, and we'll open the drawing room for refreshments. Fairmore is plenty big enough, but I wish everyone could content themselves with dancing and stay in the ballroom."

Curtis's foot started bouncing. He didn't have time to listen for the next hour to his mother's plans, not if he wanted to be on time to his appointment with Miss Hunt. "I'll tell the footmen how many tables we will need to set up."

"And you will arrange for the orchestra?"

Curtis pushed his gloved hand through his hair. "Yes, yes. Anything else?"

"Why are you in such a hurry?"

"Who, me? I'm taking the carriage to town for some errands."

Lady Blakely eyed him strangely. "Then you shan't mind if Amelia and I accompany you. I want to personally check if all of my candles have arrived. I don't care for a poorly lit ballroom."

Curtis groaned. "We have a second carriage. Perhaps you and Amelia might take it to town."

"I knew you would suggest it. You have been altogether too secretive the last few days. There is absolutely no reason we cannot go together. Is there?"

"Cannot a man desire privacy and solitude? I don't remember you going to town with Father for any reason." Lady Blakely frowned deeply enough to make Curtis regret the comparison. His father was a kind and generous man, but Father and Mother's relationship had always been strained. Curtis needed to fix his verbal error before he ruined his mother's morning. "All right. You and Amelia may come with me to town." The words almost hurt to utter, but the last thing he wanted was for his mother to ferret around and discover his acquaintance with Miss Hunt. His mother was nothing if not persistent.

Lady Blakely's smile returned, but her eyes were still absent of light. "Thank you, Curtis, dear. I will tell Amelia to dress quickly."

Now what was Curtis to do about Miss Hunt? Only one thing came to mind, and she would no doubt think him mad.

Ivy stood once more on the threshold of Grandmother's room. "I brought a book of poems to read aloud."

Grandmother seemed weaker, if possible, but her white brows arched with curiosity. "I won't listen to anything too ridiculous."

"Of course." Ivy sat on the edge of the chair beside Grandmother's bed. She opened the book but could barely see the words in the dark room. Without asking, Ivy's shaking fingers pulled the drapes back, letting in a burst of light.

Grandmother turned away but did not object. It was a silent victory for Ivy. She swallowed back her fear and began reading all the cheerful poems she had marked the night before. When she finally looked up, Grandmother was sleeping, but across her face was the whisper of a smile. Ivy's shoulders relaxed. Such a simple task had cost Ivy a great deal of courage. The smile was just the reward she needed.

When the longcase clock in the drawing room struck noon, she and Edith left for the bridge. Edith had little knowledge of Ivy's arrangement, and Ivy hoped the maid would go along with her plan. When they arrived at the bridge, no carriage awaited them. In the middle of the road was a note set on top of a handkerchief-covered bowl. She flipped open the note and read,

Something has come up. Please meet me tomorrow instead, same time.

Then she lifted the handkerchief to see the bowl brimming with chicken-and-dumpling soup. The savory smell of parsley and a hint of thyme accosted her senses. A laugh bubbled out. She had said soup cured everything, and he had listened!

"Never mind, Edith. We may return home, and we will come again tomorrow." The purse would have to wait. The feeling of disappointment did not follow, which was surprising since Ivy had put off her mission for two days now.

All she could think about was Lord Blakely: his wavy, ash-brown hair and the way his hazel eyes softened when he was amused by something she said. Was there more to the gesture of soup than a simple apology? No, the idea was a mere fancy of hers. There could be no friendship between them, let alone a romantic interest. Still, his thoughtfulness impressed her. She fingered his smooth penmanship, and her heart betrayed her by skipping a beat. It was best not to become attached to an idea so far from her reach.

She took her time returning to Ravencross, while Edith hurried ahead. Upon her arrival, Mrs. Talbot stood just inside, waiting for her. Had Edith discovered who had sent the soup and tattled?

"The local curate has come to visit Mrs. Hunt, and your presence is desired." Mrs. Talbot eyed the soup bowl in Ivy's hand with some suspicion.

"I will go straightaway. Could you set this in the dining room? I should like to eat it after the visit."

Mrs. Talbot's mouth pursed, but she took the soup without comment.

After shedding her layers, Ivy made her way down the short corridor to Grandmother's room, which was still full of natural light, just as Ivy had left it. Edith already sat in the chair at the end of Grandmother's bed, and a man stood not far from the door.

As she stepped inside, the young curate turned and dipped his head in a short bow. "Good morning, Miss Hunt. I hope you will forgive the improper introduction since your grandmother is too ill to see to it."

"Of course." Ivy dipped into a curtsy. "I am happy to make your acquaintance . . ."

"Mr. Perry."

Mr. Perry was bright-eyed and cheerful. He was not as handsome as Lord Blakely, but Ivy did not object to his appearance in any way.

"I am sorry to hear you arrived just as your grandmother fell ill. While it has no doubt put a damper on your trip, I hope you can still take some small pleasure in our community. Have you been to the village yet?"

"I have been to the village." Ivy glanced at Grandmother, who did not so much as perk up at the conversation so near to her. The poor woman was in a world all her own. "I had a memorable run-in with the dairyman—a Mr. Bryant." Mr. Perry had probably heard, so it was best to clear the air at the beginning.

Mr. Perry's smile widened. "I did hear a version or two of the story, though I am sure it was exaggerated."

Everyone in town must know, then. Ivy's cheeks warmed. "I doubt it." Then she whispered, "But let's spare Grandmother the details, shall we?"

Mr. Perry chuckled. "Yes, indeed."

"Did anyone ring for tea yet?" Ivy asked, realizing the hosting duties in such a delicate situation probably fell to her.

"No, but I must not keep either of you. I know Mrs. Hunt requires her rest. Please, do not hesitate to call on me should any needs arise."

"Thank you." Ivy almost asked about the purse but was struck with a sudden selfish desire to use the purse as her way to see Lord Blakely again—just once more, since they had already arranged a meeting. Then she'd ask the curate for help and put an end to her secret acquaintance.

"Good day, Miss Hunt." Mr. Perry dipped his head and excused himself.

Ivy looked at her grandmother. "What a kind man. Did you enjoy your visit with him?"

Grandmother turned her head with a glimmer of stubbornness and did not respond.

Ivy sighed and left the room. What would it take to make Grandmother warm to her? Even an occasional small smile would make Ivy's stay more bearable. She missed her sisters something fierce . . . but at least she had soup to comfort her.

CHAPTER SIX

THE FOLLOWING MORNING, IVY MANAGED to pull open all the drapes and read to her grandmother again. For a woman who seemed to prefer the dark, Grandmother had several windows and an incredible view. Ivy paused to admire the scenery. The land told the story of Grandfather's ascension from farmer to landed gentleman. This time of year, with so much brown and gray outside, it was hard to imagine fertile crops, but Grandmother was part of a great legacy—the only part of Ravencross that Ivy's father seemed to talk about with any sort of affection. Because of the feud, he'd chosen to give up all this rugged beauty.

Still, life had been good to Ivy's family. Her father had married a wealthy woman from Peterborough, and they'd made a comfortable home there for Ivy and her sisters. While their lands supported them, their lifestyle did not compare to Lord Blakely's. Not that she was thinking about him again. Or anxiously counting down the moments to see him.

"Are you going to read or stand there all day?"

Ivy grinned and sat down to read. When she stood again to leave, there was a good feeling in the room. She sensed a small change in their relationship. Grandmother did appreciate Ivy's efforts, even though she did not express it in so many words.

At noon, Ivy and Edith began their trek toward the bridge. Despite how many times she cautioned herself, she could not push back the anticipation of seeing Lord Blakely. She found herself repeating in her mind, Aunt Morris would never consent. Father would disown me. Lord Blakely is not for me!

A thrum of horse's hooves and the sound of carriage wheels grinding against the road drew near. Ivy clasped her hands in front of her and forced herself to breathe normally. The driver pulled the team of horses to a stop, and Lord Blakely stepped out. His smile caused a little flutter in her stomach.

Did she imagine a mutual spark of interest in his eyes? She forced herself to look away. She would control her thoughts and focus on finding the owner of the purse. By now someone surely missed it and was likely in need of food, rent, or perhaps winter necessities.

"Before you ask, Mrs. Pool is on the mend," Lord Blakely said.

"What a relief!" Ivy replied. Even Edith looked pleased.

Lord Blakely assisted both of them into the carriage, and his calming presence eased her concerns about being with him.

"Oh, and Mrs. Humphrey said Mrs. Pool enjoyed her soup and bread. Mrs. Pool sends her many thanks to you."

"I enjoyed a bit of soup yesterday myself," Ivy remarked, her eyes likely betraying her feelings.

"About that," Lord Blakely said with a small tinge of pink on his cheeks. "My mother and sister insisted on accompanying me to town. I think a dog is easier to shake than my mother when she has an idea."

Ivy had to bite back a laugh. "I don't think your mother would appreciate such a comparison. But I have a persistent sister, so I can imagine your predicament. No harm was done, at least not after your peace offering."

"Good," he said. "Then, we can carry on today as if yesterday never happened. I thought we would visit the Clarks first. There are several cottages beyond there, so if we are brief, we should be able to see them all today." Lord Blakely suddenly looked sheepish. "That is, if you agree."

Ivy smiled. "I would be lost without your help. And finding the owner of the purse means more to me with every passing day."

Lord Blakely seemed relieved with her compliance, and she appreciated the efforts he made to please her. He gave instructions to the driver, and they were off. The Clarks' cottage came into view a short while later. It mirrored the size and shape of the Pools' home. When they stopped, half a dozen small children piled outside.

"Look at all of them. Where can they possibly all sleep?" Ivy was amazed.

Lord Blakely helped Edith out of the carriage first, then Ivy. "You do think of the most amusing things. You look at them and feel sorry for them, where all I see is a bunch of happy, dirty children."

Ivy looked again. "They do look happy, don't they? Perhaps a little thin though."

Lord Blakely coughed into his hands, but Ivy knew he had smothered a laugh. They approached the children, and a few crept closer while others ran back inside.

"Is your father or mother at home?" Lord Blakely asked the ones brave enough to even look at him.

The door opened again, and this time a tall woman stepped out, wiping her hands on a tattered apron. She gave a little curtsy and said, "Your Lordship."

"How do you do, Mrs. Clark? We are passing through, asking if anyone has lost a purse."

Mrs. Clark shook her head. "No, not us. I don't have no purse to lose."

"Did it have lots of money?" a small boy asked.

Ivy nodded.

The boy looked at his mother. "Do you think it's the money we prayed for, Mum?"

Ivy reached for Lord Blakely's arm. "Oh dear," she whispered.

Mrs. Clark blushed and sent the boy inside with the rest of her children. "I haven't heard of any missing purse. Sorry." Then she dipped into another awkward curtsy and followed her son.

Turning to Ivy, Lord Blakely put his gloved hand on hers, making her knees feel weak and her heart race. "I . . . I can leave some money on their step." His words were more of a question, like he wanted to know her opinion.

"That would be very kind."

"It is Christmas," Lord Blakely said with a small smile.

Ivy grinned. "There is that."

Lord Blakely dug out a few banknotes and left them on the doorstep. Ivy thought she heard him say, "God bless you all." Gooseflesh ran up and down her arms, and her throat thickened with moisture. Just a few days ago, he'd seemed so timid in their search, but when he turned around, his face radiated joy. She would never forget her trip to Amorwich or this moment when a man blessed an entire family with his generosity.

❋ ❋ ❋

Never had Curtis ever given so much money away. Oddly enough, he did not miss any of it. And not because he had plenty but because he knew the Clarks' dire need. That little boy had prayed with his mother for money, and God had seen fit to use Curtis as the answer. He'd spent the last few years pushing away everything spiritual in his life, but he could not turn his back on the good he saw before him.

The footman helped Miss Hunt's maid into the carriage, but Curtis wanted a moment with Miss Hunt to himself. He stopped a few feet short of the carriage's open door and turned to her.

"Tell me," he asked her, "do you do this sort of thing for pleasure back in Peterborough?"

Miss Hunt eyed him strangely. "Yes, I always convince strangers to whisk me around the countryside and trick them out of their money."

He laughed. "No, I meant do you spend your days helping people?"

"My sisters and I spend our time arguing over ribbons and besting each other at card games, so we cannot be a very good sort of people."

"I believe you are being modest."

Her expression turned serious. "I do try to be a good person. I find it makes me happier. Generally, my sisters and I are busy with friends, visiting back and forth, and all the kindness we do possess is directed to them. I did want to help my grandmother, but I'm afraid intentions are not equal to talent."

Curtis tried to envision a gaggle of girls running around Miss Hunt's house. He thought it quite admirable for her to leave her sisters' company for her grandmother's sake. "I admit this feels new to me. My father, on the other hand, was generous to a fault. His attention to everyone else sometimes left my mother feeling like she was the least important to him. But I always wanted to be like my father. Only . . ." Miss Hunt did not rush him to finish, which gave him time to find the right words. "Only, after he died, I realized I was nothing like my father. I didn't deserve to inherit his life, nor should I pretend to be him."

"Do you still feel this way?" Miss Hunt asked, her brow pinched with concern.

"I do." He paused, wondering how much to reveal of his thoughts. Surely, there was no harm in sharing with someone like Miss Hunt, who would guard a secret likely the way she protected all those she encountered. "I haven't accomplished anything worthwhile in my life, not really. Not in comparison to others." He looked toward the carriage. "I like to play with numbers, robbing my solicitor of most of his duties. Figures are predictable, making any risks almost safe because of what I've predetermined. I take pleasure in the profits I make." He turned to her again. "I'm ashamed to say I have not seen the value in risking myself on behalf of other people."

He regretted turning their discussion to such a serious nature. Was she disappointed in the real him? He wouldn't blame her.

"Sometimes I compare myself to my sister." Miss Hunt ducked her head. "Julia is everything I wish I could be. Even my critical aunt cannot find fault in her, nor can I. But my father told me once that if God wanted me to be like Julia, He would have made me her. I have my own path to carve in life, using the gifts only I can discover. I remind myself of this every time I want to complain about my . . . freckles."

Curtis grinned. "Freckles? I hardly see more than a few." Dare he tell her how darling he thought them to be?

Her nose scrunched up. "You have your frustrations, and I have mine. But let's not let them ruin us."

"So you don't think I need to be my father to be important?"

"Importance is likely measured differently by every person," Miss Hunt said. "However, I think it is a very good thing you are not your father, for the same reason it is a good thing I am not my sister Julia."

"Your words have given me a great deal to think about." He smiled, but his thoughts were grim. Could he be a better baron? What changes would he have to make? His father would not have squandered two years as Curtis had. He sighed wistfully. "If I could only be half the man my father was, I would be a happy man."

"From what I've seen today, you are more like your father than perhaps you think." She smiled softly, and he couldn't help returning it as he helped her into the carriage.

It was true. Today he'd acted for himself, but in doing so, he'd followed the example of his father in helping someone else. The pride in such a thought enveloped him with peace. He didn't even mind that Miss Hunt's maid's incredulous stare pinned him in place, because for the first time, he'd shared an aspect of grief he'd experienced with the death of his father. Never had he talked about his insecurities before, but being with Miss Hunt made him think and do things he had never wanted to do before.

They traveled half a mile before arriving at the next tenant family's home.

"Here we are," Curtis said. Yet another cottage stood before them, and more children poured out. "Are you ready?" He couldn't imagine anyone else he would rather do this with.

"Yes, I am curious whether you will give away your estate next."

Curtis's eyes widened. "You think I am such a changed man, do you? Well, perhaps I will give away my stable and horses first. It seems more reasonable." He exited the carriage and held his hand out to her.

"Oh, good choice," Miss Hunt teased as she took his hand and climbed out to join him.

He could stand here in the bitter cold for hours if it meant more time in private conversation with Miss Hunt. But he was too much of a gentleman to force her to freeze in his behalf. He cleared his throat and motioned her toward the cottage.

Three cottages later, they'd had not an ounce of luck in finding the owner of the purse. However, each house had brought him closer to Miss Hunt. He naturally stood near her, eager to introduce her to everyone. Part of him wanted to encourage the image that they were courting. A man would be very lucky to have such a woman of strength and quiet wisdom by his side.

"I am sorry we did not solve your mystery," Curtis said to Miss Hunt on their way back to Ravencross. He couldn't help but let his eyes linger on her and appreciate how the tendrils of her auburn hair perfectly framed her face and brought out the color of her lips.

"Watching you catch that runaway chicken made our efforts worthwhile, wouldn't you say?"

Curtis chuckled. "Almost as memorable as you and Mr. Bryant's goat."

Miss Hunt giggled. "A gentleman should promptly forget any faults of a lady, whereas I see no reason the story of the chicken cannot be repeated."

"You won't tell anyone how I accidentally killed it, will you?" Curtis cringed. "I am gifting them with half a dozen more to make up for my blunder."

Miss Hunt took a finger and crossed her heart and sealed her lips. Then they both laughed again. He was sorry indeed when the carriage reached the bridge and it was time to say goodbye. Curtis climbed down first and then helped Miss Hunt down. Her eyes locked on his, and neither one of them moved. Her nearness caused his heart to sing and his pulse to race.

This couldn't be the last time he saw her. His hand moved of its own accord to cup her shoulder. "Miss Hunt, it has been a privilege to know you. To be worthy of you must be the greatest endeavor a man could seek." His breathing grew unsteady as his head dipped closer to hers, like the pull of Earth toward the sun. He needed her light, warmth, and kiss.

Her eyes closed, and she lifted her chin as if to accept his offering. His lips were a breath away from her when a squeal came from inside the carriage.

"Pardon me, miss," Miss Hunt's maid said, climbing down from the carriage, "but your grandmother would dismiss me in an instant if she knew what was going on here!" The maid put her hands on her hips. "And you, Your Lordship—shame on you! You dally with this young girl's heart when you know a match between you is impossible."

Miss Hunt pulled herself free from Curtis's grasp, creating an emptiness he had never known before. Her eyes were wide open and clear of any illusion she might have had concerning him.

"Edith, you mustn't tell," Miss Hunt pleaded. "Nothing happened."

"And nothing ever will," Edith said. "Your grandmother has been my employer since I was a young girl. I will not betray her."

Edith's staunch display of loyalty did not impress Curtis, because to never see Miss Hunt again would be unfathomable. He put his hands together and brought them to his lips. *Think, man!* How could he and Miss Hunt ever get their families to forgive years of anger? Could he hurt his own mother with such news?

"Miss Hunt . . . ," Curtis pleaded.

"I know," she said, her expression hurt but resolute. "But there is too much history to be undone." She quoted his own words. "Today was wonderful. I shall never forget it. I wish you the greatest happiness the world can offer."

Did he hear a tone of wistfulness in her voice?

Edith put her arm around Ivy and turned her away.

The only counterargument Curtis had was his own feelings. He clasped his hands up around the back of his neck and exhaled. He'd been a fool to believe they could spend time together and remain unattached. Now he'd have a permanent ache in his chest and only a few memories to sustain him. He silently cursed his family and the land that had caused the rift in the first place.

Curtis did everything he could to keep Miss Hunt out of his mind for three long days. His normal haunts and routine would not suffice. It was back to his books and numbers. But while he usually enjoyed a daily correspondence with his solicitor and several investors, now his mind could not latch on to anything. The fault was his own. When he could barely read through his newspaper without wondering what Miss Hunt would think about each article, Curtis knew he needed a change of scenery. How did a woman get beneath a man's skin so quickly? His feelings for her defied his solitary nature.

Once in town, Curtis attempted to prove to himself that he did not need her by talking to Mr. Bryant and petting his unruly goat. It did nothing but tease him with memories, especially when the first thing Mr. Bryant did was ask after Miss Hunt.

He woke up on the fourth day to an incredibly realistic dream of Miss Hunt. Her nearness was uncanny. Sweat broke out on his temples. Why couldn't he move past this? He decided a morning horse ride would be the best medicine to rid his subconscious of her image. Somehow, he ended up back at Mrs. Humphrey's. Why was he here again? He dismounted and went and knocked on the door.

"I didn't think I'd see you again anytime soon," Mrs. Humphrey said, inviting him in and seating him at her table. She poured him a cup of hot tea and gave him a warm scone drizzled with honey.

Moaning with pleasure after one bite, Curtis finished every crumb. "I didn't realize I was hungry. Your scones are incomparable. How is Mrs. Pool?"

"Still weak, but she is at least on her feet now. Her husband returned last night, and he was a mite humbled to hear he nearly lost her. He'll think twice before he up and leaves her again."

"I imagine married life is hard," Curtis said, grateful when Mrs. Humphrey dished a second scone onto his plate.

She shrugged. "It helps to marry a special person and not a difficult one."

"Sounds simple when you put it that way." Curtis chuckled. His usual society determined the measure of a person by their class, rank, and fortune. Surely, Mrs. Humphrey's classification of special referred more to their character and motivations.

"I don't think finding the right one is as hard as people make it to be. What about Miss Hunt?" Mrs. Humphrey asked. "I realize she is staying at Ravencross and is part of that family, and she does have the look, but her heart is untainted from the curse between the two families. Excuse me for saying so."

Curtis blew out his breath. "My tenants are no doubt whispering about the two of us being together."

"There is just as much whisper about how Miss Hunt has changed Lord Blakely."

"Changed me? What a notion."

Mrs. Humphrey raised her brow. "Your being seated at my table would have been highly unusual just two weeks ago. Yet, here you are, eating my scones like the great house starves you. Mrs. Clark's children are telling everyone about the money you gave them. They aren't the only ones. Seems this will be the best Christmas any of them have ever had."

Curtis propped his elbow on the table and rested his head on his fist. "You have a point. I never would have done those things without Miss Hunt."

"Miss Hunt isn't with you now, nor was she when you came early that morning to check on Mrs. Pool. I think you just needed a push in the right direction."

Maybe. Curtis hardly knew. He'd started thinking more seriously about God since he met Miss Hunt. Right now, he could imagine his father making arrangements in heaven for him to learn a lesson. But what did Curtis need to learn from Miss Hunt besides heartache? The image from his dream returned. He snapped his fingers. "The purse!"

"The lost purse? Did you think of who the owner could be?"

Curtis smiled and stood. "No, but I have a feeling that if I find the owner, I can move on with my life." And get over Miss Hunt.

Mrs. Humphrey's proud smile ushered him out the door. Curtis stepped outside onto the familiar landscape, but his eyes did not really see it. His mind was wrapped up in his thoughts. After twenty-six years of living however he pleased, he now had the desire to understand God's will for him.

CHAPTER SEVEN

IVY MANAGED TO READ TO Grandmother every morning the next week. In those moments, the veil of melancholy over her grandmother seemed to momentarily lift, but it always returned and seemed ultimately to worsen with each passing day. Grandmother had even begun to refuse her meals. Ivy sent for the doctor. She worried her lip as she waited outside Grandmother's room for his verdict.

"She is growing weaker," the doctor said, closing the door behind him. His long gray sideburns wrapped almost to his chin, and she found herself staring at them instead of processing his words. "You must prepare yourself."

Grandmother was dying. Despite the minimal conversation between them, her time with Grandmother had strangely bonded them together. Ivy decided to continue with her morning routine of reading out loud, if only to comfort herself. When she was finished, she excused herself, sat at the small writing desk in her room, and wrote to relay the doctor's words to her family.

The miser purse lay at the top corner of her desk, opposite the ink, taunting her to find the owner. This morning, the guilt, frustration, and loneliness she felt seemed too much to bear. She grabbed the purse and put it inside her reticule, determined to find Edith.

The maid was putting sprigs of dried lavender between handkerchiefs in the kitchen. Ivy walked up to her. "I should like you to accompany me to town."

Edith pursed her lips and raised her brow. "Will a certain gentleman be there?"

Ivy dismissed the urge to remind Edith of her place. Doing so might cause Grandmother to suffer unduly in her condition should Edith feel the need to tattle on Ivy. "I have no knowledge of anyone particular being in town." That part was honest, but the next was a bit of a stretch. "I should very much like to purchase some stationery and some small trinkets for Christmastide." She left out the matter of the purse because she was unsure how Edith would respond.

"Very well. I will ask Mrs. Talbot if I might go with you."

The weight of her small handbag compelled Ivy to move forward with her plan. There had to be some purpose behind her time at Ravencross, besides being thwarted in love and watching Grandmother die. Two weeks had already passed since she arrived, and there were only two weeks remaining. There might not be many opportunities left for her to find the owner of the purse, especially if Edith stood in her way.

The perpetual clouds over England seemed to part just for their walk. The sun warmed them despite the cool temperature. They crossed the bridge, and Ivy's eyes betrayed her. Her head turned in the direction of Lord Blakely's estate. Light filtered through a row of oaks, making stepping-stones of yellow on the path. It would be all too easy to follow the rays to Fairmore.

If she did, what would Lord Blakely be doing this very moment? Was he still planning on sending a goose to Mr. and Mrs. Humphrey? Had he returned to visit any of the other tenants? While she was curious, a second run-in with the dairyman's goat might be better than meeting with Lord Blakely's family, especially if Edith's and Mrs. Talbot's reactions were any prediction of more of the same. With regret, Ivy pulled her gaze back to the empty road leading to town. It felt symbolic, putting distance between her and her fantasy of love. She had to hurry to catch up with Edith, who had huffed a few steps ahead and waited for her. If only Ivy could hurry and forget Lord Blakely.

While Ivy visited the few shops, Edith busied herself with gathering a few things for Mrs. Talbot. Even without Edith's presence, there were few opportunities for Ivy to approach people about the purse. She had just stepped out of the tearoom when she met Mr. Perry, the curate.

"What a coincidence," Mr. Perry said. "I was wondering how you and your grandmother were faring. Truly, I was going to fetch my horse so I might visit Ravencross."

"Now you have no need to." Ivy's smile felt forced. "My grandmother is not well, but she seems as comfortable as possible under the circumstances."

Mr. Perry's brow lowered. "Her poor health is quite unfortunate. I haven't known her long, being fairly new to the community, but she seemed a fiery sort, and it is hard to see her brought low. It must be even more difficult for you to see her so altered."

Ivy bit her lip. "Before my visit, it had been some time since she was with our family, but I think it would be hard to watch anyone slip from this life. Forgive me. As a clergyman, you no doubt attend a great deal of funerals; you of all people would understand."

"Actually," Mr. Perry said, the tops of his high cheekbones turning a little pink, "Amorwich is my first position out of university, so I haven't much experience."

"Oh, I didn't know. You seem to have made it your home."

"Yes," Mr. Perry said. "The families here have been very welcoming. In fact, I see a lady now who has been instrumental in guiding me around the society here. Might I introduce you to her?"

Mr. Perry extended his arm, and Ivy accepted. "I would be delighted to meet any of your acquaintances." She turned and realized Mr. Perry was directing her toward Lord Blakely, who was flanked by two women—likely his mother and sister. The joy of seeing him was immediately replaced with sheer terror. Hadn't she just told herself that such an introduction was doomed from the start? A churning sensation began in her middle. Oh dear. She was about to be sick.

One visit to town with Curtis's family had not been enough, apparently. Somehow, his mother had tricked him into taking her and Amelia back exactly a week after the first time. He hoped they would not make a ritual of this. This Season was Amelia's coming-out, and Curtis ought to enjoy their time together before she married and left Amorwich. She had matured a great deal, though her dainty features would always carry a youthfulness; her maturity was more in the way she carried and expressed herself. Even so, his heart was not in their excursion.

"We already have holly, mistletoe, and plenty of pine," Amelia said. "Do you think we need rosemary for our decorations, Mama?"

"Absolutely," their mother answered. Her black ringlets bounced on the sides of her face as she walked. "But today's errand is to secure more table napkins. We ruined so many last year."

"Remind me why my presence is required." Curtis had hoped to ride up to the nearest town to send out inquiries about the purse. He seemed to have hit a dead end in Amorwich.

Mama sighed. "Do pay attention. Miss Ashworth is in town, and I had hoped to introduce you before the ball."

"And I approved of this idea?" Curtis really must have been woolgathering. He had no recollection of a conversation about Miss Ashworth. What power did Miss Hunt have over him that his rational mind was no longer working?

Amelia laughed softly. "You didn't exactly agree to meet her. I'm not even sure you heard our breakfast conversation. But here you are, so perhaps it is fate. You and Miss Ashworth must be destined to be together."

Curtis looked at his younger sister and rescinded the idea that she had matured. It was folly for her to even jest about such a notion. He didn't need to see or meet this other woman to know she was not for him. "Please keep your fanciful ideas far from the ears of our mother. I, for one, cannot stomach them." Especially since his heart wasn't free any longer. No matter how he argued against it, an auburn-haired beauty had claimed it the week before.

Curtis and his family had not been in the village a quarter of an hour before he saw the source of his thoughts.

Miss Hunt.

Her profile was fetching from this angle. Only, Curtis did not appreciate the target of her smile: Mr. Perry. If Miss Hunt should be smiling at anyone, it should be Curtis. The idea might have been a silly one, but Curtis felt perfectly justified in the selfish thought. Mr. Perry turned and caught sight of them. He said something to Miss Hunt and then offered his arm to her. Curtis's wish to see her smile suddenly vanished. They were coming his way.

He cleared his throat and tried to get his mother's and sister's attention to turn them in a different direction. "Meat pastry, anyone?"

"No, thank you, dear," Mama said. "Oh, Mr. Perry!"

Curtis cringed. He was too late. Mr. Perry and Miss Hunt stopped in front of them.

"How do you do? Might I introduce you to my charming companion?" Mr. Perry asked.

"Oh yes, you must, Mr. Perry," Lady Blakely said. "I adore meeting all those of good blood who visit the community."

Miss Hunt looked to Curtis for help, her face a little green. He gave her an almost imperceptible shake of his head so she would not acknowledge him. She quickly looked back at his mother.

"Lord Blakely, Lady Blakely, this is Miss Hunt," the curate said. "She is Mrs. Hunt's granddaughter, visiting from Peterborough."

His mother's cheeks faded from a rosy color to light pink to sheer white. She was going to swoon. Curtis reached for her, and she leaned against him while miraculously maintaining her dignity. Miss Hunt dipped into a curtsy but did not miss the obvious reaction to her name.

Flustered, Curtis motioned to his sister. "Miss Hunt, might I present my sister, Miss Park?"

Amelia curtsied, not appearing at all upset at having been overlooked by the curate. Instead, she seemed excited to see what would happen next and gave Curtis an expectant look.

It would be up to him to continue the conversation. He cleared his throat for a second time. "What do you think of Amorwich, Miss Hunt?"

Miss Hunt's eyes connected with his, and her tight expression seemed to relax. "I . . . I like it very much."

Curtis's mouth smiled of its own accord. The timing might be wretched, but he was still happy to see her. "And your family—ah, are they well in your absence?" What was he saying now? Talking of the Hunt family was a faux pas in the best of times.

"Yes," Miss Hunt said. "All but my grandmother at Ravencross. While we hope she recovers, she is very old and quite ill."

"I am sorry to hear about your grandmother," Lady Blakely said, correcting her posture. "We must be off, but enjoy your time in Amorwich."

Curtis's brow rose. His mother had been abrupt but not exactly offensive. But where did his loyalties lie? As protective as he was of his mother, he could not have allowed her to verbally injure Miss Hunt in any way.

Miss Hunt had nearly turned away when Amelia called out to her. "Are you coming to our Christmas ball?"

His mother grabbed Curtis's arm. She might have been wearing gloves, but Curtis could swear he felt her nails dig into his flesh. What had his sister done?

A worried frown crossed Miss Hunt's face, and her eyes once again darted his way. He had no idea how to reassure her.

"I could not leave my grandmother."

Mr. Perry shook his head. "Your grandmother would not want you to avoid an opportunity to interact with young company. It would be a great shame to miss one of Lady Blakely's parties."

"And you left her long enough to come to the village," Amelia added. "Surely a dance isn't much longer."

Curtis wanted to pinch his sister. What could she possibly be thinking?

"I will discuss it with Grandmother, shall I?" Miss Hunt sent him a pleading glance.

A need to soothe her anxiety prompted him to blurt, "Please do. We should love to have you in attendance."

A small smile blossomed, lessening her evident concern. "Th-thank you."

Mr. Perry beamed as if it had all been his idea and his triumph. Curtis had never disliked a member of the clergy until now. Of course, he had never felt such immense jealousy before either. But despite the backlash he would receive from his mother when they returned home, a dance with Miss Hunt suddenly sounded like the best way to celebrate Christmas.

CHAPTER EIGHT

Ivy wondered if she looked as flustered as she felt. Somehow, she managed to say goodbye to Mr. Perry and find Edith for their walk home. Thank heavens Edith had not seen her with Lord Blakely. Two antagonizing conversations in one hour would be too much for her currently sensitive stomach.

Ivy had seen him again. Under the circumstances, she could not quite appreciate it. But did Lord Blakely care to see her? If she closed her eyes, she could still feel his hand cupping her shoulder and his breath on her lips. But there hadn't been a kiss, nor would there ever be one.

At least meeting Lord Blakely's family had gone better than Ivy had expected. Mostly. Except for the part where Lady Blakely had almost fainted at the mention of the name Hunt. And Ivy had managed to avoid vomiting, which should count for something. They were not likely to send a proper invitation to the dance, so there was no reason to think on his sister's offer again. It had been a kind thought and no more.

Once back at Ravencross, Ivy was greeted by a footman and a letter. Pressing the folded paper to her bosom, she rushed to her room, where she could read it privately. A few familiar words from her family would be like a balm just now. She slid her penknife under the wax and broke the seal. Then she unfolded the letter, surprised to see it was not from her sisters but her father.

> *Dearest Ivy,*
>   *You are greatly missed at home. Your sisters are painting each other's portraits, and I daresay, neither one is at all recognizable. I am glad you are there with my mother while she is ill,*

*but I am sorry you are not enjoying the preparations for the holi-
days like you should be. Christmas has long been your favorite
and understandably so. Your sisters tell me you are trying to solve
the mystery of a lost purse. How very like you to do a good turn
for another. I commend your efforts!*

*I wanted to write to tell you the good news. Your aunt admits
she was wrong to push a match between you and Mr. Beales,
especially with both parties being resistant. She has offered
a pleasant alternative: to sponsor you for a proper Season in
London. It was no small sacrifice for you to travel to Amorwich,
so I find you deserving of the opportunity. May your days pass
quickly with the anticipation of the months of frivolity and
adventure ahead.*

With love,

Papa

A tear escaped down her cheek. This trip wasn't supposed to be so very
complicated. At least Aunt Morris would no longer push an unwelcome
match on her. If Ivy could handle being away once more, then she would
welcome a trip to London. Lord Blakely would be there too, but the city
was large enough that there was no expectation of ever having to see him
again. She wasn't sure if that was the best part about it or the worst. But it
gave her something to think about and plan for. It would be the gift she
needed to endure two more weeks at Ravencross.

"If your father were not already dead, today would have killed him," Mama
said.

Amelia glanced at Curtis for help. As much as he'd like to interrupt,
he'd learned long ago to let his mother say her piece. She often wore herself
out and then would be much more reasonable. He slyly pulled out his
pocket watch to see she had lectured them for nearly half an hour. Curtis
hoped his mother was about finished.

"In more than twenty-five years, a Hunt has not entered this house. In
the breadth of one conversation, you both managed to shame our family
name. It is hard enough to raise you children on my own, but—"

"We are hardly children anymore," Amelia interrupted. Curtis grimaced. His younger sister had not learned to wait until the storm had passed, though this one was a bit long-winded.

"And you think a few extra years of experience beyond childhood allows you to abuse your mother? What will Mrs. Hunt think? And with her on her deathbed. And what will everyone else think? That we were in the wrong all those years and that we are offering the olive branch? I feel faint even considering such an absurd notion. The entire neighborhood looks to us to set an example. It would change back the clock, and I, for one, could never go back. Those were dark times; you think lightly about them because you were not there."

His mother turned around and faced their pianoforte. Curtis took the opportunity to stretch his back. When his mother turned again, he stilled immediately.

"Well?" Mama asked, staring at him. "Do you regret your behavior? You have been as silent as the grave."

"The grave? Well, you *have* talked a great deal about dying in this conversation," Curtis quipped.

Mama stared daggers at him.

"Very well," he said. "If you truly want my opinion, you shall have it. But I'll ask you to sit down first. I have listened as patiently as possible, and now I ask you to do the same."

His mother sat down firmly on the edge of a green upholstered chair. Despite her age, she resembled a child, with her petulant frown and arms folded across her chest. Even her lace cap tilted a little to the side, likely the repercussion of so much arm waving during her lecture.

Curtis took a fortifying breath. "I was not alive during the falling-out between our family and the Hunts, but I have respected the distance you put between them and us. Now, though, however much you might be displeased by it, the invitation has been extended, and I do believe we should honor it. Miss Hunt has not wronged this family in any way. She is only passing through the area, and her presence can do no harm unless we allow it."

"But, Curtis, really?" his mother asked, despair lacing her words.

"It's Christmas, Mama." His final argument. And inspired by Miss Hunt herself.

"Christmas?" she asked, her forehead creasing in the middle.

"Yes," Amelia answered. "The celebration of the Christ child and the time of year when we try to be more charitable. You taught me that, Mama. Christmas marks the beginning of several days of celebrating for a very important reason."

Curtis watched as his mother's shoulders drew forward and her posture drooped. She sat there, clearly feeling like her world had flipped upside down.

"All right," Mama said, although her tone did not agree with her words. "Amelia may copy an invitation to send to Miss Hunt. But do not expect me to welcome her."

"I do expect you to greet her," Curtis said, "but I will not ask you to converse with her or introduce her to anyone. I will take full responsibility."

"Very well." Mama covered her eyes with her hand. "If you will do the dreadful deed, then perhaps I can manage to endure the evening."

If only his mother knew she was doing Curtis a favor. He could not have managed this without his sister's unintentional help. "Remember how important this dance is to Amelia's coming-out. You must do more than endure the evening; you must enjoy yourself."

Amelia gave him a grateful smile, then turned to face their mother. "I am sorry, Mama. I was only trying to be as welcoming as you always are. I thought you would be proud of me."

Mama uncovered her eyes. "*Proud* might not be the best word, but I understand your innocence in all this. We haven't talked about the feud for years. It's more avoided than discussed."

"What exactly happened?" Amelia asked. "Did someone kill someone?"

Mama shook her head, and for a moment, she seemed to see something they could not. "Sometimes I think death would have been easier than living with all this anger all these years." The moment passed. Her eyes sharpened into focus, and she turned to face Amelia. "Two people simply claimed a right to the same land. It was a battle of wills, and friendships were ruined. The Hunts felt they were entitled to the property, but in the end, your father claimed it in a fair and honest manner. There isn't anything shocking or scandalous about it, but still, the matter has driven a wedge between our families that I fear cannot be removed."

Amelia squinted like she was trying to see into the past. "Never?"

"Not in my lifetime, dearest. After I'm gone, you may entertain the company you choose."

Amelia frowned and looked at Curtis. He shrugged in reply. He knew that even his father, who had loved everyone he met, grew upset when the Hunts were mentioned.

Curtis had won the argument today, but the ball really had to be the last time he enjoyed Miss Hunt's company. It wasn't worth teasing himself with the idea of something more. Of course, he could justify one dance with Miss Hunt. It would offer a chance to say goodbye.

CHAPTER NINE

THE LIBRARY AT RAVENCROSS WAS a corridor lined with books on one side, leading to a small nook at the end by a window. Ivy enjoyed the selection and pictured her father reading from the same books when he was a child. For her early-morning reading, she thought her grandmother might enjoy listening to a play, so Ivy's eyes darted from row to row before catching on several works by Shakespeare. She pulled out *Romeo and Juliet*, snorted, and pushed the book back as far as it would go. Today was not the time to dwell on families pitted against each other. She selected instead *The Taming of the Shrew*, a well-known comedy. She turned to take it to Grandmother's room when the butler paused in the doorway.

Another letter.

From the moment she touched the expensive paper, she knew it was not from her family. The hand was feminine. She opened it and set it on top of the book in her arms. One line in, she sucked in her breath. A formal invitation to the Blakelys' ball.

Ivy bypassed Grandmother's room and went directly to her own. Putting the book aside, she reread the invitation. The night of the ball, Christmas night, was only three days away.

She paced back and forth in her room. *What to do?* She needed to talk to someone, and writing a letter to her sisters would not satisfy her. Their response would take days, and she needed someone now. The only one in the house she could turn to was Grandmother. She was family, and she was alive enough to listen. The corridor leading to Grandmother's room extended far enough for a girl to lose her courage, but Ivy's anxiety about the dance urged her forward.

The curtains had been drawn since Ivy's reading the previous morning. Glancing around the dimly lit room, she exhaled with relief. Grandmother was awake. Ivy crossed the room and sat gingerly on the edge of the bed. How should she proceed? She might as well start at the beginning. "Good morning, Grandmother. I went to town again yesterday, if you remember."

Grandmother did not acknowledge her, but at least she seemed to be listening. Ivy dropped her gaze to her lap. "Despite what my father says, I find Amorwich to be perfectly lovely . . . made lovelier by a, ah, particular gentleman. I rather made a fool of myself the first time I saw him." Sighing, Ivy tucked a wilted ringlet behind her ear. "He bumped against me and caught me before I fell. I am not sure why I was eager to be out of his arms then, when now, well, I would do almost anything to find myself there again.

"Perhaps our first meeting was so very memorable so we couldn't possibly forget each other. Silly, because he might not even care for me in the same way I have begun to care for him. And why would he ever think twice about me? My suggestions make him uncomfortable, not to mention my family connections—"

Grandmother interrupted. "Your connections are perfectly suitable."

Ivy whipped her head up and met the fierce gaze of her grandmother, who had hardly spoken all week. "Yes, of course our connections are sufficient." Ivy agreed only because she didn't dare contradict Grandmother.

"You care for him?" Grandmother asked in her raspy voice.

"I do, and there lies the problem. There is a ball, and I want to go, but I know it will only encourage my feelings toward him." Ivy felt a weariness of spirit from the constant effort to bury her feelings. "Sometimes the heart and the head do not agree."

"Follow your heart."

Ivy's breath caught in her throat. Grandmother did not know the name of the man Ivy cared for. "But what if Papa does not approve of my choice?"

Grandmother closed her eyes and, in choked words, said, "There isn't time for regrets."

The words burned inside Ivy with their truthfulness. She stood, realizing their brief conversation had tired Grandmother. She backed away quietly. Should she listen to her heart? Would she regret missing one last opportunity to be with Lord Blakely? The answer wasn't so simple. Her loyalty to Grandmother and Papa meant either decision would bring her pain.

※ ※ ※

Edith was pulling the wrappers from Ivy's hair to form ringlets to frame her face when Mrs. Talbot entered. "Your grandmother would like a word, miss."

"Thank you, Mrs. Talbot. I will be only a moment." Ivy's mind whirled. Did Grandmother think this was her time to die? Why else would she ask Ivy to come? "Hurry, Edith."

Edith quickly pinned back the rest of Ivy's hair into a knot on top of her head. Ivy jumped from her seat and was down the short corridor in mere moments.

She slowed her pace when she saw Grandmother looking very much alive and more alert than usual.

"Did you bring a ball gown with you to Ravencross?"

Ivy blinked. "My aunt insisted I pack one."

"Bring it here."

Without hesitation, Ivy whirled around and went back to her room. She pulled the ball gown from her small closet and brought it to Grandmother.

"Much finer than I expected."

A sheer overlay with tiny white flowers dressed up the peach satin. A thick white ruche sash tied under the bust, and delicate embroidery finished all the edges. "My aunt insisted on the expense, though I am rather partial to the color."

"Peach was always a favorite color of mine as well. This will suit nicely."

Ivy blinked several times, but she did not understand. "What do you mean?"

"For Lady Blakely's ball."

"I-I . . . ," Ivy sputtered.

"You thought I was too ill to know what was going on around here?"

Ivy shrugged.

"Well, you were wrong. I have asked Edith for a full report."

Oh dear. "I know I should never have befriended Lord Blakely."

"Never mind that. What is done is done. You will go to the ball and represent our family with the utmost dignity and respect."

Ivy absently rubbed her arms. "But who will escort me?"

"You must go alone, but I will ask a few friends to keep an eye out for you should you have any needs."

"Do you think it wise?"

"It is imperative. I'd rather not stir up the neighborhood and cause any regret behind this invitation."

Ivy couldn't begin to imagine Grandmother's motives. Had her mind gone? "Are you quite sure?"

"I'd rather not repeat myself," Grandmother said. "Now, bring me a drink of water, and let's discuss how you will wear your hair."

The pitcher of water on the dressing table seemed like a better focus for Ivy's attention than an argument. Now she would not have to make a decision about whether or not to attend. Anticipation coursed through her. She would get to see Lord Blakely one last time. Despite what Ivy had pegged her for, Grandmother was turning out to be an ally.

Curtis stood beside his mother, greeting their guests as they arrived for the Christmas ball. The weather had held, and couples from several surrounding towns were expected to come. His mother and sister had outdone themselves with their preparations. A quartet harmonized a holiday tune in the far corner, candlelight danced in the chandeliers, and several boughs of greenery offered a sweet perfume of evergreen to the air.

Instead of merely enduring the procession of people into his home, Curtis did his best to greet them with a smile. He imagined Miss Hunt being impressed by his open manner. Would she come? Oh, how he hoped she would come.

"I see you are finally coming into your role, Lord Blakely," a woman in the procession said.

Curtis's smile slipped a notch, and he forced it back into place. "Thank you, Mrs. Heversham. Please, enjoy your evening."

There was a lull in arrivals, and his mother tugged on his jacket sleeve. He turned to find himself staring into a pair of stormy eyes. "What did I do wrong this time?" he asked.

"Word is circulating about you and a certain Miss Hunt. You have been seen together several times—and at least once, you were unaccompanied by a chaperone. Please tell me this is a case of mistaken identity." Her voice trembled. "My son would never do this to me."

Guilt robbed him of words for a moment. "Mama, I can explain."

"That is a trite phrase spoken right before a person attempts to justify something idiotic they have done." Her anger bordered on emotional hysteria.

"Calm yourself, Mama. Miss Hunt and I have been attempting to find the owner of a lost purse."

Mama cleared her throat as the subject of their conversation entered the vestibule. She removed her cloak, and Curtis forgot his argument. Miss Hunt had her hair swept up in a million curls. A string of pearls rested against her throat, and her milky skin seemed to gleam. Her peach dress brought out her rosy cheeks and her auburn hair. She was simply stunning.

He turned to move toward her, but his mother grabbed his arm. "You cannot dance with her," she whispered.

Curtis pulled his gaze back to his mother. He could sense she was terrified at the idea of him and Miss Hunt forming an attachment. But could he keep from dancing with Miss Hunt? He wanted to argue, but his mother pulled away and moved toward the ballroom, which was nearer the back of the house. Would she not even greet their guest?

No one deserved to arrive at a ball feeling unwelcome. Curtis pushed away the warning from his mother more easily than he should have. Moving toward Miss Hunt, he took her gloved hand in his before she even offered it, and bowed over her hand. He lifted his head in time to see her embarrassed but pleased smile. Her eyes sparkled in the candlelight. Curtis knew at once that his logic and his heart were not aligned. To honor his mother and family would be the proper course. To have Miss Hunt by his side would be the ideal course.

"You came," he said, maneuvering her hand to his arm.

"I did. Is the cavalry going to drive me out?"

"Not if you're taken prisoner first. I hear the guard is inhumane too. He makes you dance with him."

"Does he?" Miss Hunt giggled. "Sounds dreadful."

When they arrived at the ballroom entrance together, Curtis wished everyone else in the room would disappear. "Unfortunately, this guard can dance only when he is off duty. My sister will detain you until I can make my escape. She is not as pleasant as I am, but then, who can compete with me?"

"No one, I daresay. Except for maybe Chester the goat. I did meet him first," Miss Hunt teased. "Where is your sister? I would like to know her better."

Curtis chuckled. "You two will no doubt be instant friends. She would agree a goat is preferable company to me. My brother, Esmond, is visiting friends, but even if he were here, I would not permit an introduction. He is a much better man than I am and would attempt to steal my prisoner for himself."

"Would he really?"

Curtis laughed. "Never mind that; let's find my sister." He led Miss Hunt farther into the ballroom and noticed the onslaught of stares from those in the room. Many of them would have no idea who the Hunt family was. But those who lived in the neighborhood would no doubt whisper and spread the identity of the lady on his arm. Curtis did not like to think himself anything special, but there were those who thought securing him for their daughters or for themselves would be quite the victory, and this no doubt fueled their curiosity.

Amelia pulled away from a group of young ladies when she saw Curtis coming toward her. Her face was full of enthusiasm brought on by the ball, and she smiled broadly at Miss Hunt.

"Miss Hunt, you remember my sister, Miss Park."

Amelia looped her arm through Miss Hunt's. "Go away, Curtis. I will take perfectly good care of Miss Hunt while you finish whatever official capacity Mama creates for you."

"I could be away all night if you put it that way."

Amelia gave him a commiserating look. "As long as she directs her complaints to you and not me."

"I will do my best to shoulder all the burdens of the family." Curtis bowed to them and reluctantly returned to his post by the door. His mother must have seen him slip away, for she had gone back to greeting their guests. The busier she was tonight, the more time with Miss Hunt Curtis could steal.

CHAPTER TEN

IVY FOLLOWED LORD BLAKELY'S DEPARTURE with her gaze. All her senses had been alive in his presence, and she regretted his absence. She turned to Miss Park, who was about her own age; Ivy must not accidentally call her Miss Blakely since she did not share her brother's title. Her hair was much lighter than her brother's but still brown, and her nose was small and upturned on the end. The only similarity between the siblings seemed to be a single dimple on the left cheek, and there was something about the way they smiled that tied them as family.

"Do you enjoy dancing, Miss Hunt?" Miss Park asked.

"I do," Ivy replied. "Peterborough does not provide ample opportunity, but our occasional country dances are treasured by all who attend."

"I understand," Miss Park said, "since Amorwich is not exactly bursting with social venues. Might I introduce you to my friends?"

Ivy glanced at the circle of young ladies talking and laughing a few paces away. Would meeting them put her at ease or further fray her nerves? "I suppose," she said reluctantly, "if it isn't too much of an imposition."

"They're all very kind," Miss Park assured her. "Except for the one in the green gown, though she usually means well. But before we join them, I must warn you about my mother."

Ivy brought a hand to her pearls. "Your mother?"

"I don't know how to say this, but—"

"She didn't want me to come." No one near the front hall could have missed Lady Blakely's cut when Ivy arrived.

Miss Park grimaced. "There is no one more conscientious of decorum than my mother. From what I know, your father is a second-generation gentleman, and that is perfectly acceptable in these parts. But apparently there is deeper history than even I can entirely root out."

Ivy remembered Grandmother's words about having pride in her heritage. She wasn't ashamed of her connections, but neither did they make her Lord Blakely's equal. "Why did you invite me, Miss Park?"

Miss Park looked behind her to make sure no one was listening. Then she leaned closer. "My lady's maid is the daughter of one of our tenants—the Clarks. She told me how you and my brother helped her family. My brother has not been the same since our father's death. He puts up his nose to every woman my mother suggests for him to court. To my knowledge, you are the first person my brother has shown any interest in at all. I cannot remember seeing him so happy before. I didn't tell my mother, but she is bound to find out. That's why I needed to warn you."

The air left Ivy's chest, and she nearly forgot to breathe again. "Do you mean to encourage your brother and me?"

A smile stole across Miss Park's face. "I merely provided an opportunity. There is a mountain standing between you and my brother, and her name is Lady Blakely. It will be up to you and Curtis from here on out if there is ever to be a match between you. I am at a complete loss as to how to help any further. But for my brother's sake, I would if I could."

A quick glance in Lord Blakely's direction told Ivy all she needed to know. He represented all that was fine and important. This was not her world. From the moment she'd arrived, Lord Blakely's attention had been on her, but Ivy did not deserve it. The coffered ceilings and high windows of the ballroom measured the opulence the Hunt family could never afford. They lived very comfortably, but it would take four of her houses to make up Fairmore.

"Come, I have a feeling my friends will want to hear all about your dress. It's absolutely exquisite!"

Usually, Ivy did not shy away from meeting people, but she had to mentally steel her nerves as she approached the other ladies. If Lord Blakely had been by her side, perhaps the task would not have been so daunting. She smiled anyway, remembering how Lord Blakely had done the same when facing his tenants. At least his sister accepted her. It gave her an odd sense of hope, despite how impossible a match with Lord Blakely would ever be.

At his mother's insistence, Curtis led Miss Buxton in the first set. Round and round they twirled and promenaded, and all the while Curtis searched for Miss Hunt. At the start of the second dance, he saw a young man lead her to the dance circle. There were more women than men in attendance, but from that moment on, Miss Hunt seemed to be quite the favorite.

It was just before the supper dance when Curtis finally managed to make his way to her side. At that point, he knew he could not walk the fence much longer. He would dance with her, regardless of what his mother said. If he did not, he knew he would regret it.

"Miss Hunt?" He dipped his head and stepped closer. He could tell by the way her eyes lit up that she was as pleased to see him as he was her. Several couples lined up to dance the next set. Time to be brave. "Would you care to dance?"

She bit her lip. "I would not want to upset your mother."

Her hesitation only strengthened his resolve. "Let me take care of my mother. I want nothing more than to dance with you. Please?"

Miss Hunt's expression softened. She curtsied and then accepted his arm. He pulled her in line with the other dancers, the tempo blessedly slower than normal and perfect for a bit of conversation.

"Are you enjoying yourself?"

Miss Hunt beamed. "Very much. I must thank you for introducing me to your sister. She acts like a connection to me is something to be desired. People will be looking up my family name in Debrett's book when they return home tonight. They will be utterly confused when they discover my family is not listed as one of Society's peers."

"I am glad you are being so well received."

Miss Hunt looked down for a minute and then back at him. "There are those in the neighborhood who *do* know my family. I am afraid those are the ones whose opinions will matter. I hate to think your sister will face censure for her treatment toward me. She's been nothing but kind."

"My sister will have all my thanks and more," Curtis said. He knew his behavior—this very act of dancing—would have a greater consequence than his sister's actions. Even now, several of the other dancers could hear parts of their conversation. Despite his social aversion, he didn't seem to mind, because he was with Miss Hunt.

"You seem different now from when we first met. You smile a great deal more."

"Your cheerfulness is contagious." Dare he admit she was the reason he smiled?

"Is it because you are more comfortable here in your home? I am sure that is it."

Curtis thought for a moment. "Parties are not as enjoyable for me as they are for some, but I do feel like something has changed. I will never be my father, but I feel more content in my role than ever before. Even visiting with my guests this evening has not been the chore it usually is. I believe your influence has been good for me."

"Perhaps I should accompany you to the House of Lords for the next session of Parliament," Miss Hunt said. "It's a little more intimidating than a ballroom."

Shaking with laughter, Curtis replied, "I will save you a seat. I can just see you battle for the rights of the poor like you have battled to find the owner of that lost purse."

"I can see you doing a fine job without any of my help and without any attempt to imitate your father."

"You have such confidence in me. Why?" He took both of her hands in his and spun her around until they had switched sides in the line.

"I have seen a glimpse of your heart," Miss Hunt said, her cheeks glowing.

Curtis felt his own cheeks redden. "Oh? What did you see there?"

A few steps later and he was facing her once more. She looked at him as if she could see into his soul. "I recall the way you looked at Mrs. Pool, full of compassion. The way you helped Mrs. Clark with such generosity. And the way you helped search for the owner of the purse with such diligence. Those are qualities I know you possess."

At the end of the set, the last note of music carried out to a soft end. Curtis released Miss Hunt after the last turn and bent forward into a bow. His heart thumped heavily in his chest. He held out his arm, and she slipped hers around it. He began leading her to the refreshment room but, with a burst of courage, changed course. He pulled her behind a cluster of men talking and drinking, toward a dark corner.

"This will not do," he said, his heart nearly bursting from adrenaline. "When I am with you, I forget why I cannot be with you."

Miss Hunt dropped her head and released his arm. "Surely we can at least part as friends."

"Friends? I am not even sure we can be that." Curtis wondered, not for the first time, if she shared the depth of feelings he did.

"I must return home soon," she said. "You know as well as I do that friends is all we can be."

Curtis's jaw flexed. "You can write me off so easily? Am I just another project to you? A lost purse?"

"What a ridiculous thing to say." She stepped back and folded her arms across her chest.

His heart plummeted. "I feel like a dunce." He pulled at his waistcoat, wishing he could take off the many layers. It might be winter outside, but suddenly he was extremely hot. His lips pressed together tightly. "And here I stuck my neck on the line for a silly dance and a chance for our families to come together."

"I'm sorry you took such a great risk." Her pout reminded him of the first day he'd seen her, when she'd pulled herself out of his arms. "I'd not wish to be a project for you either."

"Don't turn this around." He was the one ready to confess his love, which she was so quick to dismiss. "We could talk in circles all night, but the real reason we are at each other's throats is because . . ." Curtis cleared his throat and looked away.

"Because why?" The fight was gone from her voice like she wanted— no, needed—to know the answer.

"Our families hate each other," he finally said. "We are two different people. You are always searching for a good cause, and I want to let well enough alone. What does that tell you?"

"Excuse me, my lord," a footman interrupted, stepping closer. "A note for Miss Hunt." The young man extended a small folded paper toward them.

Miss Hunt accepted the note and flipped it open and gasped.

"Is something the matter?" Curtis didn't like the alarm he saw in her expression.

She put her gloved hands to her temples. "I . . . I have to go."

"Now?"

"I know it's sudden, but it cannot be helped." She frantically looked around her.

"Are you sure everything is all right?" Didn't she trust him enough to tell him? He would do anything to put her at ease.

Miss Hunt shook her head. "I hardly know what to think. It's my father."

"Is he ill?"

"I am the one who is going to be ill," Miss Hunt said under her breath. "My father has come to escort me back to Ravencross."

Curtis's jaw went slack. "He is here?"

"Waiting just outside."

"He isn't going to call me out, is he?" He was teasing, but his anxious tone betrayed his true concern.

Miss Hunt turned a sympathetic eye on him. "My father's never killed anyone before . . . to my knowledge. He is usually very nice, unless he is angry."

"How comforting." Curtis couldn't help the sarcasm. "We had better take you to him before my mother finds out and there is a scene."

"My thoughts exactly. He is waiting by the family carriage."

Curtis took a step in the direction of the exit but then stopped in his tracks. "He isn't by the carriage any longer."

"He's inside? Are you sure it's him? You've never seen him before." Miss Hunt stood on her tiptoes, but her height prevented her from seeing anything over the gentlemen blocking her path.

"Red hair. Furious. I have no doubt he is your father." This was his comeuppance for attempting to cross the line of friendship with Miss Hunt.

"Tell me at once—is he wielding a weapon?"

"No, but by the way his hands are fisted, I don't think he will need one."

The men blocking her view parted, and Miss Hunt could see for herself. "Merciful heavens. That is most definitely him. I've never seen such a fierce expression. Do you think it better to face him or run?"

Lord Blakely's eyebrows arched. "He is your father. Don't you know?"

"He is perfectly reasonable, until any mention of Amorwich."

Curtis scratched his neck. He would have to face Mr. Hunt—alone. "Running might not be a bad idea. You slip away in the carriage you came in. I will speak to him."

Miss Hunt swayed, and he reached out to steady her.

"What do you plan to say to him?" she asked.

"I will tell him you have returned home. Our best chance is for the carriage to arrive home before his horse can. Then you can claim you attended to be polite and no more, which is why you left early."

"That sounds reasonable. You should be in Parliament."

"I am."

"Right." She took a deep breath. "I should probably listen to such an intelligent man. But you have to promise not to fight my father."

Curtis reached for her hands, a daring thing to do while standing in the same ballroom her father now occupied, but he did not let go. He gently rubbed the backs of her hands with his thumbs, wishing for more time. "I promise not to fight him, but you'd better hurry. Go out the balcony door. There are stairs on the left that will lead you to the garden. Follow the path to the front of the house and to your carriage."

Miss Hunt did not say goodbye. She turned and fled toward the balcony door.

Curtis watched her leave, and his heart went with her. There was no time to wish back his frustrated words or to explain the depth of his feelings for her. He sighed and marched in the direction of Mr. Hunt.

The man shared the same auburn hair his daughter had, but his had gray around his temples. That was the end of their similarities since Mr. Hunt was a good head taller than his daughter and certainly not dainty like she was. Curtis had a moment more to observe the man before he reached him, and he couldn't have picked a more intimidating subject to cross. Mr. Hunt was built like a military man, with broad shoulders and a trim physique. His face was probably handsome, but not when it was contorted with anger. Curtis could match him in height but not in breadth. If it did come to fighting Mr. Hunt, which he promised to avoid, Curtis would have to pray his youthfulness would aid him.

A few people had realized Mr. Hunt was in the room, and eyes were turning and whispers flying. When Curtis reached him, Mr. Hunt was still searching every corner of the room with his sharp gaze.

Curtis took a fortifying breath. "Mr. Hunt?"

Mr. Hunt turned his seething gaze on Curtis. "Do I know you?"

Curtis ignored the question—no reason to start off with a volatile introduction. "Your daughter isn't here."

"What do you mean?" the man said, his voice raising. "Where is she?"

Anyone within ten feet whirled around to see the commotion. Thankfully, some of the sound of his voice seemed to be pulled back toward the corridor behind him and was drowned out by the music.

"Your daughter and I . . . well, we . . ." Wait, that didn't sound good. "This might be better discussed outside."

"Outside? Why, you filthy scoundrel. What have you done?" Mr. Hunt growled. He pulled back his fist, and Curtis instinctively ducked. Mr. Hunt's hand connected instead with a footman, causing the innocent man to fly backward. His plate of drinks crashed to the floor, splashing red liquid on several guests.

Curtis put his shoulder up and barreled into Mr. Hunt, propelling both their bodies back into the corridor. The butler was just walking toward them, so Curtis yelled to him, "The doors, Mr. Murray!"

The butler sprang into action and swung the doors of the ballroom closed. Then he stepped in front of them, guarding them with his body.

Mr. Hunt hit the wall on the other side of the corridor. He straightened, glowering at Curtis and Mr. Murray.

Curtis took a step back and put his hands up in the air in a gesture of peace. A little breathlessly, he said, "Miss Hunt is unharmed; I promise. I am only an acquaintance." He wished to say he hoped to be more, but first he had to survive the introduction.

"It is rather impertinent for you to introduce yourself in such a misleading manner." Mr. Hunt's hands clenched by his sides, but his eyes were no longer slit with anger.

"Perhaps the one who arrived uninvited, jumped to conclusions, and made a scene in the middle of a ballroom is the impertinent one. But since my goal is to not cause offense or a further scene, I would ask to speak to you in the vestibule so I might explain myself."

"I just want to know where my daughter is."

"I will explain that too." Curtis motioned down the corridor.

Mr. Hunt glowered. "As you will." He obediently followed Curtis to the vestibule. This kind of acquiescence was an act worth celebrating, Curtis thought.

"I appreciate your willingness to come quietly," he said.

"Cut the pleasantries." Mr. Hunt folded his arms across his chest, emphasizing the muscles there. "Where is she?"

"At Ravencross. Or almost there," Curtis said. "She left not long ago. It was kind of her to accept my mother's invitation, though the night was not without its undercurrents. Her polite but early departure was understandable."

Mr. Hunt turned to leave, but Curtis wasn't finished. He hadn't planned to say more, but he couldn't miss the opportunity.

"Wait, please."

Mr. Hunt faced Curtis once more.

"Miss Hunt is an exceptional young lady. She has done more to heal the rift between our two families than anyone else has in the last twenty-five years. The entire community of Amorwich has had to choose sides or tiptoe around the situation for just as long. You don't live here, so you don't have to suffer along with the rest of us. I don't expect you to care. But you need to know your daughter is a credit to you. I suggest you remember that when you choose how you handle this."

Mr. Hunt grunted and stalked out of the front door. Now Curtis was left to wonder why he'd sent the lion home to face the lamb without his protection. He hoped he'd made the right decision. Her father would have the ride home to cool off, but what about Curtis? How should he feel? It hurt to think this might very well be his last memory with Miss Hunt. Their time together was measured by unforgettable moments. It seemed inevitable from the beginning that he would fall for her. He could never undo their short history, so he hoped the heartache would be worth enduring.

CHAPTER ELEVEN

THE COOL NIGHT AIR ENVELOPED Ivy and gave her an immediate chill. There had been no time to fetch her cloak. Just as Lord Blakely had directed, Ivy followed the steps to the garden and to her carriage. She instructed the driver to return her home as fast as possible. The driver must have spoken with her father, for he did not spare the horses. Ivy bounced around the seat and prayed the entire way home. Once she was safe at Ravencross, she realized in her rush to leave Fairmore that she had missed her opportunity to say goodbye to Lord Blakely. She choked back a sob when she remembered their argument. Her father's words were no doubt making the parting between the two families permanent.

Edith met Ivy back in her room at Ravencross and immediately began unbuttoning her dress. Shortly after donning her nightgown, Ivy heard the arrival of her father.

"You'd better hurry downstairs, Edith, if you value your life. I will speak with my father alone." Ivy didn't think her father would harm anyone, but never had she had so much reason to worry. Edith left, and Ivy gripped the back of the chair as she pushed herself away from her dressing table. Clad in her robe, she opened the door right as her father stormed down the passage.

"Father?" She tucked herself behind the door, using it as a barrier. Never had she seen him so angry.

"Where is your common sense?" Mr. Hunt demanded, stepping inside her room and slamming the door behind him. "And under your grand-mother's roof."

"It was just a ball, Papa." Ivy couldn't stop the flow of tears. "Was it so great a crime?"

"Do you realize what you have done? You have made your grandmother and me to look like fools. I'm so disgusted I cannot begin to comprehend what happened."

"I'm sorry to be a disappointment to you," Ivy said, wiping at her tears.

"This whole mess should never have happened." Mr. Hunt shook his head. "I avoided speaking to Lord Blakely, which would have caused a dark stain on my conscience, though his son cornered me."

It took Ivy a moment to understand what he meant by son. "The son is Lord Blakely now. His father died a few years ago."

Mr. Hunt raised his brow, his surprise silencing him for a moment. "The old man died, did he?"

Ivy nodded.

"Your grandmother never told me. Though, neither of us speaks of the family."

Ivy hugged herself, realizing more and more how futile it was to have let her heart care so much. "Why did you come?"

Her father sighed and collapsed onto a chair. "Your letters describing my mother had me worried. I thought I had better come see for myself in case this was her end. Sure enough, she looks closer to a ghost than the living." He rubbed at his jaw and then ripped his cravat loose. "I should have come myself instead of sending you. This is more my fault than anything. I've avoided coming here for too long."

"And then I was missing when you arrived," Ivy said, dropping her gaze to her slippers. Her father was a handsome man, still trim and in good health, but tonight he looked terribly tired and almost ill. He had seen his own mother near death and then discovered his daughter had betrayed him. "I'm sorry," she whispered.

He leaned forward, resting his elbows on his knees. "You left early, and that ought to count for something. Lord Blakely hinted about you healing the rift between our families. What did you leave out of your letters?"

"Lord Blakely offered to help me find the owner of a lost purse." Ivy sounded sheepish even to herself.

"I see," Mr. Hunt said. "And just as innocently, you tricked him into falling in love with you."

"He doesn't love me." Lord Blakely's frustrated words came to her mind.

Mr. Hunt groaned. "We will not stay here long enough to find out. Three days, and then we are going back to Peterborough for you to pack your things, and then it's London for you."

Ivy's tears came afresh. "Yes, Papa."

He came to her and kissed her head. "Your grandmother admitted to encouraging you to go. I know this trip was hard on you, but you accepted graciously, just like you are now. I might not like what happened tonight, but I am thankful for your time with my mother. She said you have been a light in a very dark house these last weeks—said you never left her alone long enough for her to die. I can't begrudge you one little holiday party, even if it was in the home of my worst enemy." He sighed and then looked at her once more. "Goodnight, luv."

Ivy wiped frantically at the moisture blurring her vision. Once her father left, she didn't care about seeing clearly any longer and let the tears flow. Tomorrow would be upon her too soon, and then she would be forced to see a future without Lord Blakely.

Sleep eventually came like a sweet reprieve. But when her swollen eyes greeted the morning, Ivy threw the blankets back over her head.

"Morning, miss," came Edith's voice. "Your grandmother would like to see you after breakfast. I've brought a tray of food for you."

Ivy pushed back her covers and pulled herself into a sitting position. "Very well."

"I've got a special lotion to reduce the puffiness around your eyes. I will fetch it while you eat."

Edith seemed much too cheerful for such a gloomy day. Ivy ate very little, then let Edith help her dress and fix her hair. She dragged her feet to Grandmother's room, half-nervous to find her father ready to rebuke her again.

"So you're leaving?" Grandmother asked before coughing into her hand.

Ivy nodded quickly. "We must. I am sorry you are still ill."

"I feel stronger than yesterday, thanks to you."

"Me?"

"Yes, you've brought a glimmer of light to Ravencross. And not just because you opened my drapes."

Ivy managed to smile.

"Any regrets?"

Sighing, Ivy shrugged. "I didn't mean to cause any problems."

Grandmother shook her head. "Lord Blakely is much too handsome and genuine to be a problem."

That was unexpected. Ivy's smile widened. "Did you just make a joke?"

"I've been wanting to die, not laugh."

"You want to die?" Ivy walked to the chair by Grandmother's bedside and sat down.

"I have nothing to live for." Grandmother said this without tears or emotion, as if she had come upon this conclusion long ago.

"What about your family?" Ivy thought her father and she and her sisters ought to count for something.

"The family I never see?"

"Well . . . yes."

Grandmother looked down at her wrinkled hands. "I think the Good Shepherd is trying to tell me it is not time for this sheep to return home."

"Then, you aren't going to die?"

"I will someday, but not today. What about you? What will you live for?"

Ivy's eyebrows furrowed while she thought. "I will go to London, and if I am fortunate, I will marry. And I will look back on this time and think how silly I was to think a lost miser purse was worth getting between two feuding families."

"What did you say?"

"How silly it was to—"

"No, no. The lost purse?"

"Oh yes, I've been spending all my free time searching for the owner."

"Was it burgundy wool with two silver rings in the middle?"

"Yes." Ivy straightened. "And full of coin."

Grandmother started breathing heavily and clutched her chest.

"What is it?" Ivy leaped out of her seat in alarm. "Do you need a drink? You promised you would not die today."

"I'm not dying," Grandmother said, trying to steady her breathing. "At least, I do not think so. I've never died before."

"Take a few deep breaths. Shall I call for a doctor?"

"No. Just fetch the purse."

The purse? Ivy turned, picked up her skirts, and ran all the way to her room. The purse was on her writing desk, and she swept it up with one hand and pivoted back around. She was out of breath when she returned to Grandmother, who lay back with her eyes closed but was still breathing deeply. "Here it is," Ivy said, hurrying to set the purse on Grandmother's lap.

Grandmother opened her eyes, revealing a pool of tears that dripped down her wrinkled cheeks onto her nightgown. "Losing this was like losing the will to live."

"It was yours all along? I never would have thought. It meant so much to me to find the owner, and the answer was right in front of me."

Grandmother opened it and pulled out several pieces of Spanish gold.

Ivy gasped. "All this time, I never opened it."

Grandmother chuckled, her breathing slowly steadying into a normal rhythm. "Your grandfather gave this to me as our wedding gift. It was part of his prize money for aiding in the capture of a Spanish cargo ship after the Battle of Manila, during the Seven Years' War. He wanted me to spend it all on myself. Not all his fortune was made in farming, you know." Grandmother's laugh was hoarse and shaky. "We saved this last bit for a time of need, but we always had more than enough.

"After he died, I began carrying it around to bring me comfort." Her words became thick with emotion. "I couldn't remember where I left it. I searched and searched until I made myself ill with worry. I figured it meant it was time to cross to the other side to be with him."

"How do you feel now that you have it once more?"

"Your grandfather surely wants me to use the coins for a good cause. I will keep searching for the right purpose—a reason worth living for."

A sad smile spread across Ivy's lips. "You must have loved Grandfather a great deal."

Grandmother nodded. "As much as you love Lord Blakely."

Ivy's eyes widened. "It's forbidden, remember?"

"Nonsense. That is what your father thinks. But he will listen to me. Go fetch your cloak. We have a visit to make."

"But you are ill, and where would we go?"

"To see Lady Blakely."

Nothing could have surprised Ivy more. "Even I see the lack of logic behind this decision. You must stay in bed. Seeing Lady Blakely after what happened at the ball . . . well . . . it's simply ludicrous."

"I might be frail, but I am still your grandmother. Mind your betters, and fetch your cloak. And hurry before I decide it would be easier to die today."

There was clearly a renewal of wind in Grandmother's sails. The woman swung her legs over the side of the bed faster than any other invalid would have.

"Please be careful." Ivy put her hand out to help Grandmother stand.

Grandmother swayed for a second and then sat back down. "Tell Mrs. Talbot to have a carriage prepared, and then send for Edith. I will be well enough after I find my sense of balance. I know you are concerned, but God has granted me my purse and one more day on this earth. With His help, I will put everything to right."

"But what if it isn't possible?"

"Then, we shall know within the hour."

Ivy had to steady herself now. "All right. But how shall we avoid Papa?"

"We shall pray for a miracle."

Ivy was sure getting Grandmother to the carriage alive would be the miracle. But then again, she'd finally found the owner to the purse, and Grandmother wanted to fix the mistakes of her past. Perhaps miracles were not so unattainable but available for when the time was right. But even with this realization, Ivy couldn't bring herself to hope for the miracle she wanted most of all.

Edith helped Grandmother to dress while Ivy readied herself to make the call on Lady Blakely. They were making their way slowly down the stairs to accommodate Grandmother when Ivy's father met them at the bottom.

"Mama? Why are you out of bed?" He looked at his mother and then at Ivy. "Are you going out?"

"Now, son," Grandmother began. "I have been in charge of my own life for a decade, and you will not stop me now."

"Stop you?" he asked. "You are going to expire before you reach the end of the stairs. Stop there, and I shall carry you back to your bed."

"Do not think of it." Grandmother started coughing, and all of them froze until her spell passed. "It is time to move on. I'm calling on Lady Blakely."

"Did you put her up to this, Ivy?" her father asked.

"No, Papa."

"She tried to dissuade me," Grandmother said. "But I will not be stopped. It's time."

"If only that wretched family would leave the neighborhood . . . Northamptonshire . . . or England altogether. I should never have come back here."

Grandmother shook her head, taking a moment to catch her breath. "You should have come back many years ago and put this behind you.

I understand better than anyone the injustice we were served. The land and more was promised to be ours, but when they made a deal far more profitable for them, we could not enforce a verbal agreement. They were once our friends, so their change of course hurt us personally. But who is to say what we would have done in their position? Oh, my son, memories can be blinding, crippling our ability to see beyond the moment. I, for one, will no longer live in the past. What time I have left on this earth will be spent in happier pursuits. Now, give me your arm, and help me to the carriage."

Papa shook his head. "I cannot agree to this."

"You will have to forgive in your own time, but this is mine. Now, help your mother."

Papa gritted his teeth, his frustration evident. "Very well." He met Grandmother halfway up the staircase and gently scooped her into his arms as if she were nothing but a doll. He then carried her all the way to the carriage, covering her with a lap blanket and even kissing her cheek. "We have done nothing worth apologizing for. Remember that."

Grandmother sighed. "I have not been a good neighbor. I shall apologize for that."

Papa gave a single nod, then stepped back for Ivy to enter the carriage, and shut the door.

Ivy studied him through the window. Papa had put aside his own pride because of an even greater emotion—his love for his mother. Hard lines traced his brow, but under the gruff exterior was a hurting heart much like her own. Part of her wanted Papa to reach out and stop them from leaving. Facing Lady Blakely seemed like quite the frightening feat. But with a tug, the carriage wheels began pulling them out of her father's reach.

CHAPTER TWELVE

CURTIS HAD MANAGED TO AVOID a lecture by his mother all morning by keeping himself busy. Thoughts of Miss Hunt were never far from his mind. No amount of work would undo the pressure in his chest and the building anxiety of Miss Hunt leaving before he could fix things between them. Whether such an opportunity was plausible or possible to hope for, it did not matter. He yearned for it. How to attempt it was the question.

With footmen scrubbing the ballroom floors of Fairmore and maids scraping candle wax from nearly every surface, Curtis had to weave between them to leave the room.

"What is the damage?" his mother asked from the entrance to the drawing room as he stepped into the corridor. She had her fan out as if she'd been too close to the fire.

Curtis attempted a light response. "The potted fern in the back appears dehydrated—a true tragedy—but otherwise the room will be righted by the end of the day."

"I do like that fern," his mother said, stepping on her tiptoes to look over his shoulder. "I always forget how awful the day after a ball can be. However will I survive this Season with Amelia?"

Curtis waved his mother back into the drawing room so she might sit down. "You shall survive just as we all will—by sheerly enduring it."

"I want to enjoy it, not endure it."

Their butler entered the room and cleared his throat. "A Mrs. Hunt and a Miss Hunt to see you, Your Ladyship. Are you at home to them?"

Curtis's mother put her hand to her mouth and then to her hair. "Don't leave me," she said, reaching toward Curtis. "This is all your fault. I should never forgive you."

Curtis's heart leapt at the opportunity. "I'll stay, but I cannot imagine why they are here, not unless the lion I sent home last night sent the ladies to finish us off."

"What are you talking about?"

Mr. Murray cleared his throat again. "Are you receiving callers today, Your Ladyship?"

"Yes, send them in." Mother closed her fan in one smooth swish of her wrist and then stood and smoothed out her dress. "I rather feel like I'm waiting for my execution. Silly, is it not?"

The grandmother came in on her granddaughter's arm, Miss Hunt nearly carrying the weight of her frail relative. Curtis rushed forward and took the older woman's other arm, no doubt surprising both her and his mother. Miss Hunt shot him a look of gratitude, and he attempted to ease her anxiousness with his smile.

"What a surprise," Mama said when they were all seated.

Mrs. Hunt needed a moment to catch her breath. "I apologize for missing the ball, but I was indisposed."

Mama blinked rapidly, as astonished as the rest of them to think Mrs. Hunt had ever intended on coming to the ball at all. "Are you still unwell?"

"I have promised not to die today," Mrs. Hunt said.

Miss Hunt attempted to hide her laugh by coughing into her hand.

Curtis caught the gesture, but his mother did not. "You needn't trouble yourself for a visit when you are both ill," Mama said.

"Lady Blakely," Mrs. Hunt began. "I have not set foot in this house for more than twenty-five years. I do not care to discuss the reason for my offense, just the present matter. You are by far my better through marriage, but it didn't used to be that way, so let me be frank. For a community of our size to be divided is intolerable. It is time we put the past behind us. Until my granddaughter arrived, I saw no point. Now, through a little Christmas miracle, I have realized how precious our time on this earth is. Let us not squander it by fighting. You . . . have my apology . . . for casting aside our friendship." Her voice grew strained, and she cleared her throat. "I shall not overstay my welcome, but I would like you to come to tea the day after tomorrow. By then I should be more myself and will be ready to catch up on the gossip from the ball."

Silence followed Mrs. Hunt's words. Curtis exhaled slowly while he waited for Mama to reply.

"Tea would be nice," Lady Blakely finally said, and then her perfect composure broke. Her eyes scrunched up, filling with moisture, and her fan was back up and beating rapidly.

"Ivy, be a dear and help me stand," Mrs. Hunt said.

Ivy.

Her name fit her well. He could see how she wrapped herself around everyone she met and had unwittingly entangled herself around his heart.

Ivy took one of Mrs. Hunt's arms, and Curtis stood and took the other.

"I will help you out," Curtis said, glad when no argument followed. He looked over Mrs. Hunt's head toward Ivy, but she was concentrating on her grandmother. If he could only get her alone for a moment, he had so much to say.

Their pace was steady and slow, but it still did not feel like a long enough walk to the carriage. Curtis couldn't contrive a way to get Ivy to stay behind. Should he offer to ride with them home? Should he make a scene and insist Ivy listen to him? Neither felt right, but biding his time didn't make sense either. If he waited for too long, she'd be gone.

The footman stepped in and helped settle Mrs. Hunt into her seat. Ivy sat beside her, almost as if she were propping up her grandmother.

Anxiety gripped Curtis's heart. "I am glad you came." His words came out exceptionally rushed and dull. "I do hope your health returns, Mrs. Hunt. So many have been worried, and I am sure your granddaughter would be relieved."

"Stop rambling, Lord Blakely. It is obvious you would like to speak privately with my granddaughter; you may do so now."

Relieved, Curtis looked at Ivy, who only seemed surprised. "If you find it agreeable," he said.

Ivy nodded quickly. He held out his hand, and she put her small one in his. After helping her down, he pointed to his stables. "Could we walk this way? I have something to show you."

The stables were tucked behind a cluster of trees just far enough to avoid any smells. When they opened the stable door, warm air and an aroma of hay and animals welcomed them inside. After a few quick instructions, the stablehands slipped outside to give them privacy.

"Just here," Lord Blakely said, motioning Ivy over to the first stall door.

She looked inside and laughed. "Chester! Mr. Bryant's goat. I hope you did not steal him."

"No, just borrowed him for a bit of company."

"Are you so very lonely?" Her eyes sparkled with mirth.

"I am, actually." He couldn't stop staring at her. She was so beautiful. "Since meeting you, I spend more time worrying about my tenants than I do myself. You were the one serving everyone, and I merely took notes. I am finally adjusting to this new outlook on life, and I don't think I will be able to wait until next Christmas to make more changes around here. I'm even talking to goats. You do see why I hold you responsible."

Ivy seemed amused but baffled. "Should I be apologizing? I think you took your goodwill a little too far when you decided to care for the goat; however, I do think it a better choice for you than chickens."

Laughing, Curtis put his arm on the stall door and leaned a little closer to her. "I cannot help it. I think of you every time I'm with him." She smiled, and it gave him the courage to continue. "About last night—I'm sorry for our argument. The mess between our families seemed insurmountable at the moment, and I regret my words completely. Will you forgive me?"

Ivy bit her lip and nodded. "I'm sorry too. We never should have parted in anger."

"Ivy . . . may I call you Ivy?"

Ivy dipped her head with embarrassment. "If you'd like."

"Well then, Ivy. I am Curtis, not quite the same man you first met. A mite humbler, I hope, and more aware, thanks to your good influence. And you already know Chester."

"Yes." Ivy's smile made his heart swell. "How do you do, Chester?"

"I think he should be part of our family." Curtis motioned to the goat.

"Our family?"

"Yes. You, me, and the goat."

"I think we could stop after you and me," Ivy said breathlessly.

She did care. Relief lightened his heart. "Well, we could leave the goat out, but I don't think stopping after you and me is the ideal scenario. I do need an heir, you know."

Ivy's cheeks glowed a rosy hue. "Are you proposing?"

Curtis's breath grew unsteady. He reached for her, uncertain but hopeful. His hands slowly encircled her waist, reveling in the feel of her. He tugged her against him. It was just as he remembered; she fit perfectly. "Thoughts of you chase me wherever I am and even in my dreams. You've given me the best Christmas I've ever had—one of peace, clarity, and hope. I feel deep down this is just the beginning, not goodbye. I love you, Ivy. I haven't your talents to offer, just my heart and my home. Please say you'll marry me."

Ivy blinked back tears. Would she accept his humble offering?

"I promise there will be plenty of soup."

She bit back a smile and stepped up onto her tiptoes. "Your love is the only gift I want."

His stomach caught inside him, and he breathed out in relief. "You shall have my gift of love this year and for the rest of forever." He leaned down, and their lips met. Ivy tasted as sweet as Curtis had imagined she would. Her mouth was tender and soft one minute and then fiery and passionate the next, true to her personality. This was joy. This was how the crucibles of life could be endured and the aches of life diminished. Her arms encircled his neck, and he drew her closer. Together, their future would be bright.

The goat baaed, and the euphoria of their kiss broke, bringing them back to the present. He pulled back, and a laugh sparked between them.

"I guess the goat can be part of the family," Ivy said, lifting her hand to his cheek, "as long as he can show proper respect when you kiss me."

Curtis rubbed his fingers along the side of her neck. "What kiss? Hmm? Let's keep this between us until I can convince your father not to murder me. Your family means a great deal to you, and I will do my best to beg his permission."

Ivy groaned, leaning her head into his hand. "It's impossible. Wait— let's ask Grandmother to do the talking."

"She rendered Mama speechless, didn't she?" His smile dropped, and he shook his head. "No, this is something I must do on my own."

"I do hope you're right." Ivy stepped out of his arms. "I think Grand-mother would say we need one last Christmas miracle to soften Papa's heart."

"It's been a full month. How many miracles can a man ask for?"

Ivy sighed. "Is it too much to ask?"

Curtis thought back to what he knew about miracles. "The day Mrs. Pool lay ill in her bed, I learned that asking is the only way to get an answer. Say a prayer, dear girl. I want nothing more than to marry you." He dipped his head again and captured her warm, eager lips. He couldn't think this would be the last time, but he could not hold back his longing.

He escorted Ivy back to her grandmother and then returned to the stables to have his horse saddled. A pressing matter such as marriage could not be put off.

CHAPTER THIRTEEN

IVY PACED IN FRONT OF Grandmother, who sat on the sofa, and alternately clasped her hands together and covered her eyes. When Ivy and Curtis had arrived together at Ravencross, her father had taken in Curtis's unexpected appearance; his back had gone rigid and his features had hardened. Curtis had requested a private audience, and the two of them had disappeared into the small study without another word. The longcase clock in the drawing room seemed to tick louder with every passing second.

"You're not going to hurry anything by fretting," Grandmother said, though she too seemed anxious.

"I'm not fretting, not completely. I'm praying."

"That I can condone. But the Holy Father requires a little work on our part too, you know. You might try knocking your father out with a vase and then eloping to Scotland."

Ivy's gasp turned into a laugh. "Grandmother!"

"Come now, don't be too serious. I am only attempting to lighten the mood. We will know soon enough."

As if summoned by Grandmother's words, footsteps sounded outside the drawing room. Ivy stepped back toward her grandmother. Her father entered first, followed by Lord Blakely.

"I told you he loved you," Papa said, his tone anything but light.

Ivy released her pent-up breath. "But you left him alive, so that is something."

Curtis's face was unreadable.

Papa ran a hand through his hair, mussing it on one side. "Killing him might have been easier to stomach. Aunt Morris might never forgive either of us."

Ivy's breath caught. "Do you mean . . . ?"

"Happy Christmas, my girl."

So this was why she had come to Ravencross—for Grandmother, for Curtis, and for her future with both of them. A single desire to do good had blossomed into unexpected happiness. All the struggles on her journey, both of heartache and fear, had paved the way for the joy and gratitude now brimming inside of her.

Her father motioned to Curtis. "It looks like you will be traveling to London as the new Lady Blakely."

Ivy's smile could not spread any wider. She moved to be near Curtis and immediately was tucked under his arm.

"You, me, and Chester," Curtis said with a wink.

She laughed. "I don't know what to say. I can hardly contain my happiness." She turned to her father. "Thank you, Papa."

Sighing happily, Grandmother sank back into the sofa as if this news had been her best medicine yet.

Papa's frown lessened a little, but his voice remained somber. "Unlike your grandmother, I cannot forgive the past. But I can forget it enough to appreciate the advantages of a union of love for my eldest daughter—especially to a man who nearly bargained away all of his holdings for a chance with you."

Ivy's heart sank. "No. You couldn't," she told her father. Was this still about the land feud? She looked up into Curtis's eyes, but instead of seeing sorrow, she saw only pleasure and warmth.

"You know me better than that, Ivy." Her father chuckled. "He passed all of my tests. His devotion to you is complete and his lands intact. In a way, the lands I once thought would be my own will now be in the family. It's how it should be."

Ivy squeezed her eyes shut. "I think I must be dreaming. I get both of you—my family and my heart." She smiled at her father and then up at Curtis. "And the answer to my prayer."

Curtis held her close. "Happy Christmas, love."

About the Author

ANNEKA WALKER IS AN AWARD-WINNING author. She was raised by a librarian and an English-teacher-turned-judge. After being fed a steady diet of books, she decided to learn about writing. The result was a bachelor's degree in English and history. When she isn't dreaming up a happy ending for a story, she's busy living her own with her husband and adorable children.

Follow Wholesome Romance on social media for more great titles.

OTHER BOOKS AND AUDIOBOOKS
BY SIAN ANN BESSEY

Forgotten Notes

Cover of Darkness

A Family Is Forever

Kids on a Mission: Escape from Germany

Kids on a Mission: Uprising in Samoa

Kids on a Mission: Ambushed in Africa

Teddy Bear, Blankie, and a Prayer

Deception

Within the Dark Hills

You Came for Me

The Insider

One Last Spring

To Win a Lady's Heart

For Castle and Crown

The Gem Thief

The Heart of the Rebellion

The Noble Smuggler

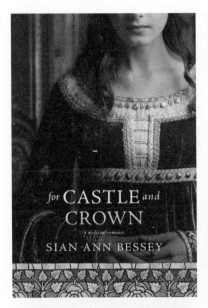

for CASTLE and
CROWN
a medieval romance
SIAN ANN BESSEY

The
GEM THIEF
SIAN ANN BESSEY

SOME THINGS AREN'T
ALWAYS AS THEY SEEM

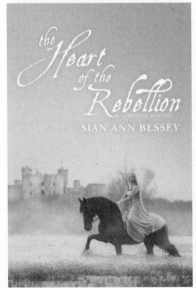

the
Heart
of the
Rebellion
A MEDIEVAL ROMANCE
SIAN ANN BESSEY

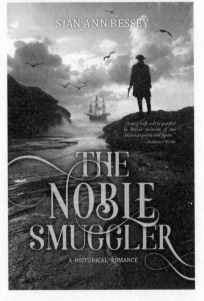

SIAN ANN BESSEY

"History buffs will be gratified
by Bessey's inclusion of real
historical events and figures."
—*Publishers Weekly*

THE
NOBLE
SMUGGLER
A HISTORICAL ROMANCE

PRAISE FOR SIAN ANN BESSEY

"Sian Ann Bessey weaves a beautiful Christmas story with vivid descriptions, a tender romance, and unforgettable characters. Amelia and Philip remind us what 'A Season of Hope' is all about."
—Anneka R. Walker, author *The Masked Baron*

"Sian is a novelist adept at taking ordinary life and love and making it extraordinary. She does this to great effect in all she writes. This story is no exception."
—Carla Kelly, author *The Unlikely Heroes* (coming 2021)

"A down-and-out family you want to cheer on and a swoon-worthy soldier! *Sigh.*"
—Krista Lynne Jensen, author *Kisses in the Rain*

A SEASON OF HOPE

SIAN ANN BESSEY

For Julie Hess,
who has worked tirelessly for many
years to ensure thousands of missionaries
she's never met receive something special for Christmas

ACKNOWLEDGMENTS

As ALWAYS, I AM GRATEFUL to my family members for their unfailing love and support and to the remarkable people at Covenant who do so much behind the scenes to bring my writing to life. I'd also like to offer special thanks to my gifted fellow authors in this anthology. Participating in this project with each of you has been a privilege and a joy.

CHAPTER ONE

Shropshire, 1816

WITH A WEARY SIGH, AMELIA Nesbitt's mother handed her the newly delivered note. "It's about Lambert again."

That wretched goat! Amelia dropped into the old armchair in the parlor and stared at the short missive, willing the spidery letters to crawl into a new configuration and reveal a completely different message. But Mr. Thomas Cunningham's note remained as terse and unforgiving as it had the first time she read it.

> *Dear Mrs. Nesbitt,*
>
> *You are hereby charged ten shillings and six pence to replace two shirts and a pair of stockings that were damaged beyond repair by your trespassing goat.*
>
> *Payment is to be made by 24th December, and this shall serve as your final warning. Should any further damage be incurred, the magistrate will be notified.*
>
> *Sincerely,*
> *Mr. Thomas Cunningham*

Amelia lowered the letter to her knee and gazed out of the window. Rain was streaming down the glass, blurring her view of the back garden, but she could still make out the woodshed up against the hedge. The somewhat dilapidated structure did indeed contain a small pile of wood, but it also housed her brother Giles's current assortment of pets, which included five chickens, a three-legged cat, and the errant goat.

The chickens paid for their keep in eggs, and the cat acted as a moderately good mouser, despite its missing limb. Lambert, however, had virtually nothing to recommend himself. He was obstinate and disobedient. He repeatedly escaped the shed, and notwithstanding the abundance of grass on this side of the hedge and the other, he preferred to dine on whatever articles of clothing Mr. Cunningham's servants put out on Woodcroft Hall's clothesline. This was the third time they'd heard from Mr. Cunningham in as many weeks, and Amelia knew full well that what little remained of their meager savings would not cover the cost of their goat's most recent wayward behavior.

Her shoulders drooped. She was to blame for this. It was she who had allowed Giles to keep the milk-white kid when Mrs. Everett, the farmer's wife, had offered it to him at the market all those weeks ago. Giles had received so few gifts during his ten years of life; it had seemed cruel to prevent him from bringing the animal home. But owning the goat was proving to be more of a punishment than a prize. Every penny Amelia and her mother had saved to provide a happy Christmas for their small family had been used to replace Mr. Cunningham's chewed-up clothing.

"Mother! Mia!" Giles burst into the parlor, water dripping off his sandy-colored hair and running down his freckle-covered nose. He held up a length of severed rope. "Lambert's escaped again."

"So Mr. Cunningham has informed us," Mother said. "Is there still no sign of him?"

Giles shook his head, sprinkling his shoulders with more water droplets. "He's not in the garden, and there's another hole under the hedge not far from the one I boarded up last week."

"Of course there is," Amelia muttered, rising to her feet. "The dratted goat thinks he's a rabbit."

Giles's brow furrowed. "Do rabbits eat gentlemen's clothing too?"

"No." Amelia could not fully hide her irritation. "I daresay a rabbit would be quite content with whatever it could find in our garden."

The corners of Giles's mouth turned downward, and he looked from Amelia to their mother. "Lambert's rather a lot of trouble, isn't he?"

"I'm afraid so," their mother said with her usual gentle honesty.

Amelia started toward her cloak hanging on the hook near the door. "We'd best go and find him before it gets dark or he does any more damage."

Her mother nodded. "I shall write back to Mr. Cunningham. Perhaps he will allow us an extension period to repay the debt, given that Christmas is almost upon us."

Amelia thought it unlikely that the tight-fisted gentleman would do anything of the sort, but she would not fault her mother's belief in his goodwill. Drawing her cloak over her shoulders, she managed a tight smile. "Surely, no harm will come from asking."

Tying the ribbons of her bonnet beneath her chin, Amelia led her brother out into the deluge. A narrow path ran from the humble cottage's front door toward the garden gate and the lane beyond. The few remaining chrysanthemums in the garden were bent low, their rain-soaked petals heavy and wilted. Most of the other flowers, which had been so vibrant earlier in the year, were gone; only the Christmas roses were yet to bloom.

Several feet to her left, Amelia could see the makeshift barricade Giles had erected in front of the first hole Lambert had created in the hedge. Not more than a yard away from it, another ragged hole was now visible just above the ground.

"I could squeeze through it," Giles said, noting the direction of her gaze and stuffing the severed rope into his pocket. "But you wouldn't fit."

Amelia shook her head. "We'll use the lane." Although it would shave a considerable distance off their walk, sending Giles onto the Cunningham property through the tangled bush was not worth the risk. She'd rather take a little longer on foot and save her mother the time it would take to mend the tears in Giles's breeches afterward.

"If we go over the stile, we can cut through the woods," Giles said, leaving the garden gate behind and taking off at a run.

His arms spun like a windmill as he careened down the steep hill. Amelia was a nineteen-year-old young lady, but she hesitated for only a moment before tossing propriety to the wind and chasing after him. By the time she reached the stone stile, Giles was already across. He stood in the wet grass on the Cunningham property, his arm extended.

"Jump," he said.

Amelia's breath caught. How many times had she stood atop this very perch as her older brother, Will, waited impatiently for her on the other side? They'd walked the mile distance from the parsonage to Woodcroft Hall more often than she could count to meet up with Will's best friend, Philip Cunningham. The boys had been virtually inseparable during their youth. Even though Will was the son of the local vicar and Philip the son of one of the most affluent gentlemen in Shropshire, their mutual love of adventure had drawn them together.

Whenever Philip had returned to Woodcroft Hall for the school holidays, he'd appeared at the parsonage the very next day in search of Will. The boys had filled their days hiking the hills, fishing the streams, or exploring the ruins of nearby Clun Castle. Although she was five years their junior, Amelia had begged to be included, and occasionally, at her mother's insistence, they had grudgingly allowed her to join them. More often than not, Will had expended most of his energy complaining about how slowly she walked or how unnecessary it was to pick flowers along their way. Amelia had simply ignored him, sometimes even managing to persuade Philip to pause long enough to study the beauty of the gorse bush blooms or the pussy willows' fuzzy nubs.

"Make haste, Mia," Giles called.

His features were so similar to Will's, but the dash of daring that had been so evident in their older brother was missing from Giles's countenance. Instead, his green eyes shone with concern. Amelia pushed past the lingering ache of loss. It had been five years since Will and Philip left, and she had a goat to catch.

She landed on the other side of the stile with a squelch. Mud stuck to the soles of her boots and formed a brown ring around the hem of her pale-blue gown. Mentally adding the need to rewash her clothing to Lambert's growing list of offenses, Amelia faced the wooded area.

"If we cut through here," she said, "we'll come out on the west side of the great lawn and have a clear view of the house."

"With all this rain, I don't suppose there are any clothes still on the clothesline," Giles said glumly. "If Lambert's not there, he could be anywhere."

Amelia was only too aware of the extensive acreage at Woodcroft. As a child, she'd dipped her feet into the lake, chased Will and Philip through the trees, and sledged down the hills. She knew full well that if they didn't spot Lambert near the house, they would likely need to call off their hunt until the weather cleared and the maids put out more clothes to dry. Without shirt bait, they could be hunting the goat for days.

"We'll just have to hope for the best," she said, making for the nearest oak tree.

Giles fell into step behind her, and before long, the trees thinned and they reached the edge of a wide expanse of green lawn. A gravel drive cut through the grass, leading to the wide front doors of a splendid three-story house. The manor was an imposing sight, built of red brick and lined with tidy rows of small-paned windows and at least half a dozen chimneys.

"Will Mr. Cunningham mind us being here?" Giles asked, glancing at the house anxiously.

"I certainly hope not," Amelia said. "He obviously wants Lambert removed, so he should be glad to see that we've come so promptly after receiving his letter."

Giles nodded, although he didn't look fully convinced. The last two times Lambert had trespassed, one of Woodcroft Hall's servants had returned him to the cottage and delivered a bill. Amelia thought it likely that this time, the goat had simply escaped capture. She placed her hands on her hips and scanned the grounds.

"If I were a goat, where would I be?"

"Indoors," Giles said. Now that they were standing still, he was shivering slightly. He'd been outside longer than she had, and Amelia guessed the rain had long since soaked through his shoes and jacket.

"I'm not convinced Lambert is that intelligent," she said. "But the stables might be a good place to start."

They hurried across the lawn and rounded the corner of the house. North of the manor, the terraced garden dropped to the lake and the gently sloping hill beyond. Amelia paused beside an ancient ash tree. She had always loved this prospect, and its beauty was hardly diminished by the inclement weather.

"Just look at that, Giles." She yearned to wander the garden and study the vast assortment of plant life. "Have you ever seen anything so lovely?"

"Um, yes. A roaring fire in the parlor," Giles said, wiping the moisture off his face with the back of his equally wet sleeve.

Amelia stifled a sigh. No matter their differences, on this subject her brothers were alike: they had no interest whatsoever in foliage.

Turning away from the captivating view, she pointed to a large building across the courtyard. "The stables."

They approached the entrance cautiously. The faint thuds and shuffle of stabled horses reached them through the closed doors, but there was no sign of the goat.

"That must be where the maid hangs the washing," Giles said, pointing to a line strung between two poles a few yards away. As he'd guessed, the line currently hung limp and empty. "If Lambert's that taken with Mr. Cunningham's shirts, he'll likely stay close by, hoping for more."

Circumventing the growing puddles, Amelia started toward the other side of the stable. The roof overhung the wall by about ten inches. Surely, that was distance enough to shelter a kid from the rain. She'd almost reached the back of the stables when she heard a scurry of feet and saw a flash of white streak past her.

"Giles!" Amelia called.

Her brother darted after the goat. Amelia turned, running across the courtyard to cut the speeding creature off before he reached the shrubs. Lambert saw her coming and veered left. Giles followed, and Amelia kept running—through the puddles, across the shifting gravel on the drive, and onto the wet lawn. A crow took flight from the upper branches of the ash tree, swooping low and cawing its displeasure at the commotion. Lambert swerved away from the large black bird and ran headlong into Amelia. Caught off-balance, Amelia's feet slid on the sodden grass and she tumbled to the ground. Lambert bleated frantically, his legs becoming more and more tangled in Amelia's skirts.

Giles pounced on him. "Got you, you naughty goat," he said, yanking the kid off Amelia and pinning the wiggling animal between his legs as he attached the severed rope from his pocket to the short piece still hanging around Lambert's neck. "Are you hurt, Mia?"

"No." Amelia stood slowly and brushed her hand over the grass and mud plastered across her cloak. Her bonnet had fallen back, and her golden-brown curls had come loose from their pins. She could feel them hanging around her neck in wet strands. "But I pray no one from the house was watching that performance; otherwise, my pride will be severely injured."

Giles grinned. Cinching the knot tightly, he rose to his feet. "It was a splendid catch."

She took an unsteady step toward the drive. "I'm glad you thought so." Her left elbow throbbed mercilessly, but she managed a weak smile. "Perhaps following the drive might be better than going home over the stile since we have Lambert in tow now."

"Very well." He eyed the goat sternly and tugged on the rope. "Say your farewells to Woodcroft Hall, Lambert. You are never to return."

❄ ❄ ❄

Philip Cunningham had not felt this cold in more than five years. Having fully acclimated to the heat of the West Indies, he found Britain's winter weather had come as an unpleasant shock. It had been two days since he left his ship in Liverpool, and the rain had yet to abate. He had long since lost feeling in his fingers and struggled to grip his horse's reins. Water was dripping off his hat, and his cloak felt more like a heavy wet blanket than protection from the elements. The temperature had seemed to drop a degree with every mile he'd ridden inland from the dock, and he had to believe it would not be much longer before the coming of night turned the rain to snow.

Upon reaching the Four Crosses Inn, he turned off the main thoroughfare and guided his mount onto the road that led through the small village of Morton Abbott. The residents appeared to have taken refuge from the worsening weather, the market square empty of stalls and customers. A thin black-and-white dog standing beside the old well was the only one to observe his passing by.

The road bent slightly to the right, and up ahead Philip spotted the church spire. He tensed, bracing himself for his first sighting in years of the parsonage located beside the small graveyard. How different his return to Morton Abbott would have been if Will were here. Facing the Nesbitt family after all that had happened would be one of the greatest challenges that lay ahead of him. It weighed on him as heavily as the dread of his upcoming reunion with his father.

Philip allowed his gaze to rest on the small redbrick parsonage that had been the setting for some of his fondest childhood memories. His mother had died when he was very young, and over the years, his father had become more and more distant from his only son, voicing displeasure or disapproval far more freely than praise or affection. If it were not for his friendship with Will Nesbitt, Philip did not know how he would have survived those difficult growing-up years. Will's parents had treated him as another son, opening their home to him whenever he was back from school and showing him what life was like when a family's cornerstone was love.

The ivy that clung to the parsonage walls had grown considerably whilst he'd been gone. A couple of the upper-story windows were almost completely covered by the dark-green leaves. Philip's brow creased. If he remembered correctly, those were the windows to Amelia's bedchamber. Amelia—or Mia, as he and her brothers had called her—had always loved anything that grew in the ground, but he was surprised she would allow the ivy to block so much light from her room.

A second glance showed him that the entire garden wore an air of neglect. Bushes were overgrown, and tall weeds had sprouted along the short path that led to the front door. The rosebushes beneath the parlor window, which had been Amelia's pride and joy, were misshapen and still wore the dead heads of blooms long since past their prime. It was possible Amelia had married and moved away—she was of age by now—but he was sorry the family had been unable to maintain the property as he recalled it.

The blank windows reflected none of the warmth he remembered at the parsonage, but a thin plume of smoke floating above the parlor chimney told him someone was home. He was duty-bound to make his first stop Woodcroft Hall, but tomorrow morning, after he'd met with his father, caught up on sleep, and was dressed in dry clothing, he would return to the parsonage to speak to the vicar and his family. There was much they needed to know.

The road narrowed into the lane that ran along the fringes of his family's estate. On the distant hillside, he could see a cluster of tenant cottages and behind them the small parcels of land farmed by the cottages' occupants. Woodland separated the arable fields from the lane, and tucked into a tiny break in the trees was the old gamekeeper's lodge.

A year or so before Philip had left Woodcroft Hall, and after months of complaining about the leaking roof, the gamekeeper had moved to one of the newer cottages on the other side of the park, leaving the lodge unoccupied. But judging by the gleaming windows, the tidy garden, and the smoke coming out of the chimney, someone was in residence now. Philip glanced at the roof as he passed. The light was fading, but as far as he could tell, no repairs had been made on it since the gamekeeper had left. He frowned. Surely, water would be entering the house on a day like today.

The sound of voices coming from the bottom of the hill diverted his attention from the old lodge. Two people were walking toward him, their heads lowered against the rain. As they drew closer, Philip realized that one was a woman. Her cloak and the lower six inches of her gown were splattered in mud. Beside her, a boy was leading a goat on a rope.

"Good evening," he said.

"Good evening, sir," the woman replied, but her face remained averted. The boy, however, looked up at him, curiosity shining in his eyes.

Instantly, Philip was transported back to the morning of his twelfth birthday. He'd received a surprise package from his uncle in Jamaica that contained an intricately carved wooden turtle. As soon as breakfast was over, he'd raced to the parsonage to show the gift to Will. His friend's expression as they'd studied the gift together had been the mirror image of this boy's.

Something in the hedgerow attracted the goat, and the animal strained against the rope. The boy turned his attention to pulling the recalcitrant creature back on course, and the moment was gone. Philip gave himself a mental shake, shifting his gaze from the child to the road before him as he continued forward. Only when he reached the sharp bend at the base of the hill did he look back. The woman had disappeared, but the boy was leading the goat through the gate that led to the gamekeeper's lodge.

CHAPTER TWO

TAMPING DOWN HIS MOUNTING TREPIDATION, Philip faced the front door at Woodcroft Hall. He drew back his shoulders, took a deep breath, raised the brass knocker, and let it fall. Moments later, he heard the shuffle of slow feet, followed by the drawing of a bolt. The door opened to reveal the manor's aged butler.

"Good evening, Atkins," Philip said.

The elderly man stared at Philip, then blinked twice to expel his shock. "Master Philip," he said, opening the door wider. "Welcome home."

"Thank you." Philip stepped inside and offered the old butler a genuine smile. "It's nice to see you again, Atkins."

"And you, sir. May I take your hat and cloak?"

Grateful to be rid of the sopping items, Philip handed them over. "I rode ahead of my trunks," he said. "They should arrive sometime tomorrow."

"Very good, sir. I shall notify Mrs. Atkins to have your bedchamber made ready."

Philip gave him a grateful nod. The well-trained butler asked no questions; he simply accepted Philip's unexpected arrival with composure. "Is my father in his study?"

"Yes, sir. Would you have me announce you?"

Philip shook his head. "I daresay he'll know me, even though it's been a few years."

Atkins's lips twitched. It was the closest the man ever came to a smile. "Yes, sir."

Turning from the butler, Philip surveyed the hall. The familiar scent of beeswax hung in the air. After the vivid sights, sounds, tastes, and smells of the West Indies, the familiarity of his family home nestled amongst Shropshire's rolling green hills soothed his travel-weary soul. Generations of family members silently watched him from their gold-framed portraits on the walls, and the candelabra on the table at the base of the sweeping staircase flickered. There were not many truly happy memories for him in this vast house, but it was his home nonetheless. It was where his ancestors had lived and raised their families, and for the first time, he felt a connection—to those who'd gone before and to the manor itself—and an unexpected sense of homecoming assailed him.

"Will there be anything else, sir?" Atkins was watching him, still holding Philip's wet outer clothing.

"No, thank you, Atkins."

Shaking off his unexpected sentimentality, he started across the hall, his boots clicking rhythmically against the black-and-white tile flooring.

As Philip approached the second door on the left, his footsteps slowed. His father's response to his return was unlikely to be as measured as the butler's had been, but Philip knew it was past time for this reunion. He wondered if his father would ever understand how much the last five years had changed him.

When he'd left home, he'd been an inexperienced and unhappy young man in search of adventure. The West Indies had offered him adventure, certainly, and working alongside his mother's brother on his sugar plantation had afforded Philip the highest quality of island living. But his escapades had come with a price. Philip had also experienced challenges and the unimaginable hardship of losing his best friend—and along the way, he'd found himself.

Gathering his courage, he knocked on the door.

"Come." His father's voice was unmistakable.

Philip opened the door and walked in. To the right, his father's desk took up one corner of the room. Papers and ledgers lay in untidy piles upon its surface. A quill stood upright in a small bottle of ink, blotting paper beside it. The desk chair was pushed back and empty; books lined the wall beyond. The dark-green curtains at the windows had yet to be drawn, but the light was fading fast and much of the room was in shadow. Most of the light came from the candles standing on either end of the mantelpiece, and the blazing fire below. Two armchairs were positioned before the fire, one of them occupied.

Philip faced the gray-haired man and inclined his head politely. "Good evening, Father."

The shock in his father's eyes quickly turned to anger, and he rose to his feet. He had lost weight, Philip noted. His face was thinner than it had been before, and his waistcoat hung loosely across his chest. His lips were pinched together tightly, and his ice-blue eyes were fixed on Philip with the intensity of a hawk preparing to pounce. Philip planted his feet and braced himself.

"After all this time, you considered it unnecessary to write to inform me of your intention to return, did you?"

"I have discovered letters traveling between the West Indies and England are as often lost as they are delivered," Philip said evenly. "I did write to you before sailing from Kingston, but it would appear my missive did not reach you. For that, I apologize. But since I rode to Woodcroft Hall immediately after my ship docked, I felt there was little point in sending a note from Liverpool. I knew I would arrive before the post."

"You take a lot for granted, boy. Whatever makes you believe you are still welcome here?"

Philip held his father's gaze. "Nothing more than hope, sir."

His father gave a contemptuous snort. "Hope? Relying on hope will get you nowhere."

"I beg to differ, sir. Hope has seen me through a great number of trials. Without hope, I would have been lost."

"Your grand adventure wasn't all it was cracked up to be, then?" In a twisted sort of way, his father seemed pleased.

"On the contrary. It was far grander than anything I could ever have imagined, but many of my greatest experiences followed times of sacrifice and suffering."

Something that looked remarkably like pain flashed through his father's eyes. "You do not need to travel halfway around the world to experience suffering," he barked.

"I agree," Philip said.

His response seemed to take his father aback. The older man muttered something under his breath, then walked over to the window and gazed out at the dark, stormy sky. Philip remained in his same spot, waiting.

Finally, without turning to face him, his father spoke again. "You'd best have Atkins inform the cook immediately if you intend to stay for an evening meal."

Philip's shoulders relaxed a fraction. "Yes, Father."

❄ ❄ ❄

Philip had forgotten how quiet it was at Woodcroft Hall. He had awoken to silence. No feral roosters crowing or stray dogs barking. No chatter of plantation workers passing his open window or the sound of his uncle's cook singing as she cut up fruit for the morning meal. Even the patter of rain on the roof—that had continued long into the night—had now ceased.

He started down the wide staircase toward the drawing room, passing two maids along the way. They gave him polite nods and continued upward, their feet making no sound on the wooden floor. The servants, it seemed, were trained to maintain the quiet.

The smell of bacon greeted him as he stepped into the drawing room. Food was set out on the sideboard, but somewhat to his relief, his father was nowhere to be seen. Philip's evening meal the night before had been a torturous event consisting of a lecture on his wayward behavior and his uncle's mismanagement of family funds, followed by a discourse on his father's prerogative to entail the estate upon whomever he pleased.

Philip was still unsure whether his father had intended to threaten him with a change to his will or to inform him of modifications already made. Either way, the diatribe had been both exhausting and discouraging. If his father had only bothered to ask about his experiences in the West Indies or his future plans now that he was returned to England, the man would have learned his son had in fact worked hard, invested well, and come home a wealthy man in his own right.

Finishing his food quickly, Philip left the drawing room in time to see Atkins exiting his father's study, a note in hand.

"Have it delivered right away," Father called after him.

Atkins paused, glanced at the writing on the letter, and nodded. "Yes, sir."

"And call for my coach."

"Yes, sir," Atkins repeated, inclining his head before turning to leave.

Philip crossed the hall to take the butler's place at the study doorway. His father was standing beside his desk, a sheaf of papers in his hand.

"You are leaving?" Philip asked.

"I am." His father set the papers in another pile. "I have an appointment with my tailor in Shrewsbury."

It seemed an unusual errand for his father, who'd never had much patience for fashion or shopping. "I wish you well with it," Philip said. "I plan to call at the parsonage this morning."

"Mr. Snell is known to spend most of his mornings visiting parishioners. You would be better served to wait until the afternoon."

"Mr. Snell? Who is Mr. Snell?"

"Why, the vicar, of course." His father began walking toward the door, his interest in the conversation already waning. "Did you not say you were going to the parsonage?"

"Yes, but my intention was to visit Mr. Nesbitt."

"Mr. Snell is the vicar of Morton Abbott now." Atkins reappeared at the doorway, and Philip's father accepted his hat and traveling cloak from the butler with no apparent concern for how the news would affect his son. "Mr. Nesbitt died almost three years ago," he said matter-of-factly.

"He died?" Philip could barely form the words through his shock. "How? What has become of his wife and family?"

"The influenza took him, I believe." Father put on his hat and gloves. "The family was given a few weeks to make alternative arrangements before Mr. Snell took over the parsonage and all parochial duties in the village." He frowned. "Mrs. Nesbitt approached me to ask if there were any tenant cottages available at Woodcroft. There weren't, of course. But she was desperate, so I told her that for a small fee, they could stay at the old gamekeeper's lodge."

Understanding came one painful punch at a time. The untidy garden and untamed ivy at the parsonage suddenly made sense—as did the tended flowerbeds at the gamekeeper's lodge. The boy he'd passed in the rain. That had to have been Will's younger brother, Giles. He'd been no more than five years old when Philip had left. And the woman with Giles? Had that been Mrs. Nesbitt or Amelia? And how were they surviving in that rundown old house?

"That place was virtually derelict when the gamekeeper moved to the cottage on the other side of the park."

His father shrugged. "They were glad for a roof over their heads, and they've voiced no complaints."

"That roof is full of holes! Blast it all, Father. Do you truly care so little for your fellow man?"

"Who are you to talk to me about caring for others?" The pain Philip had seen in his father's eyes the night before had returned, and bitterness coated his tongue-lashing. "You left without so much as a by-your-leave, and you took no thought to ever inform me of your well-being." Setting his jaw, he turned away. "Like it or not, my boy, we are more similar than you believe. Your lack of concern has been brutally apparent for years."

His father walked out of the study and crossed the hall without looking back. Philip stared after him, wondering if there were any way to fill the emptiness he felt.

CHAPTER THREE

AMELIA STOOD POISED OVER THE bucket in the parlor. The moment the water droplet from the ceiling hit the liquid within, she whisked it away, replacing it with an empty bowl before the next drip fell. After placing a scrap of fabric in the bottom of the bowl to mute the plink, plink, plink of dripping water, she carried the heavy bucket out through the front door. The rain had stopped, for the time being, but the ground was already saturated. Moving a little farther from the house, she emptied the water beneath the dogwood trees.

A sound at the garden gate caught her attention, and she turned to see a young man coming toward her. She recognized him immediately. Peter was a footman at Woodcroft Hall, and his arrival here with letter in hand could mean only one thing.

"Morning, Miss Nesbitt," he said.

"Good morning, Peter," she said. "Is that for my mother, from Mr. Cunningham?"

"Yes, miss."

Amelia stepped closer. "She's inside the house. Would you like me to give it to her?"

"If it's no trouble, miss," he said.

"Not at all. Thank you for bringing it so promptly."

"Happy t'do it, miss." He handed the letter to Amelia, bobbed his head, and turned back the way he had come.

With the empty bucket in one hand and the letter in the other, Amelia returned to the parlor. Her mother was seated in her favorite chair beside the fireplace. There was no fire burning—they would wait to light one until this evening, when the temperature in the house became unbearably cold—but with the window behind her, the seat gave her the best light to work on her sewing projects.

"Mr. Cunningham has written," Amelia said, crossing the room to hand the envelope to her mother.

Mother set down the gown she was altering and reached for the letter. "He responded quickly."

"Yes." Amelia watched anxiously, both hands now clasped tightly on the handle of the bucket.

She had thought on their dire financial situation long into the night. Her late father had left a legacy of generous giving. Unable to see a parishioner suffering without stepping in to give assistance, he had given of his own means to succor others in times of need. At his death, those who loved and appreciated his goodness had been plentiful; his monetary resources, however, had been severely lacking.

Despite its leaking roof and drafty doors and windows, the gamekeeper's lodge had been a blessing. The Nesbitt family had relocated from the parsonage with precious few possessions but with the comfort of being yet surrounded by those who knew and cared about them. The villagers had done all they could to help. Mrs. Reeve, the village dressmaker, hired Amelia's mother to sew for her whenever possible, Amelia had been offered a stall at the weekly market to sell the flowers she grew so well, and parcels of food occasionally arrived on their doorstep from friends in the village. Nevertheless, every month proved to be a struggle to make ends meet.

Amelia was discouragingly sure it would be impossible to raise sufficient funds to pay their rent and the bill for the damaged clothing before Christmas. Mistletoe, holly, ivy, and Christmas roses were the only things she could sell at the market until the first snowdrops showed their heads in February or March. And with the holiday only three days away, her mother had already completed the Christmas ball gowns requested by Mrs. Reeve. It was highly unlikely that further moneymaking opportunities would present themselves in the immediate future.

"Well?" Amelia asked.

Her mother looked up from the letter, a hint of tears glistening in her eyes. She shook her head. "He will not give us an extension," she said. "He wishes the debt paid in full by Christmas Eve."

The blow left a hollow ache in her chest. It was so terribly unfair. "Mr. Cunningham could buy those shirts ten times over and still eat roast pheasant for dinner every day." Her indignation rose. "He has a piece of coal where his heart should reside."

With trembling hands, Mother refolded the letter and slid it back into the envelope. "Hush, Amelia. You should not speak of him so. Mr. Cunningham is well within his rights to ask for prompt payment."

"It's Christmastime, Mother. And he knows our situation." Amelia swallowed the lump in her throat. They would likely be homeless and penniless by the end of the month. "He's an odious old man."

Folding her hands on her lap, Amelia's mother faced her. "What would your father say to that?"

"Really, Mother. This is not the time to resort to platitudes." Her burgeoning fear for their future almost smothered the guilt pricking at her conscience.

"Amelia."

Somehow her mother's chastisement was all the more cutting because of her brevity. Amelia's grip on the bucket tightened, and she dropped her head.

"Forgive me." She took a shuddering breath. "It's just that . . ."

"What would your father say?" She heard her mother's earnestness; the answer to this question truly mattered to her. "What did he teach you?"

Why was it suddenly so hard to recite the words she'd memorized at her father's knee? "'Love your enemies, bless them that curse you, do good to them that hate you, and pray for them which despitefully use you.'"

Amelia's mother reached out and took her cold hand in her own. "I do not know how we will manage any more than you do, my love, but if I learned anything from your father over the twenty-five years we were together, it is that if we will only do our part, God will surely do His."

"You truly believe that?"

Her mother squeezed her hand. "I do."

Amelia sighed. "I shall never be as good a woman as you are."

"Ah, now, that is something I do *not* believe." Mother smiled. "I shall let you in on a little secret, but you must never divulge it to Giles." Leaning closer, she dropped her voice to a whisper. "I have been praying for Lambert for weeks. That pest of a goat has been despitefully using us ever since he arrived, and I'm heartily tired of him."

At the look of exasperation on her mother's face, Amelia laughed. She could not help it. Before long, her mother was laughing too, and after the worry Amelia had experienced over the last twenty-four hours, it felt rather wonderful.

"Three eggs today!" Giles called as he burst in through the door carrying his precious load. "And even better than that, Lambert has not escaped the shed."

"Good news indeed," their mother said, exchanging a last conspiratorial smile with Amelia before rising to her feet and setting her sewing on the table. "Perhaps some griddlecakes are in order."

Giles's eyes lit up. "Now?"

Mother chuckled. "If you will help your sister finish emptying the buckets abovestairs, I will start the batter."

Giles needed no further motivation. Setting the basket of eggs on the table, he hurried into the passageway. "Make haste, Mia," he called back to her.

"You must be hungry," Amelia said, following after him.

"I'm always hungry," he said.

He spoke cheerfully enough, but as he mounted the stairs ahead of her, Amelia couldn't help but notice how thin his legs had become. He'd need more-substantial meals than a few griddlecakes and watered-down soup if he were to grow as tall as his father and brother had been. Amelia stifled a sigh. She'd best start praying for Mr. Cunningham right away.

There were two leaks in the roof above Giles's bedchamber and one over the room she shared with her mother. When they'd replaced the three buck-etsful of rainwater with empty ones, Amelia sent her brother to join their mother in the kitchen while she went back outside to check on the Christmas rosebush. If there were enough blossoms to make a few bouquets, perhaps Mrs. Hathaway at the Four Crosses might be willing to buy some to decorate the inn's large front room. Amelia would approach her about it before market day. Whatever the innkeeper's wife did not want, Amelia would try to sell at her flower stall. Any purchases, no matter how small, would help.

The air was cold and damp. Wrapping her cloak about her more tightly, Amelia looked up at the cloud-laden sky. Was more rain on its way? Or would the moisture fall as snow this time? She would need to remember to ask Giles if the animals had sufficient food and water in the shed to survive a day or two, should a snowstorm hit.

The clatter of hooves on the road drew her attention. A lone rider was approaching, coming up the hill. She glanced at the gentleman curiously.

She did not recognize him as one of the local gentry, but his coat appeared to be very fine, and his chestnut horse was no working animal. Turning away before the gentleman caught her watching, she walked across the wet grass to the Christmas rosebush. Half a dozen creamy-white flowers were in bloom, and at least two-dozen buds were within a few days of sharing their beauty with the world. A few hours of sunshine would do the trick. Amelia looked upward again. There was no sign of a break in the clouds.

Behind her, the garden gate creaked open. She swung around. The gentleman who'd been riding up the lane had dismounted outside the lodge. He'd tied his horse to the gatepost and stood on the path to the door, staring at her. He was tall, and his dark hair curled slightly beneath the brim of his hat. Although she could not immediately place him, there was something about him—something vaguely familiar.

"May I help you, sir?"

He stepped closer, and she saw his lips curve upward. "I should have guessed that after all these years, you would still be tending your beloved flowers, Mia."

Amelia's heart began to pound. There were only three people in this world who'd ever called her Mia—Giles, because he'd been unable to pronounce her full name when he was young; Will, simply because it was easier; and Philip Cunningham, because that was how Will had introduced her when they were children.

"Philip?" she whispered.

His smile widened. "I had hoped it had not been so long that you would have forgotten me."

Amelia bit her lip as tears filled her eyes. "It's really you?"

"Yes, Mia." His smile disappeared. "I only wish . . . I truly wish Will were with me."

She shook her head, and the moisture collecting in her eyes spilled down her cheeks. "It is enough that you have come."

"Thank you," he said, his voice suddenly husky with emotion.

This was hard for him, Amelia realized. He had loved Will as deeply as Will's own family members had, and he had likely been unsure of the Nesbitts' response to him returning without their son and brother.

"Come," she said, starting for the door. "Mother is inside. She will want to see you, as will Giles." She smiled then. "You will find him much changed, I think."

Philip followed Amelia into the gamekeeper's lodge. He would need to work harder to control his feelings. Returning to England without Will had been hard; coming to see Will's family was harder; accepting Amelia's gracious welcome despite the loss her family had experienced might be the hardest of all.

Ahead of him, Amelia entered the small parlor. He stepped inside, instantly noting the bucket near the door that was catching water dripping from the ceiling. His jaw tightened, and he quickly surveyed the rest of the room. The Spartan furnishings were worn, and despite the cool temperature, no fire burned in the grate. A pile of fabric sat upon the only table in the room, the needle, cotton spool, and pincushion beside it suggesting it was a sewing project of some sort. A single candlestick stood upon the mantelpiece beside a narrow vase filled with dried lavender—Amelia's touch, he had no doubt. He removed his hat and turned to see that she had taken off her bonnet and cloak and hung them on a peg near the door.

She smiled and extended her hand for his hat. "May I take your hat and cloak?"

Philip tightened his grip on his hat and tried not to stare. Now that Amelia had removed her cloak and bonnet, he could see her clearly for the first time. Her fair hair was pulled up in a simple knot, but soft curls framed her heart-shaped face. A few renegade freckles dusted her nose, a testament to the time she spent outside with her flowers. Her peach-colored gown, although obviously not new, accentuated her figure perfectly. The gangly young girl who had tagged along on his and Will's adventures all those years ago was no more; the young woman before him was nothing short of stunning.

"Philip?"

At her concerned expression, Philip realized he had yet to answer or offer her his hat. Cursing himself for acting like such an idiot, he slid his cloak off his shoulders.

"Yes, thank you." He took off his gloves and handed her his hat. Their fingers brushed, energy from their brief physical contact hovering in the air between them as she hung up his cloak beside hers.

"Would you care to take a seat?" she said.

From somewhere at the rear of the house, he heard voices and the clatter of dishes. If the Nesbitts' situation was as dire as he imagined it to be, it was doubtful they had any hired help. Mrs. Nesbitt was likely working in the kitchen.

"Have I come at an inconvenient time?" he asked.

Amelia tilted her head slightly, and he recognized the way her small nose scrunched as she thought something through. "Actually, if you are the Philip I remember, I believe you may have chosen the best possible moment to arrive."

"Why is that?"

"Mother is in the kitchen. The moment she knows you are here, she will stop what she is doing to join you in the parlor." Her eyes twinkled. "On the other hand, we could dispense with all polite protocols and relocate to the kitchen, which would be much closer to the hot griddlecakes."

Philip grinned. After five years in the West Indies, he had become altogether too comfortable with ignoring social conventions. Besides, no one made griddlecakes as well as Mrs. Nesbitt. "When it comes to your mother's griddlecakes, I can guarantee I have not changed a bit," he said. "Lead me to the kitchen."

Amelia laughed, and Philip discovered he liked the sound very much.

Leaving the parlor, they walked down the short cold passageway to the door at the end. Amelia opened it and led him into the small kitchen. A boy sitting at the square wooden table came to his feet as they entered, and Philip's breath hitched, his feet stopping of their own volition. It was the same boy he'd seen on the road the night before—the one who had reminded him so much of Will.

"Mother, Giles," Amelia said. "We have a visitor."

At the stove, a woman turned from the hot pan she was watching. Much of her lilac-colored gown was covered by a white apron, and a mobcap sat upon her gray hair. Her eyes—the same color green as her sons' eyes—widened, and her spatula fell to the counter with a clatter.

"Philip!" she cried. Crossing the room in four short steps, she wrapped her arms around him. "You're home." She looked at him tenderly. "And just in time for Christmas."

Philip swallowed hard. This homecoming was so different from the one he'd received at Woodcroft Hall, and it rightfully should have been Will's. Giles was gazing at him with the same silent curiosity he'd shown when they'd passed each other the night before, and Amelia's sweet smile caused an unexpected ache in his heart.

"I'm terribly sorry, Mrs. Nesbitt," he said. "About Will and Mr. Nesbitt. I learned about the vicar only this morning."

"They were both difficult losses," she said, "and we miss them still, but life has a way of pushing you forward whether you like it or not." She turned to her young son. "Giles, this is Mr. Philip Cunningham. He was your brother, Will's, closest friend."

"The one who went to the West Indies with him," Giles said.

"That's right," Philip said, bracing himself for what Giles might ask next. He was prepared to talk of his experiences there, of Will's death, and his own grieving and guilt, but he had not imagined the conversation occurring within minutes of their reunion.

"Are you related to the Mr. Cunningham who keeps sending us notes for payment on the clothes Lambert eats?"

Whatever Philip had been expecting, it was not this. "Ah . . ." He looked to Amelia. Her face had turned a rather pretty shade of pink. "I fear I may need help answering that question. Am I, Mia?"

"Yes." Her voice was barely above a whisper.

"The griddlecakes!" Mrs. Nesbitt cried, releasing her hold on Philip's arm and darting back across the room to the stove. "Sit down, Philip. You shall have the next one."

CHAPTER FOUR

As far as Amelia could tell, Philip Cunningham had thoroughly enjoyed his griddlecake, but he had limited himself to one. Each griddlecake that had come off the hotplate since then had somehow ended up on Giles's plate. The boy consumed them as though he hadn't eaten in a week. Truth be told, he hadn't been eating enough for a lot longer than that, and Philip had probably guessed as much.

She watched Philip now as he conversed with Giles. It was obvious that her younger brother was rapidly falling under the man's charm. It was hard not to. She'd done the same as a young girl. Philip had always been kind to her. He'd been the one willing to listen when she'd wanted to share something with the boys and had often slowed his pace to allow her to catch up when their longer legs had outdistanced hers. The fact that his dark hair and eyes, broad shoulders, and sun-darkened skin gave him the swarthy look of a ridiculously handsome pirate only made his treasure trove of tall tales from a faraway land all the more enthralling.

Giles sat with one elbow pressed to the table, his chin cupped in his hands, and his eyes glued to Philip. "How big was the snake?" he asked.

Philip paused, looking thoughtful. "Between six and seven feet long, I'd say. It was wound around the lower branch of the tree, so it was hard to tell exactly, and I decided it would be best not to linger long enough to see it unfurled."

Giles's eyes widened to the size of saucers. "Were you scared?"

Philip chuckled. "The Jamaican boa is not poisonous, so I never felt my life was in danger, but he was certainly big enough for me to leave well enough alone."

Amelia's mother offered Philip a cup of tea and began pouring one for Amelia. "Would you tell us about Will?" she asked. "We received your letter telling us he was ill with a high fever, but it was not until months later that we learned he had not survived."

Instantly, the spark in Philip's eyes died. "I have relived those horrendous weeks more times than I can count. Perhaps if I could have found something or someone to blame other than myself, the memories would not have haunted me so." He stared at the brown brew in his teacup as though he could see the past in the steaming liquid. "I am the one who encouraged Will to participate in the venture, and I am well aware I can never make restitution for taking him from you."

Mother reached across the table and placed her hand over his. "Philip, that is not your load to bear or forfeit to pay. Will wished for his adventure as much as, or more than, you did. You and your uncle enabled my son to live his dream. It ran its course more quickly than any of us would have hoped, but it was his, and he wished for it with his whole heart." She paused, suddenly looking wistful. "Did he walk the beach at sunrise and eat a coconut or see a crocodile?"

Philip's lips quirked upward. "He did. He loved the warm sand, was not very taken with the taste of coconut, and spotted a small crocodile in a ditch only a few days after our arrival in Jamaica."

Mother's countenance glowed. "Well then, he managed what he set out to do."

"He was fascinated by the sugar plantation," Philip said. "Every part of it—from the local workers to the crop in the fields to the bookkeeping. He did not mind the blazing sun or scorching heat; he simply put on his hat each morning and went to work.

"One day, my uncle asked us to scout out some untamed land that he owned a few miles from the main plantation." Philip gave a ghost of a smile, the memories obviously still vivid. "Will was in his element, exploring the jungle and spotting exotic birds and reptiles. But three days later, he did not come down for breakfast. Overnight, his temperature had risen alarmingly. He complained of aches in his head and his joints, and then came the rash. The locals diagnosed it as breakbone fever. My uncle brought in the doctor, but there was nothing he could do." Philip gave a gutted sigh. "Will was gone a week later."

For several seconds, there was silence in the kitchen. Amelia felt a tear drip down her cheek but did nothing to prevent it from falling onto her gown.

At her side, her mother took an unsteady breath. "Thank you, Philip," she said.

"I wish it had been different," he said. "I still miss him."

Mother managed a sad smile. "That's as it should be, I think. Time helps ease the awful pain after our loved ones depart, but they are never forgotten. It is well that we miss them still."

"I miss Father," Giles said unexpectedly. Amelia looked helplessly at her brother. Giles had been so young when Will left—he barely remembered him—but the loss of their father had been more recent, and she knew all too well how much it still stung.

Philip immediately turned to the boy beside him. "What do you miss most about him?"

Bless Philip. A glance at her mother's face told Amelia that Mother had been as stunned—and therefore as momentarily dumbstruck—as she had been by Giles's admission.

Her brother shrugged. "He took me fishing, and he told the best stories. He could fix things better than me or Mother or Mia." He glanced at his mother as though afraid his disclosure would offend her. "I think he'd know how to stop the roof from leaking and how to keep Lambert from escaping."

"Who is Lambert?" Philip asked. "Is this the one who eats clothes?"

Giles nodded solemnly. "He's my goat. And he keeps digging holes under the hedge and going to Woodcroft Hall to eat Mr. Cunningham's shirts off the clothesline."

Philip turned his attention to Amelia. "And you have been receiving bills for this? From my father?"

Amelia tried not to squirm beneath the intensity of his gaze. Was her present discomfort the price she paid for calling Mr. Cunningham "odious" earlier this morning? And why did the older man's demands suddenly not seem so unreasonable?

"Yes," she said, "but he is well within his rights to ask for remuneration. Apart from the damage done to his clothes, our goat was trespassing."

Philip muttered something under his breath and rose to his feet. "Giles, would you be good enough to introduce me to Lambert? I don't claim to be anywhere near as skilled as your father, but I know how to wield a hammer well enough. Perhaps, between the two of us, we can contrive a way to outwit your goat."

"Yes, sir, Mr. Cunningham." Giles jumped up with alacrity. "I'll show you where to find the tools."

"Philip, you don't need to—"

Amelia's mother stood and placed a firm hand on her shoulder, stopping her protest midsentence. "Thank you, Philip," Mother said. "Your assistance with Lambert would be most appreciated."

He gave a small nod. "I'll have someone here to look at the roof within the week," he said, and with the heels of his polished boots sounding a march against the red-tiled floor, he followed Giles out of the kitchen.

"Mother?" Amelia's confusion infused her voice. There were any number of laborers in the village whom they could have asked for help, but without the means to pay them, her mother had refused to impose their problems upon anyone. But now she was effectively encouraging Philip to see to those things.

"It will be well, Amelia," her mother said softly. "Philip needs this as much as we do."

"Try the latch now," Philip said.

Giles grasped the small handle, pushed the metal bar upward, and grinned. "It's much better."

"Is it tight enough to prevent Lambert from bumping it open again?"

"Yes, sir. He's strong, but he's not that strong."

Warily, Philip eyed the skittish kid standing in the corner of the shed. Since the willful animal had hatched such an ingenious escape plan more than once, it was unlikely that his foray onto Woodcroft land had been mere chance. Lambert was a wily creature.

"You'll have to watch him when you enter the shed," Philip warned. "If he's anxious to be outside, he'll be waiting for an opportunity to escape."

"I'll be ready for him," Giles said confidently.

"Good lad." Philip handed the boy the tools he'd used. "Now, if you'll put these back where they belong, I'll be on my way."

They walked together toward the house. The wind was picking up, and Philip pressed his hat more firmly to his head.

"Will you come again soon?" Giles asked when they reached the path that led to the garden gate and Philip's waiting horse.

Warmed by the hope in his voice, Philip nodded. "I shall be back before the week is out."

Giles smiled widely. "That would be grand."

Philip chuckled. "Good day, Giles."

"Good day, Mr. Cunningham," he called, already running toward the front door.

Philip crossed the short distance to the garden gate and untied his horse. He mounted quickly and studied the old lodge from his elevated position. There were at least half a dozen spots where tiles were missing from the roof. Surely, that meant there were more leaks than the one he'd noticed in the parlor. Drawing his shoulders back, he turned his horse around and started down the hill, his thoughts full of the Nesbitts, of Will. They'd left their homes and families with such hope, such eagerness for adventure.

There had been truth behind his father's words this morning. That was likely why they had cut so deep. Philip had not shown him the common courtesy that should be afforded one's elders. Their relationship had been so poor when he'd left for the West Indies that Philip had honestly believed his father would be glad to be rid of him. Perhaps he'd been wrong. He had not the slightest idea how to bridge the gaping chasm between them, but now that he was home, there was no excuse for any further negligence— with regard to his father or the Nesbitts.

He considered what little he'd learned about the Nesbitts' situation from his short time in the lodge and his interactions with Giles at the shed. The rather shabby furnishings, lack of wood in the fireplace, Giles's worn breeches, and the limited fare at the kitchen table all spoke of a severe scarcity of funds. Giles had told him that his mother took in sewing projects from Mrs. Reeve. That would account for the pile of blue silk and thread he'd seen on the small table in the parlor.

Apparently, Amelia ran a flower stall at the weekly market. Surely, that would bring in very little money in the dead of winter. And yet, with Christmas coming and Lambert's recent penchant for eating fine white shirts, this was the very time they needed it most. He frowned. His father's unexpected trip to the tailor's in Shrewsbury suddenly made sense, but that the Nesbitts were footing the bill did not. The cost of half a dozen new shirts would barely make a dent in his father's books, whereas, if he guessed aright, a payment of that amount would see the Nesbitts destitute.

It was a tribute to Mrs. Nesbitt that despite her drop in social standing, she remained the faithful, loving woman she'd been as the vicar's wife. Her hair had grayed since he'd seen her last, but in all other ways, she appeared to be unchanged. Giles, of course, had altered a great deal. Philip would not have recognized him if he didn't look so much like Will. He had formed an attachment to the young boy already.

Then there was Amelia. To say he felt a connection to her would be a gross understatement. Their shared history was a bond, certainly, but that could not fully explain his response to seeing her again for the first time. His initial shock had quickly transformed into an intense awareness. Indeed, he'd been hard pressed to keep his gaze off her. She'd always had expressive eyes, but never before had he been so warmed by the joy or so gutted by the sorrow he'd seen in their depths. The thought of spending more time in her presence both thrilled and terrified him—and he'd not felt those emotions simultaneously since he and Will had stepped off the ship together in Kingston.

He guided his horse through Woodcroft Hall's main gates and started up the long drive. Elm trees, tall but leafless, lined his way, and through the skeletal branches he spotted the first snowflake he'd seen in five years. It swirled to the ground, only to be followed moments later by another. Philip gazed heavenward. The clouds were hidden behind a mass of twirling white flecks. He grinned, his thoughts instantly turning to the joyful days he'd spent playing in the snow with Will and Amelia.

"Come on, girl." He touched his heels to his horse's side. "Let's get you inside. I have a sledge to find."

CHAPTER FIVE

DUSK WAS FALLING, AND IT was still snowing. Amelia stood at the window watching Giles launch snowballs at the shed. The regular thump, thump, thump against the wall was undoubtedly giving the chickens fits, but he was having such a marvelous time playing in the frozen wonderland, she was reluctant to call a halt to his fun.

She glanced over her shoulder. Her mother was sitting in her favorite chair, her needle flying in and out of the blue fabric on her knee, a small smile playing across her lips. It had been that way ever since Philip had made his surprise appearance earlier today. It was quite remarkable. Nothing about their situation had changed—with the exception of the latch on the shed door—and yet Philip's arrival seemed to have infused them all with new hope. For a few short minutes, he had transported them all to a warm tropical island, and Will had seemed wonderfully close. The past had felt less tragic and the future less unsure.

"I shall not be much longer," Mother said, interrupting Amelia's musings. "Would you warn Giles that it is almost time to come inside?"

Amelia nodded, reaching for her cloak. "I'll tell him."

Pulling on her gloves, she opened the door. A gust of cold air blew a swirl of dancing snowflakes into the lodge, its icy touch brushing her cheeks as she stepped outside. Already, the gradually darkening sky was turning the blanket of snow a pale shade of pearly blue. Grasping a fistful of fabric in each hand, she raised the lower portion of her gown a few inches and waded through the deepening powder.

"Giles," she called.

Her brother looked up from the pile of small white cannonballs he'd been shaping by the hedge. His nose and cheeks were pink, and his eyes shone with excitement. "Look at all this snow, Mia. It will be deep enough to make an enormous snowman by morning."

Amelia laughed. "I believe it already is."

Giles looked around eagerly. "Perhaps you're right."

From beyond the hedge, the rumble of wheels reached them. Curious as to who would be out riding in such a storm, Amelia moved closer to the gate. The sound, magnified against the silence of the falling snow, was increasing rapidly, and before long she could make out the muted clatter of horses' hooves and the creak of leather. A carriage pulled by two black horses crested the rise and started down the hill toward them.

"That's Mr. Cunningham's carriage," Giles said, joining her at the gate. "And it's moving at quite a clip."

"It is indeed." Amelia watched the coachman hunch lower on the box seat as the vehicle continued downhill. "He must be trying to get home before it's fully dark."

The carriage quickly moved out of sight, and Amelia was about to turn away when the rhythmic sound of rolling wheels faltered abruptly. One of the horses gave a terrified whinny, and an awful grinding sound followed. The crack of a whip and a man's shout rent the air seconds before an almighty groan ended in an ear-splitting crash. Amelia flung open the gate and raced into the lane.

"The carriage has overturned," she cried in horror. The vehicle lay on its side, the wheels spinning. "Go and tell Mother," she urged as she started running. "Hurry, Giles!"

She did not look back. Keeping to the grass verge and grasping at branches in the hedgerow to steady her when her feet slipped, she half-ran half-slid down the hill. The horses strained against the tangled harness, their panicked brays drowning out any other sound, but by the time Amelia reached the accident, a man had stumbled to his feet.

"Are you hurt?" she called.

"Nothin' worth fussin' over, miss." The coachman was clutching his left arm. "It's Mr. Cunningham we need to worry about."

Amelia clambered onto the side of the carriage. It was coated in ice crystals. Numbing cold penetrated her gloves as she slithered forward. "Mr. Cunningham! Can you hear me?" She grasped the door handle and yanked it back. It slammed against the side of the vehicle. "Mr. Cunningham?"

He moaned. Behind her, the coachman's attempts to climb up were being hampered by his injured arm. Gripping the edge of the doorway,

Amelia slid into the gaping hole. Hanging by her fingers, she stretched her toes downward. She could not feel the other side of the carriage, but she had to be close. It would not be a frightening drop unless she landed upon the injured gentleman. She called his name again.

"Mr. Cunningham?"

The answering moan came from her left, so she swung right and let go. She landed on her feet, and thankfully, no one was beneath her. Dropping to her knees, she looked around the shadowy vehicle. Mr. Cunningham was sitting not more than a foot away, his back against the carriage roof, his face pale in the dim lighting.

"Are you hurt, sir?"

"Who are you?" His voice was faint, but she was relieved that he responded.

"I am Miss Amelia Nesbitt," she said.

"Who?" He raised one hand to his head, and she saw a dark trail of blood running across his brow.

"Amelia Nesbitt," she repeated. "I live at the gamekeeper's lodge and happened to be outside when your carriage overturned."

Outside the carriage, one of the horses whinnied again, fear evident in its high-pitched cry.

"The horses," Mr. Cunningham rasped. "I am well enough, but Pickford must see to the horses."

Assuming the coachman's name was Pickford, Amelia rose. "Mr. Pickford, can you hear me?"

"Yes, miss." The man must have been near the door.

"Mr. Cunningham wishes you to see to the horses right away."

"Very well, miss."

She heard him slide back the way he'd come and returned her attention to the gentleman beside her. "Rest assured, Mr. Cunningham, your coachman is seeing to the horses," she said. "What of your injuries?"

He leaned his head back. His eyes were closed. "I hit my head," he muttered, "but my confounded ankle has fared the worst."

"Do you think it is broken?"

His eyes remained closed, but the blood from his forehead had now reached his collar. "Regardless of whether or not it is broken, it is unlikely to hold me upright."

Amelia glanced upward, her lower lip caught between her teeth. Snow was swirling through the open doorway. Perhaps if the carriage had been free of ice and Mr. Cunningham could stand to his full height, the gentleman may have been able to pull himself free. With neither of those advantages, however, all hope of getting him out unaided was gone.

"Amelia!" It was her mother's voice.

"I'm in the carriage," she called back.

Thuds sounded as her mother climbed onto the upturned vehicle. "How is Mr. Cunningham?" Mother said when she reached the doorway.

"His head is bleeding, and he has injured his ankle."

Her mother lowered a blanket to her. "Take this," she said. "Keep him warm, and if you can find something to wrap around his head to stem the flow of blood, so much the better. I've sent Giles for help. He went through Lambert's hole in the hedge, so it should not take him long to reach the manor."

Relief filled Amelia. If Philip were at home, he would know what to do. "What of the horses?" she called.

"Mr. Pickford has removed the harnesses. They are standing free of the carriage."

"Have him go to Woodcroft," Mr. Cunningham said, his voice staccato as he spoke through his pain. "Must get them out of this weather."

"Mr. Cunningham wishes Mr. Pickford to return them to Woodcroft right away," she called.

"Very well. I shall tell him." The carriage shuddered slightly as Amelia's mother dismounted, and through the open door she heard the muffled sounds of her mother and Mr. Pickford conferring and the fading jingle of the harness as the horses moved away.

"Mr. Cunningham, do you have anything I can use to bandage your head?" Amelia asked.

He was silent, and for one panicked moment, Amelia wondered if he'd lost consciousness. Then he raised his hand and tugged at the fabric around his neck.

"Cravat." His voice was weakening. "Already ruined."

Hesitantly, Amelia reached for the length of white silk. With a gentle tug, she untied the bow and leaned forward to unwrap it from around his neck. Mr. Cunningham shifted one leg slightly, his soft moan evidence that the discomfort in his ankle had not lessened.

Pulling the long strip of fabric free, Amelia quickly wrapped it twice around Mr. Cunningham's head, careful to place the width of the fabric across the cut on his forehead.

His next moan was deeper.

"Forgive me," she said. "It is not my intention to hurt you further."

He snorted. Amelia considered it the best response she could hope for and cinched the cravat with a tight knot. She noticed a fat bundle tied in brown paper and string lying nearby and reached for it.

"I am going to raise your leg," she said. "If we keep it elevated while we wait, it might lessen the swelling." Amelia set the bundle beside his leg. "On the count of three," she said.

She counted down slowly, then carefully lifted his booted leg and slid the bundle underneath.

He released a hissing breath. "No more."

She placed the blanket over him and slid back a few feet, pulling her knees up and wrapping her arms around them. Snow was beginning to accumulate within the carriage, and the temperature was dropping with the coming of night. It would have been more sensible to close the carriage door above them, to keep out the moisture and the cold, but Amelia felt less trapped with the sky still visible.

They'd been waiting in silence for some time when Mr. Cunningham stirred.

"How long has it been?" he asked.

Amelia had heard nothing outside since the horses left and could only assume her mother had needed to help the injured coachman or had returned to the lodge for something.

"I cannot tell for certain, sir," she said, "but I would hope someone will be here soon."

She tightened her grip around her legs, willing some warmth into them. If they waited much longer, she would be too cold to be of any help to Mr. Cunningham. Suddenly, she heard a faint cry. Raising her head, she strained to hear more.

"Over here, Mr. Cunningham." It was Giles.

"I see it, lad."

Philip. He had come. Struggling to her feet, Amelia reached out to steady herself against the carriage seat as the vehicle rocked from side to side.

"Father!" Philip's silhouette appeared at the opening, a lantern in his hand.

Amelia fought back tears of relief. "He has injured his head and ankle."

"Bless you, Mia. Your mother is on her way back from the lodge with a sledge to help transport him," he said. "Can you stand, Father?"

"Worth a try," Mr. Cunningham whispered.

Philip studied the opening, then turned to assess whatever lay behind him. "Giles," he called. "I will need you to hold on to my legs as I lean into the carriage."

Giles? He was but a boy. "Is there no one else to help?" Amelia asked.

"Others are coming," Philip said. "Atkins was assembling some of the grooms and footmen as I left. We will need them all to right the carriage, but whereas Giles and I cut through the woodland, they will undoubtedly have to take the road, and you have both waited in the cold long enough already."

Amelia had no desire to argue the point. "What would you have me to do?"

Rather than answer her directly, he spoke to Mr. Cunningham. "Father, are you able to stand long enough for me to grasp your arms and pull you out?"

"Possibly," he said.

"Allow me to help," Amelia said. Moving gingerly, she reached for the gentleman's elbow. "On the count of three."

"It hurt abominably the last time you counted to three," he growled.

"I daresay this will hurt more," she said. "But the reward will be escape from this carriage."

His response was a disgruntled mumble, but he slowly rolled onto his hands and knees. Using the carriage seat for leverage, he drew up his torso and planted his uninjured foot on the side of the carriage currently functioning as the floor. She reached for his right arm.

"Ridiculous," he muttered through gasps.

He was not happy, but he did not shake her off, so Amelia counted to three and lifted. She staggered sideways, and he wobbled on one leg, but they remained upright.

"Well done," Philip said. Amelia looked up. He must have set the lantern down somewhere close by. By its faint glow, she could see the snowflakes swirling and could tell he was lying on his stomach, his shoulders hanging over the opening, his arms extended. "Take my hands, Father."

Mr. Cunningham hesitated. "You cannot . . ." He hung his head. "The weight will be too much for you."

"Father, the longer you delay, the harder it will be." He shifted slightly. "I have the strength; you need only trust me."

Without another word, Mr. Cunningham reached for Philip's hands. Amelia stood beside him, watching as Philip clasped him tightly. "Ready yourself, Giles," he called. Then, with a grunt of exertion, he raised his father into the air.

One moment, Mr. Cunningham was suspended above her, and the next he was gone. Voices, thuds, and vibrations filled the hollow carriage. Amelia stood, watching the opening. At last, Giles's face appeared.

"Mr. Cunningham's in a bad way, so Mother has gone to make up a bed for him at the lodge," he called down to her. "The younger Mr. Cunningham is helping him onto the sledge. As soon as his father's situated, he'll be back to get you out."

"Tell him to get his father indoors first," Amelia said. "Mother must see to his head wound right away."

"But it will take some time to pull him up the hill."

"Which is why you must go now," Amelia said. "I am well enough here. Go and assist them, Giles. It will be faster with two of you pulling."

Giles was already moving away from the doorway. "We shall make haste, Mia," he called. "You have my word." And then he was gone.

Amelia wrapped her arms around herself. Though her companion in the upturned carriage had been an injured, taciturn old gentleman, he had been company. Remaining here alone, in the dark, was considerably more frightening. She dropped to the floor and reached for the discarded blanket. They would return soon. Surely they would.

CHAPTER SIX

PHILIP DID NOT KNOW EXACTLY how much time it had taken to settle his father in the Nesbitts' parlor; he only knew it had taken too long. He'd seen Mrs. Nesbitt's worried glances out of the window as she'd handed his father a cup of hot tea. Philip's sense of urgency was as great as hers; Amelia had been out in the cold for far too long.

With a lantern to light his way, he hurried down the hill toward the snowy mound that was the upturned carriage. The men and fresh horses from Woodcroft had yet to arrive, but he could hear voices on the wind coming from across the fields. He could only hope they were near. A fresh layer of powder had already covered the trampled snow around the carriage. He climbed onto the spokes of the wheel, cleared the snow off the side of the vehicle, and crawled to the opening.

"Mia!" Silence. With his heart pounding in his chest, he moved the lantern into the doorway and strained to see through the darkness. "Mia!"

"Ph-Philip?" A bundle in the corner shifted.

"Yes." He lay on his stomach. "Can you reach for me?"

"I'm so c-c-cold." She did not move.

Dear heavens, what had he done leaving her behind? "Please, Mia." He set the lantern down and lowered his arms. "Let me take you home."

Sluggishly, she came to her feet. She teetered sideways, reaching for the carriage bench to steady herself. "I cannot . . . I cannot—"

"Yes, you can. A few steps closer," he encouraged her. "Now raise your arms."

She released her hold on the bench to lift her arms, but she could not reach him. Hooking his feet around the carriage wheel, he edged a few inches lower. She shifted toward him, and he did not waver. He caught her small hands and pulled. She cried out as her feet lifted from the carriage, but he kept pulling until her head and shoulders cleared the opening. Crawling backward, he drew her out with him. She cried out again, and this time he released her hands and wrapped his arms around her, drawing her close.

"Forgive me, Mia."

She buried her face in his chest, her arms snaking around him as he lifted her off the vehicle.

"S-s-so c-cold," she said again.

"I'll take you home. You can sit by the fire and have some hot tea."

She nodded. "D-don't let g-go."

"I won't." He tightened his hold on her.

From around the bend, a pale light appeared, and through the snowfall, Philip made out a handful of men, their heads lowered against the blowing snow. They carried shovels and crowbars, and two of them were leading horses.

"Over there!" one of them shouted.

They looked up, and suddenly they were moving toward him with new purpose.

"The carriage is empty of people," Philip called. "Set it right the best you can, and take it back to Woodcroft. Mr. Cunningham and I will remain at the gamekeeper's lodge tonight. In the morning, if the storm has passed, send the sleigh to the lodge. Mr. Cunningham has injured his leg and will need assistance returning home."

Philip heard the mumbled words of assent, but he had already turned away. He trusted the men to reclaim the carriage and clear the road. They had no need of him. Leaving the lantern for the men, he started up the hill as quickly as he dared. If the servants noticed who was in his arms, they would likely assume he'd returned from the West Indies having forgotten the correct standards of behavior between a gentleman and a lady. Or perhaps all such protocols were void during snowstorms. It made no difference to him. No matter how improper it may seem, he was not releasing his hold on Mia.

Mrs. Nesbitt was waiting for him at the door. She opened it and ushered him inside, her hand reaching out to pull her daughter's hood back. Amelia stirred, but her eyes remained closed.

"She is in dire need of dry clothing and a warm fire," Philip said. "I promised her hot tea as well."

Mrs. Nesbitt did not hesitate. "Would you be so good as to carry her to her bedchamber, Philip?" she said, taking the candle from the nearby table and starting up the stairs ahead of him.

Philip followed her into a small room with a bed, a chair, a writing table, a wardrobe, and a bucket for catching drips coming from the roof. The freezing conditions outside had temporarily stopped the leak, but they had also chilled the bedchamber. He glanced at the single log burning low in the fireplace. The small flames barely gave off any heat.

"Is there more wood?" he asked.

She nodded. "I'll have Giles get some right away."

"Let me do it." He did not want to release Mia, but he knew he must. Doing something practical to help would save him from pacing the passageway until he knew she was recovered. Mrs. Nesbitt seemed to understand.

"Thank you, Philip." She waited for him to gently set Amelia on the bed before untying her daughter's cloak. "The extra wood is in the shed."

Philip recognized his dismissal, and with one last long look at Amelia's pale face, he exited the room and headed for the front door and the shed beyond.

❄ ❄ ❄

The cottage was quiet. Philip leaned his head back in the armchair in the parlor and gazed at the glowing embers in the fireplace. A few feet from him, his father lay sleeping on the sofa. Mrs. Nesbitt had wrapped Father's head and ankle in clean strips of muslin and had situated him as comfortably as possible with a pillow for his head and a thick woolen blanket to keep the chill of night at bay.

When she had not been watching over Philip's father, the vicar's wife had been caring for Amelia. By the time Philip had returned to the bedchamber carrying a generous load of wood, Amelia's wet clothing had been hanging on a clothes rack to dry, and she was bundled in multiple blankets. Her blue eyes had followed him as he'd crossed the room and set the logs beside the fire. He'd hoped to talk to her, but Mrs. Nesbitt had whisked him out of the room the moment his delivery was made, and no one else had been allowed in ever since.

He was in no position to press Mrs. Nesbitt, but his sudden and overwhelming desire to protect Amelia and to be beside her was making it difficult for him to concentrate on anything else. The fear he'd experienced when he'd received no answer after calling her name into the overturned carriage went far beyond neighborly concern. And the sense that she'd been exactly where she belonged when he'd held her in his arms had yet to leave him. It was as though their childhood friendship had suddenly awoken from a five-year hibernation, having used the time to grow and develop into something much more.

Giles had nobly offered Philip his bed for the night, but quite apart from the fact that the boy was obviously exhausted, Philip had thought it better to remain with his father. Mrs. Nesbitt had given the gentleman willow bark tea to help offset the pain in his ankle, but the medicinal effects of the brew were unlikely to last all night.

Philip glanced at his father's shadowy form on the sofa. Up until now, he'd always blamed his father for their lack of connection, but perhaps it was time he accepted some responsibility too. He'd emotionally shut himself off years ago and had made no attempt to repair their relationship ever since. He sighed. Things could have ended very differently after today's accident. Although injured, his father was still alive, which meant Philip had been offered another chance to make things right between them.

As though he felt Philip's gaze, his father turned to face him, the whites of his eyes shining in the faint light. He cleared his throat. "I appreciate your efforts at the carriage. I was not sure you would come."

Did his father truly believe him to be so unfeeling? "There was never any question."

"I am grateful to hear it." He paused. "I did not think you would ever return to England either."

"It was always my intention to come back," Philip said. "Spending time in the West Indies helped fulfill my lifelong dream to see the world, but Woodcroft Hall is my home."

"Woodcroft Hall has not been your home for far longer than five years." Regret tinged his father's voice. "There has been little love within its walls since your mother died, and although I have been with the Nesbitts for only a few hours, already I see why you consistently favored being at the parsonage over the manor."

"The Nesbitts are uncommonly good people," Philip said, "and Mr. Nesbitt was the best of men. I was always made to feel welcome in their home, but that is not the only reason I spent so much time with them." He looked away, unnerved by how difficult it was to share the deep heartache he'd carried since his youth. He'd never admitted to it before, but he knew that if he wished to start afresh with his father, it would take honesty and a clean slate.

"I truly believed you wished me gone," he said. "When I was a boy, you showed little patience for having me underfoot, and as I grew older, it seemed I caused you more disappointment than happiness." He forced himself to continue. "I should have talked with you before I left for the West Indies—and written to you while I was away—but I assumed you did not care."

"I may have been a poor excuse for a father, but I have always cared."

"As have I," Philip said. He met his father's eyes, barely daring to hope. "We both have need to make changes, but perhaps it would be worth our efforts to try."

"I have no delusions that I can become a new man overnight." Unprecedented emotion coated his father's voice. "But if we can agree to practice patience along with change, there may be hope for us after all."

"I thought you did not believe in hope."

His father pondered that for a moment. "Consider it a first step toward change."

Philip chuckled. He could not remember ever laughing with his father before. "It's a laudable step," he said. "I shall have to work hard to match it."

"Don't be ridiculous," his father replied. His unyielding tone of voice was all too familiar, but it now held a hint of gladness. "It cannot be done."

A gust of wind rattled the window, and Philip was reminded of something else he was determined to change. "In the spirit of being more open," he said, "I should tell you that once the snow has cleared, I aim to have the lodge's roof repaired."

Father's gaze shifted to the bucket in the room. "The leaking roof is the reason for that receptacle, I assume."

"It is. And there are more in other rooms." He leaned forward. "Father, it is not fitting that those who have shown us both great kindness should have to live in such conditions—especially on our property and at Christmastime."

His father grunted. "You believe this old place worthy of the cost of repair, do you?"

"If someone is to live here, most certainly."

"Very well," he muttered. "The roof shall be repaired as soon as it is accessible."

Relief coursed through Philip. He had successfully crossed one hurdle—now if he could only cross the next, far greater, one.

"I had also thought that, until that time, we should invite the Nesbitts to stay at Woodcroft Hall."

There was a moment of stunned silence. "That is a ludicrous suggestion. Do you have any idea how inconvenient that would be?"

"To whom?"

"Everyone," his father said tersely. "It would mean extra work for all the household staff."

"Mrs. Atkins's skills as a housekeeper have been grossly underutilized for more than a decade, and as we are talking of three guests, not an entire house party, I do not think she will feel overrun."

"Overrun? That's it exactly." He attempted to sit up but then abandoned the idea with a moan of pain. "If I wished to find any peace in my own home, I would be forced to sequester myself in the study."

Philip was not yet ready to back down. "Forgive me, but the house currently feels more like a mausoleum than a home, and I was under the impression that the study was by far your favorite room anyway."

"The fact that it is my favorite room has no bearing upon this discussion whatsoever." His father's voice was starting to sound more like a growl. "It is my house, and I wish it to stay that way."

"Would you not rather have it be your *home*?" Philip said. "Spending Christmas there with family and friends would go a long way toward achieving that goal."

"Balderdash," his father said. "It would simply make my head ache even more than it already does."

Philip took the hint. He had planted the idea; at this point, he could only pray it would take root and his father would set aside his stubbornness and act upon it.

"You must rest," he said.

"It is impossible to sleep with such discomfort in my ankle," his father grumbled.

Philip rose to his feet. "I believe Mrs. Nesbitt left some more willow bark tea out for you."

"Brandy would be preferable."

With a shake of his head, Philip started for the passageway. Patience. He had promised to show patience. He stopped at the doorway. "I fear brandy is not to be had in this kitchen," he said, "so I shall fetch you some tea."

CHAPTER SEVEN

AMELIA AWOKE BENEATH A PILE of blankets. Wiggling one arm out of her warm cocoon, she reached out to touch the other side of the bed. It was empty, and the chill on the sheets suggested her mother had been gone for some time. She opened her eyes to discover daylight streaming in through the curtains. She pushed herself upright and looked around the room. The fire was out, but the clothes she'd worn yesterday hung on the rack before the fireplace, and as soon as she saw them, memory came flooding back. The overturned carriage; Mr. Cunningham's injuries; her long, lonely vigil in the cold; and Philip's return to rescue her.

She pressed her hands to her cheeks as a new warmth filled them. Philip had held her so close, had made her feel safe—precious, even. And she had wrapped her arms around him tightly. A small sigh escaped her lips. Something between them had changed. She never wanted to feel that numbing cold again, but Philip's embrace was another matter entirely.

Voices and the sound of scraping reached her from outside. Grateful for the distraction from her disconcerting thoughts, she slid off the bed, and with a blanket wrapped around her shoulders, she tiptoed across the cold floor to the window. Moving the curtain back a few inches, she looked outside. Snow, bright and sparkling, coated the world. Tree branches and bushes bowed under its weight. The hedgerow and garden shrubs were nothing more than lumps and bumps beneath a covering of white.

Immediately below her window, Philip and Giles were working side by side, clearing a path to the shed and the garden gate. Giles said something and Philip leaned on his shovel and laughed. Giles joined in, and even though Amelia could not hear their joke, she smiled too. Philip was good for Giles.

The glass was becoming foggy. Grasping both corners of the blanket in one hand, Amelia wiped the window clean with the other. The movement must have captured Philip's attention, because he looked up, his eyes instantly meeting hers. She caught her breath. He raised his hand in greeting. She smiled, tightened her grip on the blanket, and let the curtain fall back into place.

Leaning against the adjacent wall, Amelia wrapped her arms around her waist as though she could somehow capture the feelings that fluttered inside when Philip looked at her. She closed her eyes and groaned softly. The handsome gentleman may be good for Giles, but unless she managed her emotions better than this, he may prove to be quite the opposite for her. Surely no wealthy young man with a sense of adventure would be interested in anything more than brotherly friendship with the penniless daughter of a local vicar.

In the distance, church bells rang, and with a start, Amelia realized it was Sunday. Hurrying to the wardrobe in the corner of the room, she took out her pale-yellow gown. If the small amount of progress Philip and Giles had made in clearing the knee-deep snow were any indication, they would not make it to church in time for today's service. Nevertheless, ten o'clock in the morning was long past time she make an appearance downstairs.

Following the sound of her mother's voice to the parlor, Amelia entered the small room to find her mother sitting in her favorite chair, pouring a cup of tea for Mr. Cunningham. The older gentleman was reclining on the sofa, and his wrinkled clothes suggested he had been there all night. There was no sign of his cravat, but a fresh bandage was wrapped around his head and another around his ankle.

"Amelia!" Her mother rose and crossed the room. Taking Amelia's hands in hers, she studied her carefully. "How are you feeling?"

"I am well," Amelia said. "There is really no excuse for my laziness."

"Nonsense." Her mother led her to a nearby chair and indicated that she be seated. "After what you endured last evening, you needed the rest."

"Forgive me for not rising to greet you, Miss Nesbitt." Mr. Cunningham pointed to his ankle. "As you can see, my movement is somewhat limited."

Amelia nodded. "Of course, Mr. Cunningham. I hope you are improved from your ordeal yesterday."

"The pain in my ankle is much the same, but my head is clearer." He frowned. "It was wretched luck the carriage overturned as it did, but I daresay I should not have received such prompt assistance had I been elsewhere. I am grateful for your part in my rescue, Miss Nesbitt."

She inclined her head, hoping her discomfort was not obvious. "My role was very small," she said. She had not really thought upon who was occupying the carriage when it turned over; her actions had been purely instinctive. Indeed, the fact that she'd been called upon to aid the one man she felt least inclined to feel charitable toward would seem to be a manifestation of either God's chastisement or His humor. "I am glad Philip was able to remove you from the vehicle so quickly," she added.

"Yes. His arrival was most timely."

The older gentleman lapsed into silence, and Amelia's mother handed her a cup of tea. In the passageway, the front door opened. Boots clattered across the tile, and Giles's chatter floated into the parlor on a draft of cold air. Amelia turned to see her brother lead Philip into the room.

"The path is clear all the way to the gate," Giles announced proudly. His cheeks were pink and his hair disheveled.

Mother smiled. "Thank you, dear. And thank you, Philip. The tea is ready, and now that you are here, we shall toast some bread."

Giles needed no second bidding. He took his spot on the stool beside the fireplace and reached for a toasting fork. Philip, however, moved to stand beside Amelia, his concerned dark eyes searching hers.

"Are you well?"

She nodded. "I am."

He accepted a cup of tea from her mother and took the seat beside Amelia. "I had forgotten how quickly cold weather becomes dangerous," he said. "That you suffered so severely because of my mistake has tortured me ever since I left you in the carriage."

"But you returned as soon as you could," Amelia said. "You carried me home safely, and I am grateful."

The tension in his shoulders eased, and his lips curved upward. "I would not have wished to bring you back any other way."

Amelia felt the color creep into her cheeks. She lifted her teacup to her lips to avoid looking at him, but his soft chuckle told her that her traitorous complexion had betrayed her.

Philip would not have believed that a simple parlor breakfast of tea and buttered toast would be one of the best he could ever remember having, but it was. Giles kept them all entertained with grand fish stories that bordered on the absurd, followed by tales of Lambert's exploits with the chickens and the three-legged cat. Mrs. Nesbitt topped off every teacup religiously and ensured that even Amelia had more than one piece of bread.

Amelia had spoken very little since he'd sat down beside her. Perhaps he should not have teased her about carrying her home, but the sweetness of her blush afterward had made it worth the risk. Surely, she would not have reacted that way if she'd been completely impervious to his touch.

His father had been watching the interactions in the parlor with undisguised bemusement. The pleasant conversation and ready laughter were a stark contrast to the deafening quiet or caustic comments that attended meals at Woodcroft Hall. Philip could only hope his father found the change agreeable or, even better, that he might desire something similar in his own home.

When everyone had finished eating, Mrs. Nesbitt lifted the large family Bible off the table beside her and handed it to her daughter. Amelia gave her an understanding smile, opened the book, and began to gently turn the pages.

"Mr. Nesbitt loved the Christmas season for the opportunity it gave us to remember the birth of the Christ child," Mrs. Nesbitt said. "Every year, on the Sunday before Christmas, we would gather in the parlor at the parsonage and he would read to us from the Gospel of Luke. It did not matter that we would hear the same sermon again on Christmas Day; he claimed it gave us longer to ponder on the miracle of the season."

"He told me he loved the story more with each telling," Giles said.

His mother smiled tenderly. "He did say that, didn't he?"

"And now Mia says it."

"She does indeed."

A touch of pink returned to Amelia's cheeks, but she kept her eyes on her mother.

Mrs. Nesbitt turned to the two Cunningham men. "Amelia usually does the reading in the evening, but seeing as the snow has prevented us from attending today's church service, I wondered if you gentlemen would mind if we did it now."

Philip's father cleared his throat. "By all means," he said.

"Even if you've heard it before, you might like it better this time," Giles informed him.

Philip had rarely seen his father look more uncomfortable. Smothering a smile, he winked at Giles. The boy was a breath of fresh air, and the lifeless rooms at Woodcroft Hall would benefit greatly from having him around.

"I should like very much to hear it," Philip said.

Mrs. Nesbitt gave a pleased smile and nodded at Amelia. "Go ahead, dear."

Amelia raised the book slightly. "The Gospel according to St. Luke, chapter two, beginning in verse one," she said and read, "'And it came to pass in those days, that there went out a decree from Caesar Augustus, that all the world should be taxed . . .'"

Philip leaned back in his chair and listened as Amelia read the familiar words, the melodic cadence of her voice drawing him in to the well-known account. He glanced around the room. Giles appeared spellbound, his countenance brightening each time the shepherds were mentioned, and Mrs. Nesbitt listened in serene silence. It was his father's face, however, that arrested Philip's gaze. The older gentleman's habitual scowl was gone, as were the lines usually chiseled into his forehead. There was a softness in his expression that Philip had never seen before.

Barely daring to move for fear that he would break the spell, Philip watched as Amelia finished the reading and closed the Bible. His father took a deep breath, his shoulders sagging.

"Did you like it?" Giles asked.

Father offered the boy a weak smile. "Very much. What did you think of it this time?"

Giles pondered the question. "I think I'm more like one of the shepherds this year than I was last year because now I have a goat."

Philip's father pursed his lips. "Ah yes, the shirt-eating goat."

Giles's face fell. "I don't know what got into him, sir, but it won't happen again. The other Mr. Cunningham has helped me mend the latch on the shed door, and Lambert hasn't escaped since."

"I'm glad to hear it." The gruffness was back in Father's voice, and Giles seemed to droop on his stool.

"Mr. Cunningham," Amelia said. Her grip on the Bible in her lap had tightened, and she was studiously avoiding looking at Philip. "With regard to the payment for your damaged clothing, I intend to talk to Mrs. Hathaway at the Four Crosses to see if she would be interested in purchasing some Christmas roses and kissing balls for the inn. If you would be willing to delay our payment due date from Christmas Eve until the end of the month, I feel sure we would have sufficient to cover the cost."

Christmas Eve! That was tomorrow. Philip's thoughts veered abruptly from Amelia and kissing balls to something far less pleasant. Had his father truly demanded payment from this good family by then?

"I would like to make another suggestion, if I may." At Philip's voice, all heads turned to him. "Decorate Woodcroft Hall instead." Philip ignored his father's shocked splutter and kept his eyes on Amelia. "I do not remember the last time the manor was dressed in greenery for Christmas. It's long overdue, and I should very much like to pay you to do it this year."

Amelia's gaze darted to his father, but Philip did not look his way. "You . . . you wish to pay me to decorate your home?" she said.

"Yes." He could sense her indecision. "Please, Mia. I would not have the slightest notion of how to go about it."

"It would be far easier for you to accomplish the task if you were all in residence," Philip's father said. This time Philip did turn. Their eyes met, and he recognized the effort this was taking the taciturn man. Philip gave him an encouraging nod, and he seemed to take heart. "Philip and I discussed the matter last night," he continued. "The lodge is in need of a new roof, and until the task is complete, we feel it would be best if you were to stay at Woodcroft Hall—as our guests." His brusque voice wavered. "Or for Christmas, at least."

Mrs. Nesbitt was the first to recover from the shock of receiving such an invitation. "That is extremely generous of you, sir."

Philip's father looked almost as aghast over what he'd just said as was everyone else. He shifted uneasily. "It's the least I can do after the care you've given me. Besides"—he glanced at the bucket—"I have a responsibility to maintain the properties on my land."

"Can I bring Lambert?" Giles asked.

Instantly his father's glower returned. "Absolutely not."

Giles looked stricken. "I don't think I can leave him or the other animals in the shed by themselves for that long."

"Not to worry, Giles," Philip said. "I'll walk over with you every day to check on him and the chickens and the cat."

"Even if there's more snow?"

"Especially if there's more snow. Then we can take the sleigh."

Giles perked up immediately. "Can we ride the sleigh today?"

Philip laughed. "One of the grooms is coming to pick up Father in the sleigh. If your mother agrees, you may all ride back to the manor with us."

"May we, Mother?" Giles's enthusiasm was contagious. Even Philip's father no longer appeared so grim.

Mrs. Nesbitt smiled. "I think that sounds rather splendid."

Giles gave a whoop of delight, and Amelia shot Philip a grateful look. "Thank you," she whispered.

He met her eyes. The air between them hummed. He wished he could tell her that she and her family had already done more for him than he could ever repay. But now was not the time nor the place. The shift in his father's stance was still too new, too unsure.

Instead, he inclined his head and offered her a small smile. "Not even goats should be forgotten at Christmas."

CHAPTER EIGHT

AMELIA SLID HER LEGS OUT from under the covers of the large four-poster bed, a soft smile playing at her lips. It had not been a dream, then. This beautiful bedchamber with its damask draperies, ornate furnishings, and stunning oil paintings was real. And that meant her family's arrival at Woodcroft Hall in the sleigh yesterday and the delicious dinner they'd enjoyed afterward had truly happened too.

She slipped her arms through the sleeves of her dressing gown and crossed the colorful Persian rug to stand at the window. Blue skies and bright sunlight shone down on the sparkling white landscape. The terraced garden appeared as deep snowy stairs leading down to the ice-rimmed lake beyond. With a chorus of honks, a *v*-formation of geese flew over the lake, the shadow of their distinctive flight pattern following them across the frosty expanse until they reached the woodland.

Amelia studied the distant trees and wrinkled her nose in thought. Although beautiful, the snow would make choosing and cutting just the right evergreen boughs difficult. Finding mistletoe might be even more challenging. She'd noticed some a few weeks ago amongst the branches of a hawthorn tree near the gamekeeper's lodge. Perhaps that would be the best place to start her hunt for the greenery she would need to decorate the manor.

Moving quickly to the small trunk she'd brought with her from the lodge, Amelia pulled out her warmest petticoats and stockings. No matter that the manor's fireplaces burned hotter than the ones at home, she would need many layers if she was to spend much time in the woods today.

When Amelia was dressed and her hair pinned, she left her bedchamber and descended the wide curved staircase in search of her family members. The sound of male voices led her to the drawing room, where a buffet breakfast had been laid out on the sideboard. Philip and Giles were talking together at the table, the mugs of steaming drinking chocolate and plates of pound cake before them seemingly forgotten as Giles listened with rapt attention to Philip's description of life below deck on a large schooner.

Amelia stepped into the room. Philip immediately came to his feet, and Giles scrambled up beside him.

"Good morning, Mia," Philip said.

"Morning, Mia," Giles echoed.

Smiling at her young brother's burgeoning hero-worship of Philip, she inclined her head. "Good morning, gentlemen."

Giles looked mildly confused; Philip's eyes sparkled with humor.

"I trust you slept well," Philip said.

"Very well, thank you," she replied.

"I should say so." Giles was eyeing his previously forgotten breakfast with new longing. "We've been waiting for ages for you to get up."

Amelia raised an eyebrow. She had not thought she was excessively late. "Have you been awake long?"

"Yes." Giles gave up on waiting for her to take a seat and dropped onto his chair again. "We went to feed the animals hours ago."

Philip's cough sounded remarkably like a smothered laugh. "It may have been closer to three-quarters of an hour, but time does tend to drag when you are waiting to go sledging."

"You're going sledging?"

"Yes," Giles said excitedly. "Mr. Cunningham said he'd take me to the hill he used to sledge down when he was a boy. We picked up my sledge at the lodge when we fed Lambert and the chickens. He found his in the carriage house two days ago."

"I told Giles we should wait to see if you'd like to join us." Philip smiled at her. "I seem to remember sledging was one of your favorite activities."

Amelia had adored sledging with Will and Philip. They'd flown down the hillsides, reveling in the competitive races as much as they had in the speeds they reached. It was one of the few times the boys had considered her an asset. Each had wanted her to ride with him to gain the advantage of a little extra weight.

"I thought we were gathering greenery today."

Philip nodded. "We are. Or rather, the gardener and a small army of footmen are. I sent them out this morning, thinking if they made short work of it, there would be plenty of time to decorate the house this afternoon." He frowned, suddenly seeming unsure. "I hope that meets with your approval."

"Of course!" Amelia had not dreamed she would be given so much help with the undertaking.

He smiled and her stomach fluttered. "Then, will you come sledging with us this morning?"

"Yes," she said, and was rewarded by grins from both Philip and Giles.

She seriously doubted sledging was on any approved list of activities for young ladies to engage in with eligible young men, but how could she resist?

"You'd best get something to eat right away, then," Giles said, raising his cup. "The drinking chocolate is marvelous."

Amelia moved to the sideboard. "Has Mother eaten already?"

"Yes. She just left to go to the library," Giles said. "Mr. Cunningham encouraged her to find a new book there. She seemed pleased."

Amelia wasn't exactly sure which Mr. Cunningham Giles was referring to, but she realized she had yet to ask Philip about his father. The older Mr. Cunningham had retired to his room as soon as they'd arrived yesterday, and although Philip had sent for the doctor to come as soon as the roads were passable, she'd heard no update on the gentleman's condition.

"How is your father?" she asked as she turned toward the table with her plate of food.

"He's still abovestairs," Philip said, taking his seat as Amelia took hers. "But as he's complaining about virtually everything, I believe it fair to say he is back to his old self."

"Has the doctor seen him?"

Philip nodded. "Dr. Jefferies arrived first thing this morning. He maintains the head wound is already showing signs of healing, and as far as he can tell, there is no breakage in the ankle. He advised Father to keep off his foot for a few weeks, but whether that will actually happen remains to be seen."

"Perhaps if Giles clatters through the house loudly enough, it will persuade your father to keep to his bed," Amelia said.

Philip chuckled. "A worthy suggestion."

"I don't clatter," Giles said. "I just have places to go in a hurry."

"Exactly right," Philip said, his lips twitching with amusement. "Like sledging hills."

"Yes." Stuffing the last of his pound cake into his mouth, Giles pushed his chair back with nothing less than considerable clatter. "Quickly, Mia. It's time to go."

Philip laughed. "Give your sister a few minutes to collect her outerwear, lad. She can meet us in the hall at the top of the hour."

❋ ❋ ❋

Philip had forgotten the thrill of barreling down a snow-covered hill. The grating of the metal runners cutting through the packed snow blurred in the rushing wind as he raced Giles and Amelia to the line of trees below. Giles whooped with delight as he and Amelia inched Philip out for another win.

"Three out of three!" Giles shouted, offering Amelia his hand and helping her off his sledge.

Amelia laughed. Her cheeks were pink with cold, but her eyes sparkled with excitement. "You've lost your touch, Philip," she teased. "All that hot weather in the West Indies has ruined you."

Philip grinned. "When do we inform Giles that you are the reason he keeps winning?"

"Mia has nothing to do with it. I'm the driver," Giles said.

At Giles's look of consternation, Philip placed his hand on the boy's shoulder. "It's a fact, Giles. Whichever sledge Mia chooses to ride wins."

"Nah." Giles started back up the hill, dragging his sledge behind him. "I can beat you even if Mia's on your sledge."

"I accept your challenge," Philip said with a laugh. He turned to Mia. "Are you willing? It will be just like it was years ago."

"I think he should be humbled before he crows any louder," she said.

He grinned. "My thoughts exactly."

Giles was already seated and waiting on his sledge when Philip and Amelia reached the crest of the hill. "Mia will start us off," the lad said.

"Very well." Philip positioned his sledge and offered Amelia his hand. "You get on first, Mia. I'll climb on behind you."

He waited until she was situated at the front of the sledge, then sat down at the back. There was significantly less room for the two of them than there had been more than five years before, but he found he didn't mind at all. With his arms on either side of her, he held on to the rope. "All right," he said.

Amelia tensed. "Ready, steady, go!"

Philip and Giles pushed off simultaneously, and the sledges shot down the hill.

"Woohoo!" Giles cried, passing the first tree half a length ahead of them.

"Catch him, Philip," Amelia urged.

"Oh, we shall." Philip eyed the steepening slope ahead. This was where the heavier load's momentum would come into play. "Hold on tight."

She leaned back against him, and their speed began to build. Within seconds, they'd made up the distance between the two sledges and were inching ahead. He glanced to his right. Giles was crouched low, his sole focus on the finish line.

"Philip! Watch out!"

At Amelia's cry, he looked forward. A rabbit had darted out of the trees and stopped directly in their path midway down the hill. Acting instinctively, Philip yanked the rope to the left. Giles whooshed ahead, and the petrified rabbit tore back into the trees. In one swift movement, Philip released the rope and wrapped his arms around Amelia. The sledge ploughed directly into a bush, turned onto its side, and tossed them into the snow. They rolled once before coming to a stop with Philip on his back and Amelia pressed against him.

"Mia?" Her bonnet was askew and he could not see her face. Praying he'd broken her fall, Philip touched her shoulder. "Mia. Are you all right?"

She stirred. Placing her small hand on his chest, she raised her head. Her bonnet fell back, and her eyes, the same color as the sky, met his. His breath caught.

"Yes," she said. "Are you?"

He took an uneven breath and reached up to gently brush some snow off her cheek. "Yes." Dear heaven, she was beautiful. "At least, I thought I was." His gaze flitted to her lips. "But perhaps not."

"Oh." He saw her lips move, though barely a sound emerged.

"I was wrong, Mia." He swallowed hard. "This does not feel anything like it did years ago."

"No," she whispered. "No, it does not."

Philip was fairly sure his heart was no longer functioning as it should. He touched the soft curls escaping her pins. She held perfectly still, her gaze not leaving his.

Then, from somewhere nearby, Giles's voice reached them. "Mr. Cunningham! Mia! Are you hurt?"

Sudden awareness of their compromising position flashed across Amelia's face, and she pulled away, scrambling into a sitting position a few feet from him just as Giles came into view. Trailing his sledge back up the hill behind him, the boy was panting hard. He looked from Philip to his sister to the upturned sledge.

"What happened?"

Battling an irrational feeling of loss, Philip rose and began brushing the snow off his breeches. "A rabbit." He glanced at Amelia. She was retying her bonnet ribbons. Was it his imagination, or were her fingers trembling?

"A rabbit?" Giles scanned the area with a worried frown. "Did you hit it?"

"No," Amelia said. "Philip managed to steer us out of its path."

"And into a bush," Philip said grimly.

Giles stepped over to the bushes to right the upturned sledge and moved to examine the runners at the front. Philip walked over to Amelia and offered her his hand.

"Are you certain you survived our tumble unscathed?"

The brim of her bonnet hid a good portion of her face, but she placed her hand in his and allowed him to help her to her feet. "I thought so at first," she said softly.

He waited. "But now you are not so sure?" She did not reply, but neither did she withdraw her hand from his. Philip squeezed it gently. Of all the risks he'd ever undertaken, this one was by far the most terrifying. "It would be quite remarkable if we were both suffering from the same complaint, would it not?"

"Yes." Her voice was low. "It would, rather."

Placing the tip of his finger beneath her chin, he raised it until he could see her eyes. He smiled hesitantly, and she responded with a shy smile of her own. His heart—which had already been pummeled quite enough for one day—quickened once more.

"I don't believe your sledge sustained any real damage," Giles called from the bushes.

Philip stifled a groan. "Would it be wrong to coax Giles into sledging back down the hill alone?"

Amelia nodded. "I believe so."

"Even if I were to claim the West Indies robbed me of all sense of propriety?"

She nodded again, but this time he saw amusement in her eyes. "Even then."

He sighed. "Very well. I shall postpone the remainder of this conversation until I am sure he is otherwise engaged."

"Do you wish to walk or ride the rest of the way down?" Giles said, approaching them with both sledges in tow.

"Ride," Philip said and reached for the rope to his sledge.

"I was hoping you'd say that." Giles grinned. He situated his sledge next to Amelia. "Climb on, Mia. I'll have you to the bottom in no time."

Amelia hesitated for a fraction of a second, and then she climbed onto Giles's sledge. Curbing his disappointment, Philip pointed his sledge downhill and took his seat. Now was not the time, but his chance to talk alone with Amelia would come. He would make sure of it.

❄ ❄ ❄

The gentle hiss of runners cutting through the snow accompanied Amelia, Giles, and Philip as they slowly made their way back across the fields to the manor. Giles and Philip walked side by side, pulling their sledges behind them. Amelia followed a few feet farther back, vaguely aware of Giles's questions about tropical fruits and animals while all too aware of the man answering them.

She probably should have continued the ride down the hill with Philip, but when Giles offered to take her, she'd seized the opportunity to collect herself and calm her turbulent emotions. Unfortunately, the one minute it had taken to reach the base of the hill had not been long enough. She was in almost as much turmoil now as she had been when Philip had held her close and suggested his feelings for her had changed as much as hers had for him.

Philip had not spoken to her after they'd dismounted the sledges, and Giles had been more than happy to monopolize his attention since then. It was probably just as well. With her thoughts so muddled, she was likely incapable of a coherent conversation.

To her left, a long snowy mound rose above the blanket of snow. It was the stone wall that marked the beginning of Woodcroft Hall's gardens. Almost of their own volition, Amelia's steps slowed. Philip paused his conversation with Giles and turned around.

"This is your special place, Mia. Would you like to stop?"

"You remembered." She met his eyes, her heart swelling in wonder.

He smiled gently. "Of course."

"Remembered what?" Giles asked.

Amelia kept her eyes on Philip. "Is treacle pudding still your favorite food?"

"I beg your pardon?" Confusion clouded Philip's expression.

"Notwithstanding all the new and exotic foods you tried in the West Indies," she pressed, "does treacle pudding remain your favorite?"

She watched as understanding lit his eyes, and she caught a hint of a smile on his lips.

"Without a doubt," he said.

"And do you still detest cabbage almost as much as brussels sprouts?"

His smile widened. "Absolutely."

"Brussels sprouts are disgusting," Giles said. "No one likes them."

"I do," she said, but she was not looking at him. "Philip could tell you that."

"I could indeed," Philip said. "And unlike me or Will, she also likes gooseberries."

Amelia smiled. Philip had always paid her more attention than either of her brothers had done. He'd been gone for five years, yet he knew her still. And what was more, she knew him.

Giles frowned. "What does eating brussels sprouts and gooseberries have to do with stopping here?"

Philip took pity on him. "This has always been your sister's favorite place to view the gardens," he said. "When we were young—no matter the season—if we passed by, she'd want to stop and look."

Giles walked closer to the wall. "But there's nothing to be seen now but snow."

"And yet, it's so very beautiful," Amelia said, moving to stand beside him so she could more fully appreciate the prospect.

Giles studied the gardens below, his frown still in place. "But what about the treacle pudding and brussels sprouts?"

"Do not concern yourself with them, lad," Philip said. "Particularly as the mince pies and evergreen boughs waiting for us at the manor will likely need all of your attention."

"There are mince pies?" Giles's excitement knew no bounds.

"I've never known Cook to miss a year," Philip said.

Giles waded through the snow to reclaim his sledge. "Mince pies, Mia! We must hurry."

Philip chuckled. Still holding the rope to his sledge in one hand, he offered Amelia his other arm. "As exciting as mince pies are to a ten-year-old, I would guess your interest leans more toward the greenery," he said. "Shall we go and see what the men have gathered before Giles and I join them to bring in the Yule log?"

Amelia nodded and slipped her arm through his. "I should like that very much."

CHAPTER NINE

THE SERVANTS HAD DONE A marvelous job. Henry, the head gardener, had known exactly where to locate and how to cut the holly, ivy, and sweet-smelling pine boughs. To Amelia's delight, he'd added bay, laurel, and mistletoe to the selection of evergreens, and despite the thick layer of snow, he'd even managed to find a handful of newly bloomed Christmas roses.

The footmen had traipsed after him through the grounds, gathering the greenery into crates, which they had then brought back to the manor. Mrs. Atkins, the housekeeper, had uncovered some ribbon, wire, and string, and under Amelia's direction, three maids were dispersing the festive boughs throughout the manor, filling the quiet rooms with the sights and smells of Christmas.

"You have made Woodcroft Hall look lovely, my dear," Amelia's mother said as she entered the dining room, where Amelia was using the long table to create the decorative boughs. "The main hall, in particular, is quite transformed."

Amelia smiled. "Thank you, Mother. It's such a magnificent space—with the grand staircase and tall ornate ceiling—it surely deserved to be dressed up for the season."

"Well, you have certainly done it justice," her mother said. "And I have no doubt the Cunningham men will agree."

Through the open door, Amelia could see the entrance to Mr. Cunningham's study. According to Mrs. Atkins, his valet had assisted the older gentleman there this morning, and as far as Amelia could tell, he had yet to exit. Tightening her grip on the ribbon around the arrangement of Christmas roses before her, she glanced at the brightly colored holly berries woven through the fragrant pine boughs she'd set on the dining room

mantelpiece. Would Mr. Cunningham approve of the festive transforma-
tion? Would he consider her efforts sufficient to pay off their debt?

"I hope you are right," she said.

Mother gave her an encouraging smile. "I believe Christmas Eve is the
perfect time for an extra measure of hope."

From out in the hall came the sound of the front door opening, and
male voices, loud and exuberant, immediately filled the air.

"The Yule log is here," Amelia said, hurrying across the dining room to
stand at the doorway.

Sure enough, four footmen were walking across the hall in a line, carrying
an enormous log on their shoulders. Clearing the way before them, Giles
was practically skipping with delight, and Philip was bringing up the rear.
They disappeared into the drawing room. Across from Amelia, the study
door opened and Mr. Cunningham stood framed in the doorway, a crutch
beneath his arm.

"What is the meaning of this infernal din?" he growled, looking into
the hall. Atkins had already closed the front door, but an icy draft was
creeping down the passageway. "And who is to blame for letting in all this
cold air?"

"Good afternoon, Father," Philip said, reappearing from the drawing
room. "You will be pleased to know the Yule log is in position in the
fireplace."

The footmen slipped silently by, their faces averted. Giles scampered
after them but came to a halt at the study door. "Happy Christmas Eve,
Mr. Cunningham," he said. "Did you see? We've put the Yule log in the
drawing room. Oh, and Cook has all the mince pies and the Christmas
pudding ready, and she showed me the goose we'll be having for Christmas
dinner, and Mia has decorated your whole house." He paused to take a
breath. "Isn't that exciting?"

"I believe *exhausting* would be a better word," the stunned gentleman
said. "Do you ever slow down, young man?"

Giles cocked his head to one side and contemplated the question. "I
suppose so," he said. "When I'm asleep."

Humor filled Philip's eyes, and his lips twitched as he manfully tried to
hold back his laughter. Amelia's mother slipped past her.

"Mr. Cunningham has a valid point, Giles," she said. "It would not
hurt to spend a few quiet hours before dinner, especially if you wish to stay

up to see the lighting of the Yule log." At Giles's crestfallen expression, his mother smiled. "Perhaps a game of chess, if Mr. Cunningham has a set we might use."

"Chess?" The gentleman was obviously surprised. "You play chess, young man?"

"Yes, sir. My father taught me."

"Are you any good?"

Giles grinned. "Rather. I beat Mother every time."

"It sounds as though you are in need of stiffer competition," Mr. Cunningham said. He studied Giles thoughtfully. "I pride myself on being quite good myself. What do you say to taking me on?"

Amelia was not sure which of the other adults was most stunned by Mr. Cunningham's suggestion, but her mother recovered first. "That's very good of you, Mr. Cunningham," she said.

The gentleman acknowledged her thanks with a nod. "To the library, then." He fixed Giles with a stern look. "And there is to be no running between here and there."

"Yes, sir, Mr. Cunningham." Giles paused. "Will you be very cross if you lose? Crosser than you are normally, I mean?"

Amelia held her breath, her mother looked aghast, and Philip had a sudden cough. Mr. Cunningham leaned forward on his crutch and waggled his finger at Giles. "If I lose, I shall give you another of my shirts for that blasted goat of yours."

Giles beamed and Mr. Cunningham made a noise Amelia had never heard him make before. It sounded remarkably like a chuckle. But before she could be sure, he limped down the passageway with Giles following after him, a subdued skip in the boy's step.

Philip watched his father and Giles disappear into the library with a combination of incredulity and thankfulness. He had long lost count of the blessings he'd received through his association with the Nesbitt family. The recent glimpse of positive change in his father was yet another to add to the list. Was it so wrong of him to hope for one more miracle? One that would make him the happiest and most fortunate of men? He glanced at Amelia. She stood at the dining room doorway talking to her mother. He stepped closer.

"I believe I will reclaim the book I started reading in the library earlier today," Mrs. Nesbitt was saying. "It might not be a bad thing to be close by should something go amiss with the chess game."

"A wise decision," Philip said. "Take it from a former opponent—my father will not make this easy for Giles."

Mrs. Nesbitt smiled. "Ah yes, but there is a shirt for Lambert in the offering."

Philip grinned back. "I hope he wins it."

"We shall see," she said, starting down the passageway toward the library.

He turned to Amelia. "Forgive me for not saying something sooner. I caught sight of the decorations in the hall when we brought in the Yule log. You have transformed the house."

"Mrs. Atkins and the maids were extremely helpful in setting everything out around the manor. All that remains now is to finish making a flower arrangement for the dining room table and to put together a . . . a kissing ball."

"Ah, of course, every house needs a kissing ball at Christmastime." Philip was quite sure he should not take so much delight in seeing Amelia blush. "And have you decided where the kissing ball is to be placed?"

"I . . . ah . . . I had thought maybe in the hall."

He nodded. "A good choice." He gestured down the passageway. "Shall we look for a spot together?"

They walked into the spacious hall. Cream-colored ribbons and red holly berries festooned the dark-green ivy winding up the sweeping banister. Pine boughs lay across the sideboard, their pungent scent pervading the vast room, and a flower arrangement made of Christmas roses and laurel leaves sat in the center of the table.

"It's magnificent, Mia."

She must have heard the awe in his voice because she offered him a shy smile. "I am glad you are pleased."

He stepped closer, reaching for her hands. "I would venture to say my feelings are considerably more profound than that." Her deep-blue eyes met his, and he found it impossible to look away. "Mia, I . . ."

A knock sounded, and she started, instantly pulling her hands free. Releasing a frustrated breath, Philip turned toward the front door just as Atkins appeared out of nowhere to open it. A lone man, bundled in warm clothing, stood on the doorstep. He handed Atkins a letter. "A delivery for Mr. Philip Cunningham," he said.

"Very good," Atkins replied. He accepted the letter and held the door open just long enough for them to watch the courier hurry back to his horse.

Philip crossed the hall quickly. A missive delivered on Christmas Eve, and through such snowy conditions, was surely of some import. Without a word, Atkins handed him the envelope, and with a brief bow, he disappeared again.

"Forgive me, Mia," Philip said. "I should probably read this straightaway."

"Of course," she said. "I shall return to the dining room. I must finish in there before the servants need to prepare the table for the evening meal."

As she slipped away, Philip broke the seal. He read the letter quickly, his smile widening with each line.

"Mia, wait!" She stopped and turned to face him. "Come with me to the library," he said. "I would like you and your mother to learn the contents of this letter at the same time."

"Does it affect us?" Worry lines instantly creased her forehead.

"It does," he said.

Saying nothing more, he took her hand and started toward the library. Her small slippered feet could barely keep up with his long stride, but he did not slow until they entered the room. A brief glance told him that his father and Giles had started their match. Already a handful of pawns lay abandoned at the side of the board. Not far from the chess players, Mrs. Nesbitt sat in an armchair, a book open on her knee.

"Forgive the interruption." Philip released Amelia's hand as all eyes turned to him. "A letter just arrived by courier, and I think it important that Mrs. Nesbitt read it without delay."

Mrs. Nesbitt paled. "Does it bear bad news?" she asked.

"Not at all."

She rose to her feet, and he handed her the letter. Amelia stepped to her side, and at an approving nod from her mother, she, too, began to read. There was a minute of total silence. Then Mrs. Nesbitt looked up, and there were tears in her eyes. Philip glanced at Amelia. She was staring at him, her expression a heart-wrenching blend of disbelief and hope.

"Tell me exactly what this means, Philip. I must not misinterpret a letter of this importance," Mrs. Nesbitt said.

Philip could not curb his smile. "It means you have a significant amount of money coming to you."

She placed a hand to her cheek. "This solicitor . . . he says the money is Will's. How is that possible?"

"Will earned a good salary during the short time he was in Jamaica. It was always his intention to return to Morton Abbott and use the money to help ease his family's financial burdens. Although there was precious little I could do for Will when he became ill, I did make him a promise that I would invest his money and ensure it came to you.

"I was not willing to risk sending Will's death certificate to my solicitor in London whilst I was still in the West Indies. If it had become lost, there would have been no way to retrieve it. So I waited until my ship reached Liverpool and sent it from there, along with a letter of explanation."

Philip pointed to the paper in Mrs. Nesbitt's hand. "What you have before you is my solicitor's reply, assuring me that with Will's death certificate in hand, he can now transfer all funds in William Nesbitt's name to his closest living relative—which is you."

Mrs. Nesbitt's hand was trembling. "But this amount." She looked at the letter again. "It cannot possibly be this much."

"Fortunately, my investment has paid dividends. The amount listed is correct."

She dropped back into her chair. "How can I ever thank you?"

He grinned. "Perhaps you could make your homemade griddlecakes again."

Mrs. Nesbitt smiled through her tears. "Yes. And next time, you shall have more than one."

"I congratulate you on your good fortune, Mrs. Nesbitt." Father's attention remained on the chessboard as he spoke. He hovered his hand over his rook before lowering it to the table as he reconsidered his move. He cleared his throat, finally turning to look at Philip. "Sound investing is an uncommon skill, son. It is encouraging to see the man you have become by following your own path."

Philip's throat constricted. "Thank you, Father."

His voice was barely above a whisper, but his father nodded, acknowledging he heard it, and that was enough. Then his father slid his queen across the board and glowered at a wide-eyed Giles.

"Well don't just sit there, lad. Make a move." Father's gruffness was almost enough to hide the emotion in his voice. "I'll have your bishop next if you don't mind what you're about."

Giles blinked, looked down at the chessboard, and slid a pawn over one square. "Check," he said.

Philip took a steadying breath, and with a slight bow directed toward Mrs. Nesbitt and Amelia, he left the room.

❄ ❄ ❄

Amelia sat at the dressing table, staring unseeingly at her reflection while the maid Mrs. Atkins had assigned to her tweaked one more curl.

"Lovely, you are, miss. Really lovely."

"Thank you, Evelyn." Amelia shook herself from her stupor. "You've done wonders with my hair."

"'Appy to do it, miss." She paused. "Will you be needin' anythin' else?"

"No, thank you." Amelia stood. "I think I'm ready."

The maid smiled and bobbed a curtsy. "Good evening, miss."

Amelia ran a hand over her slate-blue evening gown. It was not new, but there was enough wear left in the satin to be presentable. Her fingers faltered on the ribbons at her waist, realizing for the first time that once Philip's solicitor successfully transferred Will's money, there would likely be sufficient funds to buy herself and her mother several new gowns, along with new breeches for Giles.

Her shock over the staggering news still lingered. She had watched through her tears as Philip had walked out of the library. Relief that their financial situation was no longer dire had certainly played a part in causing those tears, but it was Mr. Cunningham's statement that had been her undoing. She had a fairly good idea how much his praise meant to Philip; watching him leave without a word to anyone but his father had confirmed it.

She'd not seen Philip since. After a hard-fought battle, Giles had finally conceded the chess match to Mr. Cunningham but was already planning a rematch on Christmas Day. Amelia's mother had remained in the library but had not turned a single page in her book after reading Philip's letter. The small smile affixed to her face had been enough to reassure Amelia that she was well, so Amelia had returned to the dining room to finish her work there.

The Christmas rose and laurel leaf arrangement had not taken long to complete, but she'd spent extra time making the kissing ball just right. Cook had sent up some dried apples to add to the holly, ivy, mistletoe, and rosemary, and Amelia had used the leftover ribbon to decorate the top. When the last ribbon was tied, she'd handed it off to Atkins, who'd promised to have it hung somewhere in the main hall.

The clock in the passage struck the hour. She was late. Stepping out of her bedchamber, Amelia hurried across the landing. From somewhere belowstairs, she heard Giles's excited voice and the rapid tapping of his feet running against the tiled floor. It would undoubtedly require more than one injunction from Mr. Cunningham to slow Giles's pace, but the thought of the older gentleman's crotchety disposition no longer filled her with irritation or dismay.

Hoping she would not be the last to appear for dinner, she started down the stairs. The hall below was empty. Candles flickered, casting long shadows across the evergreen boughs. The smell of melting wax blended with the heady aroma of fresh pine and rosemary. She reached the lowest step and paused, closing her eyes and breathing in the scent of Christmas.

"You look beautiful, Mia."

With a start, Amelia opened her eyes. Philip moved out of the shadows to stand at the bottom of the stairs. Dressed in a pair of tan breeches, with a black jacket over his pinstriped waistcoat and crisp white shirt, he was by far the handsomest man she had ever set eyes upon. He extended his arm to her, and her heart began to pound. As though drawn by an invisible thread, she placed her hand in his and walked down the final step until she was standing before him.

"I did not mean to be late," she said, unaccountably breathless.

He smiled. "We have a few minutes yet. Father is currently trapped in the drawing room with Giles, who is determined to discover Father's winning strategy before their chess match tomorrow. I believe he said something about needing a Christmas gift for Lambert."

Amelia laughed softly. "It may be more than a few minutes, then."

"That is certainly my hope." He took a deep breath, his dark eyes searching hers. "Mia, I had no idea the affection I felt for you when we were children could so rapidly grow into the feelings I have for you now." He reached out and gently touched her cheek. "I do not know quite how it occurred, but I have come to realize I am falling desperately in love with my best friend's sister."

"You are?" Willing her racing heart to slow, she met his gaze.

"Completely and undeniably."

She rested a trembling hand upon his chest. "I am glad," she said softly. "Because over the last few days, I have found myself falling in love with my brother's best friend."

With elation shining in his eyes, Philip slipped his arm around her waist and drew her closer. "I think perhaps my heart has always belonged to you," he said. "I simply needed to come home to discover it."

She leaned in to him, and he lowered his head, his lips teasing her with their nearness. Her fingers reached for the soft dark curls at the base of his neck. His arms tightened around her, and then he was kissing her, and there was nothing or no one else in her world but Philip.

"Mia," he murmured a little while later. "Where exactly is the kissing ball?"

"I . . . I don't rightly know." In her current state, Amelia was not sure she could find the front door. She pulled away slightly. "I gave it to Atkins to hang somewhere in the hall."

"Perfect," he said.

She looked up at him. "Perfect?"

"Yes." He reached for her hand. "In case you hadn't noticed, we are now inexcusably late for dinner, so we are going to search the hall until we find it."

"Won't that make us even more late?"

"Undoubtedly. But it's Christmas Eve, and everyone knows that if we stand beneath the kissing ball, tradition demands that no matter the hour, I must stop to kiss you." He was already scanning the room for the decoration.

Amelia could not contain her smile. "Tradition demands it."

"Absolutely," he said, his grin widening as he spotted the suspended ball of greenery not more than six feet away.

They crossed the distance in three steps, and with the kissing ball immediately above their heads, he wrapped his arms around her once more.

"Happy Christmas, Mia," he said softly.

Joy filled Amelia as she threaded her arms around his neck. "Happy Christmas, Philip," she said.

And then, because tradition demanded it, he kissed her again.

ABOUT THE AUTHOR

SIAN ANN BESSEY WAS BORN in Cambridge, England, but grew up on the island of Anglesey off the coast of North Wales. She left her homeland to attend Brigham Young University in Utah, where she earned a bachelor's degree in communications with a minor in English.

She began her writing career as a student, publishing several magazine articles while still in college. Since then she has published historical romance and romantic suspense novels, along with a variety of children's books. She is a *USA Today* bestselling author, a Foreword Reviews Book of the Year finalist, and a Whitney Award finalist.

Although Sian doesn't have the opportunity to speak Welsh very often anymore, she can still wrap her tongue around *Llanfairpwllgwyngyllgogerychwyrndrobwllllantysiliogogogoch*. She loves to travel and experience other cultures, but when she's home, her favorite activities are spending time with her family, cooking, and reading.

You can visit Sian on the web at sianannbessey.com or on Facebook at Sian Ann Bessey-author.

Follow Wholesome Romance on social media for more great titles.

OTHER BOOKS
BY CARLA KELLY

REGENCY
Summer Campaign
Marian's Christmas Wish
Miss Grimsley's Oxford Career
Mrs. McVinnie's London Season
Libby's London Merchant
One Good Turn
Miss Billings Treads the Boards
Miss Whittier Makes a List
Mrs. Drew Plays Her Hand
Reforming Lord Ragsdale
The Lady's Companion
The Wedding Journey
With This Ring

THE SPANISH BRAND
The Double Cross
Marco and the Devil's Bargain
Paloma and the Horse Traders
The Star in the Meadow

ST. BRENDAN
The Unlikely Master Genius
The Unlikely Spy Catchers
The Unlikely Heroes (coming in 2021)

CHANNEL FLEET
Marrying the Captain
The Surgeon's Lady
Marrying the Royal Marine

The Unlikely
Master Genius

The St. Brendan Series
FIRST TIME IN PRINT

CARLA KELLY

The Unlikely
Spy Catchers

The St. Brendan Series
Book 2

CARLA KELLY

Regency
Royal Navy Christmas

CARLA KELLY

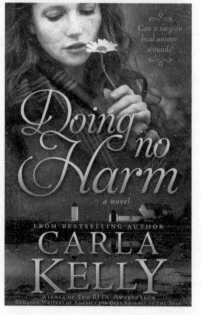

Can a surgeon
heal unseen
wounds?

Doing
no
Harm

a novel

FROM BESTSELLING AUTHOR
CARLA
KELLY

WINNER OF TWO RITA AWARDS FROM
ROMANCE WRITERS OF AMERICA FOR BEST REGENCY OF THE YEAR

PRAISE FOR CARLA KELLY

"Carla Kelly has a strong historical voice that resonates in her heartwarming story 'Christmas by the Sea.' Readers will all want to be part of the Crenshaw family!"
—Anneka R. Walker, author *The Masked Baron*

"The spirit of Christmas abounds in Carla Kelly's heartwarming tale of love, kindness, and miracles."
—Sian Ann Bessey, author *The Noble Smuggler*

"Carla Kelly is a master at drawing you into the heart and soul of the lower-class Regency world!"
—Krista Lynne Jensen, author *Kisses in the Rain*

CHRISTMAS BY THE SEA

CARLA KELLY

In memory of Valoy Jensen, a woman much like Margaret Crenshaw.
Also to my mother, Dorothy Baier, who was just such a navy wife.

CHAPTER ONE

EVEN THOUGH HE HAD BEEN away for two years, Joshua Crenshaw, a surgeon in the Royal Navy, would have made it to his own bedchamber in the dark, if he hadn't bumped into a packing crate.

He knew his wife, Margaret, wasn't one to rearrange furniture. There shouldn't have been a packing crate between the front hall and the stairs. Should he worry? He was too tired to worry. What he wanted was to go to bed, and soon.

But now his foot hurt. Had Josh not uttered an oath of some width and depth, he could have crept to bed in silence. His most recent trip around Cape Horn—an unheard-of one week instead of the typical three—had still furnished him with new expletives, because no one liked the Straits of Magellan.

The consequence to his outburst? When he limped upstairs, his wife was waiting in the corridor, brandishing the cutlass he had left behind before shipping out on a voyage of exploration up the western coast of North America.

"Not one step closer." She sounded like she meant it.

"Megs, it is I," he whispered, knowing there were three children stashed somewhere on this crowded floor.

"J . . . Josh?"

"Aye, sweetheart. Joshua Crenshaw, age thirty-six, still with all my hair and other accessories, requesting and requiring permission to climb into bed with you. We made a quicker voyage than expected. Captain Barlow was certain we would not make port until 1812, but here I am." He grinned in the dark. "In fact, our profane captain declared our rapid transit a miracle."

The weapon dropped with a clatter—*oh, please sleep soundly, children*—and she was in his arms in seconds. Two years was a long, long time.

"My love, why is there a packing crate in our front hall?" he asked. She smelled deliciously of roses, a far cry from brine and tar, and my word, he was grateful.

"It will keep, husband."

It did.

But into every pleasant interlude some rain must fall, apparently. It fell on Surgeon Crenshaw at about four bells in the morning watch—six of the clock for land people—in the form of a book slammed against his face over and over, with its wielder's accompanying gruff admonition: "This is Mama's bed! Who are you?"

He opened his eyes, or tried to, to see a smallish girl with curly hair, book in hand. As he covered his unbattered eye, his wife threw herself across him. She grabbed the book and the perpetrator in one smooth motion, pulling his irate daughter to her side of the bed.

Josh sat up, bewildered. The last time anyone had intended him harm was when a French prisoner took exception to the amputation of his crushed leg. His suddenly active patient had brandished a knife in his face as Josh tried to screw down the tourniquet. The result produced an interesting scar on the surgeon's cheek, sutured after the amputation because first things first.

His left eye started to throb. He touched it gingerly and knew his innocent daughter—she must be nearly three— had just blacked his eye. *I am home*, he thought. *Dear me.* Josh Crenshaw was nobody's fool. He kept a prudent distance. "Millie, I'm your father," he said to the pretty child. All she lacked was his wife's superabundance of little freckles to be utterly entrancing.

Megs had the matter well in hand. "We've talked about Papa, Millie. Remember?"

His child gave him another glare, but she nodded. And persisted. "But Mama, your bed!"

"I know," Megs said in her comforting way. "He doesn't have a bed of his own, so he sleeps with me when he is in port."

"Send him away," Millie demanded.

"I dare not. I like him," his wife said. "See?"

She tucked herself close to Josh, careful to keep her skeptical daughter on her other side. He put his arm around Margaret and kissed her cheek.

"I like her too, Millie," he said. "She cooks good food and sings off-key in an endearing way."

"I do not sing off-key," his sweet wife said, adding more minor damage by gently flicking his temple with thumb and forefinger. *Oh, these Crenshaw women.*

She did sing off-key, but he never minded. "She also tucks me in at night, as I am certain she does to you."

Millie looked at him in a more kindly way. Of course, his eye was swelling shut, and the room was still dim, so he might have been wrong. "Does Mama read to you?" she asked.

"No, but I don't mind," he said, hugely amused, even though his eye hurt. "You have a remarkable right hook, Millie. If you were taller, I would pit you in the ring against Gentleman Jackson."

She frowned at that and cuddled closer to her Mama. Josh took his wife's hand and kissed it, which earned him another glare from his daughter.

Megs was quick to notice. "Now, Millie," she said firmly, "Papa is home for . . . for . . . how long, my love?"

"Three weeks at best," he said. "Scuttlebutt says we will be assigned to blockade duty."

"Is that good or bad?" his wife asked, ever practical.

"Depends. We will be off the coast of France and Spain and more likely to make port now and then," he said. His left eye had closed completely. "On the other hand, the blockade is boring, which makes sailors careless and more prone to accident. I'll be busy."

"What in the world will it take for the Corsican monster to surrender?" Margaret asked, getting up. She whispered in her daughter's ear, set her down, gave her a gentle swat on the seat, and turned her loose into the corridor.

"I have it on good authority that our irritating enemy wants to conquer Russia," Josh said. "I mean, why not? There it is. Let's see what the Cossacks of the steppes do to him, shall we?"

Megs nodded. She dampened a cloth in the water pitcher, returned to bed, then applied the cloth to his injured eye. She glanced at the murderous book beside him. "My love, you were assaulted by *Sense and Sensibility*. It's a delightful story. Your brother managed to procure me one of the first copies."

My brother, he thought. *My charming, wealthy, all-too-accessible brother. I'd almost rather see him take a flying leap than Napoleon.* "How nice of him."

"That was tepid." For a lovely moment, Margaret rested her head on his chest. "I've missed you dreadfully. I'm glad you're home early."

His arms tightened around her. "So am I, but satisfy my curiosity, please." He kissed the top of her head, so handy there on his chest. "You'll have to eventually tell me why and where we are moving."

"In the general tumult of your arrival, I forgot to tell you." She tried to inject a little dignity into the moment. "Oh, stop laughing! We're moving because I found the perfect house for us," she said. "I wanted to consult you, truly I did, but where were you? I plunged ahead on my own."

CHAPTER TWO

JOSH HAD NO OBJECTION. His family was overcrowded in their current domicile, located a street away from Plymouth's Barbican district, unpretentious and inexpensive. Surgeon's pay was respectable, but Josh's percentage of any prize money was modest.

"Can we afford this?" he asked anyway.

"Aye," she assured him. "You gave me latitude in the matter of funds while you are gone, as long as your brother approves."

"I did," he agreed. "Corny likes it too?"

"He does." She kissed his cheek. "I know you like Salcombe."

He did, no question. Salcombe was an unassuming village on the Devon coast, but a place he liked. Granted, he would have preferred to be party to the initial decision, but she was right. Who knew when he would be home again?

Still, he liked to tease her. "Megs, if I had come home one month from now, closer to when I was expected, would I have found no forwarding address from you?"

He wasn't prepared for tears. "Don't ever tease me like that, Josh," she murmured. "Please don't."

Touched and chastened at the same time, he wiped her eyes with his fingers. "Forgive me, dearest. This life of ours does take a toll, doesn't it?"

"Aye, it does," she agreed. "It's good to have you back, but we do have to get used to each other again, don't we?"

"We do. I hope it's fun."

Josh mulled over the matter as he heard his two older children running down the corridor. All he wanted was a quiet Christmas with his darlings. He craved a chance to regroup, loll on the sofa, revise enough sea stories to satisfy their children and not terrify Margaret, kiss her now and then, eat Christmas pudding, and visit a few neighbors.

Megs was right though. There was always that initial hesitation, unintentional but there, when he returned from sea essentially the same but different because fleet actions, horrendous wounds, and too little comforts for the ill and dying all took their own toll. And that was only his view. His family lived other lives while he was absent.

He cast aside the thought of moving and the changes in his wife when Jane and Timothy pulled up sharp in the doorway, shy. He stared at them, fascinated and a little shy himself. Who were these wonderful, hesitant creatures? They were his children, two years older certainly, and he loved them.

He motioned them closer; they didn't fail him. Her eyes wide with delight, his daughter sat beside him. Jane looked him over as if assessing what two years of sailing in strange waters had done to him, then decided he passed muster. She let him envelope her in an embrace and cried, as he knew she would.

"Papa, we worry," she admitted. Three words, but they said everything; he understood.

"I could tell you not to worry, but we live in a dangerous world," he said. "I'm here now and so happy to see you."

He held her off for a moment for a good look. She was taller and possessed that peculiar dignity of childhood. "Heavens, are you eight?" he asked.

"You know I am, Papa," she told him, even though he wasn't so certain. He glanced at his wife, who was subduing laughter. Megs would probably tease him later about not knowing their ages. He would bow his head and take her gentle scold, knowing he could never tell her how a two-year voyage with young men and some powder monkeys not much older than Jane could turn an entire crew into his children.

"I know you are eight. I disremembered that you were so pretty though," he added.

It was true. More than their other children, Jane was a pleasant blend of the two of them, with Megs's straight auburn hair and graceful gestures and his brown eyes and height. She was bright, too, but that also was both of them. His own family could make snide remarks about Margaret Murphy's less-than-exalted social background, but no one could fault his wife's intelligence. She had married him, hadn't she? What better proof did a husband need?

Next came Timothy—Margaret's image—with his abundance of Murphy freckles, sturdy build, and a certain Gaelic shrewdness, even at age six, that no Crenshaw possessed. Timmy plumped himself down on the bed and leaned back against Josh with a sigh that went right to his father's heart. He held up his bandaged finger. "You weren't here when I needed you, Papa," he said, going right to the core of the matter, as Megs tended to do. "Mama had to take me to Mr. Reese for repair, and he smells of barley water."

"Should I inspect Mr. Reese's work? Redo it, if need be?"

Timothy giggled. "No, Papa." He could be generous, also like his mother. "I was brave enough for one time, but I cannot vouch for another."

Josh laughed and hugged him. "There are men on my ship who fear me, too."

"I don't fear you, Papa," his son said. His eyes filled with tears. "What I do is miss you."

It was food for thought, Josh decided as he shooed them out and dressed, finding an older uniform in the back of the closet. Hmm. He had lost weight on this last voyage.

Once presentable, he carried his mound of dirty shirts and linens to the washroom off the scullery, careful in the front hall not to trip over the packing crate—no, it was three packing crates—that hadn't budged. Megs would send his briny clothes to the laundress. She had informed him that although their maid of all work and Polly in scullery could do his washing, there was a woman widowed by Trafalgar who needed money. If he knew Margaret—and he did; oh, he did—she would find a way to pay more than the going rate.

He left the kitchen and saw Millie peeking around the breakfast room door, which told him he might win her heart. Jane took Josh's hand as he stood in the doorway, suddenly indecisive about his own hearth and home, where the floor didn't pitch or yaw and no one ran out the guns for practice. She tugged on his hand, not to mention his heart, and he leaned down.

"Papa, please sit by me," she said. He did, aware that Megs had decreed that the Crenshaws wouldn't traipse from sideboard to table in the way of gentry but would sit at the table and pass dishes around, which she remembered from her childhood home in sleazy, devil-may-care Portsmouth. "We never stood on much ceremony," she'd told him, and that was that, because neither did he, to the dismay of the more-exalted Crenshaws.

There was bacon—plenty of it—and eggs. Here came the coffee pot, brought in by Mrs. Simpson herself, their cook and the widow of his former captain's steward, who beamed a welcome-home-from-sea glance at him.

Millie, who seemed to want a hand in everything, followed, and Margaret herself carried in the rice pudding, then helped her daughter onto her higher chair. *You're too far away, my love,* Josh thought as she seated herself next to their youngest across the table from him. Soon the food was prayed over and circulated, and everyone began to eat.

And forgot about him. Timothy asked his mother whether he had to go to school at the vicar's during Christmas now that Papa was home. Jane followed her mother's succinct reply in the affirmative with a question of her own about a need for new hair ribbons. Between bites of bacon, Timothy and Jane discussed the vicar's announcement about caroling, and Margaret tended to Millie.

Josh watched them, dismayed, then reminded himself that after a long absence, they needed to reintroduce themselves. He knew their familial reacquaintance would come. He ate in silence, angry with Napoleon Bonaparte because Boney's twenty-plus disruptive years had made Josh a guest in his own home.

Megs noticed his silence first. With a significant look at her daughter, she asked Jane to trade places and sat beside Josh. "There now," she said quietly. "This is better."

It was, until he heard the front door open and a booming voice ring out. "Good morning, my lovelies! Am I late for breakfast?"

Ah, Cornelius. So Corny was in the habit of breakfast at Chez Crenshaw? Josh wasn't prepared for the way his two older children leaped up from the table and ran into the front hall, already pelting one of Plymouth's better barristers with greetings.

"Pass the jam, please." Megs said it calmly, but even though he was an often-absent husband, he heard an edge to her voice—she who was generally kind to all creatures, up to and including his relatives.

"What's wrong, Megs?" he asked, keeping his voice low because he heard his brother coming toward the breakfast room.

"Dearest, you didn't come home a moment too soon," she said in the small voice that reminded him of earlier days, when his intimidating family tried to, well, intimidate her.

"What . . . ?"

"He gave me such grief over that house in Salcombe."

"I thought you—"

"I eventually wore him down," she whispered. "Smile, dearest. Here he is. We can discuss this tonight."

"I have a better idea," he whispered back. "What do you say we go to Salcombe this morning and see the new house?"

"Yes, let's. I know you will approve of my choice."

"Margaret, you are in charge when I am at sea," he reminded her, then had the honesty to ask himself if he really meant it.

"Margaret! 'Pon my word, has the prodigal son returned? And with a black eye!"

CHAPTER THREE

READ YOUR SCRIPTURES LATELY, CORNY? Josh thought as he stood up to shake hands with his generally charming older brother. "If you think forcing superstitious sailors to drink lime juice to avoid scurvy or treating too many cases of putrid throat amounts to riotous living, then yes, I am prodigal."

"That eye," Corny murmured. "Is this where you say, 'You should see the other chap'?"

"My daughter. She wondered who the stranger was in her mama's bed."

"You chose the sea life, little brother," Corny said, with the added implication, *We warned you*, lurking unsaid.

Overlook it, overlook it, Josh reminded himself. Cornelius Crenshaw made himself completely at home. Too completely? Maybe he needed a reminder. "How is your lovely wife?"

Corny shrugged. "She is tolerable." He sighed the theatrical kind of sigh that seemed to be the special purview of barristers, designed to sway juries. "I left her scolding her lady's maid, so she is in her element." He looked around and patted his chest. "It's peaceful here, Josh."

"It is anything but that," Megs contradicted. "What have my conniving children managed to winkle out of you between the front door and the breakfast room?"

"Nothing this time," he informed her. "They wanted me to know Papa is home." He patted Josh's shoulder. "Dressed in his best, I see. Noah probably wore that uniform on the *HMS Ark*."

"Everything else wants laundering," Josh said, wishing he didn't feel like a child around Cornelius. *Find a new subject.* "What do I see but a change of venue in store for Megs and me and our little crew?"

"Ah yes," Corny said. "A change of venue." Something in Corny's eyes suggested trouble afoot, as if he had been caught between a misdemeanor and a felony. The look went away quickly, and Josh's older brother became his usual confident self. Perhaps Josh had imagined it. He did tend to get defensive around his brother and his sister.

Good thing Lucy—or Lady Lucinda Nearing, more properly—wasn't in sight too. Since marrying that wealthy priss of a husband, she had become even more pretentious. Her husband had somehow ingratiated himself with the perpetually poor Prince Regent. Roylston Nearing had loaned Prinny some welcome cash, earning a knighthood the hard way, which meant there would be no repayment except a frivolous title. Lucy could not have been happier. She ordered even her close friends to call her Lady Nearing.

"We're moving directly after Christmas, Josh," Megs said. "Your brother has already found a buyer for this house."

"I did," Corny said.

"Megs, you know I love Salcombe," Josh said, and he meant it. He had long admired its pretty row of pastel-colored houses. "Please tell me it's one of the painted houses on All Saints Way."

"Yes, it's pale blue with yellow shutters and has three more bedchambers than here," she replied. "Your crew, as you call us, will watch for every Royal Navy vessel that sails past. The market is wonderful, so you needn't worry about me coming up against a rough nautical element as I shop."

"You realize, of course," Corny reminded her, "that if you hired a housekeeper, my dear sister-in-law, you could send her to make your purchases."

Stop right there, Josh thought. *Not another word.*

Cornelius obviously was not privy to his brother's mental pronouncements, because he blundered on. "After all, Margaret, you're a Crenshaw, and real ladies don't rub shoulders with anyone in the marketplace." He said it gently enough, but the condescension told Josh that while he was away, the Crenshaws still made life difficult for Megs. Drat them.

Shut your mouth, Corny, he wanted to say, except the children were listening. *Mind your own business, you snob.* Josh felt his heart crack a little around the edges as his wife looked away, uncertain and embarrassed. "Megs likes to shop," he said quietly. "She's a dab hand in the marketplace. I couldn't be more pleased." He squeezed her hand. "Let's go see the house."

She perked up. "Yes, let's all go."

"I'll arrange a carriage," Josh said, hoping his brother would take the hint and leave.

"I have a better idea," Corny said. "In fact, that is partly why I came over so early."

"You are always here for breakfast," Timothy chimed in. "Papa says Mrs. Simpson is the best cook."

"Aye," Josh agreed, "but every morning?"

Megs nodded, and there was no overlooking her expression. The frown she directed his way told him there would be discussion on the matter later.

"I am here with good news." Cornelius clapped his hands together. "Josh, wouldn't you know that as soon as I mentioned a new house for our little brother to Lucinda, she dropped everything and insisted she would help with the details."

Oh, please no, Josh thought, aghast. He was almost afraid to look at Margaret, but a quick glance afforded him a glimpse of stark terror.

"Oh, I . . ." Words failed Margaret.

I can nip this in the bud. "Please assure her we will manage quite well and she needn't exert herself," he said, thinking of the last time Lucy Nearing had inserted herself into their lives.

Cornelius talked fast, all the warning Josh needed of approaching doom. "She's already here and staying with me, Brother. Imagine my delight! In fact, I came here specifically to warn—inform Margaret that Lady Nearing will arrive in one half hour to take her to the new house in her carriage. And here you are too, Josh. Children, won't that be a treat?"

Jane and Timothy looked at each other with something close to horror. Millie seemed impervious to the dread news, but then, she was only two and a half.

"Uncle, I think Timothy and I will manage here quite well," Jane said after a glance at her mother. "Mrs. Simpson asked me to help ice the Christmas biscuits."

"I promised the vicar I would write that essay on why England rules the waves," Timothy said, and he, the reluctant scholar who only minutes ago wanted to get out of school since his father was newly arrived.

"You may stay here, my dears," Margaret said. "Your father and I will be delighted to visit our new home with your uncle and aunt." She smiled at her brother-in-law, who was just shallow enough to think she meant it, as Josh saw the matter. "Corny, please excuse us so we can prepare for this treat. She will be here when?"

"In-in one half hour," Cornelius stammered, possibly aware that he was being played by a master. "I'll leave you now." With toast and bacon in hand, he beat a quick retreat.

Margaret sighed after she heard the front door close. "Dear me. This was supposed to be an uncomplicated move at Christmas." She nodded to Jane and Timothy. "May I trust that all will run shipshape and Bristol fashion while Papa and I go to Salcombe? We can turn Millie over to Polly in the scullery, and you can help Mrs. Simpson with the biscuits."

"I think you're masterful," Josh said to his wife when only Millie remained in the breakfast room, busy with rice pudding and unaware of the family drama.

"I'm terrified," Megs admitted. "Why is this happening? You know how your sister feels about me."

He did. His late father had informed him years ago that it was bad enough his younger son chose to go to sea as a mere surgeon when he could have at least become a physician and served a more genteel clientele, but no, Josh also had the effrontery to fall in love with the daughter of the ship's bosun on the *HMS Sortie*, his second frigate.

Josh's reasoning that Patrick Murphy was a warranted officer, the same as he was, had fallen on deaf ears. Father's lament of "Where did we go wrong?" alternated with his sister's distress of "I trust you do not expect me to include that woman in our social sphere." He knew how his family felt about Margaret Murphy Crenshaw.

In her worst moments of enduring snubs and recrimination, Margaret had asked him if he regretted his decision to marry beneath his station. He had not a single regret. He loved his profession, as taxing as it was during wartime, and he adored his wife, and so he assured her as often as she needed it.

"We'll muddle through this, Megs, and they'll go home," he assured her now. "Tell me though: did Cornelius seem startled and then genuinely upset to see me?"

"He did. I don't know why." She lifted Millie from her high chair. "Granted, you are earlier than I expected, but that is a blessing. Let's whee Millie down to the washroom, where I will divide your stinky clothes into manageable piles and send them with Polly to the laundress."

Millie quickly discovered the pleasure of a hand in each parent's grasp and a lift off the floor every four steps or so, accompanied by "Whee!" Josh's daughter gave him a charitable look, which boded well for the future.

In the washroom, he helpfully separated his clothes into piles, wincing when Margaret grew solemn over the shirts with bloodstains. Even his surgeon's canvas aprons couldn't shield everything. It was a lovely excuse, if he needed one, to take his wife in his arms, hold her close, and murmur something about the war ending eventually, and then he could resign his warrant and start a country practice.

"A practice in Salcombe, perhaps?" she asked. "Our new house has two rooms downstairs that could easily become an office and clinic."

"Hold that thought," he said and kissed her soundly, which earned a chortle from Millie, who flopped back onto a mound of clothes, apparently not minding the odor of sweat and old blood on clothes washed in briny water for two years.

"Will I be able to see the ocean from that office?"

"Aye, husband. Kiss me again, and fortify me against the arrival of your sister."

He happily obliged, aware that as soon as he got rid of his relatives, this would become an excellent Christmas.

CHAPTER FOUR

HIS SUSPICIONS ABOUT HIS BROTHER and sister's machinations were not unwarranted. In fact, one look at his sister's face a half hour later told Josh mischief was afoot. It was probably obvious to shipmen at sea that she hadn't expected him to be in Plymouth in the flesh, big as life, irreversibly there.

"Such a surprise, dear brother," she said when her carriage rolled to a stop outside Josh and Meg's little house and he and his wife came out to greet her and a shockingly subdued Cornelius. "We weren't expecting you so soon."

"Care to come in, Sis?" he asked, knowing the answer.

"Heavens no," Lucy Nearing said. "You may join us, Josh." She glanced at Megs. "You, as well, if you must."

Barbs and darts. Would it never end? "Sister, please don't," he said, taking Margaret's hand, wishing she hadn't started to tremble.

Lucy nodded to Margaret, who nodded back and kept her hand tightly in Josh's. "So delightful to see you, Joshua," she said. "You, too, Margaret, of course."

Josh helped Margaret inside the carriage, then sat beside her, wondering what kind of small talk anyone could make for the distance from Plymouth to Salcombe. He should have trusted his wife, the woman he had to leave regularly because king and country demanded it.

"Cornelius, are you ready for Christmas?" she asked his brother, who seemed to be trying to hide in the corner of the elegant but small conveyance, no mean feat.

Corny mumbled something that included an invitation to Lucy's for Christmas dinner as his upcoming treat. Lucinda shot the barrister a warning glance, which told Josh such an invitation from Lucy wouldn't be forthcoming to them.

Margaret was made of sterner stuff than both of Josh's siblings. "Josh, what a lovely view of the coast," she said, changing the subject and leaning across him to gaze at the shoreline. "I wouldn't want to live where I couldn't see the ocean."

"It's been a favorite view of mine for years," he teased, which made her laugh. "Have I told you about the time . . ."

So it went for the duration of the drive, the two of them carrying on a conversation, getting reacquainted, while Corny avoided eye contact and Lucinda ignored them. A smaller person would have wilted under the weight of his sister's disapproving glower, but Margaret was not a smaller person.

Bravo, my love, Josh thought. *Bravo.*

In some ways, Megs seemed almost a new woman, this decisive lady who had found another home and managed his affairs—their affairs—successfully while he was away on the king's business. He remembered her former shyness around his brother, but apparently Corny came to Josh's house every morning now for breakfast. And Lucinda? Some people were best left alone. Why Lucinda had initiated this drive, he couldn't imagine. If she thought to make fun of the house in Salcombe, well, that wouldn't happen, because Josh wasn't a mouse.

He sat back, pleased, until the coachman didn't turn off at Salcombe but continued on the road to Paignton.

He looked at Margaret, saw her surprise and discomfort. She spoke up before he did, even though he knew she still feared his judgmental sister. "Lady Nearing, will you please get the coachman's attention? We missed the turnoff to Salcombe."

"We're not going to Salcombe," his sister said in her most my-decision-is-final voice. "Cornelius and I have found a more suitable house for our little brother."

Margaret's sudden intake of breath went straight to Josh's heart. She turned her face to his sleeve.

"Lucinda, please stop this carriage," he said, easing his arm around Margaret, who seemed to be trying to burrow inside his uniform. "Margaret has chosen a house in Salcombe, and I want to see it."

"No."

"That's it? No?" he asked, dumbfounded.

"Cornelius, explain the matter to our little brother."

Josh let go of his wife and opened the door of the moving coach.

"What are you doing?" Lucinda demanded as her voice rose to an unpleasant screech.

He leaned out of the open door. "Stop the carriage," he ordered the coachman, knowing his surgeon-during-battle voice was beyond anything Lucinda could produce.

The carriage stopped. Without a word, Josh let down the steps and held out his hand for Margaret. "Come, my love. I can use the exercise. We're walking to Salcombe to see a house."

"Say something, Cornelius!" Lucinda demanded.

His brother, the brave barrister, couldn't look at him. "We—your sister and I—decided on a more suitable house in Paignton. We purchased that for you instead."

The only sound was the creak of harness and the hiss of breakers on the shore.

"You bought a different house from the one my wife wanted?" Josh asked, stunned.

"We did what was best for you and your children," Lucinda replied.

"You have no idea what is best for us," Josh snapped.

No answer. Lucinda looked away, and Cornelius suddenly found the coach lining fascinating.

"Had you no inkling of this . . . this underhanded dealing?" he asked Margaret, keeping his voice low, for her alone.

"None. He never dissuaded me, never said a word," she replied. "Goodness, it's humiliating to think how excited I was about the perfect home for us."

She did something next that a younger Margaret never would have done, and he loved her all the more for it. She stepped close to the carriage and looked Cornelius Crenshaw right in the eye. "To think you've been eating breakfast at *my* table with *my* children for months on end and permitted this. Shame on you."

She closed the carriage door with a decisive click as Lucinda shouted something about, "Like it or not, you own a house in Paignton now," then, "I know what's best for my brother," then something else mercifully swallowed up by the screech of low-flying gulls curious to know what was going on.

Josh offered his wife his arm. She crooked her own through his, and they started walking toward Salcombe. "It's not far," she said, then dissolved in tears. "I didn't mean this to be such a Christmas," she said, then stopped and wept into his chest.

The carriage hadn't moved, but Josh got Megs in motion, tears and all, away from his abominable, perfidious brother and sister. He pulled out a handkerchief, and she snatched it from him. She wiped her eyes with a fierce gesture, blew her nose like she meant it, then glared back at the vehicle.

"I've been played for a fool," she said, and he heard all her embarrassment. "What's more, Corny could do it and get away with it because women have no say in the purchase of property." She stopped and looked at him. "And now we have a house in Paignton to pay for?"

"They seem to think so," he said, his heart sinking. His brother had betrayed him, and it stung. "How could they do that to you?"

She tugged him into motion this time. "More easily than we knew, obviously. I'm sorry, Josh. I truly am. You should have looked a little higher for a wife."

Break my heart some more, he thought, sad beyond belief. "I never needed to look anywhere else," he said simply. "I love you."

"Probably not the smartest thing you ever did," she retorted.

He heard the tiniest glimmer of his own Margaret then, the woman he knew without a doubt could manage life successfully during his lengthy absences.

"It was, actually," he told her as they strolled along. "I have no regrets." He stopped and took her by the shoulders. "No more breakfasts for Cornelius."

She smiled at that, then dabbed at her eyes. "We're in a spot, aren't we?"

"I suppose we are."

He did love Salcombe, the little village close to the sea, with those rows of pastel-hued houses putting such a cheerful face to time and tide. Providing the wind was in the right quarter, he thought of all the times he had seen Salcombe from the deck of a frigate, knowing he was nearly home with those he loved best.

"Which house is it?" he asked. "I still want to see it."

"Why not?" she asked in turn, gallant again and almost but not quite cheerful. She pointed up to the pale-blue house with yellow shutters at the end of the row above the high street. "There, on All Saints Way, you know, where there used to be that ruin of a church. The house is probably empty and locked, but we can look in through the windows."

Tears came once more, the kind sniffed back. With a deep ache in his heart, Josh knew how much Megs wanted the blue house with yellow shutters. He held her close, even though a disapproving matron frowned at them from the Oceanview Tearoom on the high street.

"What are we going to do?" she asked.

Her humiliation was so great she couldn't even look at him—what he feared had happened. "We're going to see this house you want," he told her, his hands cupping her face. He raised her chin gently so she had to look at him. "None of this is your fault, my love. Not one thing."

It took too long for his peace of mind for his wife to nod in agreement. He set her in motion once more, clasping her firmly around the waist and not stopping until they stood in front of the house in question.

His heart sank. It was perfection and precisely the house he would have chosen, too. Strange that roses should be blooming by the door. Didn't they know it was December? Odd, that.

"I thought it was empty," Megs said. "I think someone lives here." He felt her sigh. "I hope whoever owns it now likes it as much as I do."

She turned away, but then the door opened.

"Do I have company?" Josh heard.

He stopped Megs and looked back to see a small man, hair white, eyes kind. He was by no means handsome, but he had an air of capability about him.

"I watched you slow down and stop," the man said.

"My wife was interested in buying this house," Josh explained. "Thought she had, in fact. It appears you have purchased it instead. Good holiday to you, sir."

"Come in, come in," the man said and gestured for them to join him. "I am merely a caretaker. Would you like to see inside?"

Josh looked at Margaret, who had perked up. "Yea or nay, love?" he asked.

She hesitated, then nodded. "I'd like that, sir, if you don't mind."

"Not at all. Come in."

CHAPTER FIVE

"I am Mr. Paul," the old fellow said. "I'm here until the owners assume possession. And you are . . . ?"

"I am Joshua Crenshaw, a surgeon in the Royal Navy." Josh indicated Megs. "This is my wife, Margaret. We live in Plymouth."

"Home from sea?" Mr. Paul asked. He gestured toward the chairs pulled close to a pleasant fire.

"Aye, sir, but we should not encroach upon you."

Mr. Paul shrugged. "Why ever not? I'm twiddling my thumbs here and don't mind a diversion."

"I'm reluctant to trespass on your goodwill, sir," Josh said, "but would you mind if we looked around? We won't be long."

"I think it a delightful idea, Surgeon Crenshaw." He turned to Megs. "You've been through the house, haven't you?"

"Aye, sir," she said. "I thought we had bought it, but my brother-in-law and sister-in-law had other ideas, apparently."

Mr. Paul shook his head over that, then brightened. "Since you've been here before, please, show your husband around." He touched his back. "I'm older than I look and would rather sit here by the fire."

To Josh's relief, Megs smiled. "Let me help you to your chair," she said and did just that, easing Mr. Paul back among his cushions. "Can I get you anything?"

"Hand me that book, if you please," he said, pointing.

She did, after looking at the title. "*Sense and Sensibility*?" She laughed, which further calmed Josh's heart. "I have a funny story for you. It explains my husband's black eye."

She told him about the morning's jolt for Josh, when his youngest child had clobbered him with Megs's copy of that very novel. "Josh is back from two years away, and they need to be reintroduced to each other."

"Long journeys will do that," Mr. Paul said with a laugh. "I've made a few in my day. Go on, you two. Look around."

Taking Josh's hand, she walked him first to the two rooms off the breakfast room. "These would have been perfect for your office and clinic, my love."

The rooms overlooked the street and, beyond that, the Channel. On days when no one needed his particular services, he could have enjoyed the view and looked back on his years in the fleet, provided Boney ever yielded.

"You're right, Megs," he said. "I can see you with your knitting in here, keeping me company during lulls in great hordes of patients seeking my service."

"I would have loved it," she agreed, "even though I know you are teasing me."

"Me? Never."

They looked at each other and laughed. His heart felt more at ease as she relaxed and perhaps forgot about his abominable relatives—either that or she hid her humiliation well. It was hard to tell with Margaret Crenshaw.

The breakfast room, with its view of the back garden—or at least, what the back garden would look like in spring—made her sigh. She shook her head over the kitchen. "So much room in here" was her comment. "There is an actual dining room, but I doubt we would ever be so formal."

"Probably not," he agreed. "We're breakfast room sort of people, aren't we?"

Six bedchambers upstairs made him sigh too. *Room for everyone and then some*, he thought. *What a pity it won't be ours.*

They stood for a long time in the larger bedchamber that overlooked the street and Channel. Megs leaned against him. "I wish" was all she said.

"At least we have our home on Motte Street," he began, then stopped as the prospect of a terrible calamity flapped home to roost on his shoulder like an unwanted albatross. "Megs! You said there was a buyer for our home. Do you think . . . ?"

She put her hand to her mouth, her eyes wide and terrified. "I haven't signed anything."

His own expression hardened. "Apparently you don't need to sign any-thing, where my relatives are concerned. We . . . we need to get to Carter and Brustein immediately."

He grabbed her hand, and they ran down the stairs.

Mr. Paul looked up in surprise from his chair by the fireplace. "Is something the matter?"

"Everything, sir," Josh said as he snatched up his wife's coat from the chair where she had draped it. "My dreadful relatives may have sold our house in Plymouth out from under us. Where can I find a conveyance? We must hurry to our countinghouse."

For a man who said his back pained him, Mr. Paul leaped from his chair and darted out the front door with remarkable dexterity. "I'll be only a minute," he called as they looked after him in amazement.

Josh helped Megs into her coat and had barely slung his boat cloak around his own shoulders when Mr. Paul returned, all smiles. "Done. There is a conveyance just down the street coming this way. Wait here." He held up his hand. "Deep breaths, you two."

One more deep breath and a post chaise pulled up smartly to the curb. Josh reached for his wallet as he started down the steps. Mr. Paul stopped him. "I already took care of that."

"Oh, but—"

"Don't argue with an old man," Mr. Paul said, sounding remarkably like someone who expected to be obeyed. "Just send me a message to let me know what happens." He smiled. "This will turn out better than you think."

It was an odd comment from someone who knew nothing of their circumstances, but Josh felt the smallest bit of optimism. *I am an idiot*, he thought next.

"We will, sir, and thank you," Megs said as Josh hustled her into the post chaise.

"Where, sir?" the postilion said as he flexed his whip, determination writ prominently on his face. Mr. Paul must have paid him a tidy sum.

"Carter and Brustein in the Barbican. It's two blocks from the Drake Hotel," Josh said. "Spring 'em."

"Aye, sir," he said.

The man was as good as his word. Josh knew he had never made a trip faster. Megs clung to his hand as they raced along. He saw the fear in her eyes.

"What was I thinking?" she said softly. "All I wanted to do was make a better home for you when you are in port. What if we are homeless?"

He held her close as she cried, and he wished Cornelius and Lucinda to outer darkness—at the very least, he wished them some discomfort in their condescending, complacent lives. Apparently he owned an unwanted house in Paignton now, but he had no desire to see it. Perhaps after Christmas they could put it up for sale. If they were lucky, it would sell soon and they wouldn't be homeless for long.

His thoughts were hardly comforting, so he said nothing. But that wouldn't do; Megs was feeling low and blaming herself. "We're together, dearest," he reminded her. "Our children love us—at least, Jane and Timothy love their papa. I fear Millie isn't too happy with me."

His reward was a watery chuckle. "Oh, you," Megs said from the depths of his boat cloak, where she had burrowed a comfortable spot. "Millie will succumb to your brass buttons and general air of competence, same as I did. I suppose you will tell me this will be something to think about and laugh over in years to come."

"I sincerely hope so," he said and kissed her hand. He had to smile too. "No matter what happens, it's still better than an amputation during a typhoon."

"Or a kitchen floor covered with honey," she chimed in.

"When was that?"

"Two weeks ago. Millie loves sweets."

They were both laughing when the post chaise came to a smart stop in front of Carter and Brustein's countinghouse. The postilion pulled down the step and wished them a happy Christmas. He was gone in a flash. Before Josh opened the door to the countinghouse, he looked back, wondering how a chaise and two horses could disappear so fast.

All was calm and quiet in the countinghouse, a balm to his soul. He asked the clerk if he could speak to Samuel or David Brustein, hoping his Jewish accountants hadn't left Plymouth during this most Christian of holidays.

He and Megs sat where the clerk indicated. Margaret admired the handsome dark paneling and looked down at the Turkish rug underfoot. "Beautiful," she said.

Maybe when this interview was over, Josh could inquire about such a rug for their own sitting room. If they still had a house.

"Surgeon Crenshaw, such a pleasure to see you."

Josh looked up, happy to ignore his unprofitable thoughts. He stammered out their dilemma as David Brustein listened and nodded, then ushered them into his office. He shook his head over the rest of the story, giving Margaret his most sympathetic attention as she tried not to cry.

"I'll get your records," he said. "One moment."

One moment stretched into two and then beyond. Josh reminded himself that patience was a virtue. He was starting to dispute that tried-and-true platitude when Mr. Brustein returned, file in hand and a smile on his face.

"No money has changed hands over your house on Motte Street. I see no evidence of a contract. Perhaps your brother was waiting until after the holiday to bring this to my attention."

Margaret closed her eyes in relief. Josh felt an absurd urge to burst into tears. He stifled it. He didn't wish to disappoint Megs.

"Can you make a note in my file disavowing anyone from disturbing my account here?" he asked. "More specifically, please negate Cornelius Crenshaw's power of attorney."

"Consider it done," Mr. Brustein said. "I fear the matter of the house in Paignton is out of my control, however. Documents were signed only two days ago."

"All of that done without my wife's knowledge," Josh said. "Have we no recourse?"

Mr. Brustein shook his head. "Alas, no, because your brother's power of attorney was still in effect at the time of the signing." He looked closer at his notes. "Your money hasn't been transferred yet to the seller, but your brother signed the contract. I'll have to honor it, sir, when someone claims it by presenting the deed."

"Live and learn, I suppose," Josh said, almost seeing his prize money from years in the fleet drifting away on little fairy wings. "We'll sell it again."

"The market isn't too sanguine right now," David Brustein cautioned.

"Time and tide, Mr. B.," Josh said. He held out his hand. "We'll manage until the market improves."

Josh and Megs strolled home arm in arm. His eye started to ache, and he looked forward to lying down with a cool cloth over it. *Hmm.* "If I lie down on what is obviously only your bed, according to our youngest offspring, d'ye think she'll thrash me again, dear Megs?" he joked.

"I'll defend you," his wife replied. "I'll move the candlestick, too, just in case."

They were laughing when they opened the front door. The laughter stopped when Jane, usually their calmest child, rushed up, worry etched all over her face.

"Thank goodness! Papa, we need you." She looked over her shoulder. "Timothy, bring him in here."

Him who? Josh felt his shoulders rise in tension, a sensation he was all too familiar with from sudden emergencies.

Timothy carried in a puppy, muddy and thin, possessing a woeful countenance and a dangling leg. "He showed up on our doorstep. Papa, we need you in just about the worst way."

$\mathscr{C}$HAPTER SIX

HIS CHILDREN NEEDED HIM. HIS self-sufficient, resilient children, who never knew when he would fetch port and didn't know him as well as he would have liked, needed him. All the distress of the day's misadventure left his shoulders. What did it matter that he was about to lose a significant amount of his prize money to a house in Paignton no one except his brother and sister wanted? Timothy and Jane needed him, and he was in his element, even if it was merely over a dog.

He knelt in the front hall. Timothy deposited the wretched little pup into his arms. "Can you spare a towel or two, my dear?" he asked over his shoulder. "Perhaps a washrag and basin of warm water?"

"Only if you carry him through to the washroom," Megs said. She looked closer. "He has a sweet face."

Jane and Timothy exchanged glances. *Oh, wifey, you are in for it,* Josh thought gleefully, well aware of Megs's refusal to acquire a dog. She had never given a reason, but he knew when to pick his battles, and he wouldn't pick one over a pet.

He would be noncommittal; it wouldn't do to pretend too much interest in actually giving this pup a home. "Yes, a sweet face," he said, striving for neutrality. "I'll see what I can do, children."

"I'll be right back with a towel," Megs said. "Timothy, you fetch a basin of water. Hurry now."

"We thought about asking Uncle Corny for help, but he doesn't know anything," Jane told him, which made Josh chortle inside. She touched the little beast's floppy ears. "Uncle Corny doesn't like dirty things, either." She looked at him. "You don't mind, do you?"

"Not at all, my dear. You should see some of the sailors and Royal Marines I have cleaned up after a battle before I can even get to their wounds. Serving the guns and working the sails are a dirty business."

He could tell from her expression that she had never considered that aspect of his life and work. Why should she? Her mama ran a taut ship here at home, where cleanliness was prized, meals were always on time, bedchambers were warm during the winter, and Father Christmas always brought gifts, even if they were modest. What did Jane know of dirt and blood and pain? He watched her face, touched to see real sympathy cloud her eyes.

"Is it hard, Papa?" she asked quietly.

"At times." He had to be honest. "Then I remind myself what they—we—are doing to protect our dear ones here in England. I carry on for you, Jane."

If he could have set a bell jar down on the look of gratitude she gave him just then, he would have been a happy man forever. She patted his arm. "I'll help."

She did. He carried the whining pup through to the washroom, where Megs hurried in with a towel before going to retrieve more washrags. The little pup whimpered when Josh set him down, but Jane was there to pet and comfort the creature. Timothy joined her in a few minutes, carrying a basin of warm water from the kitchen. Margaret returned with the washrags, Millie peeking around her mother's skirt.

"Dab at his fur, and we'll wipe him off," Josh ordered. He lifted up a back leg. "Her. Well, missy, it appears you have run afoul of the mean streets of Plymouth," he told his terrified patient.

"Oh, Papa," Jane said. She leaned against his sleeve, and his heart was full.

"I always talk to my patients," he told her.

His girl was a bright one. "Even if they are not conscious?"

"Even then. I never am certain what my sailors can hear." He smiled. "When they call for their mothers, I kiss them on the forehead."

He heard Megs's sudden intake of breath behind him and felt her hand, gentle on his shoulder. He rested his cheek on her fingers for a moment, glad for the comfort.

Father and children worked in companionable silence, Megs and Millie leaving the others to their task. Gradually, a pup with brown and white fur emerged. She tried to wag her tail and nearly succeeded. She needed something to eat, and soon.

"Daughter, tell Mama to cook some gruel for us. Breakfast leftovers will do. Thin it with cream, if there is any."

Jane scampered off, and Timothy continued cleaning. He had freshened the water twice and did so again after purloining another towel and washrag from somewhere. "Mama won't mind."

"She takes good care of you, doesn't she?" Josh commented. He palpated the pup's front leg gently, feeling for the break. A whimper assured him he had found it.

"Mama loves us," Timothy said, and that seemed to cover the subject. He wasn't a talkative child. Then he surprised Josh. "Mama loves you too."

"I know."

"How do you know? You're not home too often."

It wasn't cruelly meant, Josh knew. Timothy was a little boy trying to make sense of his world. "How do I know, son? Hush, little pup; I'll make it better soon. Mama writes me wonderful letters, and she treats me very well when I am here." He smiled. "She takes good care of you because she and I are in this together. That's what love is, son."

Timothy nodded, satisfied. "She reads your letters to us over and over. They make her cry sometimes, but she reads anyway. Do you read our letters over and over, Papa?"

Josh nodded, unable to speak. *If you only knew*, he thought. *I wear them out.*

Jane returned with a small bowl of gruel. The pup perked up, sniffing. "Set it by her head," Josh directed, all business again, no matter how humble his patient. "Timothy, go upstairs to Mama's chamber and fetch my medical satchel. It's next to my side of the bed."

"Do you always keep it so close?" Timothy asked.

"Always."

Jane slid the bowl toward his patient, who apparently could not believe her good fortune. She licked and lapped and made funny noises in her throat. There it was: one tail wag and another.

"I like it when my patients start to eat," Josh commented. "That usually means I'm not going to lose them. Hold her still, Janey."

His daughter held where he pointed, then gave him the full force of her smile, so like her mother's. "You gave me a nickname," she said. "I like it."

"I do too," he said. "Janey. Janey."

Timothy returned, lugging the leather satchel. Josh thought of all the fleet actions the satchel had survived. Watching his son made him wonder if

Timothy might carry it someday. The thought made him smile. He glanced at Janey, who lay almost nose-to-nose with the pup. *Or you, daughter. Times might change.*

He consulted his staff. "What would be a good splint? I need something stiff and not too long."

"Mama has butter knives," Timothy said after some thought.

"Brilliant!" Josh exclaimed, wondering if Megs would miss them. "Get me two, please. If Mama cuts up stiff, refer her to me."

And you will do what, Josh? he asked himself, confident that during the Christmas season, he could think of something.

He asked Jane to leave her post as chief comforter and get him two bandage rolls from his satchel. He watched her rummage in the bag, frowning when she saw his capital knives.

"Tools of the trade, Janey," he said. "Ah, there. Thank you."

The puppy offered no opposition as Josh wrapped her front leg. When Timothy returned with two butter knives and a grin—"Mama said she would talk to you later"—Josh applied his makeshift splints and wrapped the leg some more until the job was done.

"I doubt she will want to move much," he told his children. "Keep food handy. And there's this: when she messes, you're in charge of cleaning her bum."

"You don't have to do *that* aboard ship, do you, Papa?" Timothy asked.

"I've done it, son," he said. "I started at sea as a loblolly boy, and that was my principal task." He tightened his arm around his boy's shoulder. "Don't look so aghast! There isn't anything you can't wash away."

Except, possibly, the enmity of unhappy relatives. He had run away to sea at fourteen, which was old for the Royal Navy. From Devonport, the *Avenger* had sailed for the Orient practically on the tide. When they'd made port again in Plymouth two years later, his irate father had nabbed him. A man at sixteen by then, Josh had overridden his father's arguments that a surgeon in the Royal Navy was no life for a gentleman's son, because in his case, it was.

That heated argument dockside had led to bargaining and to a year of medical school in Edinburgh, where Josh had acquired surgical skills. A year's ward-walking at Guy's Hospital in London had followed. Medical boards had come next, followed by his warrant from the navy board as a surgeon. He had not a single regret, although his father had many. Since Josh was at sea so much, the high-in-the-instep Crenshaws found it simple enough to overlook him.

Janey found a low-sided box that she lined with two more towels, and Josh lifted his small patient inside. In a moment, the pup closed her eyes. "One of you will want her by your bed tonight," he said. "Call it ward-walking. You can take turns. If Mama has any washrags left, you'll need them." He laughed. "I doubt any of us will be bathing, since the towels are occupied."

"Papa, don't be silly," Jane scolded. "Mama never runs out of things."

No, she never did. He had known Margaret Murphy was the woman for him almost from the start. She was lovely, she was competent, and because her Irish father was a bosun, she knew the navy. The torment of Josh's life was her treatment by his brother and sister, never as heavy-handed as today. He knew he should go to her, but here he was, sitting on the washroom floor with his children. Janey cuddled close on his one side, Timothy on the other. Was ever a long-absent father so fortunate? The blessing was he knew Megs would understand.

Now she was stuck with a puppy. "We should name Pup something better," Josh said. "She is a girl, after all."

"Let's call her Grace," Timothy suggested.

"Grace? Papa, doesn't that mean elegance or good breeding? You said she came from the mean streets of Plymouth," Janey said. She turned to Timothy. "Why Grace?"

He shrugged. "I like it."

"We'll let her aspire to something better than the mean streets," Josh said. "Grace it is."

He hoped Janey and Timothy would not be upset when he told them they weren't moving. He knew he couldn't—or shouldn't—explain the unkindness of relatives to young ones, his young ones, so tender. Would they wonder why their Mama had objections to a house in Paignton, which, knowing his sister and brother, was probably grander than the charming place in Salcombe? They didn't need to know their favorite uncle Corny could be so devious. Thank goodness he and Megs had been able to deflect any sale of the overcrowded house they now lived in.

He looked at Grace, exhausted from her splinting and probably wondering what she was doing in this strange place. He couldn't help a rueful smile. He and his complicit offspring had shoe-horned in a dog that, from the size of her paws, was not going to grow up small. Grace indeed.

Megs, Megs, I'm glad you love me, he thought. *I'm complicating things.*

CHAPTER SEVEN

CROWDED THOUGH THEY MIGHT BE in the breakfast room for their delayed dinner, Josh looked around with real satisfaction at his family. He wondered idly if the Admiralty would object should he jump ship and stay with these lovely people.

But there were sterner matters to deal with. Megs had given him the nod, so he knew it was his job to disappoint the children about the house in Salcombe. She was right to make it his responsibility. After all, the odious Crenshaws were his relatives. He set down his spoon.

"Children, there is no way to gild this. We can't move to that house in Salcombe," he said. "Someone else owns it. We'll start unpacking tomorrow."

Janey's shoulders drooped. Timothy shook his head. He spoke with six-year-old logic. "Papa, I already measured my chamber in the new house. Everything will fit there."

"In that house, Millie would have her own room, and I wouldn't have to share," Janey said, then put her hand to her mouth. "Not that I mind sharing. It's just that she and I would probably manage better if we had our own rooms." She leaned closer. "Millie is a little bossy."

"That partly comes with being nearly three," Megs reminded her daughter. "We hate to disappoint you, but . . . but . . ."

"Uncle Cornelius and Aunt Lucinda must have misunderstood us," Josh continued, uneasy with prevarication but unsure how to explain downright cruelty and excessive snobbery to children who knew their mother was the finest woman on earth. They didn't care if she was Irish and her father had been a mere bosun. *I didn't either*, Josh thought. *Still don't.* He plowed ahead. "They thought we wanted a grander place in Paignton that we really can't afford and bought that instead."

"Then, it belongs to them," Janey pointed out with impeccable logic.

"That's the complication, daughter," he said. "For some reason unknown to any person who knows how intelligent you ladies are, our laws require men to make those decisions for women."

"But you're a man," Janey persisted. "In fact, you're our papa."

"I am indeed. I am also out at sea and hence gone for large periods of time, thanks to our current national emergency. For your mother to access what the law calls my money, an honest man with power of attorney must be more readily available—in our case, your uncle." *I trusted you, Corny*, he thought with a surprising amount of bitterness, considering he usually liked his older brother.

His son and daughter absorbed the news. "Well, that's a fine how-de-do," Janey said.

Megs chuckled. It eased Josh's heart to see genuine humor in her eyes again. She was a long way from the wife who'd cried into his shirt, standing on the road to Paignton. "We still have our home here, and we'll sell the place in Paignton. Besides, who wants to move at Christmas?"

Timothy returned to his rice pudding, the matter apparently closed in his mind. From her expression, Janey still questioned it. Josh wondered how much she already knew about the little jabs and icy stares that came her mother's way because Margaret came from a lower social sphere. He wasn't certain he wanted to know.

No one was better at turning an unpalatable subject than his wife and helpmeet, she who shared her bed with a sometimes-absent husband. "Tomorrow, let's not waste a moment in unpacking last year's Christmas wreath," she said decisively. "You and Cook have wisely iced holiday biscuits, and there is a plum pudding hanging in the pantry. Remember the wooden garland in one of the crates? What should Papa do?"

Josh thought about the house in Salcombe and the old fellow who was caretaking it for as-yet-unknown owners. "I would like to write a letter to Mr. Paul in Salcombe and invite him to Christmas dinner. Margaret, would that be a good thing? He said he was alone."

"He did. I've been thinking about him too," she said. "Do you know, I want to invite my father's friend, a gunnery sergeant from the *Euryalus*. He lives in a rooming house in the Barbican. I doubt he has too many dinner engagements, and this is Christmas we are discussing. Janey and I could take him an invitation."

"May I draw him a picture of a plum pudding and a holly wreath?" Janey asked.

"Yes! Let's clear the table once we're done and get started," Megs told her children.

"Will Uncle Corny be here?" Janey asked. "I don't know why he has never come *here* for Christmas. Should we invite him?"

"He has his own set of friends," Margaret said. "He told us that once, remember?"

Uncle Corny also has a snob of a wife who would never sit at a table with a bosun's daughter, Josh thought. He wondered how Margaret had managed, on those many occasions when he was absent, to deflect her children's thoughts from the Uncle Corny they adored, the old hypocrite.

He asked her later when the children, Millie included, were drawing Christmas invitations and he was drying dishes as she washed them since it was Cook's evening off. "Who usually has Christmas dinner with you?"

"Certainly not Cornelius," she assured him. She wiped her hands on her apron and laced them around his neck. "I remind your heirs and offspring of that chapter from St. Matthew, in which Christ invites the lame and the halt and the blind to the feast." She rested her forehead against his chest as his arms went around her. "Papa—oh, I miss him—Papa left me a list of former shipmates. I invite some every year, Gunny among them. Our children have heard wonderful sea yarns."

He held her close. "Megs, you're a wife in a million."

"I know," she said, which made him laugh and kiss her.

She flicked some suds on him after the second or third kiss.

"I'll get you for that," he said, wiping his eyes. "Probably later."

"That's what I was hoping," she said, all complacence, and returned to the dishes. "Mr. Paul is a queer old stick, isn't he? Did you have the feeling he knows more about us than is really possible since we've never seen him before?"

"I did. Who showed you the house originally?"

She put her hands into the soapy basin, which made him step behind her as a precaution. "Oh, you! I made my point with one splash. That's better. I'll just lean back a little, because you're comfortable. It was a lady. I believe her name was Priscilla. She said her husband was away." She sighed, and he felt it. It told him worlds about his own frequent absences.

"I won't always be away," he assured her.

"It was an odd name. Something like Quill." She washed another dish and handed it over her shoulder to him. "Get busy, Surgeon Crenshaw. It's been a vexing day, and I'd like someone to massage my feet tonight."

CHAPTER EIGHT

JOSH CHECKED ON GRACE FIRST thing in the morning in Timothy's room, pleased to see the pup wagging her tail and whining. Timothy went for more gruel and cream. Grace gobbled that down, then looked up, ever hopeful, in that way of dogs and children.

Millie eyed Josh with less suspicion when he tapped on Janey's door quietly and opened it. He looked around the room, neat and squared away, as he would have expected under the management of a bosun's daughter. Space was tight. He couldn't help thinking about the larger chambers at the house in Salcombe.

For one brief moment—he felt like a traitor—he thought about the house in Paignton his siblings were so set upon. Knowing them, he knew it would be large, perhaps even ostentatious. There would be room for everyone.

Satan, get thee behind me, he thought, ashamed, reminding himself of all the slights and meanness that had come Margaret's way because she didn't fit his family's idea of proper society. They never considered that she was the right wife for their little brother, who had chosen his own, less-exalted path in the working world. The unavailable house in Salcombe was perfect for *them*, Joshua and Margaret Crenshaw. What a pity his relatives would never understand.

Since Janey still slept and Millie was probably plotting world domination, he scooped up his youngest and carted her back to his own chamber, where the joy of his heart was sitting up and looking adorable, if a bit disheveled. "Your daughter," he announced. "I am off to deliver that invitation to Mr. Paul."

"You want to see the perfect house again."

"Guilty as charged, madam," he said, then plunked Millie onto her lap. "I have a nagging feeling I know Mr. Paul."

"Please extend my greetings too," Megs said. "We're hopeful he will visit us the day after tomorrow." She smiled at him with that knowing smile. "Whether we know him or not."

He procured a modest conveyance at the nearest inn and settled back, content, for a drive he enjoyed. The wind blew in coldly off the Channel. As content as he felt, he couldn't help but think about his next assignment, which would likely involve the blockade off the French and Spanish coasts. He thought about Bonaparte and wondered about boundless ambition. His father had accused him once of having no ambition because he had settled, in Father's word, for mere surgery when he could have been a more-exalted physician.

Josh relaxed, a smile on his face, despite the inevitable pillage of his modest-enough prize money funds at Carter and Brustein, their too-small house, and a falling-out with his brother and sister, which he knew was also inevitable. Perhaps the great mystery was that it hadn't happened sooner.

He had everything he wanted: an excellent wife and mother to his so-far three children; three distinctively individual little ones; and work that left him depleted, rethinking decisions and wishing for more skill and knowledge, but also firm in the certainty that every day he did all the good he could for others. He was blessed beyond measure. The thought humbled him as nothing else could have.

And what better moment to consider his blessings than Christmastime? *You, Sir, who made the lame to walk and the blind to see,* he thought with gratitude. *You, Sir, are the Great Physician. Please always be a lamp unto my feet or, maybe more needful for me, a lamp unto my hands.* He didn't think the Lord would mind a slight alteration in the text.

When they arrived at the charming pastel blue house, Josh asked the jarvey to wait and got a cheerful tip of the hat in response. *And look at that*—Mr. Paul stood in the open doorway, almost as if he were expecting a visitor. Maybe he was.

"I hope I am not interfering with your schedule," Josh said by way of greeting. He held out the invitation, writing done neatly by Janey and folded into Millie's drawing.

"Do come in. I always have time for a guest," Mr. Paul said and led him into the sunny sitting room Josh knew he wanted for his own. "Would you like some tea? A biscuit, perhaps?"

"I wouldn't presume to take up your time," Josh said, still holding the invitation. "This is for you, sir."

Mr. Paul took it, unfolded Millie's drawing, and nodded. Josh looked over his shoulder. "Mrs. Crenshaw asked the children to help her. Millie was determined not to be left out."

Mr. Paul held out the drawing. "She is your youngest, Surgeon Crenshaw?"

Josh nodded and took a better look at Millie's art. Janey had spent careful time on a drawing for the carpenter's widow who was also to be invited, after Timothy had claimed the gunnery sergeant because, as he insisted, it was "manly." Millie had done her best for Mr. Paul.

"She has a lot to learn about stick figures," Josh joked, and Mr. Paul chuckled. "Look at that, will you? She gave you a halo. Megs—er, Margaret— has been reading from the book of St. Luke lately, and I think Millie is impressed with angels. You know, the sort who bring good tidings of great joy."

"I know," Mr. Paul said. He held the drawing closer for a better look. "Who minds a halo? And there's a ship. Is that yours?"

"I believe it is, right next to this house, apparently, if the blue paint is any indication. Millie likes to pack a lot of action into a small sheet of paper."

"I'll treasure it more than you know, Surgeon Crenshaw." Mr. Paul read the invitation. "How kind of you to invite me to Christmas dinner. I accept with pleasure. Two of the clock tomorrow?"

"Aye, sir. Megs included directions." Perhaps he should warn Mr. Paul. "There will also be an old gunnery sergeant and the widow of a ship's carpenter, sir. Megs likes to invite people who might otherwise be alone. Her father, may he rest in peace, gave her a list a few years ago of former shipmates and widows who have fallen on hard times, whether through the loss of loved ones or penury. She likes to help them."

"I've heard that from others," Mr. Paul said.

"Really, sir? I didn't know you knew this shire."

"I'm here and there," he replied with a vague wave that took in Devon and Cornwall or possibly the known universe. "I have also heard good reports of you, sir, of medicine above and beyond the call of duty."

"Me?" Josh asked in surprise. "Medicine is a *profession* above and beyond that call, sir."

"Not for everyone." Mr. Paul gave Josh a deferential nod. "I can tell I am embarrassing you. Would you like to look around again? I have the feeling that is also why you are here."

"You found me out, sir. I'll confine my interest to this cheerful room, however."

"Be my guest."

He took another glance around, wishing he could have bought the place for Margaret but resigning himself. What was the point in languishing over something that wouldn't happen?

"You're having a difficult time, aren't you, Surgeon?"

It was a quiet question. Josh could have temporized and denied, then demanded to know how Mr. Paul knew of his turmoil and what business was it of his. Instead, Josh told Mr. Paul the whole story, from his love for the daughter of a bosun to his family's horror at his own descent down the social ladder to the heavy-handed way the darling of his heart had been deceived by someone who was supposed to legally look after her interests while Josh was away.

"We haven't lost our Plymouth house, thank goodness," he concluded. "I'll have to figure out how to sell the house in Paignton. It wasn't her choice. The matter has left her humiliated." He sighed. "I'm just grateful we had an extraordinarily short passage around Cape Horn and I arrived here to make sure our Plymouth house hadn't been sold yet." He shook his head over that. "Even my profane captain called that passage a miracle."

Mr. Paul smiled at that disclosure.

For what he knew had to be the last time, Josh admired the pale-yellow walls, the lace curtains, and the cheerful coal fire in the grate. He warned himself not to start mentally placing his own furniture in the better-furnished room, because that was folly. Better to simply enjoy the view one more time.

He would have succeeded, if he hadn't taken the time to look out the window at the sight of the ocean, his second home. A mariner could be content in such a place, knowing the Channel was close by. *Stop it, Josh*, he advised himself.

He turned to leave, and there was Mr. Paul, still looking so naggingly familiar. Should he say anything? Why not? The man would be his guest tomorrow, and that would likely be that. He had said he was only here as a sort of caretaker until the real owners arrived.

"Mr. Paul, do I know you?" he asked.

"I don't think we have met," Mr. Paul said, then qualified himself. "Perhaps not in person. There are other ways to meet."

"It's just that I feel quite comfortable in your presence, as though I know you," Josh explained. "Maybe it is because you put me at my ease." He couldn't help his own embarrassed grin. "You let me unload family burdens on you. It's a physician's skill I continue to work on."

Mr. Paul shrugged his service off. "I used to be an impatient fellow, hurrying about, a man with never enough time to work good or ill, and I did my share of both."

"You, sir?"

"Heavens, if you only knew. I'm a better man than I used to be. I do have an old friend, long retired, who was a physician and quite the storyteller. You should have seen him and *his* bedside manner."

"It's an accomplished skill," Josh agreed. He held out his hand. "We look forward to hosting you tomorrow. We'll be a little crowded around our table, but what is that to anyone?"

"I'm looking forward to it," Mr. Paul said as they shook hands.

The good feeling lingered on the ride home. He enjoyed the leisure, perhaps even the sheer pleasure, of being alone, with no one clamoring for his help. He mused on Mr. Paul's considering anything Josh did as extraordinary. That was the nature of medicine. Perhaps Mr. Paul's physician friend could explain that to him.

As for Margaret, Josh knew she was extraordinary. He strongly suspected that when he returned home, more than half of those lovely Christmas biscuits the children had iced yesterday would already be in the hands of other people who needed to be remembered at Christmas.

In Plymouth, he paid his driver and walked the few blocks to his house, still relishing the feeling of well-earned idleness. His good cheer abandoned him when he turned the corner of Motte and Charter and saw Lucinda's carriage in front of his house. He walked faster, then broke into a run.

CHAPTER NINE

HE NEEDN'T HAVE WORRIED.

Josh opened the front door, tiptoed down the corridor, and peeked into the sitting room. He saw the joy of his heart buttressed by their children as his sister shook a finger in Megs's face and Cornelius stood by, watching. Josh knew by the sadness in Megs's eyes that his obnoxious sister had just served another mean supper.

"The house we selected for you in Paignton is far better than any house in shabby Salcombe," Lucy raged. "You must trust us to look after your interests."

"I think you had better leave, Aunt Lucy. Mama isn't interested."

Bravo, Timothy, Josh thought, impressed with his young son.

Janey looked equally determined. "Aunt Lucy, we like it here in Plymouth," she told her aunt with a firmness that belied her eight years. They were their mother's loyal defenders, his children. He need never fear for any of them while he was away, not with this sort of competence.

"Lucinda, we made ourselves quite clear yesterday," Josh said, walking into the sitting room. "We'll remain here in Plymouth for the foreseeable future."

Cornelius sprang to life, rounding on his brother. "Why can't you see that the house in Paignton is better for all of you?" he asked. He did everything but stamp his feet in frustration.

Cornelius genuinely didn't understand. Josh began to feel sorry for him, this brother of his with a distinguished career in litigation and pots of money and a wife who barely tolerated him. *Poor Corny.* "Don't worry, Brother," Josh said in his most soothing voice. "We haven't lost our minds. It's just not the house Margaret chose. She knows how I like Salcombe; you didn't. We'll sell that house in Paignton."

Corny delivered what he obviously hoped was his best shot. "The housing market is poor right now. You'll be years finding a buyer."

"We'll manage." It was easy to seem calm; he *felt* calm. They would manage.

Lucinda felt no soothing calm, apparently. "You're being unreasonable! We are offering you and your . . . your . . ."

"My wife?" he asked. "The pretty, intelligent woman who married me?" He should know better than to egg on his sister, but he couldn't resist. Ah, the joys of being the pesky little brother.

". . . your wife the chance to move into a better society, you ninny! People will forget her origins eventually, if we do this right."

"Margaret's father was the best bosun a captain could wish for, Lucy." Josh reminded himself no one spoke loudly in his house, and he wasn't going to be the one who broke the rule. Besides, his sister was frightening Millie, whose lips trembled. "Hush, Lucy. I'm not being unreasonable. I'm making a successful marriage even better. I wish you could see that."

"Here we are, trying to raise your wife in the eyes of our circle, and you are all resisting!"

He could tell from the tone of her voice that Lucinda had delivered her last chain shot over the bow of the good ship Joshua Crenshaw. "She doesn't need raising, Lucy," he said gently. "You've worked yourself into a lather over nothing. We don't need your help. Find another project. This one is over. Good day to you both."

What could they do? He ushered his frustrated brother and his furious sister from the sitting room, wished them a happy Christmas as he hurried them down the corridor, and closed the door after them.

Millie, her finger in her mouth, had followed him into the foyer. Her eyes were filled with tears, she radiated distress, and she had come to him for comfort. He knelt and opened his arms wide. With a sigh that went straight to his heart, she fell into them. He picked her up.

"We are well, daughter," he whispered in her ear. "You don't ever have to see them again."

She put a hand on each side of his face, searching his eyes. "Never?"

"Never," he assured her. "We'll trust Mama to keep them away, if I am not here, and Timothy and Janey."

He held her close, enjoying the softness of her curls against his neck. "Papa?"

"Mmm?"

"I won't hit you again."

"That's a relief, daughter, as I plan to show up here now and then and will be in Mama's bed."

"She doesn't mind?"

"Not at all."

"I'm not certain which of you has made a conquest," Margaret said as he walked into the sitting room, Millie secure in his embrace. He held out his arm to his wife, and she hugged him too, to be joined quickly by Timothy and Janey.

"It was a mutual conquest, I believe. Of all people, Megs, you know I am irresistible to women."

He meant it as a tease, but his wife only held him tighter. Joined with his whole family after so long away, Surgeon Joshua Crenshaw, Royal Navy, knew that all he wanted for Christmas was for Boney to come apart in Russia and begin a slow decline. He hoped his wish wasn't too much of a martial nature to desire at Christmas. If things went badly for Boney, maybe in a year or two he could leave the navy and start that medical practice in Salcombe, providing they found a house there.

"Am I the only one who is famished and wants a butter-and-jam sandwich in about the worst way?" Timothy asked—practical Timothy, who was a lion when it came to defending his mother.

They needed no other urging. Margaret gestured her older stalwarts toward the kitchen but remained with Josh as he set Millie down. She teetered between staying or following the herd, then hurried down the corridor, demanding strawberry jam in that commanding voice of hers. Had she been a lad, Josh would have predicted a career on a quarterdeck for her.

Megs collapsed onto the sofa, fanning herself with her hand. Josh sat beside her, then patted his lap. She took the hint. "I didn't suspect my odious relatives would do that," he said. "I'm sorry you had to bear the brunt."

"It was Timothy," she said, making herself comfortable in his lap, her head against his chest. "Janey and I had taken the invitations to the Barbican—both Gunny and Mrs. Colyer will be here tomorrow, by the way—and Timothy was alone with Millie when they invaded."

"Our Timothy? The one who gets nervous about thunderstorms?"

"That Timothy. When we came home, he had served his aunt and uncle tea and was listening politely as your sister harangued him." She kissed Josh. "He reminded me rather forcefully of you, oh courteous man who stole my heart."

"What a family I have."

Trust Megs. "Yes, you do," she said. "Will you read Luke chapter two tonight, or shall I?"

Cook didn't complain when supper turned into bread and jam, then more bread drizzled with treacle because the man of the house liked it. In honor of Grandfather Murphy, whom all of them were missing, Megs allowed grog, well-diluted with water for those eight and younger. Millie made a face at it. Mrs. Simpson also served lobscouse to give the Royal Navy its full due.

To cap off the meal before they all grew too silly, Mama produced rout cakes. "I bought these yesterday and hid them in that empty lard tin in the scullery," she said, then smiled at her son. "Ha! Fooled you, Timothy!" In an aside to Josh, she added, "Your son will nearly commit felonies for these. In that too he reminds me forcefully of you."

Luke chapter two went down easily in the sitting room. "I've read it two Christmas Eves in a row," Megs said as she handed him the family Bible. Her eyes had a faraway look. "My father read it last winter, God rest him. Thanks to good winds and divine Providence, you are here to read it tonight."

"I wish I were here every Christmas Eve," he said, touched to his very soul. He opened the Bible and turned to that chapter of chapters. He cleared his throat. "'And it came to pass in those days, that there went out a decree from Caesar Augustus, that all the world should be taxed.'"

He let Timothy and Janey take turns. His daughter finished with "'And Jesus increased in wisdom and stature, and in favour with God and man.'" She closed the book with satisfaction.

"Two more verses, Janey," he said. Millie had fallen asleep on his lap, and her warmth was making him drowsy. Or maybe it was the grog. "Turn to Luke chapter fourteen, thirteen and fourteen, and tell me who this reminds you of."

She did as he said. He saw her read it silently first, then smile. "'But when thou makest a feast, call the poor, the maimed, the lame, the blind.'" She glanced at her mother. "'And thou shalt be blessed; for they cannot recompense thee: for thou shalt be recompensed at the resurrection of the just.' It's Mama, isn't it?"

Josh couldn't resist a little unholy glee to see his wife's eyes brim with tears. "No one but Mama."

Practical Timothy chimed in. "I know Gunnery Sergeant Boyce has one leg, and I think Mrs. Colyer is rather poor, if she lives in only one room. Who is blind?"

They couldn't come up with anyone. Josh didn't think it prudent to suggest Uncle Corny and Aunt Lucinda were the blind ones.

"Maimed?" Timothy asked, literal as always.

"Papa, that's quite a scar on your cheek," Janey said. "Are you maimed?"

They all laughed, Josh the loudest. "An Esquimau I met at a Russian trading post last year told me to spread bear grease on the wound." He shrugged. "I ran out of bear grease."

"Papa's too handsome to be called maimed," Megs said. "We'll give that one a rest, shall we?"

Everyone agreed. They settled into that peaceful mode that reading from Luke, the beloved physician, left behind.

Janey stirred. "I was going to be angry with Aunt Lucy and Uncle Cornelius forever for what they said." She looked down to contemplate the carpet until she gained control of her voice. "Now I just feel sorry for them. They don't know what we have, do they?" She was quick, but Josh already knew that.

Bravo, Janey, Josh thought. *You do understand that sort of blindness.* "No, and more's the pity. Go along to bed. Take Millie. I'll tuck Mama in."

She hesitated, then whispered into his ear. "Papa, that scripture is you too, not just Mama."

CHAPTER TEN

JOSH DIDN'T KNOW WHAT TO expect on Christmas morning in a household of young ones. The best part was to wake up his beauty with the tousled hair and give her a kiss.

"Happy Christmas, Mrs. Crenshaw. My, but your hair is a mess," he teased.

"That is entirely your fault, and you know it," she reminded him as she smoothed it down. "Happy Christmas to you, my love." She settled into his arms. "Last Christmas you were somewhere along the North American coast, were you not?"

"We were near a Russian settlement," he said. "Everyone seems to want a piece of that continent, Britannia included. The Americans are a bothersome lot though. They have established a fort at the mouth of the Columbia River. I predict trouble."

"Exotic locales."

"This is better. When does the herd get up?"

"Oh, you! Any moment."

Megs was right. Soon all three of their children sat on their bed, looking hopeful. The tableau was complete when Josh heard a thump-tap and peered in the doorway to see Grace, also looking hopeful.

"I'm impressed," he said. "Perseverance is an excellent quality in a hound and a Crenshaw. Timothy, take Grace downstairs. Mrs. Simpson will supply you with some Christmas roast I have been smelling for an hour or two. You young ladies go downstairs to the sitting room, and we will follow. Roundly, now!"

Blank stares.

"Come, come. That means move along smartly, in my navy."

Josh and Megs came downstairs in half an hour to find three remarkably well-behaved children in the sitting room. Josh smiled to see the garland of wooden beads adorning the mantelpiece, the loops haphazard. Last year's wreath was squared away nicely over the fireplace, if a little worse for wear from the packing crate. Rain spattered the windows, but that was Plymouth.

Megs went into the scullery and returned with a wicker basket of presents. It looked modest to Josh's eyes but not to his children's. They leaned forward.

"Oldest or youngest?" Megs asked.

The children consulted. "Oldest," Janey said. "Papa goes first."

He didn't expect that. It was enough to be in the orbit of these lovely beings he had created with their mother, and to know everyone was well-dressed, warm, and housed, even if the house was getting crowded. *Let me just sit here and absorb the very sight of you,* he wanted to say. *Then I'll go to the tedium and danger of the blockade with a true heart.*

"Very well," he said instead and held out his hand.

Millie did the honors, slapping a small package into his hand with the same vigor she had used to black his eye. Millie was the adamant type. He opened it and nodded to see a dip pen.

"Mama says you have to write ever so many scripts and reports," Janey explained. "We did chores for it."

"I'll think of you every time I use this," he said, "which will be at least several times a day."

"My turn." Margaret handed him a package wrapped in brown paper. He opened it and pulled out two canvas bibbed aprons. "These look sturdier than the ones the Navy Board allocates," he said, fingering the fabric. "Thank you."

"I hate that you need them, but I know you do," she told him. "May all your surgeries be successful."

"Mama next," Janey declared, and Timothy did the honors, handing her another small package.

Megs whooped when out slithered silk stockings, and garters that looked like someone's first sewing effort, possibly Jane's.

"Uncle Corny let me sweep out his office and empty his ash cans," Timothy said. He held up his hand. "I know, I know, Mama. You sent us there to work for free, but he wouldn't hear of it."

Josh laughed, but not too loud, because Megs was obviously weighing the merits of silk stockings against the virtue of a good deed. The stockings won out, to his delight. This gave him some hope for his gift to her.

The children's gifts from Margaret were the practical kind: a book for Janey, a waistcoat for Timothy, and new shoes for Millie. He doubted his wife ever wasted a copper in her household expenses. He wondered what she would do when he handed out his presents, the sorts of things a seafaring man trots home. Might as well begin.

He didn't have a package for Margaret's gift, just a twist or two of brown paper. "Here, love. This is from Brazil, where we took on water and scraped the hull of barnacles."

She untwisted the brown paper and spread it out on her lap. Her intake of breath said it all. She touched the green gem as if it were alive, then turned astonished eyes on him. "This couldn't possibly be . . ."

"It is," he informed her. "We were in Belém, on the Pará River. A lot of amazing things come downriver."

"I doubt it floated like Moses in the bulrushes," Megs said, her voice hushed. She picked up the exquisitely cut emerald and turned it this way and that. "Dear me. We're not as poor as church mice, but how on earth could you afford . . . ?"

He had her now. "My dear, you would be amazed how grateful a couple can be when someone delivers a child after four years of failure." He saw the whole thing again, the pushing, the straining, the agony of a misplaced baby struggling to live. He had small enough hands. "I really didn't expect this though."

"You amaze me, husband," she said simply and kissed him. She whispered in his ear then. "Let us consider taking this to Carter and Brustein and using it to counterbalance some of the expense of that house in Paignton."

She was right, of course. "We'll think about it, Margaret."

He had dragged in the children's presents, save Janey's, late last night from the storeroom behind the house, where the garden tools were stashed, to the scullery. There wasn't any way to wrap Timothy's gift. Josh went to retrieve it and hauled it in from the scullery, Mrs. Simpson following him because she couldn't believe her eyes, either.

The gasps said it all. He spread out the gigantic bearskin with massive head attached. Grace started to growl and then bark as she tapped and thumped her way to make her last stand between the beast's head and the children.

"Brave pooch! It's yours, Timothy. The island of Kodiak specializes in Ursa Major such as I have never seen," he told his son. "I won it in a game of whist. Too many card players don't understand basic mathematics."

Eyes wide, his son threw himself down on the bearskin. "Hush, Grace," he said. "It won't bite."

"You can't possibly top that, my love," Margaret said.

"No, I can't. Well, let me try." He had brought a package wrapped in sailcloth down from their bedchamber and now handed it to Jane. "It's more in the nature of a future gift, dearest," he said.

Carefully, his daughter unfolded the sailcloth and stared down at her lap. He knew *he* had never seen such beautiful white brocade. "Oh, Papa," she said, and it said the world.

Margaret put her arm around Jane's shoulder. "My love, I know you think boys are odious now, but someday you'll have the most beautiful wedding dress in Devonshire." She turned to Josh. "What amazing thing did you do for this?"

"There was a Russian count at Yakutat Colony, who had recently traded in China. His leg was broken in a logging accident. Compound fracture. I set it. Simple."

"Thank you, Papa," Jane said, "but setting a compound fracture, simple?"

"Never more so," he told her. It had been simple. Count Borochin's valet had poured the contents of a silver flask down the count's throat and held him close, and the matter had moved quickly enough. The count had been very grateful. "We were docked at Yakutat, and I went ashore. No rolling fire from the guns. The operating table wasn't shifting about, and I wasn't slipping in . . . well, I wasn't slipping."

His children looked at each other, their faces serious. Maybe he had said too much. Delivering a baby was one thing, rough-and-ready surgery in wartime quite another. "It's what I do," he said simply, then clapped his hands together. "Now, I did pay for this lovely thing. Feast your eyes, Millicent."

He held out a beaver pelt, a dark one, round and supple because it had been tanned by Tlingits. He handed it to Millie, her mouth a perfect *o* in amazement. His heart turned over as she rubbed the pelt against her cheek, then climbed onto his lap and arranged the pelt against his chest. She leaned back and closed her eyes. His arms went around her. "You can think of me, Millie, after Mama tucks you in at night," he whispered. "I won't be that far away, will I? Not with this."

He couldn't look at Margaret, because he heard her sniff. To his relief, someone knocked on the door.

"Ah! Dinner guests," he said. "Let us clear away our spoils and think of others, children."

Janey and Timothy scrambled to drag the bearskin behind the sofa as Margaret went to the door. Millie stayed where she was. She patted the beaver pelt, then patted Josh's cheek. He was in heaven, or as near as. Christmas couldn't possibly get better.

CHAPTER ELEVEN

GUNNERY SERGEANT BOYCE CAME INTO the sitting room, following Margaret and escorting Mrs. Colyer, whose cheeks were red from the cold wind. Her hands too. *What, no gloves?* Josh glanced at his wife, whose eyes were also on Mrs. Colyer's bare hands. He knew in his heart the widow wouldn't leave that way.

He had met Gunny years ago at a Christmas dinner before he and Margaret married. The man had been a bluff and hearty Royal Marine gunner, with a wife equally engaging. Later he had lost a leg in some nameless fleet action and then the engaging wife a few years after that. Now Gunny smiled and held out his hand, but the bravado was gone. War could do that; so could grief.

My, but Josh's older children were well-trained. Timothy took coats and hats. Millie watched suspiciously, not convinced the strangers came with good intentions. Josh knew she would grow and change under her mother's tutelage.

He took Margaret's hand and kissed it. "You are one in a million," he told her, which brought a light to Gunny's eyes.

"Her father was too," the gunnery sergeant said. "I never met a better bosun. Order out of chaos was his specialty."

"As it is my wife's," Josh said. "The apple didn't fall far from that tree."

"Hold her close, lad; hold her close," Gunny told him, sadness resurfacing.

Margaret smiled and moved ahead with his other guests toward the breakfast room, since they had no real dining room in their little house.

Josh answered the next knock on the door, and there stood Mr. Paul. "Happy Christmas to you, sir," Josh said. "Do come in."

"I appreciate the invitation." Mr. Paul looked around. "It's a cozy house."

"That is an adroit euphemism, sir. We're starting to stumble about under-foot," Josh joked. "The sitting room is full of an enormous bearskin I won in a game of whist, and my little'un won't let go of a beaver pelt I gave her."

"Did your wife like the emerald?"

Josh thought he made a creditable show of not staring at Mr. Paul. How did he know about the emerald? He smiled and nodded, then decided he must have mentioned something yesterday afternoon, when he had unburdened himself in Salcombe.

You are too young to be so forgetful, Josh chided himself. "She was properly impressed." It was easy to smile at the memory. "She even teared up a little."

He leaned toward Mr. Paul. "She is insisting I take the emerald to Carter and Brustein and leave it as a surety for a portion of that whopping sum we owe for the Paignton house."

"The one no one except your relatives wants?"

Josh knew he had mentioned that and felt himself to be on sure footing again. "The very one. I suppose she is right. It would solve part of the problem. Still, a man would like to give his wife fine things now and then." He realized then how little he knew about his guest. "Are you married, Mr. Paul?"

"Heavens no. I'd be a thorn in any woman's side with all the traveling I do."

They enjoyed a quiet laugh together, then walked into the breakfast room because Margaret beckoned them.

Dinner was a delight. The beef roast was perfection, and Mrs. Simpson had an equal knack for Yorkshire pudding. Grace thump-tapped her way into the room, sniffing the air, then found a spot by Millie, where food tended to get flung about. Josh winked at Margaret at the other end of the table when Gunny started to tell sea stories. The glumness left the gunnery sergeant as he remembered fleet actions, travel in the Orient, bartering with South Sea natives for coconuts, and helping serve the guns at the Battle of the Nile, his last fleet action.

"Papa was at Trafalgar," Janey announced. "That was a big'un."

"I don't have any glamorous stories," Josh assured them. "I was below-decks as usual, tending to the wounded." *There's no glamour on an orlop deck*, he wanted to assure them—only pain and blood and second-guessing decisions and knowing that whatever he did, it would never be enough. Still, he wouldn't trade it for the glory of the quarterdeck. His was quiet work, even if his own brother and sister thought it lowly.

He glanced at Mr. Paul, who was regarding him with something close to sympathy, which he knew he did not want. He could head it off. "Mr. Paul, you mentioned you travel, yes? It's hard to do when war restricts us, but you seem like a man of the world."

Mr. Paul smiled faintly at that. "I made a few voyages in the Mediterranean a long time ago. Was shipwrecked several times."

"Gor!" Timothy exclaimed. "Were you frightened?"

"We were too busy trying to avoid the rocks and contrary currents," their dinner guest told them. Mr. Paul looked at his host. "You, Surgeon? Ever shipwrecked?"

Interested faces, especially young ones, turned his way, expecting stories as exciting as Gunny's, stories of firing down from the tops of masts onto enemy decks. *Why are you doing this?* Josh wanted to ask his guest. *I'm just a surgeon.*

"I know you have a story," Mr. Paul suggested. "Maybe it's time to tell it."

How would you know anything like that? was on the tip of Josh's tongue. There sat his children, expecting something grandiose, some sign that their father, too often gone, was more than the quiet fellow who showed up, loved them, and left too soon.

"I do have a story," he said, surprising himself. Even Margaret leaned forward, interested. He had always tried to shield his family. Maybe he should say no more.

He glanced at Mr. Paul, who nodded and said, "It's time."

"I was in the Mediterranean, too, Mr. Paul." Josh closed his eyes, remembering the heat and the noise of battle. They wanted a story. He had a story.

"It was the *Casus Belli*," Mr. Paul said.

How did he know? "Aye, I was surgeon on the *Casus Belli*," he began. "My first voyage as a surgeon."

"I had no idea," Sergeant Boyce said. "I've heard rumors . . ."

"Believe them. We had bested the French, but we were sinking, and the pumps couldn't keep up." He glanced at Megs, whose hand had gone to her throat, her eyes troubled. "Don't worry, Megs. I survived," he said, which made the guests chuckle.

"The captain told me to put the wounded into two jolly boats, which were tied to the stern of the *Casus Belli*."

"Why, Papa?" Timothy asked.

"Captain Boothe knew I couldn't get them out in time if the ship sank. This way, they would already be in the boats."

Why was Mr. Paul doing this to him? He didn't want to remember the awful heat and the groans of the wounded. He sighed. Apparently it was his story to tell. "We lashed the jolly boats together, and I moved from one boat to the other, tending the wounded." He smiled. "I fell in once. That was embarrassing."

He hoped his little ones would laugh at the thought of Papa floundering in the water, but their faces were serious.

"When the *Casus Belli* sank, we took on as many sailors as we could without swamping the little boats. Others crowded into the cutter, and the rest grabbed on to spars and deck covers and floated." He shook his head, unable to continue.

Sergeant Boyce took up the story. "Everyone in the fleet has heard rumors. You were there! As I heard it, a French corsair—privateer to you young ones—took the *Casus Belli* crew for ransom and made them prisoners in Turkey, except for your father and his floating hospital." He shrugged. "No one wanted them. They left them to drift and die. So it really happened."

"It did."

"I would have helped," Janey spoke up. "Papa, I would have!"

"I do not doubt it, daughter," he said. "I see it in your eyes."

Margaret nodded. "So would I," she said, her voice soft. "My love, you never told me this story."

"No. It's too hard." They deserved to hear it though. "We floated for a week, somewhere south of Malta." He took a deep breath. "I lost only two patients, but I believe they would have perished anyway. A surgeon can only do so much." *But oh, how I tried*, he wanted to add, then realized he had spoken out loud.

His anguish hung in the air. Margaret left her place at the end of their crowded table, nudged his hip, and sat beside him on his chair. Millie's eyes grew big with worry.

"Janey, hold Millie, will you?" Josh asked.

"But what happened? I have to know," Timothy demanded.

"Thanks be to God, it rained," he said simply as Megs smoothed his hair. "We lay there and felt such relief. In the morning, the *Agamemnon* found us."

"And the prisoners of the Turks?" It was Mrs. Colyer, the quiet lady with chapped hands who spoke then. Even in his own misery, Josh couldn't help noticing that Gunny had draped his arm around her shoulders. "What happened to them?"

"The rich paid ransoms, and the rest died," Sergeant Boyce concluded. "It was an ugly business." Josh noticed the martial light that used to glitter in the gunnery sergeant's eyes was back. "The government wanted to hush it up. Seems someone at Whitehall was negotiating with the Turks about something or other and didn't want people back home to know. Until now, I've heard only rumors."

"That is my story, children," he added. "Maybe I should have told you sooner. My other stories are easier to bear. I'll tell them to you later, if you'd like."

They were all silent. He saw Cook standing in the doorway with Polly, the scullery maid, and the maid of all work close by. "As you were, men," he teased with a smile. His servants laughed and went about their duties.

He felt a load had been lifted from his heart. Why had he ever thought to keep his war a secret? That was the worst story of all, and he had never told it. True, the government had cautioned silence, but the matter was long over and done.

"Without men like your father, the navy would have ground to a halt years ago," Gunny said, breaking the silence. He chuckled and tapped his wooden leg. "Hear that? A busy surgeon saved my life and let me fight again another day." He pointed at Josh. "He's a good'un, and don't any of you lubbers forget."

Bless Margaret Crenshaw. She somehow managed to reroute the conversation and take it into the sitting room, where Mrs. Simpson served them Christmas pudding. Everyone played parlor games until the gunnery sergeant looked at his timepiece and slapped his head.

"Time's passing!" he said. "Mrs. Colyer, may I walk you home?"

"We will summon a conveyance," Margaret said.

"What say you, Mrs. Colyer? Will ye trust yourself to a one-legged Royal Marine?" Sergeant Boyce asked, his eyes lively. "I feel like walking. It's a fair night."

"Aye, aye," the widow replied.

Josh went for their coats, Margaret beside him. "Here." She handed him her own mittens from the closet. "Give these to Mrs. Colyer, and don't take no for an answer. I can knit myself another pair."

They waved Gunny and Mrs. Colyer off.

Mr. Paul shook hands all around and tipped his hat to them. "It was a good Christmas," he said.

"Thank you for sharing it with us," Josh replied. "Perhaps we will see you again soon. How much longer are you caretaking that lovely house?"

"Alas, my stay here is over, as of tomorrow," Mr. Paul told Josh and Megs. "I believe the new owners will take possession then."

"I hope they treat it well," Margaret said.

"I have no doubt they will. I have enjoyed this little foray into Plymouth," he said, as he started down the front steps. "I don't get out as often as I'd like, and we have to take turns."

"We?" Josh asked. Mr. Paul had a confounding way of saying little about himself.

"It's an interesting organization," their guest replied. "We seem to be busiest at Christmas. Why that is, I sometimes wonder."

"People are on their best behavior?" Margaret ventured.

"Perhaps," Mr. Paul agreed. He took Margaret's hand in his, and then Josh's, joining them together in a gesture as intimate as it was kind beyond measure. "But I suspect you two are fundamentally the same all year around."

"And boring, I suppose," Josh said with a laugh. "We're regular as clockwork."

Mr. Paul bowed to them and set off down the street.

"We didn't order him a conveyance, and Salcombe is so far," Margaret said. "I see a carriage." She squinted into the darkness. "They're hard to find on a day like this. He's fortunate."

Yes, isn't he? Josh thought. *Mr. Paul, just who are you?*

"Let's get our monsters to bed, Surgeon Crenshaw," Megs said. Arm in arm, they went inside. "I would like you to brush my hair tonight."

"Mrs. Crenshaw, what an excellent idea."

CHAPTER TWELVE

BOXING DAY MEANT NO ONE had to do anything early. Last night, Margaret had given the servants the day off, with her thanks and gifts of coins in little boxes. True to her nature, Cook wouldn't leave without boiling eggs and making buns so no one would perish with hunger on her watch.

The luxury of cuddling Megs was only exceeded by her comment, whispered into Josh's chest, that he didn't call out in his sleep or mutter last night.

"Do I do that often?" he asked, surprised.

"All the time," was her quiet answer. "Not last night."

He considered the matter and wondered. Something had happened yesterday, above and beyond Christmas. Or maybe it was part of Christmas, a part he had never experienced before. He had been touched by the oddest sort of grace, something he thought to be reserved only for dusty sermons and arguments among clergymen.

He couldn't define or explain it, except that he felt whole this morning. He wanted the feeling to last. A glance at Margaret—she had returned to sleep—further convinced Josh that his wife already knew more about grace than most, by the way she lived her life doing good, even with modest means, because that was all she had. Hers was not a life of luxury such as the unhappy Lucinda Nearing possessed. Rather, it was a life well-lived.

He also understood for the first time that the size of the deed wasn't important. He knew his sister, Lucy, contributed regularly to the shire's poorhouse, because she trumpeted the matter about. Megs Crenshaw did the small deed: the mittens last night to Mrs. Colyer; some of the leftovers to Gunnery Sergeant Boyce, who was not in straitened circumstances but who was no cook; the extra sandwich to the worker last week who cleaned a drain; words of kindness to all and sundry. He could only imagine all Megs did when he wasn't around, which was too often, but that was war.

She had settled on that house in Salcombe, partly because she knew how much he liked that little village and partly, he surmised, because she felt at home in a modest place among working people. He had married no social climber, no Society mushroom trying to push in where she wasn't wanted. He had married an ordinary woman, even a lower-class one, in other's eyes. Lying there, hands behind his head, staring at the ceiling, he understood as never before the ineffable essence of love. If there was a more fortunate man anywhere, Josh Crenshaw had no idea whom he could possibly be.

He lay there in complete comfort until he heard Grace's thump-tap outside the bedchamber door, followed by the hopeful flap-flap of a revolving tail. He got up quietly and took his medical satchel with him. Dressing gown on, he scooped up the little dog with the big paws and went downstairs, forgetting which treads squeaked because he wasn't there all that often.

To the kitchen the pair of them went, which meant Grace's tail started revolving faster. "Very well," he said and pilfered some leftover roast from the scullery. "You realize January is going to be more lean, don't you? Scraps? Eggs?"

Grace was an enthusiastic opportunist. Her breakfast complete, she offered no objection to his removing the butter knife splint and retooling her front leg with more layers of bandage. "I dare you to bend that," he said as he set her down, then watched in satisfaction as she limped about. "Give it a month. I'll inform my children."

"Papa, we'll . . . we'll stand the watch when you're away." Timothy sat beside him, rubbing his eyes. "Is that the right expression?"

"More than you know," Josh said, pulling Timothy close.

They sat together, saying nothing, just long enough to remind Josh how much he was going to miss his children once his ship took its place in the blockade.

"Was Christmas merry enough for you, son?" he asked finally.

Timothy nodded. "No one I know has a bearskin rug. I even slept on it last night."

"I did that a night or two aboard ship when the weather turned really cold."

"Papa?"

"Aye, son?"

"Were you afraid in those jolly boats?"

Was he? It was a good question. "I was at first. Some of the men were so ill."

"I mean were you afraid for yourself?"

"I didn't have time beyond the constant fear I have, even now, that I will never know enough." Josh wasn't certain such an answer was within the scope of a six-year-old, who lived in an ordered world where not much went wrong, not with Margaret Crenshaw at the helm. He knew his son was learning confidence in such a home. He knew there was a balance between confidence and courage. "If you are ever in such a place as I was then, I am certain you will do the right thing."

"Really, Papa?"

"Aye, really."

Josh gave the lad buns and boiled eggs lightly salted next, a wise move when philosophers are only six. Their discussion of what to do on a day of unbridled leisure lasted as long as a stroll into the sitting room to light a fire in the grate. Josh looked up at the mantelpiece and saw a letter.

"I didn't notice this last night," Josh said as he picked it up. "Did you?"

"No, Papa. Who is it for?"

"For me and your mother."

"Should I get her?"

"I hate to bother a sleeping wife," Josh said, which made Timothy grin. "I'll open it. It's probably a thank-you note from Mrs. Simpson for the coins."

He didn't recognize the handwriting. He read the note, blanched, read it again, and had to sit down. "Better get your mother," he told Timothy in a voice he was unfamiliar with.

Apparently Timothy was unfamiliar with it too. "Papa?" he asked, and Josh heard the fear in his voice.

It was fear easily put to pasture. "No worries, Timothy. Something interesting is going on. Get Mama."

Josh stared at the note, a smile on his face. The scientific side of his brain assured him that what he was thinking was impossible, even though he already had his suspicions. The other side reminded him anything was possible at Christmas, at least if that scientific side would jettison its skepticism.

He heard Margaret on the stairs, missing all the squeaky treads because she knew them. "Josh?"

"In the sitting room."

He held out the letter to his woman with bare feet and hair wild around her head. Timothy must have communicated something dire, because she usually put on shoes. "What's wrong?"

"Read it. No fears."

She took the letter and reacted precisely as he had done, with the addition of tears. "Mr. Paul said this about me? How can he possibly know?" she asked.

He shrugged and pointed to the next paragraph. "That is impossible," she said in a voice indicating she knew that yes, it was impossible, but oh, suppose it was not.

Timothy looked over her arm. "Mama, I can't read that writing. Who is it from? Please read it to me."

"From Mr. Paul," she said. She took several deep breaths. "He does have awful handwriting. Here goes." She cleared her throat. "What a strange way to begin a letter."

"Not so strange," Josh said. "I've read letters like this before. You have too."

"*Mr. Paul, a member of an organization especially busy at yuletide, writing to Surgeon Joshua and Margaret Crenshaw, residing in a small house on Motte Street in the town of Plymouth, in the year of our Lord 1811. Greetings and happy Christmas! I wish I could visit in person, but I have another call to make in Devonshire.*"

She looked up. "Josh, this is strange."

"A little."

She continued. "*Reports get about in my organization, and what better time to verify them than at Christmas, when He was born who made the lame to walk, the blind to see, the deaf to hear, and the beggar to not lift up a petition in vain? We take turns, my colleagues and I, in doing a little extra good at Christmas to honor our founder. It was my turn this year.*"

She stopped, in tears, and handed him the letter. "I can't."

"I can. Timothy, your mother is a watering pot," Josh said. "We haven't even come to the best part, which is this: *I was tasked with finding the right people for this house in Salcombe.*" He paused when Timothy sucked in his breath. "*Mrs. Crenshaw, you made this an easy task. Some years are harder than others, especially when nations war against nations. The organization was unanimous in its decision this Christmas. The house is yours.*"

Timothy whooped. "I know that bearskin will fit in the room I wanted!"

"What sort of organization is this?" Megs asked in amazement. "And what have I ever done?"

"The small deed, my love," Josh said. "Year in, year out, rain or shine. I have no idea what sort of organization this is, except that it seems to be a religious one. One more sentence. *The key is under the second flowerpot.*" He couldn't help smiling. "*Grace be with you,* signed Mr. Paul." He pointed out that sentence to Timothy. "I think he wants Grace to move with us to Salcombe."

"Of course," Megs said. "We would never leave Grace behind."

We wouldn't dare, Josh thought. *Mr. Paul, you're a sly one, if you're who I think you are.*

CHAPTER THIRTEEN

IN LESS THAN THIRTY MINUTES, everyone was dressed, and the buns and eggs were a distant memory. Grace came along too because, ahem, Mr. Paul had particularly requested her, according to Timothy. Margaret found a sizeable basket, and in the puppy went, carried by Jane and Timothy.

Josh wasn't even slightly surprised when they walked to the inn next to the post office and found a conveyance ready and waiting for them. The coachman tipped his hat. "'E said you'd be along sometime soon. Naw, mister, put away your purse. The little bloke already paid for a round trip. Nice chap."

"That he is," Josh said. He handed Margaret in, and she gave him a fishy stare. "You know something, Josh."

"Just speculation, my love," he replied serenely. "If I were to tell you, you'd confine me to Bedlam."

Upon request from Janey, Josh read the letter again. When he finished, his daughter said, "I doubt Mr. Paul knows the half of what Mama does all year for others. She's so quiet about it." She leaned closer. "Mama can be fierce. You should have seen her snatch our scullery maid, Polly, from that awful hotel kitchen and scold the landlord."

"Really, Margaret?" he asked, amazed and yet not amazed.

"You'd have done the same thing, Josh," Megs assured him. "I heard about the matter from a nice man named Peter who sold me fish on the dock. I did what any woman would do."

Not my sister and thousands like her, Josh thought. *Believe what you want, my love.*

She sat back, keeping her own counsel, looking out the window. "Millie, you'll be able to see little boats from your bedchamber window."

Josh knew when a subject was being changed. What a wife he had married. He whispered into her ear, "First time I saw you, I wanted to count all your freckles and catch a glimpse of your pretty ankles. You married a shallow man."

"Josh, you are certifiable," she said. "I thought you were handsome and capable from the beginning." She took his hand, and her face grew serious. "You were the best surgeon that wounded men adrift in a jolly boat could hope for." She kissed his hand and held it tightly to her cheek.

The coachman dropped them off, tipped his hat, and said he would return in an hour. "Mr. Paul's orders," he said cheerfully.

"I hope there is a flowerpot," Timothy said.

There were three. "Who does the honors?" Josh asked.

The vote was instantaneous and unanimous. "Mama."

Megs took a deep breath and turned over the middle flowerpot. A key gleamed. When Josh could take his eye off the key, he couldn't see any footprints in the soft soil. Interesting, that.

She handed the key to him. He turned it in the lock and heard the click of ownership. "In we go," he said.

They explored the house for that hour, from attic to cellar. It was completely bare of furniture, except for the lace curtains. Only two days ago he had seen an elegant settee and wing chairs in the sitting room. "Our furniture is going to look shabby indeed," he commented as he and Margaret strolled hand in hand through the rooms.

"Do you care?" she asked.

"Not even slightly," he assured her. "Someday we'll sell the Paignton house and our own house on Motte Street and cure any deficiencies."

"My emerald still goes to Carter and Brustein tomorrow," she said.

"That was my present to you," he said, knowing better than to lament the matter. She was right. "I wish I had something else for you."

They were standing in the sitting room, where their children had assembled to wait for the carriage. "Look around you, Josh. Everything I need or want is right here."

He wanted to thank Mr. Paul and his benevolent organization—whatever it was—for this magnificent gift. He had an idea, but it was a silly one, best attempted with no observers.

"The coachman is here, Papa," Janey said, tugging his uniform sleeve.

"Save me a space. I'm going upstairs for another look out the window."

Megs didn't question him. She shepherded their children outside and blew him a kiss.

He walked up the stairs, noting that none of them squeaked. First door on the left opened into the room he and Megs had chosen for their own. He looked around with a sense of calm satisfaction, thinking of discussions late at night, babies beginning here, children to come tumbling in if they ever overslept.

"Boney, I wish you a poor time of it in Russia," he said out loud. "The war needs to end, because I have other plans."

He chuckled at his folly, then went to the window. "As for you, Mr. Paul, thank you. That is some organization you belong to. Who will be permitted to spread special benevolence next year? Matthew? Maybe Luke? Possibly John, although rumor has it he is still circulating about. Thank you, Mr. Paul."

Well, that was remarkably silly, he thought. *I'd bet a year's salary my own brother, Cornelius, felt remorseful and engineered this gift.*

He did owe a debt to Mr. Paul, real or otherwise. "Truly, sir, thank you for making me tell that story yesterday. It's odd, but I feel better for the telling."

No answer. He expected none. He looked down at the street below, where his family waited. At home, they would haul out the packing crates and fill them again. He wanted to see everyone settled before he sailed in two or three weeks.

He was turning toward the door when he noticed the lace curtain at the far window flutter. Thinking someone must have left the pane slightly open, he hurried to close the latch. A scrap of paper had trapped itself in the lace. He read it and smiled. "That *is* some organization, Mr. Paul. You're quite the correspondent, aren't you? Wasn't this in your letter to the Hebrews in Jerusalem?"

He read the note out loud. *"Be not forgetful to entertain strangers: for thereby some have entertained angels unawares."*

Josh ran his finger over the writing, opened the window wider, and held out the scrap. It flew from his hand. Megs would never have believed him anyway.

At eight of the clock on December 27, David Brustein's clerk ushered Joshua and Margaret into his office.

"I am pleased you have come to see me," Mr. Brustein said with no pre-liminaries. "I have something for you that will bring you relief." He folded his hands on his desk. "Pardon my manners. You first. What can I do for you?"

Margaret took the emerald from her reticule and held it out to him. "Look what Josh gave me for Christmas."

"That's a beauty," the accountant said. He held up the gem to the light. "No flaws. I'd say your husband has excellent taste."

"You'll give me a swelled head, Mr. Brustein," Josh said in protest. "I don't want her to do this, but Mrs. Crenshaw insists. Would you cast about in that way of yours and see if you can find a buyer? That should offset some of the expense of that house in Paignton. You told me once that you have a brother in the diamond trade in London."

"I do indeed, but we won't require his services," Mr. Brustein said. He handed the gem back to Margaret and held out a letter of his own. "This is why I am so delighted you came to see me this morning. This was pushed under the door."

Please don't let it be bad news, Josh thought in alarm.

"No need for a long face, sir. It's a letter from the man who owns the Paignton property. Apparently he has changed his mind and wonders if we can cancel our sale. He wants you to allow him to regain his property. Your choice, sir."

Mr. Paul, you sly dog, Josh thought. *You did say in your mantelpiece note that you had more business in Devonshire, didn't you?*

He could be casual about the matter. He could be suave. Instead he whooped out loud and kissed Megs's hand with a loud smack as Mr. Brustein roared with laughter.

"I thought you'd be pleased," the ordinarily formal counter of everyone's money said when the three of them had subsided to weak giggles.

"Where do I sign?" Josh said, which set Margaret off again. "Anywhere? Everywhere?"

"On the bottom line, of course."

They walked home in pleased silence, stopping at their favorite bakery for leftover iced Christmas biscuits because good fortune or not, Margaret Crenshaw was a frugal woman. They ate a few, then saved the rest for their children.

"Such a Christmas this has been," Megs said. She pressed her tongue to her handkerchief and wiped sugar off Josh's cheek. "What a miracle."

Egad, did she suspect? He hoped not. Somehow, this whole business was between him and Mr. Paul. "Miracle?" he ventured.

She tucked her arm through his. "You said it yourself, my love, or at least, your captain did. No one travels the Straits of Magellan in one week. It's unheard of. It's a miracle."

"Heaven bless me; so it is," he agreed.

EPILOGUE

The blockade off Ushant, March 1812

AN AVULSION, BROKEN LEG, NASTY catarrh, earache—probably the most common deepwater ailment—and an endless nosebleed later, Josh Crenshaw dragged his sorry carcass to the deck, got nodding permission from the captain, and pulled hand over hand up the ladder to the quarterdeck.

Careful not to get between the captain and the wind, he sat in the empty canvas chair with a massive "aah" and pulled out Margaret's first letter since he arrived on the blockade. Usually mail was quicker, but this was the season of storms, and Josh kept his expectations low. A respectable mail pouch had arrived today, making everyone happy. He had saved this letter, marked *Number One*, until he could be free to read it in one sitting. Numbers two through six were waiting too. Megs wrote often.

She began as good navy wives always began: *All is well, my love, as of February 1. I trust the same is true for you.*

All was well. He was sleeping better, for one thing. A smile on his face, he read through one close-written page about their children's antics, and the happy news that modest as Salcombe might appear, the village boasted an excellent grammar school.

The instructor takes not only boys but girls, so Janey is in her element, Megs wrote. *Parish funds pay some of the bill. Because there is a preponderance of sailors' children, more is paid for by Trinity House, which I do not understand but do appreciate.*

Bravo for Trinity House, those watchdogs of lighthouses and coastal buoys and widows and orphans and whatever else suited their fancy.

I need only pay a small sum for books.

"Good for you, Megs," he said.

Now for the good news, she had blazoned across the onionskin sheet. *Who should approach me, and so shyly, but Sergeant Boyce? He wants to buy our Motte Street house! Josh, it appears he has been walking Mrs. Colyer home from chapel, a temperance lecture, a demonstration of gypsy dancing (something called flamingo, but surely that can't be right), the library, and Mrs. Holly's Tea Room and Sundries. Mrs. Colyer (I'm to call her Evie now) consented to wed Gunny, and he needs a house.*

This was good news.

His offer was close to your own estimate, so I agreed immediately. Mr. Brustein said he would sign for you since women are not to be trusted. Honestly, Josh, why do men think women are not bright?

I don't think that, he told himself, even though he knew how to spell *flamenceau. If you had been allowed to follow your lead, Megs, we wouldn't have had those scary moments about the house in Paignton.*

She wrote, *I wore my emerald necklace to church yesterday to celebrate.*

Another banner headline followed: *Corny came to breakfast! He showed up one morning this week. He took my hand and said, 'Why should we dictate what makes the two of you happy? Forgive me.' He turned to go, but I ushered him to a seat instead. (We had bacon that morning.) I forgave him a long time ago, but he probably wouldn't believe that if I told him.*

"He probably wouldn't, Megs," Josh told the letter as the paper rattled in his hands. The wind was changing.

He finished the page. *Josh, I suspect Corny finagled the purchase of our home here in Salcombe with Mr. Paul. He must be too shy to mention his generosity.*

Josh knew that was the logical answer. He didn't have to believe it, however.

The wind shifted. Josh eyed the captain, wondering if the enemy ships would come out to play, if the wind blew from the east. Not yet? He turned back to his letter and followed the arrow to the other side.

Best news for last! he read, and it was. *It should come as no surprise to you, my darling, that I find myself increasing. We did make rather merry over Christmas, didn't we? Mid-September should find me in confinement. I'm happy for more space in our lovely house.*

Who wouldn't smile at that? They certainly had made merry. He hoped she wouldn't be too nauseated this time. He had probably used up all the miracles allotted to him, but it would be splendid to be in port when the next Crenshaw put in his or her noisy appearance. So far, he had only been present for Janey's birth.

The captain was reading a newspaper from his mail pouch. He motioned to Josh. "Bad news from Russia," he called. "At least, bad news for Napoleon. It was a terrible retreat."

Josh gave the captain a wave and turned back to Margaret's letter. *If this one is a boy, perhaps we could name him Paul. It's something to consider. I wish I had Mr. Paul's address. He might like to know.*

She signed with her usual flourish and a little drawing. He looked closer and chuckled. It was Margaret in profile with a little bulge and a tiny footprint inside the bulge.

He pocketed the letter and walked to the railing. *There you have it, Mr. Paul,* he thought, or prayed; perhaps it was both. *All is well on All Saints Way in Salcombe. Boney had a poor time of it in Russia, and I am still sleeping better. My patients are content enough, but I do not like avulsions. Margaret will be confined sometime in September. Yours most sincerely, Josh Crenshaw. P.S. Visit us again, if you're ever in the neighborhood.*

ABOUT THE AUTHOR

WELL-KNOWN VETERAN OF THE HISTORICAL fiction and romance-writing field, Carla Kelly has authored many books, short stories, and articles for various publishers. Through the course of a lengthy career, Carla has earned two RITA Awards from Romance Writers of America for Best Regency of the Year; two Spur Awards from Western Writers of America; three Whitney Awards from Storymakers; and a Lifetime Achievement Award from *Romantic Times*.

Carla's interest in historical fiction is a byproduct of her lifelong study of history. All her jobs—newspaper feature writer and columnist, ranger in the National Park Service, public relations work in medical centers and a hospice, contract researcher, university professor—have either involved history or writing or, happily, both at the same time.

Carla tired quickly of writing about the usual dukes and peers that clutter Regency romance, preferring to focus on ordinary people. Never too comfortable in overheated ballrooms, she prefers a Royal Navy frigate in a following sea with the stunsails out; a campaign with Wellington's British Army in Spain; or a U.S. Army campaign during the Indian Wars. She's equally at home in America's Southwest of the eighteenth century when Spain ruled—the Spanish Brand series—or at a school in devil-may-care Portsmouth for workhouse lads, as in the St. Brendan series.

She likes the challenge of joining fact to fiction in a manner that is truthful, interesting, and utterly reliable as the real deal. She knows accurate history and compelling fiction are highly compatible.

Follow Wholesome Romance on social media for more great titles.

OTHER BOOKS AND AUDIOBOOKS
BY KRISTA LYNNE JENSEN

Of Grace and Chocolate

The Orchard

Falling for You

Love Unexpected: With All My Heart (contributor)

Kisses in the Rain

Christmas Grace (contributor)

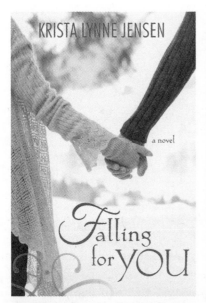

KRISTA LYNNE JENSEN

a novel

Falling
for YOU

Love Unexpected

Three Romantic Novellas

With All My
HEART

ANITA STANSFIELD, KRISTA LYNNE JENSEN
SHERYL C.S. JOHNSON

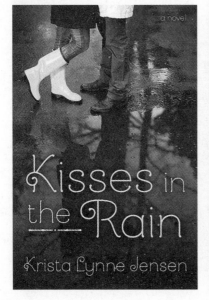

a novel

Kisses in
the *Rain*

Krista Lynne Jensen

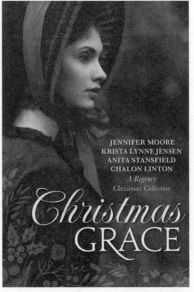

JENNIFER MOORE
KRISTA LYNNE JENSEN
ANITA STANSFIELD
CHALON LINTON
*A Regency
Christmas Collection*

Christmas
GRACE

PRAISE FOR
KRISTA LYNNE JENSEN

"'Expectations at Canterwood' will reunite eager fans with the Stanhope family in this romantic and witty Regency Christmas tale by Krista Lynne Jensen. I finished the book with a smile and a wistful sigh."
—Anneka R. Walker, author *The Masked Baron*

"A beautifully told Christmas story filled with romance, humor, and healing."
—Sian Ann Bessey, author *The Noble Smuggler*

"With its message of peace and joy, Christmas seems to turn everything even more special, including love. Krista proves this with 'Expectations at Canterwood.'"
—Carla Kelly, author *The Unlikely Heroes* (coming 2021)

EXPECTATIONS AT CANTERWOOD

KRISTA LYNNE JENSEN

In memory of my grandparents Wendell and Nada Anglesey,
who started out with nothing and now have everything

ACKNOWLEDGMENTS

I'D LIKE TO THANK MY Covenant family; my editor, Kami Hancock, my friend Samantha Millburn; and my fellow writers for always encouraging me. The world is a better place with your compassionate, creative minds in it. Thank you, Brandon and kids, for everything. You are my heart. Merry Christmas, everyone.

CHAPTER ONE

MARINA ROWLEY HAD INDEED PANICKED. She'd caught her first sight of the man with whom her parents were encouraging her to make a match, had darted away from the drawing room before anyone had taken notice of her, and was now pressed into a winter privet hedge out of doors. Her hand pressed to her racing heart as the privet branches poked her hair and back. She'd taken no thought to fetching her bonnet and had only her shawl about her shoulders. She shivered but not from the cold.

Well, perhaps a little from the cold.

Before her journey with her mother and father from the shores of Scarborough, Yorkshire, to the village of Longhorsley in Northumberland, her mother had told her she believed the gentleman was a seasoned dragoon just returned from war. The invitation mentioned only his name and that the Christmas house party was being held in his honor. Marina's younger sister—who had begged to spend the holiday with a friend and was indulged—had teased her about him being old. Marina's father had optimistically declared that Marina was well out of the nursery herself.

But this . . . The soldier she had just seen for the first time since her arrival at Canterwood the previous day had to have been at least five and fifty. Her own father was not yet fifty. The brass buttons on the soldier's uniform strained under his copious belly, and his gray hair frizzled in massive clumps on each side of his otherwise shiny pate. Marina had no more detail than that, as she had fled the hall without any rational thought.

Her shoulders slumped and her heartbeat slowed to an uncomfortable thudding. Though she'd felt censured for reaching her twenty-fourth year without an offer, the man in uniform she'd spied in the drawing room made her want to insist she was still meant to dine in the nursery. She instantly felt a pang of guilt. Aside from his age and wild hair, the man had not appeared to be unpleasant. Was she really this shallow?

She grimaced. Yes. She was.

She stomped her foot on the gravel walk. Twenty-four or not, bespectacled or not, opinionated or not, she should not have to settle for marrying a man more than twice her age. Should she?

"Are you well, miss?"

Marina jumped and turned, tiny branches of the hedge catching her hair. "Oh!" Her hand shot to her head as she looked upon a man in a rough brown coat and a flatcap—a gardener or stablehand, perhaps. "Yes, quite well. That is . . ." Her neck began to burn with embarrassment. "I seem to be caught."

He searched beyond her. "Doing . . . what?"

She closed her eyes, wishing to be anywhere else. "No. I'm caught. My hair—in this privet."

He stepped forward. "Allow me to help." He paused and looked toward the house. "Or I can fetch your maid, if you prefer."

"No," she cried as he moved away. "Please. Don't alert anyone. I already feel like an utter fool. I'm sure I can get free in a moment." She gingerly pulled at her coif, but the movement only loosened the pins holding it all together. "This can't be happening." She removed her spectacles and slid them into the back of her glove so as not to knock them to the ground.

"Might I ask what you're doing without a coat?" he said. "You are a houseguest, correct?"

"Yes. Our hostess, Mrs. Ophelia Stanhope, is my cousin. We arrived yesterday for the house party." She blew out a breath. "And if you must know, I was hiding. The decision was rather sudden, and now I'm paying for my childishness." She winced at the irony and tugged once more.

"You are Miss Rowley?" he asked.

She paused and did what she could to face him. "I'm afraid so." Whomever he was, the servants must have been given a detailed guestlist.

He assessed her for a moment, then looked at the house and back to her. "If you'll allow me, I can at least snap the twigs holding so tightly to your hair and free you that way. I'll not lay a finger on you. You have my word."

She read his intent expression and, having no better solution, nodded.

He stepped forward and reached for the hedge. She immediately felt his warmth and drew in a steadying breath. He smelled of wool and horses. The snapping of small twigs followed.

He adjusted his angle. "Might I ask from what—or whom—you were hiding?"

"It was a shock, that was all." She held as still as she could, her face surely rose-red now. "I did not expect him to be older than my father."

"Who is older than your father?"

"Why, Lieutenant Richard Stanhope, Lady Teresa Stanhope's brother-in-law."

He paused. Then the snapping continued. "You mean Lady Teresa's son."

"No, I think not. I met Lady Teresa yesterday, and that would be impossible. She is aging—beautifully, I might add—but cannot be the mother of the man I saw."

"You are free." He stepped back, scrutinizing her.

She lifted her hand back to her hair, feeling the remains of privet twigs, and stepped away from the hedge. "I can't thank you enough." She raised her shawl over her head, covering her hair completely, and replaced her spectacles on her nose. For the first time, she took a good look at the man who had rescued her.

Her breath stilled as her gaze met eyes so pale they could be green or gray. They intensified under dark-blond brows and wind-tossed hair streaked with a paler blond. A scruff of a beard darkened his jaw.

"Shall I escort you back to the house?"

She blinked. "Oh. No. I shall say I went for a walk and then return to my room." She glanced at the house. "It's nearly time to dress for dinner, I imagine."

"And . . . what of the lieutenant?" he asked, concern in his expression.

"Do you know him?" she couldn't help but ask.

He nodded.

"Is he a good man? Kind?"

He opened his mouth, then closed it. Then opened it again. "I believe he is. At least, he tries to be. He can be a brute at times, I suppose."

"As can most men." She sighed and straightened her shoulders. "Well, I'll do what I should have done at the first: hold my judgment." She glanced again at the house. "But I might also pray he finds me to be too young." She bit back a grimace. "Which is the opposite of what my mother prays for before every ball—that the gentlemen do not find me to be too old. I don't *feel* too old." She turned back to her rescuer. "Forgive me. I'll say no more. I trust you'll say nothing of this. You've been very kind. Good evening."

Before he could say anything more, Marina hurried to the house. If she timed it well, she could brush the twigs out of her hair herself and have the lady's maid start fresh on a simple twist for dinner.

CHAPTER TWO

RICHARD STANHOPE WATCHED SOMEWHAT DAZEDLY as Miss Rowley departed. The silence left by her absence was akin to the silence after a battle—the kind that left one questioning what had just happened.

He'd missed yesterday's arrivals due to an appointment in Newcastle and had returned earlier that afternoon. His mother had made sure he knew the guest list for the Christmas house party, making an especial point— in her subtle way—that his sister-in-law's cousin Miss Marina Rowley was unattached, somewhat of a wallflower, and would likely appreciate a "friendship," which he'd interpreted to mean a courtesy. As the reluctant guest of honor of this particular party, he'd of course be as hospitable and welcoming as he would be to any of the unattached ladies who had been invited. He was wary of offering anything more.

He had not, however, expected to find Miss Rowley caught in a hedge-row, hiding from a person he could only guess to be his uncle Hubert, a staunch colonel in the Fifth who wore his regimentals whenever the occasion allowed. Why she had assumed Uncle Hubert was him was inexplicable.

He scratched his head and started for the house, intent on taking the long way around to the front doors. He'd no sooner taken two steps when he was called from behind.

"Lieutenant."

He turned and quirked a smile. "Vicar."

His friend grinned.

Addressing his childhood friend Tom Langley as a vicar was likely the oddest sensation he'd experienced since returning home from war. That and addressing Tom's wife, Julia, as *Mrs.* Langley. Tom had taken a living and a wife while Richard had been away fighting. Richard would admit to no one that he felt a measure of envy, but he'd quickly come to appreciate the couple's easy company and peaceful home on the days when he needed to clear his head of the noises of battle. Tom had proven his enduring friendship by lending an ear when Richard needed to share what he could never speak of to his mother or burden his brother with.

"I thought I might find you out here," Tom said as he caught up to him. "Successful trip?"

"Could be. Took the new stallion out." He shook his head. "So strange. After seven years of riding cavalry mares, I'm reminded that the Arab stallions' power is astonishing. This one's temperament is steady, too."

"He'll make a good stud, then?"

"I believe so." His gaze wandered in the direction of the Canterwood stables, now held and run by his elder brother, Frank. This was Richard's plan: sell his commission and start his own breeding stables, producing and caring for horses instead of riding them to their deaths. He had no more desire for soldiering. He'd paid. His friends had paid. Napoleon had been defeated. He felt the need to be industrious, productive—to make a life.

"I can see the wheels turning in that head of yours. It's a good idea, Richard. You've the knowledge and experience for it."

Richard nodded. "I'm thankful for your support. I only need to talk to Frank. And that prospect frightens me almost as much as this house party does. Why my mother thought this necessary is beyond me."

Tom chuckled. "Need I remind you that your mother does as she pleases and seldom without reason?"

Richard arched a brow. "That's what I'm afraid of." Two years ago, Tom had fallen victim to his mother's brilliant mind when he was thrown into a scheme with the Stanhopes' governess, the now Mrs. Langley.

"I have three words for you, my friend." Tom counted off on his fingers. "Beware. The. Children."

Richard laughed. "Is that scripture?"

"It should be."

Frank and Ophelia's three children, Alger, Sophia, and Helena—now thirteen, eleven, and a precocious seven—had played a heavy part in bringing Tom and Julia together that Christmas. They'd boasted of it to their uncle without reserve.

Tom slapped Richard on the back, and the two men resumed their walk to the house.

Richard watched the house warily. "I have . . . a conundrum. I've stumbled into awkward circumstances with one of the houseguests, and I've no idea how to put it aright without further . . ."

"Awkwardness?"

"Exactly. Have you met Miss Rowley?"

"Ophelia's relative? No, not yet."

"Neither have I."

Tom studied him. "Easily remedied. Have Ophelia introduce you."

"Therein lies the awkwardness. And potential mortification of Miss Rowley, if I've judged her correctly."

"I'm not following."

Richard stopped and rubbed the back of his neck. "I've met Miss Rowley but have not been introduced. A few minutes ago I found her in need of a minor rescue, which I executed with utmost propriety. But while helping her, I learned she has mistaken someone else for me, and without knowing I was me, proceeded to tell me, in her distress, that she wished *not* to become—er—acquainted with me but was nevertheless determined to be gracious with the person who is not me but whom she believes to be me."

Tom stared.

"I believe, in the moment, she thought me a servant."

"The real you? Or the other you?"

"The real me."

Tom looked him over and nodded as if at least that made sense. "I'm still not following, but let me ask you this: Did you at any point tell her she was mistaken?"

"Yes. That is, I tried to assure her I was my mother's *son* and not her *brother*. But she didn't believe me."

"You introduced yourself, and she still didn't believe you?"

"I didn't introduce myself."

"Why not?"

"Because it isn't proper."

Tom rubbed his forehead, then broke into quiet laughter. "I'm at a loss regarding this fascinating triangle, but I'll help however I can."

Richard huffed in frustration and continued walking. "The only reason I knew who she was is because she mentioned being Ophelia's cousin. So, you see, there was no formal introduction—"

"And she took you for a stablehand."

"Presumably."

"And believes somebody else is you."

"You're getting it. And now we shall surely meet before going to dinner—"

Comprehension lit Tom's face. "—and very publicly she will learn who you are and be mortified by her mistake."

"Exactly."

"And you don't wish that for her."

"Of course not."

"But you do wish for her to know who you really are."

"I do."

"And that you are certainly not a stablehand."

"It is respectable work, but yes."

"Is she pretty?"

Richard's foot paused on the first stair. "What?"

"You heard me."

Richard recalled the medium-height girl with medium-brown hair and medium-brown eyes hidden behind round spectacles. But then she'd turned to him, her neck long and graceful, her cheeks flushed, and she'd removed her spectacles, and her eyes had become searching—trusting. He'd broken the twigs caught in her hair, and his fingers had accidentally brushed tresses so silky and thick they had almost shocked him. She'd smelled of orange blossom.

When she'd put her spectacles back on, the glasses had tried to transform her back to the medium girl he'd thought she was before, but they'd failed.

"Richard? Are you with me?" Tom snapped his fingers in front of Richard, grinning.

Blinking, Richard pushed Tom's hand aside. "She's pretty, in a way. She is . . . rare. But that's not the conundrum, is it?"

"No, I suppose not. But it makes things a bit more fun."

"What vicar talks this way?"

Tom placed both hands on Richard's shoulders and squeezed. "Friends first, Richard. Always friends first."

Whether he was overtired or his nerves were strung tight over this party, Richard's eyes misted at Tom's words, and he cleared his throat. "It's good to be home, friend."

"It's good to have you home."

CHAPTER THREE

MARINA STOOD WITH COUSIN OPHELIA in the drawing room before dinner. Her hair was smooth and twigless, and she wore a new gown, but she couldn't seem to settle. Her toe tapped as she anticipated when Lieutenant Stanhope would appear. Her mother watched the doors from her position before the hearth, until she gave Marina a pointed look. Marina turned away from the doors, feigning disinterest. She knew her mother's designs—they were the same as they always had been: catch a husband for her eldest daughter despite Marina's long list of shortcomings.

A young woman with pretty hazel eyes and honey-brown hair approached Ophelia, her belly round with child.

"Mrs. Stanhope," she said, "I wonder if you might introduce me to your cousin." The young woman openly watched Marina with a smile. Ophelia took Marina's arm.

"I'd be delighted. Miss Rowley, this is Mrs. Langley, our vicar's wife and a dear friend."

The women curtsied.

"Now that I think on it," Ophelia said, "you two should get along splendidly, for both of you are witty, intelligent, and have a knack for avoiding oysters on your plate."

Mrs. Langley grinned.

"Excuse me, ladies," Ophelia said. "Mrs. Strom is summoning me again. She and her daughter seem very fond of me."

"I'd wager they're very fond of the lieutenant," Mrs. Langley said.

Marina frowned, now searching out the Stroms.

"That too," Ophelia said with a mischievous smile and left them.

Mrs. Langley took Marina's abandoned arm in hers. "I've been eager to meet you, Miss Rowley. Are you enjoying your stay at Canterwood?"

"Yes, I am. The grounds are lovely, even in this cold."

"They are. I admit winter in Longhorsley has grown on me. And Canterwood's orchards are especially magical when the snows come. Have you met the children yet?"

"Only the two oldest, when they were little things. Mama told me the youngest made a brief appearance at tea to play a song for her grandmother on a miniature harp. I'm sorry I missed it."

Mrs. Langley laughed. "That would be Helena. She'll work her way into a house party however she can manage. I'm sure that's the only reason she agreed to pursue an instrument, the little schemer."

"You know the children well?"

"I was their governess."

Marina's eyes widened. "Oh."

Mrs. Langley grinned. "You needn't be shocked. My husband and I are quite well suited. And the Stanhope family practically shoved us together, for which I am forever thankful." She blushed, beaming.

"You are in love with your husband," Marina remarked.

"I am. But tell no one, Miss Rowley." Mrs. Langley squeezed her arm. "A vicar in love? Scandalous."

Marina was surprised to find herself at ease with this woman. "Please, call me Marina."

"If you'll call me Julia." The vicar's wife embarked on a turn about the room with Marina in tow. "I must confess, Marina, one reason I requested an introduction is because it frees me to introduce you to others. Mrs. Stanhope and Lady Teresa are quite busy, and we must be sure you are properly acquainted with members of the party." As she spoke, Julia steered her toward the doors leading to the corridor. "Is there anyone you've not met yet? Oh, I know." They reached the doors and stepped through, leaving the majority of the guests. "I'm sure you haven't met my husband. He was just out here in the passage near the library with a few other members of the party."

"I should like to meet him."

"You know, my husband is the very good friend of—"

"Good evening, Mrs. Langley."

Marina's heart leapt to her throat as Julia halted. Before them stood Lieutenant Stanhope, executing a bow over his broad girth.

"Good evening, Colonel," Julia said with a curtsy. "I hope you are well."

Colonel? Had he been promoted at the end of the war?

"Can't complain, can't complain." The man eyed Julia with a gleam. "And who is this treasure?"

Marina was having difficulty looking at the man directly. She couldn't seem to decide on an expression of any sort, though her cheeks had heated a good deal.

"May I introduce Miss Rowley? She is a relative of yours, sir. Mrs. Stanhope's cousin."

Marina mustered her courage, finally meeting the man's gaze. "How do you do, sir?" She curtsied.

"Quite well, thank you."

"Miss Rowley, this is Colonel Rathbone, the late Mr. Stanhope's brother-in-law."

Marina gaped.

"Quite shocked by the connection, I see." The colonel rocked on his feet. "Ties that bind, Miss Rowley, ties that bind—whether you approve of your relations or not, eh?" He chuckled good-naturedly. "I do hope for your approval, miss. I aim to make this a most pleasant house party. Now, I must be off to find my wife before she begins to think I am lost. Which I was, but do not tell her."

Marina curtsied again, feeling equal measures baffled and relieved as the colonel moved past them and down the corridor. She swallowed. "He seems pleasant."

"He is a good man. Now, let's find Mr. Langley before they call us all to dinner." She pushed open a door to a spacious library with a fire crackling in a hearth across from the door.

Marina furrowed her brow in thought. "Julia, if that man I just met is Colonel Rathbone, then who—?"

"There you are, dearest."

Marina turned toward the source of the warm greeting, and Julia sped forward to greet a man who must have been her husband.

"I've brought someone to meet you," Julia said and beckoned Marina forward.

Mr. Langley watched her expectantly. He was just taller than his wife, with deep-brown hair and wide, dark eyes. Together they made a handsome couple, and not for the first time, Marina wondered whether there were someone who might stand beside her and elicit the same observation from any random observer.

"My dear, this is Miss Marina Rowley. She is our hostess's cousin from Yorkshire. Miss Rowley, my husband, Mr. Langley."

Marina curtsied with a smile as he bowed. "Vicar, I'm pleased to meet you. Your wife has made me feel most welcome."

He smiled, studying her. "I'm glad to hear it, Miss Rowley. She has that way with people." He tenderly regarded his wife, then nodded to his right. "I should also like to make an introduction, as I gather you've not been introduced."

Marina lifted her brow as he gestured to a darker corner, from which emerged a man she'd not noticed before. A man whom, as he entered the brighter part of the room, she recognized with a start.

"Miss Rowley, this is Lieutenant Richard Stanhope—Frank Stanhope's younger brother and guest of honor, newly returned from war."

No words formed on Marina's tongue as she beheld the same man who had released her from the twigs entangling her hair—the same man she'd confessed to hiding from and of whom she'd vowed to withhold judgment. "Lady Teresa's *son*," she whispered.

He bowed, watching her as if she'd fall to ashes if he moved too suddenly—which she might. His pale green-gray eyes held her gaze. He'd shaved, and his light hair was combed back from his forehead. Gone were the rough coat and flatcap, and instead he wore a dark cutaway jacket and plum waistcoat. And in his eyes she saw . . . amusement.

Her fists balled, and she stepped forward. "You—you brute!"

The instant panic in his expression warned her that perhaps she'd mis-read him, but she was too confused, too ashamed to alter her course. "How could you? How could you just stand there and allow me to—" She remem-bered they weren't alone and glanced at Julia and the vicar, who looked stunned. She could feel her decorum crumbling. "Did you tell them? I asked you— I trusted you—"

"Miss Rowley, please, if you'll let me explain—"

"Now? Now you'll explain? I have never been so humiliated in all my life. And that is saying something, I assure you."

He took a step toward her. "I meant to remedy the misunderstanding as soon as I could."

She felt the sting of tears and removed her spectacles. "But not before you had a good laugh." She glanced at Julia, who was vigorously shaking her head. "I'm such a fool."

Picking up her skirts, she turned and fled the room, everything fuzzy. In the corridor, instead of turning left, back to the other guests, she turned right. Two doors down she found a small, empty music room and let herself in. Sniffling, she crossed to a narrow window overlooking darkened pastures and blurry lights from the expansive stables' lanterns. She leaned forward, pressing her forehead against the cool glass as a fresh wave of humiliation washed over her. "Nicely handled, Marina," she mumbled thickly. "Now you need only hide in your room for the remainder of the party." Another tear slipped down her cheek.

"I hope that won't be necessary, my dear."

Marina turned with a gasp at the gentle, matronly voice.

Just inside the doorway stood a lovely, stately older woman, with Julia just behind her.

Marina hiccupped. "You—you've brought Lady Teresa into this debacle?" She swiped at her tears, and Julia hurried forward with a handkerchief, pressing it into her hands.

"She did no such thing," Lady Teresa said, following Julia. "I saw you leave the library in distress and followed, worried for one of my guests. My dear, whatever is the matter?"

"I—" Marina's mouth froze; the words wouldn't come. How would she explain this to such a woman? She covered her mouth with the kerchief and turned a pleading expression on Julia.

"Lieutenant Stanhope will not follow," Julia said quietly. "He only sent me after you with his handkerchief."

Marina abruptly pulled the linen from her mouth.

Julia continued. "Truly, I only knew he wanted an introduction, and he wanted it away from the crowd of guests. I was delighted to help. Please, believe me, Marina. I meant no malice. I don't believe the lieutenant did either. He feels horribly."

"My Richard?" Lady Teresa asked. "He is the cause of this distress? Julia, what has happened? Tell me this instant."

Julia looked to Marina, as if to say she wouldn't speak without Marina's permission.

Marina dabbed her eyes and replaced her spectacles. The worry on the older woman's face fed her resolve, and she steadied herself. "Nothing happened," Marina said. "That is to say, there was a mix-up, all my own misunderstanding, and your son tried to remedy it with the help of the vicar and his wife. It's all a bit clumsy, and in my humiliation, I fled." The memory of that flicker of amusement in Lieutenant Stanhope's expression flashed in her mind, and she swallowed back more tears. Another memory pressed her mind, of his careful hands freeing her from the privet as he distracted her with quiet questions. She dropped her chin. "I'm sorry to have disturbed your evening, Lady Teresa."

"It will only disturb me if you continue to take all the blame in this—this whatever it is. We shall get to the bottom of it and make it right."

"Oh no, my lady. I assure you, I will be well now." Marina tried to muster a resolute, if not happy, expression. "With your permission, I'll freshen up before I come to dinner. Only give me a few minutes."

"Of course, my dear. We have plenty of time before dinner is called. Julia, please see Miss Rowley to her room."

Marina almost protested but held her tongue.

Julia and Lady Teresa shared a look, and then Julia put her arm through Marina's, more tentatively this time. "Let's both of us freshen up, shall we?"

Marina allowed Julia to lead her up a back staircase to the guest rooms, and then they were standing in front of Marina's door.

"Would you like some company, or shall I leave you in solitude?"

Marina peered at the woman. She wanted so much to like her, to trust her. "Were you in earnest? You only wished for me to meet Lieutenant Stanhope as he requested?"

Julia nodded, her eyes wide. "I knew nothing of any previous misunderstanding. The lieutenant is my husband's best friend since childhood. The Stanhopes treat Tom as family. Richard—Lieutenant Stanhope—made a simple request that I was happy to fulfill." She frowned. "Honestly, I thought perhaps he . . . that you . . . that there might be a special—" She stopped herself, tilting her head expectantly.

Marina felt her cheeks heat up. "There is nothing special."

There never was.

Julia studied her, then nodded to the door. "Come. I'll not leave you, and after we've splashed rosewater on our faces, we shall go down to dinner together. Let the men stew."

Marina nodded, then smiled.

CHAPTER FOUR

"RICHARD CHARLES STANHOPE, EXPLAIN YOURSELF."

He cringed. Tom stepped away. *Turncoat.*

Richard's mother's elegant silhouette filled the doorway. As she approached, the flickering light of the fire lit her face. She'd aged while he'd been away, but her strength still burned brightly. Right now, it was searing a hole into his chest.

"In Richard's defense," Tom began, "he was doing his best with a rather awkward conundru—" He halted his explanation under the lady's stony gaze. "I'll just—ahem." Tom receded into the dim corner with a bow.

Richard rolled his eyes. They were nine again. He appreciated the effort though. He bowed. "Mother."

"Well?"

All right, then. Feeling like he was further betraying Miss Rowley's trust, he told his mother everything, leaving out the part that he'd been utterly distracted by the woman ever since meeting her.

"What's made it worse," he said, "is that she thought I was laughing at her. I assure you, Mother, I would not do that."

"Then, what was it the lady mistook in your expression?"

Richard paused. The truth was seeing Miss Rowley again had heightened the sense that they'd shared something, just the two of them, in the hedge, however briefly. The memory of that connection had brought a smile to his lips before he could stop it. He cleared his throat. "I believed we were clearing up the misunderstanding. I was eager to do so, for her sake and mine. The idea pleased me."

His mother drew in a long, deep breath, then slowly released it. "The poor girl."

"The poor *girl*? I helped lead a regiment of dragoons into Waterloo, managed to get most of them out again, and yet I have no idea how to set this right. And, I might add, I did nothing wrong."

"Except lead the girl to think your uncle was you."

"I did not lead that."

"You didn't stop it."

"That's what I was trying to do in here, where she would not be under the scrutiny of a roomful of strangers!"

"Well, now she knows. And she might never come out of her room."

"That is fine with me." He clamped his mouth shut too late.

His mother's gaze deepened. "I hope you don't mean that," she said. "Do you have any idea how it feels to be pushed toward a situation as life changing as marriage and be terrified by the prospect yet helpless to change it, all the while trying to be gracious enough to make the best of it? Richard! She thought she was to entertain the attentions of your Uncle Hubert! *Hubert*, the dear man! I do not fault you for her mistakes, but you do own a measure of responsibility for allowing the misunderstanding to go as far as it did."

He could not argue with her there. He hadn't considered how dire Miss Rowley believed her prospects to be, even as he'd witnessed her hiding in the winter garden. He pinched the bridge of his nose and sighed. His desire to alleviate Miss Rowley's discomfort had completely backfired, and he was at a loss as to how to fix it. "What do you want me to do, Mother? Tell me, and I will do it." Obviously, he and Tom were not the experts in the room.

"You will walk into dinner with her. You will sit next to her and put her at ease with questions about herself. What are her interests? Her joys? You will invite her for a ride in the morning, and if she does not ride, then you shall go for a walk. You will include her in conversation with our guests— including your delightful uncle—until she is comfortable in this home. Tomorrow is the Christmas Eve ball. You shall request a dance, perhaps two dances—"

"Mother—"

"*Two* dances. And you will introduce her to the children—"

Richard glanced at Tom, who mouthed, THE CHILDREN with wide eyes.

"—and have them lead the both of you in a Christmas activity of some sort. In short, you shall make her forget this entire debacle and make her holiday here one she will treasure always. Am I understood?"

He swallowed. "Yes, Mother."

"Good." She gave Tom a pointed look, then turned. "Dinner is in ten minutes. I suggest you ready yourself for battle."

Seconds passed in silence after she left, until Tom whistled low.

Richard knew what the sound meant. Tom had realized what Richard's assignment truly was.

He was to court Miss Rowley.

Richard entered the drawing room with Tom just as his brother, Frank, stood to gather the guests' attention in front of the dining-room doors. As he welcomed the guests, Richard surveyed the room until he found who he was looking for. The gown of shimmering blue gauze over muslin Miss Rowley had been wearing earlier could not be missed. Neither could the matching ribbon woven through her dark pinned curls, nor the way a few of those curls caressed her back. She glanced over her shoulder, catching him staring, and immediately dropped her chin. She leaned in to Julia's shoulder, and at her words, Julia narrowed her gaze at Richard and Tom.

"That can't be good," Tom murmured.

Richard silently agreed.

"—my brother, Richard, is home."

At the sound of his Christian name, he turned his attention to Frank.

"Seven years he has served his country, earning the rank of First Lieutenant of the Fourteenth Light Dragoons—a Stanhope horseman the family could not be prouder of. This Christmas house party is in his honor, despite his protests." A chuckle ran through the room. "We hope you enjoy yourselves during your stay. And to Lieutenant Richard Stanhope"—Frank lifted his glass, and the others who held drinks followed suit—"welcome home, sir. I know I speak for all of us when I say our gratitude for your safe return is immeasurable." Mother dabbed her eyes. "May your career in His Majesty's Guard take you far. Ladies, if you were hoping to catch the lieutenant in his uniform this evening, I'm afraid that pleasure will have to wait until tomorrow's ball." Frank arched his brow and grinned at his brother. Richard gave him a slight bow, trying to ignore the knot in his chest conjured by Frank's words. The guests toasted, drank, and cheered, and dinner was announced.

Richard wasted no time. He'd learned hesitancy could cost gravely in battle. Focusing on a task before him had carried him through many a campaign. So he moved with purpose, not knowing how he'd be received, and bowed in front of Miss Rowley, his focus solely on her.

"Miss Rowley, will you do me the honor of allowing me to escort you to dinner?"

Her cheeks reddened. Glancing around, she lifted her hand to touch the single pearl at her neck. He could feel the room's curiosity. He hadn't considered that, but of course after Frank's toast they'd be watching his next move with interest. Oh well. This was part of it.

"I don't think—" she began.

"Please," he said, quietly. "Allow me this. I assure you I am in earnest."

She drew in a slow breath and curtsied.

He offered his arm, and she barely rested her hand upon it. She glanced back at Julia, who was taking Tom's arm but giving Richard a look of warning he imagined had worked well in the nursery. They passed Miss Rowley's mother, who whispered frantically into her husband's ear. He heard the words, "younger man" and "catch." Miss Rowley's hand on his arm tensed.

Richard followed his family into the dining room and pulled out a chair for his dinner partner. She sat, and he took the seat to her left, next to his mother on the end and across from Frank, Ophelia, and Mr. McKay, a Scotsman Frank often did business with. Richard had learned the man had a keen eye for good Northern brood mares.

Introductions were made, and soup was served.

"You look lovely, Miss Rowley," Mother said. "I did not tell you before, but that color is divine on you."

Miss Rowley gave a modest nod. "You are too good, Lady Teresa."

"Not too good," Mother said, lifting her soup spoon. "I am just right."

Richard watched Miss Rowley attempt to suppress a smile. He leaned toward her. "It's better if you accept that about my mother right now. It will save you a lot of trouble in the end."

She lifted her spoon. "I'll remember that, sir. And what of you? I've heard it said that you're a good man, though the source was questionable."

He nearly choked on his soup as Mr. McKay chuckled. Richard patted his mouth with his napkin. "I believe, if memory serves, it was asserted that I *try* to be good. Trying counts for a lot, I should think."

She blinked at him. "Mm, and so does honesty."

He glanced at his mother, who seemed to be enjoying her soup too well. He changed tack. "What are your favorite winter pursuits, Miss

Rowley? I've been gone for a few years, but I did not forget our winters in Northumberland as long and cold. How do you pass your time in Scarborough?"

She eyed him as if to assess his sincerity. "The winters in Scarborough are milder, being on the coast and more south. If you must know, I like to explore the beaches and the bluffs in the winter. They are not crowded as they are in summer."

"You don't say," Richard said. "No sea-bathing in December?"

She hesitated an intriguing fraction of a second. "Not by most, sir."

He smirked, and she returned it. A fighter, this one.

"What else do you like to do?" he asked.

She swallowed her soup. "Silhouette portraits."

"Really? Fascinating."

She gave him a dubious look.

"I'm sincere. I've never known a person to do them, although I have seen those of my niece and nephew in the portrait hall."

"Those are mine, sir, from a very long time ago."

"Now I shall have to go take another look."

Her brow rose. "Whatever for?"

"Well, it makes a difference, doesn't it? When one knows the artist?"

She huffed. "Do you claim to know me?"

He lowered his voice. "I'm trying."

She said nothing and returned to her soup. He glanced at his mother, whose return expression told him to keep trying. Following command at Talavera had been simpler than this.

He took a breath and steeled himself. "What of the Season?" he asked. "Do you go to London?"

She paused midsoup, her expression suddenly shuttered. "I've been to London for the Season several times. I find it exhilarating and exhausting." She met his gaze directly. "The people are at once convivial and conniving, and it becomes difficult to know whom to trust."

The set-down was not undeserved, and he felt the heat of it. He remembered her expression as he'd freed her from the hedge—so open and grateful. No wonder she'd reacted as she had to his poorly handled reveal. She was no stranger to duplicity.

His desire to regain her trust rose like a hot-air balloon.

"Did you ever go to London, sir?" she asked. "Before you left for war?"

"Only once."

"And how did you find it?"

He thought for a moment. "At the time, I found it exciting. Something to do every evening, new faces, the promise of a smile from pretty girls—" He paused and cocked a brow. She smiled at him facetiously. He chuckled. "My father brought Frank and me along to Tattersall's bloodstock auctions. To me, that was better than any of the pomp of the *ton*." He sobered. "Looking back now, after being at war, it all seems rather silly. Still, it's what we fought for, in a way. To preserve our traditions, our opportunities to be silly." He glanced at Mother and covered her stilled hand on the table. "I left for the dragoons soon after, and a year after that, Father passed on. My memories of him sharing his passion for horses with us that Season rose to the top of everything else."

Miss Rowley's expression softened. "I'm glad you have something so dear to connect with your time there."

Mother squeezed his fingers and let him go. He squared himself to the table, unsure what to say next. "I'm sorry your experience in London has been . . ." He faltered.

She sifted through her main course with her fork. "Fruitless?" she asked, a glint of challenge behind soulful eyes.

He wished to remove her spectacles and gaze more deeply into those eyes. He wondered why exactly she needed the specs. "I can't say I'm sorry about that."

Surprise flitted across her expression, and a blush touched her cheeks.

"But I am sorry you've met with those who are not what they seem. From the short time I've come to know you, your frankness deserves better. Far better."

She stared at him openly until he grew uncomfortable. She blinked and refocused on her own plate. She spoke softly. "I admit to being hasty—at times—in jumping to the wrong conclusions about a person."

At that admission, Richard felt it easier to breathe. "Speaking of mistaken identities, might you help me with something? What, in your opinion, is the best course of action to gently correct a person, should she—or he—mistake a person for someone they are not, particularly when they say things making it impossible for the other person to immediately admit who they truly are? Should the error be left alone so as to spare the one who jumped to the wrong conclusion their possible humiliation—only out of kindness and confusion, of course, and not mockery—or should the person be set up for instant mortification?"

He heard an "ahem" from Mother and looked up. His mother, Frank, Ophelia, and Mckay all gaped at him.

McKay stabbed at his pork. "How've you been feeling since coming home, laddie? Stanhope mentioned you were wounded in Salamanca. Head injury was it?" He arched his brow and took his bite.

"You know it was my ribs, McKay." Four broken.

Quiet laughter came from his right, and he glanced to see Miss Rowley grinning into her napkin. "Forgive me, Lieutenant," she said, still trying to quell her amusement. She pressed her lips together and composed herself. "I shall give your question some thought."

"You understood him?" McKay asked.

She smiled warmly at McKay. "I understood his question. It is still to be determined whether or not I understand *him*."

McKay laughed along with the others and leaned toward Richard, pointing with his knife. "Keep this one about, laddie. Apparently, she understands *dunderheid*."

Richard glared at McKay, and Frank laughed harder. Still, Richard believed he'd gotten his point across. The situation had been nearly impossible. Miss Rowley had to see that now.

CHAPTER FIVE

MARINA FINGERED A FRESH ARRANGEMENT of holly and ivy on a table as she waited nervously in the front hall in her soft-green riding habit. Mother thought the color drab, but it reminded Marina of the morning sea, and for that, she loved it.

"Good morning, Miss Rowley."

She jumped at the lieutenant's deep voice and caught her finger on a holly leaf. She drew in a quick breath at the pain and pressed her finger to her thumb, but no skin was broken. She blushed as she pulled her glove on. "Must you keep doing that?"

"Are you hurt?" he asked as she turned to him. He wore his rough brown coat again and held a short beaver instead of the flatcap. Ridiculous, the difference a hat could make in helping discern a person's station. As the lieutenant looked her over, Marina's heart gave a singularly hard thump at the realization that his eyes, too, matched the color of the morning sea.

She shook her head. "Not a scratch. Only startled." She curtsied, not knowing what else to do.

He bowed. "Good. Forgive me for startling you. Are you ready, then?"

She nodded and stepped forward when he gestured to the door. What was she doing here? When the gentlemen had joined the ladies after their port, Lieutenant Stanhope had once more approached, to her surprise, and asked her to join him for a ride through Canterwood's grounds in the morning. She could not turn him down, for she loved to ride, and the horses were of great interest to her, which she'd kept reminding herself as her mother had lectured her all the way from Scarborough about Marina's "purpose" in coming to the party. She couldn't very well feign disinterest in riding at her first opportunity and have to go the rest of the party declining other invitations if any came. Besides, what a hypocrite that would make her—pretending to be something she wasn't. The lieutenant had praised her frankness, so she would be frank. And frankly, she was no great horsewoman, but she was a good one, and Canterwood's reputation for horses of beauty and solid temperament intrigued her.

But the fact that the lieutenant had sought her out for a ride this morning puzzled her. To say they'd had a rough start was a severe understatement. She still harbored a measure of anger toward him.

"You are quiet this morning," he said as they walked toward the stables. "Are you contemplating my question from dinner last night?"

"You mean when you asked me how on earth anyone could turn away scalloped oysters?"

"No, though I am still flummoxed."

"I thought I was being discreet. I didn't wish to offend my hosts."

"No offense taken. One needn't eat every dish from every course—we'd never get up off our chairs—only, you'd arranged the food on your plate so there was no room when the oysters came around."

"You saw that?"

"Is it the scalloped part of the dish or the oysters you don't care for?"

She blinked, still working out the part where he'd watched her move her food. "The oysters. I've never liked them. Very unpatriotic of me, I know, though I do love halibut and cod and all kinds of fish. I did eat the sole. It was lovely."

"Yes, it was. One of my favorites. Nice trick, that. Maybe I'll try it the next time cauliflower comes on the menu."

She searched for more to say, but were they really to go on talking of fish and cauliflower? Because frankly, the fact that *any* man had sought her out for a morning ride puzzled her. It had simply never happened. She'd been asked on group picnics and walks with two or three other couples. Once, she wasn't even sure which gentleman was accompanying her.

"You never answered my question," he said.

"Hmm?"

"About how to address a certain misunderstanding. You said you'd think on how best to go about handling it, since my attempt so thoroughly failed."

Oh yes. That. She stopped walking, and he halted next to her. She knew what she needed to say, and her heart skittered. "Lieutenant, last night I stayed awake for some time going over that conversation in the hedges. You tried to correct me, didn't you?"

He pursed his mouth and toed the gravel path with his boot. "Too gently, I think."

"Perhaps. But I didn't give you much chance. It was a horrible situation, and I was—am still—quite mortified." She felt her cheeks grow warm again. "I—I accept that you tried your best. I've no idea what I might have done in your stead."

"You would have been more forthright."

She blinked at the unexpected observation. She could not dispute it. "You make it difficult to argue, sir."

"Do you wish to argue?"

"Yes."

He laughed. "I deserve that."

"I can't argue with that, either."

He sobered. "Do you still believe I was mocking you?"

She studied him for a moment—all she allowed herself—and looked away. "Have you ever experienced a terrible thing so often you come to expect it? And when it doesn't happen, you convince yourself it must be happening anyway?"

At his lack of answer, she peeked at him. He watched her intently but was also somewhere else.

"I'm rambling," she said to break the tension. "Mother says I ramble."

He blinked then, as if waking. "Not at all. Have you heard the term *battle hysteria*?"

"When soldiers believe the war is still happening around them?"

"It's just as you described. Perfectly."

"How awful." Marina watched him for a moment, wondering that he, of all people, might understand. She inhaled the crisp December air to clear her head and perhaps cool her cheeks. They resumed walking.

After a few moments of awkward silence, he spoke. "I find I enjoy your rambling."

She shook her head. "I am infamous for driving conversation to a standstill, and since it's just the two of us, I'll try to refrain. Trying counts for a lot, I hear."

He smiled, and it shone on him like winter sun. "It does. But I must assure you, we'll not be riding alone." He paused before the immaculate stables.

"Well, we'll have a chaperone, of course," she said. "I assumed one of the stablehands would—"

"Uncle!" A small girl with bouncing auburn hair ran at the lieutenant. She skidded to a halt just before she might've hurled into him. "We're ready for our ride." She eyed Marina and bobbed a curtsy with a grin. This was without a doubt Ophelia Stanhope's child.

Marina glanced beyond the girl to a stableboy waiting next to a strawberry dappled pony. An older boy and girl held back near their own horses and watched with interest. Algernon and Sophia, no longer little things.

"Miss Rowley, have you met my niece Helena?"

"I've not had the pleasure." Marina curtsied. "How do you do, miss?"

She bobbed. "Very well, thank you. I'm looking forward to our ride. Uncle Richard said we're to roam far and wide. Perhaps all the way to *Scotland*."

"That far?" Marina leaned forward. "I hope he packed a picnic."

The lieutenant cleared his throat. "I made no mention of Scotland, merely Byrness."

The little girl giggled, for Byrness was almost as far.

He motioned the other children forward as they laughed. "Alger, Sophia, come greet your mother's cousin Miss Rowley. You've met before; did you know? She created your cherubic silhouettes that hang in the portrait hall. How she managed to render you both angelic is pure magic."

Marina glanced at him, wondering at both this playful side of him with the children and his enthusiasm over such a meager artistic talent.

"Oh," Sophia said, her eyes wide, "do you still make silhouettes? Could you show me?"

"I'd be delighted to," Marina said, somewhat taken aback by the request. "We'd need the proper supplies."

Sophia turned and took Alger's arm. "That's what I can make Mother and Father for Christmas."

"Wonderful," Alger said. "Now I won't have to listen to you go on and on about what to get them."

Sophia frowned. "At least I have an idea now. You're still drawing a blank."

"Only because I'm waiting for brilliance to strike." He turned and executed a gentlemanly bow to Marina. "Pleased to meet you, cousin. I've heard Mama mention you with fondness many times. Welcome to Canterwood." He bowed again.

As Marina curtsied, she peeked at Lieutenant Stanhope and found him covering a grin at the boy's formality. "Thank you, Alger," she said. "Your mother and I were closer as girls, when we both lived near the sea. I always looked up to her. It was she who taught me how to play graces, and I taught her how to dig for clams."

Helena's brows shot to the sky. "Mama knows how to dig for clams?"

"She does. She got quite good at it, too."

"I can't believe it."

Marina laughed at the girl's bewildered expression. "I'm sure there are a lot of things you can't believe your mother can do. It's easy to forget our parents were children once. I can't for the life of me imagine my mother playing marbles, but my grandfather told me once that she was unconquerable. Don't tell her I told you that."

Helena giggled.

Marina lifted her head to catch the lieutenant watching her. She straightened and adjusted her jacket. "Now, children, which horse is mine? You do have a horse or two somewhere abouts, correct?" She looked blindly about.

Helena clasped her hand and tugged as the others laughed. What surprised Marina was the deep, gentle laugh coming from Lieutenant Stanhope. The sound seemed to roll through her like a gentle wave of the sea, lifting her onto her toes and setting her back down again, only not quite as steady in the sand as she had been before.

Oh dear.

Quill, the horse Marina had been given, rode sturdily beneath her in the winter-gold countryside awash with morning fog. Marina rubbed the mare's withers, and Quill huffed good-naturedly. "You are a fine lady, aren't you?"

Helena rode next to Marina. "Quill is a sweetheart. That's what Papa says. That's why we chose her for you."

"She's lovely." Quill's buff coloring gently melded into long brown legs. "I imagine all of your horses are fine."

"Not Phantom. He's atrocious. Tulip won't go near him."

Lieutenant Stanhope drew up on the other side of Helena. "He'll come along. Phantom has good lines."

"Well, he's forgotten them, then."

The lieutenant smiled. "Brutality will do that. Good thing your father found him when he did. He's in better hands now, and he'll grow to know it."

Helena sighed. "I hope he does. He's in the prettiest stables in the world. If I were a horse at Canterwood, I wouldn't be cranky at all. I'd run and frolic and eat oats and let the stableboys brush me down until I fell asleep standing."

Marina grinned, stifling a laugh.

"Well," the lieutenant said, "let's leave that for Tulip and Quill and hope the best for Phantom, shall we?"

Helena wrinkled her nose. "I'll try. He's awfully cranky though."

"Do you know what my father would say?" he asked her.

"Tell me."

He leaned forward on his horse, as if to reveal a great secret. "He would say that sometimes all a body needs is someone to believe in him."

Helena's brows rose. "Ohh, I know that one. When Sophia was nervous about playing her pianoforte for Grandmama's spring musicale, I told her I knew she could do it. And she did!"

Sophia, who was riding ahead next to Alger, turned at hearing her name and now smiled at her little sister with a look so appreciative that Marina almost missed her own younger sister. Almost.

"You see?" the lieutenant said. "You're already wise beyond your years." He glanced up at Marina, catching her watching him far too intently. The corner of his mouth lifted, and instead of a soldier, she glimpsed the young man he might've been before he left for war.

She straightened, feeling her cheeks go red, and nudged Quill onward to catch up with Alger and Sophia, composing herself as she went.

"Miss Rowley—" Sophia began when Marina rode next to her.

"Marina, if you please. After all, we're cousins. I cooed at you when you were the size of a loaf of bread."

Alger chuckled at that.

Marina leaned forward. "And you, Alger, were the size of a tom turkey and twice as much trouble."

Sophia laughed. "A turkey."

Alger rolled his eyes.

"What was your question, Sophia?" Marina gave Quill another pat.

"I've been wondering about what you said about Mama digging for clams."

Oh dear. What box had she opened with that bit of knowledge? "Yes?"

"You live at the sea."

"Yes, I do. I saw your mother often before her family moved from Whitby to Skipton."

"Last time we went to the coast, I was only barely beginning to draw." Sophia blushed and concentrated on the path before her. "Now that I'm older, I do wish to paint the sea."

"Artists come to Scarborough from all over to paint the sea, with their easels set up right on the sand. I've seen as many as a dozen artists on the beach on any given day."

"That many! Out where everybody can see?"

"Yes. People can stroll by and even watch for a bit if they'd like."

Sophia's hand pressed to her heart. "Oh, I'm not sure I could do that."

"Well, there are plenty of more-secluded viewpoints. Suppose I speak with your mama about having you come visit? As an artist's study?"

The girl sat straight in her saddle, her face lighting up. "Would you?"

Marina laughed at her sudden energy. "I cannot promise you anything, but I'll try."

"I hope Mama says yes. I long to see it again."

"It is a sight to behold. But nothing can describe the sounds of the seaside, the rhythm of waves crashing upon the cliffs or breaking upon the sand, the cry of gulls and barking of seals—"

"Seals?" Alger exclaimed.

"Oh yes, seals and minke whales and sometimes you can see porpoises."

Alger's eyes grew large. "Porpoises? Perhaps you could ask Mama if I should come along. You know, as a chaperone."

Sophia turned to Alger. "You, my chaperone?"

"That's what I said." Alger puffed out his chest.

As the two older children carried on about who needed to chaperone whom, Marina fell back again, already considering how to approach Ophelia about the matter.

The lieutenant drew up alongside her as Helena's pony hurried past so she could catch up to her siblings. "It might've been wiser to speak with Ophelia before bringing the idea up to the children."

"Do you think so?" Marina gave him a shrewd look. "Sophia's enthusiasm cannot be bottled now, and I happen to know how much that young lady pulls at her mother's heartstrings." She lifted her brow, and Lieutenant Stanhope laughed heartily.

"Wiser indeed." He settled back into his seat. "I'm learning never to underestimate you, Miss Rowley."

"Now who is wise, Lieutenant?" She hid her smile but couldn't help glancing his way. She immediately regretted it, as he was studying her intently again, making it difficult to keep her defenses fortified. She dropped her chin. "Why do you look at me that way?"

"I was wondering how wise it would be to ask for your help with a personal matter."

She adjusted her grip on the reins, her heart fluttering uncomfortably. "Be warned, Lieutenant. It is said *true* wisdom comes to us when we realize how little we understand."

"That is Plato."

"Some think *him* wise."

He smiled. "Is that a yes or a no?"

She stilled, unsure. "Why would you ask me?"

He held her gaze for an uncomfortably long time.

"Uncle?"

Marina and the lieutenant turned their heads toward Helena, far in front of them.

"May we run?" she called.

He sat up in his seat. "You may gallop elegantly."

Helena giggled, urging her pony onward.

Marina drew in a needed breath. "I think I'll join them."

CHAPTER SIX

RICHARD WATCHED ON THE VERGE of frustration and amusement—a sensation he was becoming used to associating with Miss Rowley—as she rode with the children, their laughter reaching him.

He was in no hurry to catch up yet. One minute they'd been pleasantly bantering back and forth, and the next, she'd shown him that look again. The one from the hedge—searching, asking him to be trustworthy.

He'd seen that look before as his men had ridden through towns already razed by battle. Women with their arms around their children; a lone boy huddled and hungry in the rubble; a young woman shivering with fear, clutching her shawl about her—all had worn the same vulnerable expression. He could do so little, and all of them had been left behind to make what they could of their wrecked lives.

What was it that made Miss Marina Rowley look at him that way? Surely, she'd not been through battle. The idea repulsed him. He shook it away and urged his horse to catch up with the jovial group.

"Uncle," Helena called out to him, "we're being very elegant and dashing in our galloping, are we not?"

The children held their heads high, their brows lifted, and Alger held one fist on his hip, his elbow jutting out smartly. They slowed in fits of laughter, catching their breath.

"I daresay," Richard said, "I've never happened upon a more elegant group of riders in my life. And that's saying something, considering my former profession."

Miss Rowley turned at that. "Former?"

"Is that what I said?" He checked himself and shook his head, attempting to cover his slip. "Too long without the uniform, I suppose." It had been cleaned for the ball but had been wearable for days now.

She eyed him but said nothing further.

"I don't suppose any of you are hungry," he said, changing the subject. "I heard Cook has made her rich molasses cakes."

Sounds of the affirmative rang through the air.

"Well, if you're not hungry, then on to Scotland!"

"We *are* hungry!" the children exclaimed.

"Oh, very well." He made a show of sighing deeply. "Miss Rowley? The children have spoken. We hie back to the house."

"Agreed, sir." Her lips pursed in an impish manner. "We do hie."

The remainder of the ride passed as pleasantly as it had begun. As the children and Miss Rowley turned in the direction of the stables, Richard called to his nephew. "Alger, hold up a bit."

"Yes, sir?"

When he reached the boy, Richard dropped his voice. "I'm to ask you . . ." He paused, glancing toward where Miss Rowley rode, sure and with pleasure, the feathers on her riding cap swaying as she laughed with the girls. "I—that is, Miss Rowley and I—are to join you in a Christmas activity this week."

Richard didn't like the way Alger grinned at him.

"It is an assignment from my mother," he continued. "To keep Miss Rowley entertained."

Alger's brow lifted, and he nodded as if he were sixty years old, with eyes that saw further than they should. "I like Cousin Marina. She doesn't talk to us like we're still in our nappies."

"Who talks to you like that?" Alger was big for his age, and except for some roundness lingering in his cheeks, was shedding most signs of boyishness.

"Miss Balfour and Miss Hughes. Especially when they're together."

"Ah." He could picture that. The girls—now ladies—had always been what Frank termed "gushers"—fawning gigglers over anything they deemed dear. "Don't let it bother you. Another year at Harrow, and you'll shake them."

Alger sat a little taller in his seat.

"Now, about something for Christmas. Is there anything we might be included in?"

"Let's see." Alger assumed a thinking expression. "We've had our Christmas play early—you know that—on account of the house party and

Mama thinking it not suitable for so many guests. You were an excellent innkeeper, by the way."

"It was my pleasure." He was struck by how this was the same Alger who'd clambered up his back to reach the higher apples in the orchard trees. That was eight years and forever ago.

"Because of the house party, the coal and firewood collection for the poor with Mr. and Mrs. Langley has also been done."

"You've been busy."

"Grandmama is a force in her desire for efficacy."

Richard quirked a smile. "Quite."

After another moment, Alger's expression brightened. "I have it. Miss Rowley has already promised to help Sophia with her Christmas present to Mama and Papa. Why don't you help us with our gifts too? Helena always bites off more than she can chew, and I—well, I'm a bit stumped this year, to tell the truth."

Richard considered. He was no artist, but he'd learned from his father to work with his hands. "I think that a fine idea, Alger. When shall we meet?"

"The sooner the better. Would there be time before everyone readies for the ball this evening?"

"We'll discuss it at tea with Miss Rowley." Richard felt a weight lift. He was checking off the requirements on his mother's list faster than he'd believed possible. "My thanks to you, Alger. I knew I could count on you."

"Aye, sir." He gave a sharp salute, grinned, and urged his steed onward to join the others.

Richard brought his horse to a halt. The salute, coming from a face so fresh and young as Alger's, brought forth a jumble of faces, each of them young, hopeful boys willing to follow command for King and country. Each of them dead.

"Sir?"

Richard blinked. How long had his horse been standing here in the cold?

"Sir?" A stablehand—Peter—sat astride one of the mares. "The children sent me after you. They said you were to be joining them for tea and cakes. Demanded it, they did. You know how they are."

Richard acknowledged Peter with a nod and cleared his throat. "H-how long ago?"

"Quarter hour, sir?"

"Of course. On my way." He squeezed the reins, very aware of the slight tremor in his hands. It would pass. It always passed.

After stabling his horse, he entered his childhood home now filled with the scent of Cook's rich molasses cakes and a slow-roasting venison that would appear on tonight's dinner plates. He inhaled deeply, and the smells steadied him. He deposited his hat and gloves with their butler, Nelson, did his best to avoid other guests, and made his way through the conservatory to the small adjacent music room, where the children sometimes took their morning tea. He paused at the sight before him.

Midmorning light filtered in through the narrow windows, landing on Helena, who sat at her little harp, plinking out "Greensleeves." On a low bench next to her sat Miss Rowley, leaning forward in rapt attention despite the teacup and saucer she held in her lap. Her gaze was fixed on Helena's fingers as if Helena's playing depended upon Miss Rowley's concentration.

Helena finished playing and Miss Rowley drew in a breath as if a spell were broken. She then set her cup and saucer down on the bench and clapped with fervor, Sophia and Alger joining in from across the room. Helena's dear face lit up in a grin. Richard clapped as well, immediately drawing the attention of the entire room, which had not been his intent.

"Uncle Richard," Helena said, standing, "Peter found you." Miss Rowley stood as well.

He chuckled. "Indeed. I apologize for my tardiness. My penalty is missing the first part of your lovely song." His gaze roamed to Miss Rowley's, her round spectacles resting primly on her nose. She'd changed from her riding habit into a white muslin gown with some sort of flowery stripes elongating her figure and accentuating her not-so-prim curves. He cleared his throat and glanced at the tea table. "Have you saved me a cake? Or is cake forfeiture another penalty?"

Miss Rowley spoke. "We thought you might be engaged elsewhere, so we began without you. There is cake left, despite Alger's efforts. May I pour you some tea?" Without waiting for his response, she moved to the tray and prepared him a cup. "If you'd like, we can send for more cakes. They are wonderful."

Alger lifted his head from the book he was reading. "I had three."

"One will do, thank you," Richard said, watching her move to pour tea and settle a cake onto a plate before offering it to him. He'd seen the ritual performed hundreds of times throughout his life; it was all so very British. But just now, after losing himself out there in the cold, the warmth of this scene and the unassuming domesticity of it enveloped him, and he felt peace.

Miss Rowley lifted a brow. "Are you well, Lieutenant?"

He shook himself. "Yes." He stepped to her and took the cup and saucer. The cup clattered in the exchange, and Miss Rowley's hand slipped beneath his to steady it. "Thank you," he said, though it came out under his breath as her warmth spread up his arm.

Her focus stayed on the cup, her cheeks blooming in soft rose. "Are you steady now?" she whispered.

He wasn't sure how to answer, as her touch had his pulse leaping around his chest cavity like a wild hare. What was this? Who was this Miss Rowley? He swallowed and straightened his posture. "I believe so."

She nodded and slipped her hand from his. As she turned to retrieve her tea and retake her place on the bench, Richard nearly called her back. But he had no proper reason to. She stared into her tea until Helena engaged her in conversation.

He was about to take a seat near the fire grate when Helena's next question stopped him. "Why do you wear spectacles, Marina?"

Richard took a seat nearer the conversation.

"Helena," Sophia interjected in a hushed tone, approaching her sister. "That is impolite."

"I was only curious. Nelson wears specs, but he is very old. And so does Widow Kittering. She's *ancient*." She turned to Miss Rowley. "You aren't old at all."

"Tell that to Society, my dear." She grinned. "Perhaps you'll start a revolution."

Helena's brow wrinkled in confusion, and Richard had to cover his own smile. "Is it truly impolite?" the child said, looking between her sister and her cousin. "I only wondered what makes people wear them if they're not old. I like them on our cousin. She looks dashing."

Miss Rowley released a befuddled laugh. She seemed to be avoiding looking in Richard's direction at all. Her voice quieted. "It is an honest question, and I'll give you an honest answer. When I was thirteen, just Alger's age, I had an accident and hit my head quite hard. I survived it, but afterward my eyes wouldn't focus as they ought. My eyeglasses help fix that.

I must wear them, you see. Unless it's close up, everything is a bit blurred without them."

"Ohhh," Helena said with reverence. Then she turned to Sophia, chin lifted. "It was an *honest* question, Sophia."

Sophia tilted her head. "Even honest questions can make others feel uncomfortable." She sat down next to Miss Rowley and linked elbows with her. "I'm glad your spectacles help," she said.

Miss Rowley looked down at the chestnut-haired girl. "So am I."

Sophia nodded. "And Helena's right. You do look dashing."

"Thank you, girls." Her response came in a whisper, so soft Richard barely heard it.

Ever so briefly, her gaze flickered toward Richard, then was anywhere but his for the rest of tea, even when they arranged to help the children with their gifts later that afternoon. He felt its absence.

CHAPTER SEVEN

MARINA'S MOTHER ENTERED HER ROOM just as Marina was to go downstairs for a poetry reading. "Mama, you didn't even knock." She had hoped for a few minutes with Ophelia after the reading to discuss Sophia's visit during the summer months.

"Oh, tosh, I'm your mother. Now, tell me." Her mother sat her curvaceous self on a chair by the fire and smoothed her skirts. She leaned forward, eyeing Marina, who still stood mere steps from the door. So close to freedom.

Marina sighed and strode to the chair opposite her mother's and sat. She, too, leaned forward. "Tell you what?"

"Tell me what? *Lieutenant Stanhope*, that's what. He has singled you out and is in pursuit. Do you deny it?"

"Yes, I do, Mama," she said steadily, though hearing her mother's words knocked her unsteady. "Lieutenant Stanhope only reintroduced me to my young cousins; that is all. I had a wonderful time with the children. The lieutenant hardly spoke with me." Even as she said the words, her thoughts ran back over her conversations with him, his laughter, the startling jolt from their touch when she'd steadied his hand under his teacup. She pushed the memory away. "He was pleasant but not *in pursuit*." Was he? Would she even know if a man truly was in pursuit?

"Oh, come now. We both know you're not a timid girl, except when it comes to courtship—"

"That's because I've never been courted—"

"That is untrue. Why, Mr. Oliver—"

"Mr. Oliver pretended to court me to make Anne St. George jealous."

"And it only worked because you were a true rival."

Marina stood, fists balled. "It worked because the idea of courting me was so ridiculous she couldn't stand it."

Her mother gaped.

Marina sat again and let her frustration go. "It's true, Mama. You know it. And it wasn't the only time I've been made a laughingstock. Mr. Scott, Mr. Jennings, Sir Montagu—all potential suitors either on a dare or playing at some joke." She swallowed down tears. She need not shed them again over those *gentlemen.*

"Well, if it weren't for your accident—thirteen is already a terrible age, and then to have to put spectacles over your lovely face just as you were blooming—"

"I could have died, Mama."

"And whose fault was that?"

Marina had grown weary of this old conversation, so familiar she knew every part. She skipped to the end. "The fault was mine. Had I not gone to the water that day, against your wishes, I would not have to wear these spectacles in order see, and I would have been snatched up by now with two fat grandchildren on my lap. Is that right?"

Her mother had the audacity to look compassionate. "You are slipping splendidly into womanhood, Marina. You just hide it behind a sharp wit, taciturn replies, and a quick temper."

Don't forget wire frames, Marina thought. She straightened, considering. "I've been told since I was a young girl that it is a shame I have to wear eyeglasses."

Her mother nodded sadly.

"A *shame,* Mama. I am something to be ashamed of, with only myself to blame." She paused at the revelation. "No wonder I hide. No wonder I do not trust why Lieutenant Stanhope speaks to me." She stood again, shaking with things still unsaid. She took a deep breath as her mother remained blessedly silent. "No *wonder* I am timid of being worth anything to a man—if I have any worth at all." Marina swallowed, shoving aside her fears as the girls' words from that morning returned to her. *You look dashing.* She allowed those simple words to give her strength. She smoothed her skirts.

"If you'll excuse me, I'm to attend the poetry reading downstairs. Perhaps I'll perform Wordsworth's 'The Thorn.' *That* ought to charm the room." She turned toward the door, feeling braver. "'By day, and in the silent night, When all the stars shone clear and bright'"—she pulled the door open, reciting the dreadful, haunting poem—"'That I have heard her cry, Oh misery! oh misery!'" She stepped out into the hall and shut the door behind her, closing her eyes against the dumbfounded look on her mother's face. "'Oh woe is me'—" She turned and bumped into a solid form wearing a gray waistcoat and charcoal coat.

Strong hands gripped her arms, keeping her from losing her balance completely. She looked up into the pale-green eyes of Lieutenant Stanhope. Of course.

"'Oh, misery!'" he said, finishing the poem for her, one eyebrow arched high.

She was stunned into silence, both confused and mortified.

"Do you often quote Wordsworth so passionately as you wander from your room?" he asked.

She blinked and nodded back to her door. "Only when my mother is in there."

"Ah." He nodded gravely as if he understood overbearing mothers. "Allow me to escort you to . . ."

She lifted her brow.

". . . the poetry reading," he finished when she did not.

She swallowed, very aware of his hands still encircling her arms, keeping her from falling over like soft dough. "Thank you."

Gently, he let go of her, as if to make sure her feet were steady under her. When she took his offered hand, he wrapped hers around his arm and leaned toward her. "Will your mother follow?"

She found the wherewithal to answer. "I've likely shocked her into stone."

He glanced around as they reached the top of the landing. "Wordsworth will do that, radical romantic that he is."

She paused, and he stopped, watching her expectantly. "Sir, why were you outside my door just now? We aren't to meet the children until later."

He shook his head. "I—"

At the sound of Marina's door clicking open, they looked at one another, eyes wide.

"We must go," Marina urged in a whisper.

They dashed down the stairs as quickly as they could, Marina taking care not to trip on her skirts. They turned at the next landing and continued down another flight to the main level, where the grinning lieutenant led her not to the conservatory but next door to the little music room, where they'd been with the children that morning.

Both of them collapsed in silent laughter so as not to alert anyone in the adjoining room to their presence.

"Sir," she said, catching her breath and fighting for composure, "we musn't be in here alone."

"I know, I know," he said, holding his side. "I just couldn't rush us into the conservatory out of breath, now, could I? We've escaped your mother. Go ahead." He motioned for her to leave through the door connecting the two rooms. "You'll enter at the back of the room from here. No one will notice."

She moved to the door and turned, hesitating. "Thank you," she said again.

He straightened and bowed. With raised fist he whisper-shouted, "'Oh misery!'"

She suppressed a real laugh, finally composed herself, and opened the door. The bright, warm room was situated just as he'd said, and she slipped through the doorway without notice, taking a seat in the back, near a jungle of ferns. She folded her hands calmly in her lap, but her heart raced above the poem being recited from the front of the room, and it stayed that way for far too long, her own words echoing back to her: *I do not trust why Lieutenant Stanhope speaks to me.*

And she didn't trust it. But she couldn't help enjoying it. *Blast.*

After the poetry reading, Marina sought out Ophelia. Her cousin stood conversing with Lady Teresa, so Marina held back, waiting until the ladies had finished. But Lady Teresa had other ideas.

"Miss Rowley," she said and held out a hand in invitation to join them.

As Marina approached, she felt the attention of several of the other young ladies upon her and, at a glance, interpreted their expressions as censure. Marina lifted her chin and crossed the remaining space. "Yes, Lady Teresa?"

"Hello, my dear. Did the lieutenant find you?"

"Er . . . yes?"

"Good. I stepped out earlier, and he was just there, so I sent him to tell you the poetry reading had begun. Are you enjoying your stay here? I hope the quality of your visit has improved."

"Yes, thank you. I spent the morning with the children." She turned to Ophelia. "They are delightful."

"They are quite the lot, the three of them," Lady Teresa said with affection. "I'm sure the girls are still at odds with Alger's often being away at school."

"Perhaps at times, Lady Teresa," Ophelia countered. "But Helena seems to take it upon herself to make up for his absence." She laughed, shaking her head. "Sophia doesn't get much of a respite with a demanding sibling older and younger than her." She leaned toward Marina with a shrewd look and lowered her voice. "You were not only with the children. My brother-in-law also mentioned being delighted with the *entire* group."

Marina willed her cheeks not to pink. "Speaking of your brother-in-law, I have been tracing my memory and cannot recall you ever mentioning him in the few correspondences we've exchanged over the years."

"Did I not?" Ophelia frowned. "Strange. I'm sure I would have at least mentioned his leaving for war and his return in the party invitation. We have not written letters very regularly, have we? I'm sorry for that."

"Do not be. Any letter was a welcome reminder of our childhood. I'm glad we can pick up as though no time was lost, aren't you?"

Ophelia nodded. "That is the blessing of true friendship."

Marina smiled, then frowned. "The odd thing is I do remember you mentioning a brother going to war. But his name was Charlie." She looked between Lady Teresa and Ophelia as their brows furrowed. Fear pricked Marina's heart. "Oh, I hope I haven't stumbled upon a family tragedy."

"No," Ophelia said, grasping her arm. She laughed. "Oh, goodness, no. I guess I did mention Richard after all. Charlie was his nickname as a young boy. His middle name is Charles, you see. It took Frank a long time to relinquish it, long after Richard had left it behind. I knew him as Charlie then and apparently referred to him as such."

"Oh!" Marina exhaled in sudden understanding. "So when you referred to a Lieutenant Richard Stanhope returning from war, I—"

"—didn't have any idea whom I was referring to?"

"No. Only some relative."

They laughed. Oh, would that Marina had known before coming.

Lady Teresa smiled at her most compassionately. Marina could only thank the stars the woman still had no idea what had happened out in the privet hedge.

Ophelia's brow furrowed. "Is everything . . . all right . . . between you and the lieutenant?"

"Oh. Yes. That is to say, he has been very . . ." What was the word she was looking for that would describe what the lieutenant was without leading them to think more than they ought? Charming? Compelling? Engaging—no, not *that* word. "*Gracious.* He's been gracious in showing me some of Canterwood."

"Gracious, indeed." Ophelia lifted a brow.

Marina needed a swift change of subject. "Ophelia, I should like to ask you to consider allowing Sophia to come stay at Whimbrel Manor this summer. She has a wish to paint the sea. It might give her some of the respite you mentioned."

"How kind of you to offer. My goodness, it's been too long since she's been. Most of our recent family travel has been to Scotland or to the south, depending on where horse business takes Frank. She does love to paint. I shall speak with my husband. I see no reason a girl of eleven shouldn't have an adventure with her grown cousin. After all, you and I had many adventures, did we not?" She smiled, and Marina knew she'd won.

"We did indeed."

Then Ophelia's smile broadened. "Perhaps the lieutenant could be her escort."

"Oh! Oh." *Drat.* Marina felt her cheeks go straight to red. She swallowed against her suddenly dry mouth. "As a matter of fact, Alger offered to be her escort when I mentioned porpoises."

Her cousin's eyes glinted with humor. "He did, did he? There goes her respite. Well, I shall speak with Frank. I'll let you know how it turns out."

Just then a murmur of delight spread through the room as a group of gentlemen, including Lieutenant Stanhope and Mr. and Mrs. Langley, entered. Julia spied Marina and left her husband's side but was detained from joining her friends by two older women as the younger ladies swarmed the lieutenant like bees to a sunflower—if bees were to giggle behind silk fans. The gentlemen made their bows, and Marina watched Lieutenant Stanhope smile and converse. He caught her watching and raised his fist.

She quickly averted her eyes and snorted a laugh, then pressed her lips together to prevent further impropriety. She faked a dainty cough into her hand. "Pardon me. A sudden dry throat."

Ophelia appeared to be unfooled. "I'll get you some refreshment." She smiled and left Marina with Lady Teresa, who gently touched Marina's arm.

"I do hope you are sincere when you say you are enjoying your time here, Miss Rowley," she said. "We wish our guests to feel our joy and share in it."

The group surrounding the lieutenant burst into laughter, and Marina nodded toward them. "Then, I believe you are successful, Lady Teresa." She returned the older lady's smile. "And I am having a perfectly amiable time. The past is in the past. Truly."

Marina's mother entered the room then, and Marina felt a heavy reminder that not all was amiable. For the first time since they'd left Whimbrel Manor, she wished her sister were with them. She was always a good buffer between Marina and Mama. They locked eyes, but instead of approaching Marina, her mother turned to explore a grouping of lemon trees framing a trellised bougainvillea.

"I hope you're looking forward to the ball this evening," Lady Teresa said.

"Oh. Yes, of course." Marina attempted to hide her weariness of balls. "I'm sure it will be delightful."

"It will be my son's first in many years."

"Does he like to dance?"

"He used to."

"And now?"

"We shall see. I imagine a measure of that depends upon the lady standing up with him."

Marina nodded. "One's partner can have a great deal to do with how one enjoys the dance."

"Well then, I hope you each enjoy the ball immensely." The woman lifted her brow and smiled, a hint of mischief in her expression reminding Marina of the lieutenant.

Marina blinked, unsure what to say. She managed a "Thank you, my lady" as Ophelia appeared.

"Here is your tea, darling," she said, offering her a dainty cup. "I added honey."

"Thank you." She sipped her tea. "I'm sure this will help."

"Are you not feeling well?" Julia asked as she joined their group, making Marina feel a bit surrounded.

"Good day, Julia. I'm well. Just a dry throat. Ophelia is an attentive hostess."

Ophelia grinned like a tiger. "That I am. Now, Lady Teresa and I have to see about preparations for the ball. What do you plan to do with yourselves?"

Marina lowered her teacup. "I promised Sophia I'd help her with a Christmas project, so I'm off to the nursery."

"That is very good of you," Ophelia said.

"It will be my pleasure."

Lady Teresa smiled. "May I ask what project?"

"I believe that is a secret, my lady."

"Is it a secret from me?" Julia asked. "It's been a long time since I've visited the nursery."

Marina grinned. "If you can keep a secret, then I should be happy to have your company."

"I took care of those children for a full year. I've kept secrets galore."

After finishing the tea, Marina followed Julia to the nursery. Julia and the current Stanhope governess worked at the table with the girls, who painted their silhouettes with a brick of black watercolor paint and brushes.

The lieutenant stood behind Marina as she sketched lines on ivory wove paper for Alger's silhouette. "It's astonishing how quickly you work. I'd have guessed we'd be up here for hours."

"If I'd had my black paper and snips with me, I'd have saved us a step. I've seen cutters finish a piece in under three minutes. But this way the children get to be more involved in painting themselves, which will add to the gift, don't you think? Hold still, Alger. You can look when I'm finished."

"Alger and I will procure frames for each, won't we, lad?"

"Aye, sir."

"You've captured him. Look at that stout chin. The girls' likenesses are remarkable as well. You've quite a talent."

Marina blushed. "'Tis a poor man's art, sir."

"Nonsense. If I were to try one, the likeness would more resemble the coast of Ireland than its subject."

She stifled a laugh, as did Alger. "Well, I've had a lot of practice, and I do enjoy it. I suppose that counts for something."

"Having something to enjoy counts for everything," he murmured.

She looked up at him, her pencil paused over the paper. His expression had grown serious as they studied one another.

"What do you enjoy, Lieutenant?"

"I believe I'm figuring that out."

Breathing suddenly became a thing Marina was very conscious of. She turned away from the lieutenant and tried to focus again on the task before her. She cleared her throat, pushing her spectacles higher on her nose. "Alger, lift your chin just a bit—there. I'm nearly finished."

A knock at the door sent the room into a slight flurry as its occupants attempted to hide their gifts. The governess cracked open the door and peeked out, drew her head back in, and addressed Julia. "It's Mr. Langley."

The room seemed to sigh in relief.

Julia nodded and said, "Let him in," and Marina and Alger stood.

"Good afternoon, ladies." The vicar bowed. "Gentlemen. I've come to collect my wife. My goodness. Look what you've been up to. Lieutenant, did you do these?"

"You know I did not. They are Miss Rowley's work."

"They are fine indeed." The vicar rested a hand on Sophia's shoulder, and she beamed up at him. "Your parents will treasure them."

He came over to look at the progress on Alger's silhouette. "You've made him a man," he said, flashing Marina a smile.

"It was not difficult. He is well on his way."

Alger couldn't have stood taller if he tried.

"Well, I'll let you get back to it." He glanced at the lieutenant. "You look cozy in here. We missed you downstairs. McKay and Colonel Rathbone played the most spirited game of chess I have ever observed."

"I can't say I'm sorry I missed that," he answered, folding his arms.

"The lieutenant found us the right paper and paint," Marina said. "He's been most supportive."

"I wouldn't expect any less." Mr. Langley paused. "I enjoyed a conversation with your father, Miss Rowley. He speaks very fondly of you."

"Does he?" she asked, her heart warming. "That is very fortunate, as I am very fond of him." It was true. Her father's kindness and humor often settled her after her mother's rebukes.

The vicar laughed and went to Julia to help her stand. "Come, my dear. We must return to the vicarage."

"Will we see you at the ball tonight?" Marina asked.

"I'm afraid not," the vicar said with an apologetic smile. "We'll have a quiet Christmas Eve at the vicarage. I have a bit of parish business to attend to, and I believe my wife needs to rest."

"Oh, rest, rest. The fact is I have no ball gown that fits me," Julia said, pressing her hand into the small of her back. "I do wish I could come. A ball is always exciting, whether I dance or not."

Marina couldn't agree. That sensation of being overlooked again and again whilst joyful music played was not in the least bit exciting. The only thing worse was being asked to dance by a gentleman who had eyes and ears only for another.

Julia gripped both Marina's arms and kissed her cheek in a sudden and unexpected show of affection. She whispered, "Where did you go? You looked so sad just now."

Marina shook away her melancholy and stood straight. "I'm sorry I won't see you tonight." Marina found she meant it. Julia was fast becoming a dear friend, and those were precious to Marina. "Rest well."

"I will." Julia nodded to the lieutenant. "You'll see that she's not alone tonight, won't you, Lieutenant?"

The lieutenant opened his mouth to speak, but Marina cut him off. "I won't need looking after. I've spent many a ball on my own." She winced. That wasn't what she'd meant to convey at all. "What I mean to say is it is not the lieutenant's responsibility to look after me. I'm sure, as the guest of honor, his company will be much sought-after."

Julia lifted her brow at Lieutenant Stanhope as if to challenge him in this.

He took Julia's hand and bowed over it. "Your friend will not be neglected, madam. I have every confidence Miss Rowley will enjoy herself tonight, with or without my help. But having said that"—he turned to Marina—"might I take this moment to request the first dance, Miss Rowley?"

Julia smiled expectantly between them both, and Helena giggled. At the sound, Marina glanced behind her to find all three children grinning at her.

She quickly turned back to the lieutenant. She curtsied, her heart skittering but wary. "Of course you may, sir."

With that, the Langleys bid them happy Christmas and farewell, and Marina managed to finish Alger's silhouette and set him up for painting it in. It was decided that as soon as Alger finished, the children would join their uncle on a trip into the village to purchase suitable frames and be back in time for early dinner before everyone retired to ready themselves for the ball.

"I do wish we had snow," Helena said. "We haven't yet been able to use the sleigh, and I adore a sleighride, don't you, Marina?"

Marina smiled. "My first sleighride was two years ago, the last few winters being so terribly cold in London. We rarely get snow in Scarborough, but that year, it was cold enough that the Thames froze solid. Did you hear of the Frost Fairs?"

Alger nodded. "Father told me of them—how the river became a festival with tents and booths and a dance. People even roasted pigs over fires right on the ice." His eyes grew large. "Were you there?"

Marina nodded, smiling at the memory. The lieutenant pulled out one of the small chairs and folded himself into it, watching her with interest. She continued. "My father secreted me away without my mother knowing. He wished for me to see it with my own eyes, as he believed it might not happen again. That made it doubly exciting, I suppose."

"What was it like?" Sophia asked.

"We had to be careful when we walked, but it wasn't as slippery as I thought it would be. Children pulled toboggans, and people bowled at pins. Like Alger said, booths of all kinds were set up for selling trinkets and toys so you could say you'd bought something *on* the Thames."

The lieutenant chuckled. She was starting to like that sound.

"My father bought me chestnuts roasted with sugar, and hot chocolate, and we ate our treats near a band playing Bach. It was a lovely adventure, and when I got home, I promised myself that on the same evening every year, I would eat roasted chestnuts and drink hot cocoa before bed."

"How wonderful." Sophia sighed.

"What day was it?" Helena asked.

Marina blinked, suddenly aware that she'd been staring out the lace curtains at the winter sky, lost in envisioning the memory. "The second of February."

Helena turned to her governess. "May we have roasted chestnuts and drink hot chocolate on the second of February?"

The governess smiled. "After that story, I think we'll have to."

"I wish you could be here with us then, Cousin Marina."

"I wish that too." She sat back and caught the gaze of the lieutenant. "What is it, sir?"

He gave his head a slight shake. "Only . . . thank you, for sharing that bit of home."

Of course. He would have been far away that year, fighting on a horse somewhere with a sword. "You're home now, sir."

"Yes," he said. "You keep reminding me."

"I do?"

"Yes. Thank you for that as well."

CHAPTER EIGHT

RICHARD FIDGETED WITH THE CUFFS of his sleeves, and Frank lifted a brow in his direction. He stopped and grasped his hands behind his back, only to bring a hand forward again and offer it to the next guest to be greeted into the ballroom by his family.

He bowed. "How do you do, Miss Balfour? You're looking lovely tonight."

Miss Balfour, all four-and-a-half feet of her, shook with giggles and curtsied behind a fan wafting so fast he felt the breeze. She looked as if she might say something in return, but she only giggled again as her father pulled her along, nodding to Richard.

The room was already becoming warm with guests and the hundred lit candles on the chandeliers and along the refreshment tables. The garden doors had been cracked open, but those were on the other side of the room, below the orchestra's balcony. Canterwood's ballroom was not large, and it looked as though Richard's mother and Ophelia had set upon filling it up well and good.

Frank cleared his throat, and Richard stopped fiddling with his cuffs again. He'd never had a problem fidgeting with his uniform, no matter what shape his nerves were in. He straightened his coat and stood tall. If his training had given him anything, it was the ability to stand at attention.

Frank leaned over. "A bit on edge tonight?"

"Not at all." Richard spoke sardonically. "The dragoons held balls every evening, you know, just after drills. Ensign Trent was especially light on his feet. It was the delight of the war—aside from the complete lack of female partners."

"Not on edge at all, then," Frank muttered. "Good." He straightened. "Mr. Templeton, Mrs. Templeton, welcome. You know my brother,

Lieutenant Richard Stanhope of the British Dragoons? Miss Templeton, Miss Cecelia Templeton, welcome."

Richard bowed and nodded. After the Templetons had moved into the ballroom, he leaned toward Frank. "Did Mother invite any gentlemen to this ball? The young women seem to outnumber us."

"I'm sure the numbers will work themselves out."

"Very reassuring." He searched the incoming group of guests, uncertain what exactly he was looking for.

"She hasn't come yet," Frank said.

"Who?"

"Whoever it is you're searching for."

Richard refused to respond and settled back on his heels, determined not to appear as upended as he felt.

Several more guests were greeted, including a group of wiry young gentlemen who were barely out of the nursery when Richard had left for the war. As they entered the ballroom, he heard Miss Balfour giggle from somewhere in the crowd. How many more people were coming? Surely he wouldn't be missed if he were to slip out through the garden doors and escape.

"Lieutenant?"

He turned and stilled. "Miss Rowley."

She stood in a deep-red column of delicate silk velvet that hugged her every curve before falling to the floor. Her simple adornments—a long gold chain looped twice around her creamy neck and thin gold-ribbon braids wrapping her hair up in loose curls—drew his eyes to small garnets shimmering at each ear. Her spectacles sat upon her straight nose, and she watched him, her gloved hand resting in Frank's, who had turned to him, waiting.

Frank wore a smirk.

Richard ignored it. He took Miss Rowley's hand from Frank's and bowed over it. "Good evening, miss."

"Good evening, sir." She curtsied, lifting her dress to the side with her free hand. The candlelight caught in every soft fold.

He caught himself staring in silence. He glanced at Frank, who was conversing with another guest. He dropped his voice. "I—the children and I found the perfect frames for your silhouettes. They are wrapped and ready for tomorrow."

She kept her voice low as well. "Thank you for your help."

"It was my pleasure." He stumbled with his words, not wanting to release her yet. "You're enchanting," he said. He'd meant to say she *looked* enchanting, but there it was.

She eyed him skeptically, a smile playing at her mouth. "Thank you, sir."

"I am sincere. I've been anticipating our dance."

"Have you? You won't have to wait much longer."

"True, though I fear it will be over too soon."

The look of skepticism didn't fade as she searched his face. "I may be horrid on my feet. Then our dance might seem interminable."

He laughed, and she broke into a smile—a rare thing to behold. "We shall see, then, won't we?" he said.

She curtsied again, pulled her hand from his, and waited nearby as her father greeted him next with a bow. The man had dark hair and eyes like his daughter and a similar spark of life in his countenance.

"Mr. Rowley, how do you do? And where is Mrs. Rowley?"

"I am quite well. However, Mrs. Rowley has taken powders for a headache and is resting. She hopes to join us later."

"I'm sorry to hear she isn't feeling well. I hope she recovers soon."

"Thank you."

"Have you been enjoying your stay?"

"Indeed, I have, but more importantly, my daughter has." He patted her hand. "Thank you for allotting her time with the children today. She has spoken of nothing else. She's always been good with little ones."

"Papa," Miss Rowley warned.

"A man can brag about his daughter."

"No," she said, not without affection, "he cannot." She tugged on his arm, and Mr. Rowley smiled at Richard and leaned a little closer.

"He can. And anytime you want to listen, I'll brag on."

"Papa," Miss Rowley repeated, firmly this time, and her father followed.

Richard laughed silently, composing himself as he watched Miss Rowley walk away in her red velvet.

His mother had been entirely mistaken. Miss Rowley was anything but a wallflower.

With that thought, he turned and happily greeted the remaining guests while avoiding his brother's discerning eye.

The ball commenced with a simple English country dance. Miss Rowley was *not* horrid on her feet. But whenever she dared a glance at Richard, she seemed a bit startled to find him looking back. A fortunate side effect of this game was her lovely blush, which prompted him to coax a smile from her by speaking, whenever the dance allowed for conversation, of mundane things like challenging the purpose of an aspic or wondering whether the sea was blue because it reflected the color of the sky—or was it the other way around? Or inquiring whether she'd ever tasted a kumquat.

During a turn, her fingers gripping his, she broke into a gentle laugh and shook her head. "Sir, I know nothing of kumquats. I feel my whole existence has been a sham."

They separated, but he kept his focus on her until they united once more. "Kumquats are severely underrated. I shall have to remedy the gaping hole in your life created by their absence."

As they separated again, she threw him a look as if to question his sanity. "Pray do, sir," she said. "For what is life without a kumquat?"

"Ah yes. Socrates."

She broke into a full, lovely laugh, and he joined her—likely too heartily for decorum—but then he found they'd reached the head of the line again, and the dance was over. Too soon.

As he took her hand to lead her off the dance floor, he noted several pairs of eyes watching them—watching her—most of them male. He ignored the tightening he felt in his chest from their perfectly understandable reactions. That was why he'd asked her for the first dance, after all: to set a precedent for other gentlemen. He had no doubt she would be dancing for the remainder of the evening.

As they approached a group he recognized, Ophelia met them with a smile. But before she could speak, two of the younger gentlemen who had strutted in earlier appeared quite suddenly and asked Ophelia for introductions to Miss Rowley. Bows were made, and then the young man nearest Miss Rowley requested her next available set. Not to be outdone, the second young man stepped forward and asked for the supper dance.

Richard's gut sank. Despite his mother's strong encouragement, he'd had no intention of asking Miss Rowley for a second dance. To do so would risk rumors of an attachment, though this was a country ball, and rules about such things were more lax than in the city. Still, as the request was made, Richard couldn't help but feel he'd let an opportunity for more of Miss Rowley's company slip by.

"Miss Rowley," he heard himself say as the first young man led her away.

She looked over her shoulder and stopped. "Yes?"

"Might I . . . ?"

She tilted her head, her curls shifting. "Yes, sir?"

The young man frowned and adjusted his grip on Miss Rowley's fingers. Richard glanced at Ophelia, who watched him with brow raised high.

He drew himself up. "Might you save me the waltz?"

The room seemed to hush. He didn't drop his gaze even as heat crept up his neck.

Her large brown eyes blinked, and her lips parted slightly. Then she curtsied. "I will, sir."

He bowed, and before he could say more, the young man pulled her away to dance a quadrille.

The second young man faded away, and Richard felt the curious stare of Ophelia.

He took a breath and faced her. "What?"

"Nothing. Well, no, not nothing. Definitely something. Something quite interesting."

He searched fruitlessly for something to say in response. *My mother made me do it* sounded very childish in his head. "Could I get you some punch?"

"No, thank you. But I would like to dance." She looked casually over the dance floor. "Perhaps if we hurry, we can join Miss Rowley's square."

He scowled yet held out his hand, and she took it, grinning.

CHAPTER NINE

Marina had never danced so much at a single ball—perhaps at all of them combined. Even when her mother appeared just before supper, looking rested, Marina had time only to greet her and was swept away before she could answer any questions. Her father simply smiled, looking pleased, even chuckling at the bewildered expression on his wife's face.

Supper was pleasant enough. A Mr. Dewhurst talked of Cambridge and hunting—he was very passionate about the hunt. He never asked about Marina at all, but she was used to that. She scarcely would have noticed but for two things: One, Mr. Dewhurst was, at least, speaking to her and not to someone on his other side, and two, Lieutenant Stanhope had been asking her questions almost since they'd met. It wasn't that she'd become accustomed to the questions. She'd just come to appreciate the lieutenant's interest. So, whenever she opened her mouth to offer her own opinion or experience, she noticed when Mr. Dewhurst spoke over her or moved on to another subject.

Every so often, she'd catch the lieutenant's eye at the other end of the table. Once, he winked, and she'd caught herself smiling through her next several bites as Mr. Dewhurst described his dogs.

After supper, Marina found herself listening intently between sets for the waltz.

Her mother startled her at her elbow. "Having a good time, my dear?"

Marina nodded. "So this is what a ball is supposed to feel like."

Mother sighed. "It is not the crush at Almack's—"

"Mother, we're at Longhorsley, not London."

"I was going to say it's quite a success. The Stanhopes throw a lovely party. And I was right about that dress. You always lean toward the greens and blues, but red is your color. Lieutenant Stanhope can't keep his eyes off you."

"Shh, Mother." Alarmed by her mother's declaration, Marina looked about, catching a raised brow or two from those nearby. She lowered her voice to a whisper. "Mother, you know nothing of the sort. Show some restraint."

At least her mother lowered her voice to match Marina's. "I've done nothing other mothers are not doing."

"That doesn't make it right."

Her voice rose again. "Lieutenant Stanhope has asked you for two dances, has he not?"

Marina closed her eyes, wanting to escape through the nearest doors. "Oh, why must you do this?" she muttered.

"She's not wrong," a deep voice behind her said.

Her mother turned, and then her expression grew smug. She dipped into a curtsy. "Lieutenant Stanhope. We were just speaking of you."

Marina turned slowly, collecting her composure. There he stood, tall and handsome in his uniform and watching her with suppressed amusement. She dipped into a curtsy. "My mother was speaking of you, sir. I merely wished to sink into the floor."

"Oh, tosh." Her mother tapped her arm with her fan, not gently, and then addressed the lieutenant. "I assure you, sir, that behind those spectacles is a sweet, *accomplished* young lady."

The lieutenant frowned and looked between the two women, and Marina dropped her shoulders in defeat.

"Your daughter wears spectacles?"

Marina's chin came up.

"Really, madam, I had no idea." He offered Marina his elbow, and stunned, she took it.

He leaned toward her. "Consider me an alternative to sinking into the floor?"

She heard the opening strains of a waltz and smiled, her pulse ticking up pleasantly. They left Mother still puzzling out whether or not the lieutenant was in need of eyeglasses himself.

Though grateful for the escape, once Marina stepped onto the dance floor she was struck with sudden panic.

The *waltz*.

"You're not going to run to the hedges now, are you?" he whispered.

"Is it that obvious?"

He smiled and lifted her left hand in his. "Have you waltzed before?"

She swallowed as his other hand drifted around her waist. "Yes." Twice. "But it's been a long time." Three years. She daintily lifted her skirt with her right hand.

He cleared his throat. "It's been seven years for me, but for a few balls held during training. Let's focus on what's really important."

"What's that?"

He began to sway her in time with the music. "I get to hold an enchanting woman in my arms with some propriety."

She blushed, glancing around. "I thought you were going to say not stepping on one another's toes."

"That too. Ready?" With that, he launched them both into the throng of couples.

They spent the first minute finding their footing and laughing at a little trip here and there.

"I think we'll have less chance of colliding with those more expert than ourselves if we stay near the center of the throng," he said, steering them away from a couple with far-reaching steps and arched arms.

"They look so elegant."

He looked down at her. "So do we. Only less outwardly so."

She smiled up at him, and he smiled back, just as he'd done during their first dance. And just like before, his gaze didn't wander to beautiful women more adept at conversation, flirtation, or . . . waltzing. She was fairly sure that if she said something, he would listen.

"I believe we're getting better," he said.

She blinked and nodded. "Miracles happen."

He looked ahead just long enough to lead her through a turn and then brought her back to him, returning his gaze to hers. "I'm remembering now."

"Well done, Lieutenant."

He smiled "It takes two to waltz, Miss Rowley."

"Indeed, it does."

"Might I ask you a question?"

"If I may ask you one."

"Very well. But I'll go first."

"If you insist."

"I know *my* excuse. But something puzzles me. Why has it been so long since you've waltzed?"

Her smile faded. It was a thoughtless question, but she wanted to believe he hadn't meant any harm. Still, the question dredged up unpleasant memories. "As you said, Lieutenant, it takes two to waltz. And since it is unseemly for a lady to ask a gentleman to dance, it has been some time."

He studied her with a frown, and she looked to the floor, at the feet of other dancers—anywhere but at him.

"Forgive me," he said. "It was clumsy of me to ask. I did not mean to cause you pain. Only, I cannot fathom why any man would pass you over when there is dancing to be done."

"Are you in earnest, sir?" She looked back up at him.

"I am, wholly."

She decided to tell him a little. If it scared him off, at least she would know his true colors. "Believe it or not, I have a reputation in London."

His brow lifted.

"It is not that kind of reputation," she said and glared at him.

He suppressed a smile.

She sighed, and he turned her out again, deftly bringing her back in, and if she was not imagining it, holding her a little closer.

He spoke into her ear. "What is this reputation?"

Dash it all, he'd raised gooseflesh on her arms. "I am outspoken, my wit is too sharp, and my eyeglasses apparently mean I am spinsterly and wish only to read books and study sermons." There. She'd said it. Let him make of it what he would.

"Do you read books?" he asked.

"Well, yes, but that's not the point. A young man with eyeglasses is instantly judged to be an academic, while a young lady is relegated to—as they say—the shelf."

He studied her, as if not knowing what to make of her.

"Now you must answer my question," she said, her truth-telling fueling her courage.

"Ask it."

"Why did you ask me for a second dance?" She did not let her gaze waver.

"That is simple," he said. "I do not find you spinsterly."

He led her through a series of turns, this time keeping her tucked close against him, and then ended with another spin outward before he spun her back in. "At all," he said.

"Be careful," she said, not a little breathless. "You might ruin my reputation."

"I believe that is the point, Miss Rowley."

The waltz faded. The lieutenant's gaze was direct, with no sign of insincerity. For a moment, she daren't breathe.

An instrument's sudden trill and a tremor through the crowd pulled her attention as the room came to life. A clock struck midnight.

The lieutenant stepped back, still holding her hand, and bowed low. When he rose, he grinned. "Happy Christmas, Miss Rowley."

She pulled in a breath and, delighted, laughed. "Happy Christmas, Lieutenant."

CHAPTER TEN

BY THE END OF THE ball, Marina's feet had ached and she'd been so tired she barely remembered climbing the stairs. Her mother had kept a hand on her back and made sure she'd reached the right room before leaving Marina to undress and collapse under her quilts, dreaming of gentlemen—a certain gentleman—and pretty gowns and waltzes.

It had been a glorious evening, and Canterwood had woken up—gradually—Christmas morning to trees, grass, and windowpanes laced with frost.

Gratefully, church was held midmorning. The vicar's sermon was sweet and simple and held most of his congregation's attention. The Stanhope children had waved at her from their family bench, and Lieutenant Stanhope had given her a nod, as had several other gentlemen she'd danced with the night before. She could feel her mother swell with pride. So that was what it took.

After church, the Stanhopes hosted a Christmas luncheon that included the young vicar and his wife. When the sumptuous meal was over, Julia found Marina in the drawing room, where tables had been arranged for games, and asked for details of the ball. Marina recounted everything but particularly downplayed the lieutenant's second dance.

"I know what he was doing. After others saw us dancing, my evening filled up. He was seeing that I enjoyed myself."

"And did you?"

Marina couldn't downplay her smile. "Nearly every minute."

Julia clasped her hands. "You must show me the gown."

Marina was more than happy to indulge her. As they left the drawing room, however, they met Ophelia and Lady Teresa just entering.

"Where are you two headed?" Ophelia asked. "Staying out of trouble?"

"I'm a vicar's wife. What trouble could we be into?"

"You ask that as though I don't know you taught my children how to tie a pair of boots together by the laces and then call the sleeping owner to wake up and come quickly."

Lady Teresa chuckled quietly.

Julia assumed an innocent expression. "I did not teach them how. I merely mentioned it was a trick my father used to play on us."

"And your father was a vicar, correct?"

"Well, yes."

"You see my point, then."

Julia sighed. "I concede."

Marina laughed. "I was only going to show Julia my gown from the ball."

"Oh, my dear, you were lovely." Lady Teresa put her hand to her chest.

Marina dipped her head. "My lady, you and Ophelia were radiant. I believe everyone had a wonderful time. I've heard so many compliments. Well done."

"Thank you. I trust you found your partners adequate?" She gave Marina a knowing look.

Marina blushed. "Yes, quite so."

"And it made the dancing all the better?" Lady Teresa watched her more carefully than the question warranted.

"Yes, my lady."

The older woman smiled as if she knew a great secret.

Ophelia rested her hand on Julia's arm. "Well, if you're going upstairs, I'll tell you what I was just about to announce to the room. Some of the ladies intend to explore our little wilderness—despite the bitterness of the day—at the hour. Would you care to join them?"

Lady Teresa glanced toward the windows. "The weather is rather fine, though frigid."

"Are you going?" Marina asked.

Ophelia shook her head. "I've got to see about the servants' gifts for tomorrow. Having a house party over Boxing Day is a bit of a trick. The servants have the day off."

"It will be interesting, to say the least. But I'm sure we'll manage." Marina put her hand over her stomach. "You've certainly fed us well enough to last us through the next several days."

"It is our pleasure. And Cook, at least, has insisted on taking her day off after our guests have gone—bless her for that. In any case, I won't be joining the outing. But please, don't let that stop you from going."

"A walk sounds lovely, bitter or not." Julia sighed. "I do love your woods."

"Enjoy them, then," Ophelia said. "Only, take care, Julia. You have a few months yet, but don't overdo."

"I'll be as careful as a cat," she replied.

Ophelia inclined her head, and she and Lady Teresa excused themselves, discussing Boxing Day as they left.

Julia turned to Marina. "Do come with me. I need a good walk." Her hand went to her firm, round middle. "Everyone keeps telling me I must be still. Rest. Do as little as possible. I'm going mad with inactivity." She sighed heavily, then gripped Marina's arm. "I know! I'll ask my husband to come along, and he'll have to ask the lieutenant. No one can deny me the exercise with you by my side and two gentlemen at my back, can they?"

"They might try," Marina answered with a smile.

"We've enough time to go upstairs and ooh and aah over your gown, and then you can change into your boots and retrieve your warm things," Julia continued. "I'll hurry and tell Tom of our plan first."

Julia didn't take much time and soon returned to where Marina stood just outside the drawing room doorway. Marina glanced back toward the gentlemen and found the lieutenant watching. His gaze warmed her, recalling to her senses how it had felt to be held by him as they'd danced. She immediately chastised herself for the response, even as she flickered a smile his way before going upstairs with Julia on her arm.

CHAPTER ELEVEN

WITH MOST OF THE GROUP already ahead of them, Richard and Tom trailed behind Julia and Miss Rowley, allowing the women to set the pace, their breath making puffs in the chill. Back in the drawing room, the other ladies had been jovial, flirtatious, and coy, but they had also begun to pull on Richard and pet him until he'd wished to quit the space entirely and stay to his rooms. He'd remained undecided when the other ladies had invited him on the exploration, so they'd left while he and Tom waited for the two ladies ahead of them now. It struck him how at ease he felt with these three friends—he would certainly count Miss Rowley as a friend—in his company.

"There have been murmurs of you asking Miss Rowley to dance last night. Twice." Tom lifted a brow at him. "Some of the mothers are considering their next moves in turning your eye to their daughters."

"Do vicars give heed to that sort of thing?"

"You've been warned, my friend."

Richard conceded with a smile. He looked above him at the stretch of rare blue sky, then to Miss Rowley, and found he didn't care what other mothers were scheming—only where his own mother's directives were taking him.

"Have you spoken to Frank, yet?" Tom asked, changing subjects.

Richard frowned. "Not yet."

"The longer you put it off the prouder he'll become of your future in the King's Guard."

"Yes, he's insufferably proud of me."

Tom chuckled.

Richard sighed. "I won't put it off much longer. I wish to tie up a few loose ends so I have better footing when I go to him. If it weren't for this house party, I'd have done it by now—spoken to my mother—all of it. But with guests here and some obligation every time I turn around, I haven't found the proper time. I don't wish to upset the applecart. At least, not with such a broad audience."

"The Stanhopes are a busy lot these days." Tom clapped his hand on Richard's shoulder. "It is a tricky thing. But you'll find the time. And the courage."

The courage was the thing. Richard had mustered it countless times, shouted it to his men on the fields of battle and whispered it holding their hands as they died. Yet . . .

"Ask yourself this," Tom said. "What would you do if you had no expectations placed upon you? We *are* younger sons, you and I. We have choices—more than do our eldest brothers, anyway. Imagine—a clean slate. Consider it and find your courage there."

The question, asked outright like that, gave Richard pause.

At that point, Julia veered off the main graveled walk to a narrow dirt path worn into the longer grasses.

"Dearest," Tom called. "Where are you going? The woods are this way."

Julia and Miss Rowley waited as the men caught up. "I wish for Miss Rowley to see the reflecting pond. 'Tis the perfect winter day for it, with everything painted silver."

Richard couldn't argue. "'Tis a long walk. Are you sure you're up to it?"

Julia set her forearm across her middle and smiled. "I can rest at the gazebo." She turned to Miss Rowley. "The woods are grand in any weather, but the reflecting pool is not so accommodating. We must take advantage of this calm while we can." She turned to Richard. "Wouldn't you like Miss Rowley to see it?"

Miss Rowley smiled. "Perhaps he'd rather follow the entourage ahead. They seem to like him a great deal."

Tom chuckled. "They'd miss him dearly. I heard Mrs. Strom whisper to Miss Strom that if the girl turned her ankle just so, the lieutenant would be forced to carry her all the way back to the house."

Miss Rowley turned to Richard. "What a sacrifice."

Richard cleared his throat. "Yes, well, it seems we've no choice. If I'm not in their company, there is no need for Miss Strom to turn her ankle, thus causing her undue pain." He motioned the ladies forward through the tall grasses.

"Quite heroic of you," Miss Rowley said with not a little irony as she passed him.

"I've been known to rescue a damsel once or twice. The last one was caught in a privet, if I recall."

She shot him a look and he quelled a genuine laugh.

After the path rose and then descended into a dale hidden from view of the house and most of the grounds, the grasses cleared, and Richard watched Miss Rowley pick up her skirts and her pace toward the reflecting pool.

"Oh," she said softly. "It's lovely. Like two skies." She passed the open gazebo without so much as a glance as Tom helped Julia up the steps and to the bench inside. Richard hesitated.

"Go on with Miss Rowley, Lieutenant," Julia said, shooing him on. "She's so taken with the prospect she might fall in. We can't have that, can we? You'd be forced to carry her all the way back to the house."

He shook his head, nevertheless striding after Miss Rowley.

"I shall not fall in," Miss Rowley said as he drew nearer. "But I might build a shelter on that knoll, be as still as I can, and just breathe."

"You'd get hungry."

"Not with such tranquility to feast on." Her cheeks were rosy with the walk and the bite of winter.

"So tranquility, yes; oysters, no."

"Precisely." She took a deep breath and released it in a sigh. He followed her gaze.

The prospect was indeed tranquil. The rectangular pool was more of a man-made pond, lined with flat stones found in the stretches of land that were now pasture and running grounds. Richard and Miss Rowley stood under a tall white beech tree centered at one of the narrow ends of the pool, and at the other end, where they now faced, rose a set of semicircular stone steps, framed by two garden urns. Beyond the steps lay a short frosted lawn. A white-laced, ivy-covered arch rose above it all, sheltering a marble statue. All of it reflected perfectly still in the water. Two skies.

"Is that Pegasus?" Miss Rowley asked, motioning to the statue.

"My father liked to think he was perpetuating the myth in his own way, with good, strong horses. My mother was fascinated by the stories of Pegasus, so Father built this garden for her and planted this tree the year he brought her to Canterwood."

She looked above them at the white branches. "He loved her, then." It was more of an observation than a question. "He must have, to have made her something so romantic. I can imagine love in this place."

Richard, suddenly very warm, cleared his throat. "My mother, the youngest of three daughters and a son, was intended for a much older man she barely knew—an earl like her father. She defied convention and chose my untitled father, who—with his charm, integrity, and *wealth*—won over her parents. He did love her. Very much." As a youth, he'd taken for granted his parents' love for one another. Now that he'd been out in the world, he realized what a treasure it was.

"I did not mean to pry," she said. "It's only . . . well . . . my parents didn't—don't . . ." She closed her eyes and shook her head. "At least, I wonder if they . . ."

"It's too rare an occurrence, isn't it?" he asked, saving her from having to finish the indelicate sentence.

Her shoulders relaxed, though her eyes remained on the ground as she nodded.

"Expectations," he said mostly to himself and looked over the glassy water, the silver and blue sky.

"Expectations?" She lifted her gaze.

He offered his arm. She took it, and he led her forward on the path encircling the pool.

"Earlier," he said as they strolled, "Tom asked me what I'd do if I had no expectations put upon me, if no one pushed me to continue in the dragoons and on to His Majesty's Guard."

She paused in her step, and he followed suit. "Do you not wish to continue on that path?"

His mind whirled as he searched for a careful answer. "No. I do not." That was not careful at all.

Instead of withdrawing her hand and stepping away in disappointment, she stayed. "Then, what shall you do next?"

He smiled. "It is not so easy. The other day I asked if you would help me with something . . . a personal matter. You asked why I would ask you. The truth is I'm not sure. I hardly know you, but I . . . I trust your opinion."

"My opinion?"

"If you wouldn't mind. Tom is far too biased, and I can't quite go to my family yet. You seem a rational person—"

"Tell that to my mother—"

He smiled. "And someone who can keep a secret."

Her eyes narrowed.

"Only for a little while. I know how you value honesty. It all must come out soon."

"You have me in the grips of suspense, Lieutenant. I'm afraid I must be your confidante, or I shall never sleep again."

He chuckled and tugged her forward to resume their stroll. He took a deep breath, knowing that once he began, his words might tumble out like rocks down a steep hill without any control over how or where they'd land. His heart hammered, and he glanced around as if he needed a place to take cover.

She pulled him to a stop again. "Lieutenant, what is it? It can't be that dire."

True concern in her expression spurred him to speak. He swallowed and shook off his fears. There would be no harm in telling Miss Rowley. "I have an inheritance set aside from my mother, you see. She made sure it was never made part of the Canterwood estate." He drew in another breath and squared his shoulders. "I would like to take that, sell my commission, and purchase the finest horse property I can afford in Northumberland. I could then buy an Arab stallion, the likes of which no one has seen before, and a bevy of sturdy north-country brood mares and start my own stables." The idea sent a thrill through him that wearing his uniform had never given him. Miss Rowley's deep brown eyes showed interest and encouragement, and his words came easier. "It wouldn't be as big as Canterwood, of course—perhaps not ever. I've learned all I can from my father and out in the field. I'm sure I could make it work. But—" He stopped.

"But—the expectation?" Her brow rose.

"Precisely."

"And you would be placing yourself in competition with your brother."

He nodded. "If I'm to succeed. But it wouldn't have to be that way. I'm confident we could work out a way to do business that is beneficial to both of us. I've always felt Canterwood is my legacy too, though not in the same way it is my brother's. I hope for its continued success as much as I hope for my own."

"Of course. This is your family home, your father's work. You say you're confident you can work something out?"

"I have some leads. I've spoken with a solicitor. And McKay. He's been giving me advice for starting up. But that's tricky."

"Because he's your brother's man."

Richard nodded, relieved she understood. "He's respected my need to be discreet until I've decided. But I don't like asking that of him."

"And you've no more desire to be a soldier at all?" she asked. "By all appearances, you are a good one."

He looked beyond the pond, beyond the surrounding hills. "I've seen enough good men and horses die in battle. I want to give both a better purpose—a chance at a good life. I want to produce and nurture living things." He met her gaze directly, and a thump of his heart startled him, along with a clear thought.

He wanted a family.

He searched her expression for her thoughts, and she returned his attention as she had before—with that look of suspicion mingled with hope. He took half a step closer. "You don't trust easily, do you, Miss Rowley?" he asked with caution.

She swallowed, and her voice grew hushed. "I have reason not to trust."

"Because of the duplicitous nature of the *ton*?" He needed to be careful here not to scare her off. "Last night—"

"Last night was wonderful. A dream." She resumed walking. "I have you to thank for that. I'm still questioning whether or not it was real."

"All I did was ask you to dance. It was my pleasure to do so."

She eyed him warily, a hidden smile there at her mouth.

He still couldn't understand how Miss Rowley had come to be labeled a spinster just because of a pair of eyeglasses. "Is there more?" he asked. "As to why you don't trust easily?" They had reached the opposite end of the pool and stood in front of the Pegasus statue.

"You asked my opinion, Lieutenant—goodness, do you even wish to be called that?"

She was avoiding his question, but he nodded. "I am still a lieutenant, Miss Rowley. I'm still filling that role to the best of my capability, as always."

"Of course. But it sounds as though you've made up your mind," she said. "What do you wish of *me*?"

"I was hoping you might suggest the best way to go about speaking to my brother. And perhaps tell me if you think the whole idea to be mad."

Her brow rose, and then she broke out into such a glorious smile he couldn't help but match it.

"Why do you smile so?" he asked.

She shook her head and turned to walk toward Pegasus. "Do you know what is mad? Perseus slew Medusa, and from the monster's awful remains a beautiful white-winged horse sprang forth and flew to the Gods." She turned to him, sobering. "And war. War is mad. I don't know the things you witnessed, but I listened to reports and read papers, afraid even in the safety of my sheltered life. I know my small mind cannot imagine the true horrors of war." She stepped back to him and rested her hand on his arm. "It is not madness to want to make something beautiful from something monstrous. It's . . . *divine*."

Her words transfixed him, her small hand strong, grounding him even as his heart raced. She gazed at him through her spectacles.

"Can you see at all without your eyeglasses?" he asked quietly.

She blinked. "If I'm close to something."

"I was hoping you'd say that." Carefully, he reached up, lifted them off her nose, and folded them in his hand.

"W-what are you doing?" she whispered, her eyes searching his.

He touched her cheek. "I'm looking at you," he whispered back. "And wondering what it might be like to kiss you."

"Oh," she said breathlessly, her lips forming a perfect invitation. Her gaze slid to his mouth.

"Are you wondering the same thing?" he asked.

"What it might be like to kiss me?"

He grinned.

"Your smile is quite dazzling; did you know?" she asked. "It's frustratingly difficult to keep up one's defenses when it appears."

"I'll remember that." He leaned toward her, giving in to the intense pull between them.

Her eyes grew large. "Charlie," she suddenly proclaimed, breaking the spell he'd been under.

"What?" he asked. He blinked and shook his head.

"You were Charlie," she said as she took her eyeglasses from his frozen hand and put them back on her nose. "Ophelia wrote to me of you when you left for war, only she called you Charlie. She was very concerned. And your brother was very proud."

"Yes . . . proud," he said, wondering what had just happened to bring about this abrupt change in the direction of their—er—discussion. It was probably best, but *hang* best—the woman had him mesmerized. He rubbed his chin. "Yes, I was Charlie until Eton, when I no longer wanted the nickname. But Frank continued to call me that, no doubt to remind me that to him I was still a boy, until—well, until I survived my first major battle." He rested his hands at his hips. "I must have finally proven I was man enough for my given name."

Marina began pacing in front of him.

Marina. Hmm.

"What if it only *appeared* that your brother continued calling you Charlie to put you in your place as a boy-not-yet-a-man, but in reality, he continued calling you Charlie simply because he is protective?"

"Protective?"

"Perhaps, in reality, it was difficult to accept that you were growing up, and he wanted to hang on to some semblance of how life was before it became complicated with the responsibilities of adulthood."

"I suppose that's possible." Richard scratched his jaw. Now that he considered it, Frank had never been malicious or taunting in using the nickname. "But what does that have to do with—?"

"Perhaps your brother isn't so much proud that you're a soldier, and a good one, as he is that you are making a life—*any* life—and that you are safe and honorable." She stepped closer to him. "Perhaps he would be happy, because he is protective, with any worthy avenue you chose. Perhaps he only wishes for you to be successful . . . to be happy." Her eyes blazed with a sort of triumph, and she was a little out of breath.

The effect was dazzling.

"Miss Rowley," he said, taking her hand and bowing over it with a kiss. "Do not allow anyone, yourself included, to convince you that you have a small mind." He stood, scrutinizing her words. "You believe Frank will be understanding as long as I am pursuing a worthy living?"

"One that is worthy of his dear little brother? Yes. Does that give you courage?"

He searched inside himself. He had no certainty of her being correct. But . . . "I do feel encouraged. Eager, almost."

She grinned and squeezed his hand, as he was still in possession of hers. "I wish you the best of luck finding your Pegasus. You'll let me know how it turns out, won't you?"

He nodded, hoping she'd still be here for that news. "I'll have you to thank."

"Or to curse. I'd prefer to be thanked."

Richard grinned. "I look forward to thanking you."

He watched the color rise in her cheeks.

"You are a brute," she murmured, but the corner of her mouth curved upward as she turned and continued on the path along the far side of the pool.

He watched her go, this woman of strength and wit and vulnerability. And speed. Jolted from his reverie, he moved to catch up to her.

CHAPTER TWELVE

MARINA COULD HARDLY CONTAIN THE trip and whirl of her emotions as she walked away from Lieutenant Stanhope. She was at once full of longing for that man to put his arms around her and kiss her—at last, to be kissed—and aware of every experience screaming at her to keep her guard up. He couldn't be sincere, could he? Why would he be genuine when so many others had not? Why this attraction?

She pushed her spectacles up more securely on her nose and drew her shoulders back but found her hand pressed against her heart as she willed it to calm.

He'd considered kissing her!

No. It was just the moment. Just playful flirtation that eased the baring of his soul to her. Still, when he'd caressed her cheek, his heavy gaze hadn't seemed playful.

Be careful, Marina. He does not know the whole truth.

She dropped her hand at the sound of footsteps.

"Miss Rowley," the lieutenant said, somewhat out of breath. "It is your turn now." He matched his stride to hers.

"My turn?" she asked, hesitant to look at him.

"Yes. I must know. What would you do?"

"What would I do what?"

"With no expectations."

She halted and he did the same. Surely he was joking. "I don't understand."

"If you had no expectations put upon you, what would you do?"

"Yes, I know that part. But it's not a real question."

He frowned. "Why not?"

"Because I am a woman, Lieutenant. The idea of having no expectations put upon me is as foreign to me as the Sphinx. Everything I've been taught to pursue has had one purpose, and one purpose alone. Please do not make me state it." They had stopped beneath the long leafless branches of a weeping willow. She pushed several aside and stepped away from him, but he caught her hand. When she stopped again, he released her, but his gaze locked her into place. She prayed he would not ask her to name the purpose. The answer should have been obvious and would be gauche to speak of in present company.

"Forgive me," he said. "I do not wish to make you uncomfortable. I only thought to return what you've given to me—a new perspective. Perhaps trying to imagine it might help you in some way."

He did look sincere. And he could be right. She sighed.

He motioned to a bench encircling the willow's trunk, and she went to it and sat, trying to sort her thoughts.

"May I?" he asked, gesturing to the space next to her.

She nodded, and he took it, the warmth of him reaching her side. She knew her skin flushed, and in the cold of winter, her blood worked far too hard to make up for the chill. Indeed, she had to remove her eyeglasses because they'd begun to steam. She shook her head and stared down at them.

"I didn't mean to press you," he said, apparently sensing her distress.

She looked up at him, silently begging for the gift of discernment. "You ask too much of me, sir. I know I am outspoken and laugh too much or misjudge when I ought not to be judging at all—"

He opened his mouth as if to contradict her, but she stopped him.

"I don't know what to think of you—whether or not I can trust you with the part of me you are asking to see. There are reasons I put up walls. You say you've shared with me your hopes because you trust me, even when you can't determine why." She folded and unfolded and refolded the eyeglasses in her hands. "I want to trust you, but I can think of too many reasons why I shouldn't."

He watched her with those sea-tossed eyes. "Tell me the reasons."

"What?"

"Tell me why you hesitate to trust me."

"I—"

"I can take it." He arched a brow.

She shook her head. "You lied to me upon our first meeting."

"First impressions tend to stick, don't they?" he muttered.

"I do forgive you, but I've been lied to so many times—the distrust is residual."

"Lied to by other men?"

"By other people." She turned away. Admitting it was humiliating. But perhaps he'd understand her better—understand her need for boundaries. "It seems so trivial after your talk of war."

"Were you hurt?"

She bit her lip and looked out past the willow branches. The gazebo stood across the pool, and she could just make out its shape, the dark figures of the Langleys inside. "My heart." She dropped her head. "My pride."

"Your ability to trust."

She flickered a glance up at him. "Yes."

"Miss Rowley, that is also a wound of war. I've seen it in the eyes of those whose world has been knocked sideways. And I've seen it in your eyes too."

"The world knocked sideways," she repeated in a whisper. "Yes, that's it."

"Would you tell me?" he asked. "I wish to help relieve you of this burden."

"Why?"

"Because you've helped relieve me of mine."

"You are too confident in me."

"And you are not confident enough in me."

He held her gaze for several moments more, and then she relented. "I was a strong-minded girl when I was thirteen."

He nodded in encouragement and took her hand in his, halting her from further fiddling with her spectacles.

"I knew better than my parents, of course."

He smiled.

"Ophelia's family had moved away, and she married soon after. I saw and heard little from her after that; she was so very busy with her new life. I was still a child. My mother became determined to make a desirable lady of me, and I was determined to thwart her and pursue my own passions. Becoming a lady could wait. I was so young, and my mother's rules were stifling. The more I pulled, the harder she pushed.

"The one time I truly rebelled—truly threw off the yoke of *expectations* for my own heart's desire—led to disastrous results. I had friends, a pair of brothers near my age. We'd played together as tots. We'd adventured together, climbing the cliffs and exploring the coast, observing the lives and deaths of sea creatures, facing oncoming storms, and searching for pirates. They taught me to swim—something my father was grateful for and my mother abhorred."

Marina couldn't bring herself to look at the lieutenant. She did not want to see the expression on his face. Perhaps if she just kept going, he might leave her be. He might be shocked and dismayed, and then she'd no longer have to wonder late into the night what to do about his attentions. And part of her loathed that idea. Still, she kept talking.

"But by thirteen, merely swimming was not thrilling enough. We'd begun to challenge ourselves with diving." This time she did look at him for his reaction. His brow flickered upward, but that was all.

"We'd watch gentlemen dive off the low cliffs, and then we'd meet when nobody could see me, and we'd practice. Oh, it was terrifying and thrilling, and I was *good*. Each time I attempted to go higher, I succeeded." She caught herself smiling and drew in a breath. Then she felt her countenance fall.

"A friend of my mother's—a woman out walking her dog on the bluffs above—saw me, recognized me, and told my mother of the scandal. My mother was livid. Even my father agreed I had taken my liberties too far. I was never to see my friends again. I was to be sent away to London immediately to a boarding school for girls—a ladies' seminary. I was not to return until I'd learned what respectable behavior was."

"Were they unkind to you at the school?" he asked.

"I never went. After learning of my sentence, I locked myself in my room until the house grew quiet. Then I escaped for one last swim, one last dive, one last breath of freedom. It was all very melodramatic."

He squeezed her hand.

"There was a particular outcropping of rock I'd been eyeing since my very first lower dives. I'd told myself that one day, I would dive from that height. I'd even explored the water below to determine whether it was deep enough, clear enough of rocks. But I was only a child." She stared out over the water, immersed in those memories of what being grown up meant to a young girl.

"I'd never been swimming alone. But there's something about that age, isn't there? You believe you're invincible."

He slowly nodded. "I would climb trees. Very, very tall trees."

She smiled. "The water was familiar, encouraging, and I was full of defiance. I dived several times, as before, my confidence building with each one. Then I climbed up to that highest outcropping. I stood in what I knew was good form, watching the shifting water below. I was so high, and I would never be in that place, in that way, ever again. This was my last chance. I knew it in my bones . . . so I leapt." She felt her heart beat in her chest and relived that moment of sheer exhilaration and then sheer terror. "At some point on the way down, I realized I'd sorely misjudged the height. It was all I could do to keep my form as the water's surface barreled at me, and I screamed before I hit."

The sound of his intake of breath drew her from her memory. She blinked at him.

"What happened?" he asked, deep concern etched into his face.

She drew in a clear, cold breath. "I don't remember the next part. My father had discovered I was gone and had ridden to the base of the bluffs, where he knew we swam. He'd heard my scream just as he'd dismounted and scrambled into the water to find me unconscious with a deep gash to my head, here." She reached under her bonnet and touched the rigid ribbon of scar tissue beneath her hair. "I hadn't taken into account the distance I'd need to jump outward away from the rocks, you see, to hit the deeper water."

"Merciful heavens," he said. "You could have been killed."

Her eyes met his then, and she didn't look away. "Yes. I was spared. I came away with only a concussion, this scar, and the need to wear spectacles for the rest of my life. I lived. But I also earned something more: the censure of my mother and endless teasing from my peers through every age afterward."

He frowned. "Surely your mother was grateful you survived."

"My mother was more struck down by this contraption"—she held up the specs—"marring her eldest daughter's face than the fact that my eyes had instantly lost their ability to focus. She demanded the boys be sent away for their malicious influence. Their parents obliged, they left for school, and I never saw them again. I remember Mama crying over me one evening, and I felt compassion from her at last. But then she threw herself back and exclaimed, 'She looks the part of a spinster!'" Marina paused, her jaw tense, attempting to mask the pain so apparent in her tone. After a moment, she was able to continue.

"I defied her, and she's made sure to remind me all these years that I'm to blame for my mistake, especially when those I thought were friends or gentlemen in pursuit treated me poorly or used me. It affects the family, you see. My mistake that night affects my younger sister's prospects as well as my own."

Lieutenant Stanhope watched her, that look of concern still carved into his features. "Surely you've had true friends. I cannot imagine you not making genuine connections."

The compliment warmed her with unexpected gratitude. "Of course I have. But they are few. After continual deprecation, one grows wary of others and is selective of whom one keeps company with."

"I see. I'm honored you've allowed me to spend time with you, especially after our problematic beginning."

She couldn't help the small lift of a smile.

"And I thank you," he said, his voice quieting, "for trusting me enough to share that much of yourself with me."

Her pulse quickened but not from fear. "And what perspective am I to have gained from sharing it with you, sir?"

"I'm not sure. Forgive me. Your mother—she is wrong. You know that, don't you?"

"I believe I came to that realization, in a way, just before you found me quoting Wordsworth outside my room."

He laughed quietly and dropped his head. "Ah. Yes." He paused, looking across the pool. "What if—and please, you don't have to respond but perhaps just consider—what if your mother feels blame?"

"My mother?" Marina felt only skepticism at such a suggestion.

"Consider. It was she who lost her temper. It was she who forbade you from the water and your friends. And it was she who was sending you away. Had she not, would you have risked going to the bluffs alone that day?"

She blinked at him. "No. But I still made the choice."

"Yes. And that is your responsibility. But as you've said, you were only thirteen years of age, and she is, after all, your mother. I happen to know mothers feel very deeply for the danger their children put themselves in. They question every one of their own decisions and how they might have done things differently to prevent disaster."

"I don't think my mother is that kind of mother."

He laughed, and it was good to hear him do so. He lifted her hand and kissed it as he'd done earlier.

"Perhaps," he said, "she's not even aware of the blame she feels for that day and struggles in vain to make it right."

"I wish she'd stop." Marina did consider though. If anything, the lieutenant's words made her view her mother a little differently—with a new perspective. "Thank you, Lieutenant."

He nodded and tucked her hand into the crook of his arm, warming her fingers. "There is something else you may not want to hear."

She steeled herself. "What is it?"

Humor danced in his eyes. "You haven't answered the question yet."

"What question?"

"If you had no expectations put upon you . . . ?" he prompted.

"I'd become the most famed cliff diver in all of Europe?"

He laughed again, and she joined him.

"Somehow, I don't believe that answer is sincere," he said.

"No, it is not." She shook her head.

"Then, what is your sincere answer, my darling friend?"

She froze at his endearment. He seemed to have realized what he said and stilled as well.

She gathered her courage even as her pulse raced. Her voice trembled; she didn't want to disturb the moment with her words. "My sincere answer, if I had no expectations put upon me, would be to travel. To see the beauty and wonder of the world before it might possibly become lost to my eyes in a blur."

He slowly reached for her and cradled her face in his hand, his thumb brushing beneath her eye. He seemed to search the depths of her. She could barely breathe.

"Are you in such danger, Marina? Of losing your sight?"

Marina. She only shook her head, then shrugged a shoulder, then nodded.

"I cannot decipher that answer," he whispered. "Tell me."

Her next words terrified her. She'd never spoken them aloud. They would change the way he saw her. But she pressed on. "Perhaps not. It may take a very long time. But it's possible." She swallowed and found courage. "They've not grown worse in the last two years. But Mama—perhaps she thought it would elicit sympathy or it was a slip of the tongue—she let the possibility be known in certain circles. And nobody truly wants a blind wife."

Once more, his thumb caressed her, and then he drew her closer. He smelled of wool and peppermint, and she couldn't help but breathe him in.

Then his lips pressed to hers.

Her eyes fluttered closed in surprise and wonder at the cool softness of his lips. His nose brushed hers as he pressed again, nuzzling into her, warming her as she pressed back, learning this new sensation she'd only dreamed of. He kissed her softly again, as if searching the best way to go about it. They were all delicious to her.

"Marina," he whispered.

"Yes?"

"Marina," he repeated and pulled her closer. "May I call you Marina?"

His words against her mouth did funny things to her middle. "Yes," she said, breathless.

This seemed to bring him to his senses, and he ceased kissing her, resting his forehead against hers. Should she have answered no?

"Forgive me," he said, just as breathless as she was.

"For what?"

"For taking advantage of you."

She frowned, cautious. "Is that why you kissed me? Because you feel sorry for me?"

He shook his head fervently. "No, my darling. Because I see how brave you are."

She bit her lip, fighting back the emotion his words had pricked. How did he know? How did he know how dearly she wanted to be seen?

She tipped her chin up and received his kisses once more.

CHAPTER THIRTEEN

RICHARD PACED IN HIS FATHER'S study. But it wasn't Father's anymore. It had been Frank's for several years now. Directly after his walk back to the house, with Marina tucked neatly into his side as he fended off knowing looks from Tom and his wife, Richard had sent a summons for Frank to meet him here. He would talk to his mother afterward. He'd decided he must first meet Frank head-on. He checked the clock on the mantel. He'd been pacing for twelve minutes. Since those kisses under the willow, time seemed to be challenging him to get his life—his dream of a life—in order; the sooner the better. The sooner to have Marina at his side always.

The door behind him opened, and he turned, standing at attention—a habit.

Frank chuckled. "There's the soldier. At ease. I got your message. What's this about?" He walked passed Richard to the walnut desk, took a seat, and motioned for Richard to do the same.

Richard hesitated, feeling the need to stand. But he took the seat opposite his brother and rested his elbows on his knees, recomposing the words he'd gone over and over in his head.

"Richard? What is it?"

He looked up into the sharp hazel eyes of his brother. His father's eyes.

Richard sat up, took a deep breath, and remembered what Marina believed: Frank would be happy with any worthy avenue he chose. Richard cleared his throat. "First, I have a somewhat odd question to ask you. But please, humor me."

Frank lifted his brow.

"You continued to call me Charlie for years after I'd made it clear I no longer wished it. Why?"

Frank chuckled and shrugged. "I did, didn't I? I don't know. I guess I had a hard time seeing you grow up. If you were Charlie, then you were still my little brother—under my wing, so to speak. And then you did grow up and leave, and there was so little I could do for you from here. But you no longer needed me—not in that way. Your mettle, your leadership, and your tenacity made it easier to relinquish that responsibility I clung to so keenly. I'm proud of the man you are, Richard."

Richard stared. "Thank you." Marina was right.

Frank nodded.

With that, Richard pressed forward. "Throughout these last years of war, I considered what my future would look like—if I would have a future at all."

Frank frowned and nodded at that.

"But here I am, alive and somewhat whole. And I . . . I'm choosing another path, Frank."

His brother lifted his gaze in question. "What?"

"I no longer wish to follow a military career. I've not come by this decision easily. And yet, once I decided, I haven't looked back."

Frank tapped his fingers on the desk and grabbed a quill as if he needed something to hold. Then he tapped the pen on his desk. He rubbed his face, studying Richard.

"You'd have security in the Guard. The ability to advance."

"Is that your concern? That I have stability and growth?" He wouldn't have that starting his own stables. Not at first.

"Of course." Frank leaned forward. "What is this other path?"

Richard considered carefully what to say next. "To do what I was raised to do . . . what our father raised us to do."

Frank's look of confusion cleared, and he sat back in his chair. "Work with horses. But not cavalry horses."

"No, not cavalry horses. No more fighting with horses. No more killing. I want to breed them, raise them." The tapping of the pen resumed, and Richard watched the feather bounce. "Do you think me a coward?"

The tapping stopped. "You served seven years of your youth fighting for the protection and freedom of not only your own country but for others who could not fight on their own. Heaven knows the scenes burned in your mind that shall never be in mine. You were gravely injured, healed, and returned to battle without a glance homeward—"

"That's not true. I glanced plenty."

"And you were there, Richard, in the decisive Battle of Waterloo and helped bring an end to years of fear and destruction to thousands upon thousands of people. And you think I would call you a coward because you wish to follow in Father's footsteps as I am? He would be honored. He's likely throwing his fist into the air right now with a shout of 'Huzzah!'"

Richard couldn't help smiling at the image. His gut did a sort of flip, and emotion stuck in his throat.

Frank settled forward, his elbows on the desk again, the pen put away in its stand. He narrowed his gaze. "I can't help but wonder if the life of a horse breeder's wife would be a happier circumstance for a certain bespectacled young lady than that of a military wife."

Heat crept up Richard's neck, and he refrained from pulling at his cravat. "I-I don't—" he stammered, but then images of him and Marina riding together, planning side by side, working together for a dream, perhaps somewhere by the sea . . . He released a breath, gazing at his boots. "Perhaps," he admitted, unable to hide a grin. "But it won't be much in the beginning."

"Knowing you, you have a plan. Let's hear it. Happy Christmas, Richard. How can I help my little brother?"

Richard's smile grew.

CHAPTER FOURTEEN

MARINA ROAMED FROM ROOM TO room half dazed. A disconcerting smile kept creeping its way out, and she had to keep banishing it to avoid questioning looks.

Lieutenant—no—*Richard*—had kissed her. And kissed her thoroughly. Julia, thankfully, had kept quiet on the walk back to the house, allowing Marina space to—well, she wasn't sure. To float?

She floated alone to the conservatory, where it was quiet and warm, exploring the flora without really paying attention. But then she floated near the small door to the adjoining music room and was torn from her reverie by the sound of her own name coming from beyond.

She leaned closer to the door.

"You told me to dine with her. I did. You told me to ask her questions, to make her stay here memorable. I did. You required that I provide time with the children, that I ask her to dance—*twice*—"

Richard's words reached through her chest and pierced her heart.

No. She couldn't possibly be hearing—

"—all this to make up for causing her distress over Uncle Hubert out in the garden—"

Her blood seemed to drain down to her feet.

No, no, no. Not again. Not him. Her ears filled with a rushing noise, and she grappled for leverage before she would collapse in a weak heap there on the conservatory tile.

No. She was not the same naive girl who'd allowed her hopes to rule her trust in people. Her hand found purchase, and she breathed deeply, steadying herself, wiping at tears down each cheek. He was just a man, the same as any of them. Just a man—

She held to the doorknob to stop from falling, and now it turned against her grip and pulled her forward as she stumbled into a wall wearing a blue coat and pale-green waistcoat.

She backed away, shaking her head.

Understanding dawned on the lieutenant's face. He'd been caught. "Marina. No, it's not what you—"

"Oh, my dear."

Marina's eyes darted to Lady Teresa, standing just beyond her son, her hand to her chest, pity on her face. The woman knew—she knew everything. The privet, the mistaken identity—everything.

"You—you made him?" she asked. "You made him be nice to me?"

The lieutenant stepped forward, and Marina stepped back. "Marina, no. You misheard. I was—"

"I am *tired*," she said, shaking and swiping at another blasted tear from under her specs, "of being told what I heard and misheard, what I felt and shouldn't have felt, what I should believe and what I—what I *fell* for." She drew herself up tall. Her words came out hushed and hoarse. "Stay away from me." Then she turned and ran.

Holding in sobs until she was out the conservatory doors, down the terrace steps and into the garden, she ran until she was hidden, her breath fogging the air in ragged puffs, her throat burning from holding in her sorrow and pulling in frigid air. She tugged her shawl around herself, and as she turned into the hedges, as she bowed her head and more hot tears dripped from her chin, she quietly sobbed. She hadn't lost him.

She'd never had him.

"Marina."

She froze at the gentle hush of her name. She swallowed hard and pushed the words out. "I told you to stay away from me."

"You've said before how you are quick to judge. Please hear me out."

She squeezed her eyes shut as if that would make him go away. Make it all go away.

"My darling friend."

Oh, why did he have to sound so tender? She wrapped her shawl more securely around her shoulders, searching the hedge as if it would show her a way through. Her eyeglasses were fogging up again, and her frustration tipped over the brink.

She spun on him. "Why?" she asked. "Why would you? Why would anybody?" She ripped off her useless specs. "I am me, only myself, trying my best in this world with what I've been handed. I harm no one. Why would anybody . . . ?" She couldn't finish, and he reached for her as if she were a broken bird. She wanted to be angry, wanted to scream, but oh, she wanted to be held.

"Please listen," he asked. "Will you at least listen?"

She was cornered by her own doing. Again. She would listen, or not, by her own choosing. She gave him a small nod, shivering in the cold.

He didn't touch her, but he still held his hands out with care. "What you heard, all the things my mother asked of me—"

She winced.

"She did ask me to do them to atone for keeping the truth from you that first day right here in the privet."

She glanced around. Oh heavens, she'd run to the same spot.

"But Marina"—he touched her arm—"I didn't argue with her. I didn't fight it. I *asked* for her direction, as I was reminding her just now." He cautiously lifted his other hand to touch her cheek. "So I might get to know the mysterious, baffling, *adorable* woman in the hedges. I had no intention of spending time with anyone during this house party, and then I came upon you."

She stared, unsure, not knowing which to follow—her pounding heart or her shouting head.

He cupped her face in his warm hand. "Soon I came to realize I wanted to spend *all* of my time with you."

A tear slipped down her cheek. "How do I know whether to believe you?"

"Because after I kiss you, here, right now, we are going to do what I was about to tell my mother I was going to do. If you'll have me, we're going to find your father and let him know I intend to marry you."

Marina drew in a small gasp.

He shook his head, stepping closer. "My mother did *not* ask me to do that. She did *not* fill my head with nothing but you for days. She did *not* ask me to hope I could be enough for you. She did *not* ask me to fall in love with you." He wiped away another of her tears. "And you cannot stop me, my darling. You cannot run for cover, and you cannot blast me away." He was close now, holding her hand to his chest as he tipped his nose to hers. "Believe in me, Marina. Please believe in me."

She breathed him in, searching her heart to know the truth. His gaze, almost pained in its intensity, never left hers. He let her search, let her see him. And as she did, she saw the fear in him give way to something softer, something deeper—something more powerful than her own fear. She swallowed. "A man once said sometimes all a body needs is someone to believe in him."

He exhaled with such a look of relief, gathered her up, and kissed her breathless.

After several long moments, a rough "Ahem" pulled them apart. As they disentangled themselves and Marina slipped her glasses back on, she found, to her horror, that both her parents stood arm in arm on the graveled path, and Lady Teresa, Ophelia, and Mr. Frank Stanhope stood just beyond them, with the Langleys, of course, all of them aghast—Ophelia, Mr. Stanhope, and the Langleys delightedly so.

"Papa, I—"

"What is the meaning of this, sir?" her father bellowed at Richard.

"Sir." Richard bowed and stepped toward her father. "Mr. Rowley, I—we—were just about to seek you out. I won't delay any further. I'm asking for Marina's—your daughter's—hand in marriage. I wish her to be my wife, to have her by my side always, to—"

"Yes, I get the idea."

"I am in earnest, sir. We wish to marry. We'll live here at Canterwood until we've established a new home. And I'd like to take her on a tour of the Continent as soon as possible. She wishes to see the world, and I want to give it to her. I love her, sir. In front of these witnesses, I declare it. She seems to begin where I end. I realize that this—"

"Papa?" Marina rested a hand on Richard's arm and squeezed, quieting him.

Her father's demeanor softened as he turned to her. "Yes, daughter?"

She drew in a steadying breath, and the corner of her mouth lifted. "He is in earnest."

With that, a slow smile replaced her father's scorn. "Very well." He turned to Richard and extended his hand. "Very well." He laughed and patted him on the back.

Marina hugged her father, and the others extended their good wishes.

"I always hoped," Marina's mother spoke with emotion, "that my daughter would marry a fine man, despite—well, despite everything."

Marina's elation fell at her mother's words. But she considered what Richard had said about a mother's guilt.

Richard drew Marina closer to his side and studied the older woman. Marina felt the tension in him, but his tone remained kind. "Despite what, madam?"

Her mother flickered a look of uncertainty to her father but was met with a stern expression.

Richard continued, keeping his voice calm. "Despite these little miracles"—he touched her eyeglass frames with a tip of his finger—"that allow her to see? They are glass, like a window." He turned to Marina, taking her hand and kissing it. "Her beauty is just there looking out. Her spirit? I can't fathom the emptiness of this house party were she not alive and here and reminding me what enduring all the madness of war was for. Because that is what she does. She reminds me what to live for. What to fight for. She is life."

If Marina hadn't loved Richard before, she loved him now.

Mother sniffled. "But, I—"

"Come, Rowena," Father said, taking her hand in his arm. "Let them be. You and I will have a talk, long overdue." He paused as he passed Marina. He patted her cheek and nodded. "Dear girl."

It was enough.

Lady Teresa surprised Marina—and perhaps herself—with a fierce embrace. As the woman released her and gripped her hands, Marina noticed tears in her eyes. "I see a bit of myself in you, dear. Perhaps that motivated me to act as I did. Do not fret over what I know or what I did." She smiled, taking her son and Marina in. "None of us ends up what we start out to be. You will not be a spinster, nor he a soldier. I wish you true happiness starting now. I wish you joy. Happy Christmas, both of you." The lady straightened her shoulders, gathered her heavy shawl around her pelisse, and looked at Frank. "I wish to go to the reflecting pool." Frank stepped up with Ophelia to take his mother's arm, and the three of them continued down the gravel path, Ophelia leaning her head upon her husband's shoulder.

Mr. Langley and Julia approached, and mortification hit Marina over the fact that she'd been found kissing a gentleman, quite fervently, by a vicar—soon to be *her* vicar.

"I know what you're thinking, Marina," Julia said. "And stop it. Tom and Richard are friends first. Isn't that right, gentlemen? We are overjoyed for you."

"Friends first and always." The vicar shook Richard's hand, patting his shoulder, then bowed over Marina's hand. "But I'd also like consideration for performing the marriage. I demand it, actually." He winked and Marina smiled.

She couldn't seem to stop smiling as Julia wiggled her fingers in farewell before she and her husband returned to the house.

Alone together once more, Richard enfolded Marina in his arms. They studied one another—something she was coming to enjoy immensely.

"Why *did* you not fight against your mother's demands?" she asked. "I was a stranger to you. An odd little stranger who mistook you for someone else."

"I had no desire to fight, darling." He trailed kisses along her jaw and spoke softly into her ear. "You'd already caught me, you see. Here in the hedge."

She shivered and whispered back. "You brute."

QUOTED IN 'EXPECTATIONS AT CANTERWOOD'

The quotations on pages 298 and 299 are from William Wordsworth's "The Thorn" (William Wordsworth, "The Thorn," *Public Domain Poetry*, https://www.public-domain-poetry.com/william-wordsworth/thorn-3881).

$\mathscr{A}$BOUT THE AUTHOR

KRISTA HAS LIVED IN LUSH Oregon and rugged Wyoming, but Washington is her beloved home state. She likes to choose familiar settings for her stories and is grateful to have such inspirational places to choose from. She is a mother of six, a grandma of three, a gardener, and a cook. She loves to travel, hike, and laugh, but most of all, she lives to make the best of what she's been given.

Follow Wholesome Romance on social media for more great titles.